The
LONGEST
AUTUMN

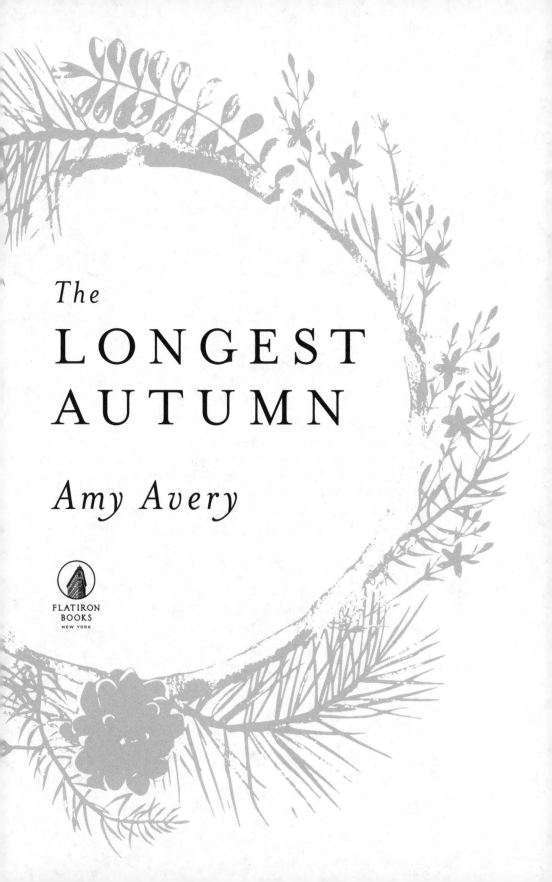

The

LONGEST
AUTUMN

Amy Avery

FLATIRON
BOOKS
NEW YORK

This is a work of fiction. All of the characters, organizations, and events portrayed in this novel are either products of the author's imagination or are used fictitiously.

THE LONGEST AUTUMN. Copyright © 2023 by Amy Avery. All rights reserved. Printed in the United States of America. For information, address Flatiron Books, 120 Broadway, New York, NY 10271.

www.flatironbooks.com

Designed by Devan Norman
Fall foliage illustration © Shutterstock / Shmakova Ksenia

Library of Congress Cataloging-in-Publication Data

Names: Avery, Amy, author.
Title: The longest autumn / Amy Avery.
Description: First edition. | New York, NY : Flatiron Books, 2024.
Identifiers: LCCN 2023025117 | ISBN 9781250896490 (hardcover) |
    ISBN 9781250896506 (ebook)
Subjects: LCGFT: Fantasy fiction. | Romance fiction. | Novels.
Classification: LCC PS3601.V4647 L66 2024 | DDC 813/.6—dc23/
    eng/20230606
LC record available at https://lccn.loc.gov/2023025117

Our books may be purchased in bulk for promotional, educational, or business use. Please contact your local bookseller or the Macmillan Corporate and Premium Sales Department at 1-800-221-7945, extension 5442, or by email at MacmillanSpecialMarkets@macmillan.com.

First Edition: 2024

10 9 8 7 6 5 4 3 2 1

For those whose careful plans and
big dreams shattered, and who put
themselves back together again

The

LONGEST
AUTUMN

C H A P T E R

ONE

The souls of the dead burn in the night sky.

An eerie light hangs over the Temple courtyard, the blue and green and violet glow of souls bobbing overhead like enormous fireflies. Some wait patiently. Others flit around me in a nervous dance, uncertain. I lift a hand to brush a passing one, its pulse like a phantom cat rubbing against my fingertips. A human face flickers at its center, but the soul darts away before I can peer too closely.

"Soon," I promise softly as I take another bite of my peach, sitting cross-legged with my back pressed against the Mirror. The fruit is small and overripe, cloyingly sweet. It's the last of the summer harvest, though heat still lingers in the air, muggy and thick as soup. Tomorrow, after I've returned to the human realm for autumn, this will be an apple, the first fruit of my season. *Our* season.

An electric tingle sparks in my belly. Anticipation, yes, but also inevitable nervousness. One would think six years of escorting Autumn would make tomorrow's ceremony routine, effortless. I don't think I'll ever banish the doubts entirely, the worry that I'm not truly fit for this duty, a mere fragile human mingling with the divine. But tomorrow I'll prove once more that I earned this, that I'm worthy, that Autumn made the right choice when he selected me. My name will earn its place on the stone monument at the corner of this courtyard. *Tirne of Autumn*, inscribed just below the previous Herald's name.

Even though it's too far to see detail in the darkness, I know the names, dozens of them. I've read them so many times, picturing mine engraved beneath. The soft brown of the monument matches the rest of the courtyard, a wide circular space framed with walls of acorn-colored stone carved in swirls and sigils. Glossy ceramic tiles of creamy white rest beneath me. Broad arches at either end bear heavy gates, though I've never seen them closed. The Temple is open to all. And in the center of it all lies the Mirror, immense and red as a ruby.

Finishing the peach, I place the pit on the tray with sticky fingers, then wipe my hands with the damp cloth folded on the side. I already polished off the seed-flecked flatbread and crisp white wine. Offerings, payment to the woman who nightly ferries the dead from their realm. A nearby soul dips closer to my empty cup. Perhaps in its mortal life, this one enjoyed wine. My god assures me the dead do not truly remember their past lives, but they are nonetheless drawn to things they once loved.

Soft footsteps echo on the tile. Right on time. A familiar figure approaches through the archway. In the darkness, he almost looks like a phantom, with his bone-white skin and equally pale hair. Gifts from his mother, Winter. The souls flit away from him, though only I can see them.

"Jaed." I sigh. Our yearly routine. "You know you shouldn't be here." Technically, he's not breaking any laws by entering the courtyard at night, but it's still taboo for anyone but Autumn or me to enter this space between dusk and dawn. The first year he came, I'd been mortified, panicked. But when no punishment fell, I'd accepted Jaed's annual illicit visit. "We could just do this tomorrow." The same admonishment, an old dance of familiar steps.

He sits beside me, folding his legs and bumping my shoulder with his own. "Tomorrow isn't your birthday. Come on. Close your eyes."

A familiar ritual. I do, holding out my hand. He presses something small and cool into it. When I open my eyes, a gemstone bead rests in my palm. Amber this year, honey-gold with a few tiny bubbles trapped inside. I hold it up, watching the light of the souls shine through it.

"Here." Jaed unclasps my bracelet, taking the bead and stringing it on before refastening it. "Twenty-six."

I turn it to admire all the beads. He'd given the bracelet to me on my eighth birthday, with eight beads. We'd replaced the cord with a longer one a few years ago, now wrapping it twice about my wrist. The beads are an incongruous assortment, each one subject to my friend's whims at the time. I have to admit, the amber looks nice against last year's orange carnelian. It may be a childish tradition, but still it makes me smile. "Thank you."

"Happy birthday." He grins as he settles himself more comfortably, adjusting his legs. Still, he doesn't touch the Mirror. He knows what it means to me.

I lean into his side, resting my head on his shoulder and twining our hands together. "I missed you."

"Me too."

I sniff. "You smell like someone else's cologne. Who did you leave sleeping in your bed tonight?"

Jaed laughs. "A new acolyte this year. You'll like him. He's excited to meet you, too. He was on kitchen duty tonight and kept swapping out peaches for your offering, determined to pick the best one."

"Well, you can tell him he chose well, and thank you."

He gives my hand a reluctant squeeze. "I'll let you finish your duty before you get a headache."

He's right. Every moment I spend in this realm, I risk one of my attacks. Back in Sylvus, the realm of the gods, I'll be safe.

"Thanks," I say as he stands and helps me up. He presses a light kiss to my cheek before sauntering away.

I turn back to the task at hand. My magic reaches outward like seeking vines, a lure to draw the last of the stray souls to me. They swarm thickly, crowding me though they bear no weight.

I usher the dead closer, a shepherd gathering her flock. "Well, come on, then." The words are gentle, encouraging. I turn to the Mirror, a masterpiece identical to its twin in Sylvus. Without a single imperfection, the bloodred glass is immense, mounted on polished black onyx a foot thick. The top curves in a graceful arch, wide enough for two people to stand before it without touching, and taller than I could reach if I stretched my arms above me. Seasonal motifs decorate the edges: summer's blazing sun, autumn pumpkins, winter-bare trees, spring blossoms. They weave together in a carved pattern of exquisite artistry. I've spent hours admiring the curves of ivy vines, the sweep of a songbird's wing etched into the stone. It is said that the Mirror's frame possesses such detail that only an immortal could ever memorize its lines and intricacies. But I think that if I try hard enough, perhaps I might, too.

Magic seeps from the Mirror like water dripping from an overfilled bucket, in the sharp, electric tang of an incoming storm. Here lies the sole portal between our worlds, the most powerful artifact in the world, and it bows to my bidding. Another thrill shudders through me, and I breathe deeply once, twice.

My entire life, the world has felt like a giant wheel, spinning slowly, and the Mirror has always been at the center. How many times have I looked into my own dark eyes painted the color of garnets?

Taking a deep breath, I pull the dead souls close once more. My hand dips into my pocket to withdraw my ceremonial knife. Acorns cast in gold twine about the handle, with a slim blade the length of my hand. In a smooth, practiced motion, I press the tip to my palm until the skin breaks. The spark of pain doesn't even make me flinch anymore. It's nothing compared to the pounding agony in my head when I linger too long here. I can feel one of the attacks starting now, a watering eye, a creeping throb in my temple. Only an hour spent in the human world, and already it crawls into my skull. Too relentless and unpredictable, these headaches, like a stalking predator ready to strike me down at any moment.

A crimson drop of blood wells against my skin, a gleaming ruby, and I flatten my hand against the glass. Icy cold numbs my skin despite summer's heat. I reach for that flicker of magic in my breast, the gift I received from the gods six years ago, but it slithers away. Grasping the power is like clutching at a tendril of smoke, but I manage to harness the elusive magic and press it into the glass. The blood seeps into the Mirror. It softens beneath my palm, and I press through. It feels like walking in water, sluggish, thick. Behind me, the souls follow.

We emerge in the palace of the gods in Sylvus, among shimmering, glassy halls never truly meant for mortals like me. But I cast the familiar scenery little more than a glance as I hold the Mirror's portal open until the last soul slips through.

The leader of a macabre parade, I usher the dead through the silent, empty palace, then beyond the heavy black door that only my god and I are allowed to open. Autumn is more than the god of his season; as the ruler of death, this is his demesne I approach. Winding obsidian stairs lead down, down, ever downward. Lights are few and far between, leaving the space dim. But after half a dozen years, I could tread these steps in complete darkness.

The stairwell ends at a circular room. As he does every night, my god awaits upon his throne, resplendent and achingly inhuman. His eyes burn and flicker like orange flames in a bone-pale face. A cloak of eternally falling leaves drapes him, its detritus littering the slick black stone of the floor. And yet all this beauty is cold, impassive as only a god could be.

I lead the souls to Autumn's well, carved seamlessly of gleaming obsidian. One by one, they sink into the murky abyss of Autumn's underworld. The realm is forbidden even to me, his Herald, at least until old age or misfortune claims my life, too. Then I will cross that border like any mortal.

When the last soul sinks into the dark, I bow to my god. He nods without a word, the ceremony complete until we repeat it again tomorrow night. And every night thereafter, until I find my own place in the underworld, my position filled by a new mortal Herald.

I ascend the steps once more and seek my bed. Already, the shimmer of magic that infuses the gods' realm eases the ache that grips my skull, scrubbing away the pain of the human world.

The human realm. Despite the threat of my headaches, excitement still flickers. Tomorrow, I fulfill my most important duty, and Autumn will return to the First Temple.

I awaken to a rapid heartbeat and a queasy feeling. Excitement more than anxiety, but both flutter through me. As my nerves settle, I don the traditional robe, the crown, and my golden belt, and leave for the Mirror's room.

My sandals echo on the smooth floors of the gods' palace, which gleams like an enormous sheet of white glass. I drink it all in. The first time I entered these halls, they'd stolen my breath away with their high arched ceilings carved in crystalline, geometric detail. Though Sylvus is a cold and impassive place, there is also a peace here that I will miss for the next few months.

As ever, sourceless light bathes the space, and my reflections stare back at me with dark, solemn eyes. Passing the fountain that ever bubbles with iridescent lavender water, I breathe in the crisp scent of its magic. Even the water here is holy, special. It's said that a mortal bathed in it would live forever. It's forbidden, of course. I can't even touch a drop of it without risking permanent banishment from Sylvus and even the human Temple.

This glory was built for the divine, not for us. We are only visitors, the four humans granted the right to live in such splendor for nine months of every year. As lovely and calm as it is, Sylvus has never truly been home. *Home* is a world away, drenched in the murmur of devotions and hymns weaving through the First Temple, the smoky scent of myrrh and clove incense. A place of soft brown stone, mortar and brick, the work of feeble, proud human hands. A vivid contrast to the hollow iridescence that surrounds me now.

The human world is touch, warmth, and comfort. Jaed's laugh, his embrace. The simple feel of hands entwined. Aside from last night's brief meeting, I've felt no one's touch save my own for nine months, and I thirst for it like water.

Soon.

Eagerness swells, quelling the anxiety. A smile tugs on my lips and my steps quicken. I lift a hand to straighten my crown of autumn leaves, a ceremonial affectation. Stray twigs tug painfully at my auburn curls. Every year, it takes ages to untangle my hair from it, but it's tradition. I can't deny it paints a pretty picture with the sleeveless crimson robe and wide golden belt of Autumn's Herald.

A voice bounces off the sparkling walls as I draw nearer to the Mirror Chamber. The goddess Winter's low contralto purr, the words indistinguishable but the tone unmistakable condescension. Autumn replies in his husky tone that invokes the rustle of leaves, a cool drizzle. "She won't be late."

I reach the open archway that leads into the Mirror Chamber. "No, she won't." I don't bother hiding the chill in my tone as my gaze latches on Winter's. Colorless, like diamonds with a single fleck of soot in the center. Perhaps it would unnerve some humans, but it has never cowed me, one raised among the gods' children.

Winter's thin lips press together. She maintains silence, her snow-pale face inscrutable, but I can practically hear her thoughts like violent music. Jealousy that I serve my god eagerly, that I excel at it. Not once have I lost a stray soul ushering the dead into Autumn's underworld. Meanwhile, her Herald is as vicious and jagged as she, sullenly performing his sole task to the letter and nothing more.

I turn my attention back to my god, who stands before the Mirror. The tension passes, and the solemnity of the situation settles once more. Autumn is dignified, impassive. His leafy crown is grander than mine, woven through with vines of beaten gold. It's a perfect match for his cloak of falling leaves. The ember-orange fire in his eyes brightens as they trace my face.

I spare a glance at the others gathered here. Spring with his rose-gold hair and wide, infectious smile, standing beside his timid Herald, eyes downcast and hands clutching one another. Winter's Herald stands tall at his goddess's side, burning with palpable indignation at my impudence to her. His eyes are as black as mine, and gleam with the sharpness of a newly honed blade.

I would not call us friends, the other Heralds and me, but we share a bond as the only human souls here, locked away from our home for months with no other company except aloof gods.

Lys, father of the Seasons and the highest of the gods, stands in dignified splendor beside the Mirror. The ghost of what might be a frown curves his mouth. He is tall, taller than any human I have met, in shades of precious metal. His hair shines like strands of fine, beaten gold, his eyes like burnished silver coins. Even his skin glows with a faint light, like a paper lantern.

Yet his glory pales before the Mirror. This close, it's overwhelming, broad as the Temple gates and nearly twice as tall as me. Summer already stands on the opposite side in the human realm, her deep brown skin perfectly accented by a golden dress and a crown of sunflowers atop her dark curls. Tinted crimson in the reflection of the red, red glass, the courtyard of the First Temple lies behind her. Worshippers have gathered there to watch me bring Autumn into their world. My world. As I approach the Mirror, Summer's Herald pierces her hand and touches it, palm flat and fingertips outspread, a smear of her blood darkening the surface. We nod to each other. Summer steps through the Mirror into Sylvus on my right, her Herald following in her wake.

Quickly, now. In a few efficient motions, I press my Herald's blade to my palm until the skin breaks. Bouncing eagerly on the balls of my feet, I touch the Mirror and pull at that indefinable flicker of power inside me. The Mirror softens beneath my touch, and Autumn passes through beside me.

I walk into the human world next. As I emerge from the Mirror's surface, my gut wrenches and flips, a sensation I've never felt during this ceremony. For a panicked moment, I fear my breakfast will heave up on the Temple courtyard. Reflexively, I clutch my stomach.

The sensation fades quickly as warm sunlight cascades over me. I drop my hand, hoping all eyes were on my god instead. A cautious, steadying breath reassures me. As I inhale, the scent of the mortal realm hits me. Summer in all its fading glory. The lush aroma of grass gone to seed, of dusty earth baked by sunlight. Since becoming a Herald, I've briefly smelled fresh-blooming roses, or winter's biting frost. My world is painted in the fragrance of the dying season, the sweetness of hay, of pumpkin and apple, the dry smell of leaves crunching underfoot. For nine months, I've only seen the Temple in the deepest part of the night to collect souls and my offering, for a handful of minutes at a time. But now three glorious months await me here. Home.

The Temple courtyard lies open to the sky. The sun is too bright, too hot. I turn to meet Autumn's fiery gaze. Only I can read him well enough to note the faint excitement in those eyes, buried deep beneath the regal countenance of the divine. He gives me a single tiny nod. A thank-you, a congratulations on a job well done. Again, pride swells within me. Another Changing of the Seasons has passed, smooth as silk.

A crowd has gathered to watch the beginning of autumn. Garbed for the occasion in hues of russet and gold, wearing masks crafted to look like fallen leaves, they cheer and applaud. The priests and acolytes kneel, Autumn's burnt-orange robes in front, icy blue and pale pink and soft gold scattering behind.

Autumn stands tall and proud, his crown gleaming at his brow. In the noonday sun, the faint shimmer of bronze gleams in his hair. Leaves swirl away from his cloak in a sudden gust of wind. In this moment, he is mighty, unknowable. His power wafts from him like ink spreading in water. Soon the earth will respond to his presence in this world, plants fading and the air growing chill.

A hush falls as the crowd awaits his traditional words of greeting.

Instead, a great crack behind me cleaves the silence.

I whirl to look, but Autumn shoves me in front of him, lifting his cloak of falling leaves to shield me. His golden crown falls to clatter on the courtyard's cobblestones. A tight pain erupts between my temples, and I cry out. It's as bad as my worst headaches, sudden and sharp and debilitating. My knees threaten to collapse, but Autumn holds me fast.

A tinkling sound scatters in the air like wind chimes. When the crystalline sound dies away, silence grasps the courtyard. The agony in my head fades as quickly as it burst, as fast as the nausea earlier.

I become suddenly, acutely aware of a warm hand wrapped around my bare upper arm.

Sucking in a sharp, terrified breath, I twist out of Autumn's grasp. I stare at the ground while a single thought screams in my mind. *He touched me. In front of everyone.* My skin burns where his fingertips pressed against my arm. It is profanity to feel the skin of a god. It doesn't matter that he made the move. The sin will be mine.

Panic scatters my thoughts. Any moment, I'll hear the angry shout. A terrified lump forms in my throat as I sweep a nervous gaze around the crowd, but no one cries blasphemy. The throng remains silent, the air crackling with tension. Crimson shards litter the ground, save the small circle of protection Autumn has formed around me.

My stomach clenches as realization settles in, and I turn to survey the scene.

The Mirror lies in pieces. Only a solid slab of black stone remains, etched with arcane symbols once hidden underneath. Scratches mar the writing, defacing the perfect etchings into something ugly.

A few shards cling to the edges. One of them falls as I watch, clinking against the tiles. It feels like a punch to my gut. I can't breathe.

This isn't happening.

"No." Autumn's voice echoes my thought, a bare whisper as he stares at the blank arch. My god's sharp profile reveals a brow furrowed in anguish. His head bows, his eyes close.

From the sea of onlookers, a single sob breaks the paralyzed hush and galvanizes the assembly. People rush forward, weeping over the bits of crimson glass, all while the priests of Autumn struggle to control a crowd that rapidly threatens to turn into a riot.

"Stop." Autumn's voice carries over the chaos, though it is not quite a shout. The humans do as he bids, compelled by the wave of magic rippling outward from his voice. "All but those who dwell here, leave the pieces here and exit the courtyard."

In a daze, people trickle out of the Temple. When the space has emptied of all but the faithful, priests and acolytes dart about to collect the shards. They seem heedless of the small cuts that spill their precious, magic-filled blood onto the tile. Someone has fetched offering bowls. Holy objects now hold the broken remnants of the most powerful, ancient artifact in the world.

"We can fix it," one weeping priestess mutters over and over again.

I don't know if they can, but I won't tell her that. Instead, I bend to help. Numbness settles over me, a heavy weight. A tear drips from my chin, and I realize I'm crying, too. I blink away the blurriness and reach for a shard. It slices into the meat of my thumb, and I hiss at the pain.

"Don't." Autumn speaks softly. When I look up, his eyes are locked on the blood welling up in the wound. At his side, his hand flexes, stretching, then curling into a fist. "Let the priests do it."

I swallow, sucking on the wound, then pressing it to my crimson robe to stop the bleeding. "Yes, Your Holiness." I'm shivering now, despite summer's heat.

"You may go. I have much to attend to."

A drastic understatement, but I'm too shaken to do anything but nod numbly and leave.

It can't be gone. I barely take in my surroundings, my feet carrying me to my room while my mind buzzes with a low hum of panic. Everything has changed. Without the Mirror, the souls of the dead will linger here until I choke on them, invisible to all save me and my god. A lesson from my training echoes in my mind. *If the dead can't descend to the underworld, they will leech life from the living in an attempt to regain what they once were.*

And if the Mirror isn't restored in time for winter, the world will be locked in an eternal season of dying. How much time remains until the winter stockpiles are used up, long before she even arrives?

We'll fix it, I tell myself desperately. We have to.

CHAPTER

TWO

"Heretic."

"Blasphemer."

"Unholy."

The priests' scorn burns like fire as they sit at the council table, hurling insults.

It is afternoon now, the Temple thrown into chaos. The midday meal was still served, but the usual cacophony of conversation in the dining hall was lowered to a worried, distraught murmur. Faces stared blankly or wept quietly.

Before I'd been summoned here to face the priests, I'd wandered aimlessly through the halls, trying to make sense of what had happened. Normally, I'd have been drinking in the feel of home: the soft walnut-shell color of the stone walls; the aroma of spiced, smoky incense; and the vinegar smell of freshly scrubbed tile floors. My sandals had echoed softly on the glazed ceramic floor mosaics, but it was impossible to feel at peace. Grief overwhelmed me, and that horrible cracking, shattering sound echoed in my head.

Until another sound had broken through my fog of sorrow, a trilling mew. "Sunshine," I greeted the plump orange tabby that trotted up to me, tail held high. He'd always been a favorite among the Temple cats. He'd flopped at my feet, and I knelt to scratch his belly. A tiny bit of comfort. "What a fine, dignified servant of the gods you are."

"Tirne!"

Jolted from my moment with Sunshine, I'd looked up to meet a smiling face, light brown with the dusty-rose hair that marked him as one of Spring's children.

"Calder." Once, we'd almost been friends. Two years older, he'd tutored me and others in mathematics when I was eighteen. The alchemist had always been shy, bright-eyed, and full of nervous chatter when he did speak, his cheeks turning a deep burnished pink for the slightest reason. He'd done so again, giving a small, uneasy bow, fingers nervously plucking at his belt. The bright green color and fine weave of his robe marked him as a high priest of Spring, and silver trim indicated his status as a member of the Temple's ruling council as well.

His eyes had darted anxiously to the floor and back up, his foot tapping. "Your presence is requested in the council chamber."

We'd come here, and I now stand between the enormous council table and the gods' raised throne, in this room once forbidden. Only the council priests and the gods enter here, to deliberate on matters of government. The Temple is a sovereign state, exempt from the Empire's rules even if we dwell within its borders. Here, the gods' word is law. And this chamber is where those laws are written.

The room is immense, larger than I thought. The domed ceiling arches above, painted with scenes of the four seasons. Though much of the Temple uses candles and fire sconces, rare and precious globes of enchanted light adorn this space. The magical lighting responds to the energy of those within the room. Right now it is icy, colder than sunlight and only half as bright. It feels like an overcast day, dreary and mournful.

An enormous rectangular table takes up the center of the room, surrounded by thirteen chairs. And on the dark surface, fragments of the Mirror gleam like rubies. Bowls of jagged pieces still perch in the corners.

The members of the council stare at me, seated in their chairs. Three Scions for each god, in a sea of the high priests' robes. Rich brown for Autumn's children, with brilliant peridot green, sky blue, and snowy white for the others. My scarlet Herald's robe stands out, but not as much as the radiance of my god. His leaf-strewn cloak rests upon his shoulders. Beneath it, a burgundy jacket shimmers in brushed silk, lovingly embroidered by his acolytes in a motif of apples amid abstract whorls.

Despite Autumn's impassive expression, the anger rolling off him is palpable to me. How can the priests—some his own children—be oblivious to it?

The highest priest, the Tharem, splutters from his spot at the head of the table. He's the only full human on the council, his robe alone a spectacular shade of crocus purple. His broad face is crimson, apoplectic. "She should be banished from the Temple for touching a god!"

"No." Autumn infuses his voice with his power, something I've never seen him do when talking to the high priests and priestesses, holy demigods. Some of them are even blood of his blood. "No skin touched skin," he lies smoothly, the compulsion in his voice giving the declaration weight. "Only my hand against her robe." His magic presses against me, warm, tingling.

The priests flinch back, murmuring among themselves, their thoughts muddled by their lord's command.

Autumn repeats, "She has committed no sin. Do you doubt the word of a god?"

Again, a muttered consultation among the priests. My fingernails dig into my palms and I hold my breath until the Tharem speaks, teeth gnashing. "Very well. She stays."

I let out a long, shaky breath, but my relief is poisoned by guilt that worms its way into my brain. He lied for me.

"Now that this business is settled," Autumn says, "we can proceed to the matter of *actual* concern." A note of disdain lies in that, and it seems it is not lost on the priests. Most of them manage to look at least a little chastised.

"The Mirror." The Tharem chokes out the word, and all eyes in the room look to the array of offering bowls lying on the table. An assortment of shards, some still smeared with priests' blood.

"Send a missive to the Emperor," Autumn says. "We'll need his decree if we're to summon those outside the faith to help."

The Tharem bows his head, his bald pate gleaming in the candlelight. "Yes, Your Holiness."

"Tirne," Autumn says, and neither his voice nor his lean, pale face gives away anything. "Before the high priests can unravel the mystery of the Mirror's sundering and stitch the pieces back together, we have questions."

"Yes, Your Holiness."

Autumn's blazing eyes search mine. Doubt lingers there. "The Mirror is broken . . . but is the magic weakened as well? Can you sense anything from it now?"

With shaking fingers, I pluck my ceremonial blade from my pocket and puncture a fingertip. As the blood wells up, I summon my magic and brush the nearest shard, questing for that spark of magic. The moment I touch it, a soft *tink* echoes through the room, and the glass splits in two.

I yank my hand away, sharp and violent.

Silence.

All eyes stare at the fragments for a long moment before hostile gazes land on me. On my face, on the traitorous hand that broke the Mirror even further.

"No," I whisper. This can't be happening. The Mirror is the center of my universe. It's my only scrap of power in this world, the cornerstone of the title and duty I worked so hard for. The one Mother trained me for.

And it's my key to Sylvus, the only place I'm free from the threat of my headaches.

"Tirne." Autumn's voice is colder than his season, the first frost as autumn gives way to winter. "Step back from the table."

With faltering steps, I do, holding my hand to my chest. I feel like I'm being strangled, my rib cage too tight to breathe. I can't stop staring at those two pieces of ruby-tinted glass.

"No," I say again with more conviction, as if uttering the word will make it true. "I didn't . . . I can't . . ."

"She did it!" Fury contorts the Tharem's features. Combined with his flushed pink skin and round face, he looks like a garvish from Kildian folklore, a twisted and vengeful creature. My aunt had once so loved to frighten me with fantastical tales of the old beasts. Right now, I'm that terrified child again, staring into the face of a rabid beast that points his finger at me and cries blasphemy.

"What did you do?" the Tharem snarls.

"Nothing! We came through the Mirror, then it just . . . broke."

The Tharem's watery eyes narrow. "And you sensed *nothing* unusual? Your attunement to the Mirror is the one gift we granted you."

That garners a wince. When I'd consumed the small vial of my god's bittersweet blood, I'd been blessed with a connection to the divine and dominion over the Mirror. It is the only bit of magic I possess.

But that nausea I felt when I passed through . . . A heavy lump forms in my stomach, worry swimming up from the depths of my mind once more. What if the Tharem is right? But I recoil from that thought. No. I couldn't have broken it. I know what I'm doing. I've performed my job without flaw for half a dozen years. If I tell them of my queasiness, it's all the proof the Tharem will need to convince everyone this is my fault.

"No. I didn't feel anything." The lie comes out a croak.

Autumn says my name once more, and my head whips around to look at him. His lips are pressed tightly together, his brow creased. And through the connection that links us, the magic of his blood that flows within me, I sense a knot of unease. Worry.

"Tirne," he says, voice soft but commanding. "You are not to touch any piece of the Mirror again." He pauses for a breath. "Without the ability to use the Mirror, your status as Herald is hereby stripped from you."

My head won't stop shaking in denial, the world going gray around the edges.

No. No, no, no, no. This isn't right. I didn't do anything wrong!

"From this point forward," Autumn continues, "you are to resume the station and duties of an acolyte while we examine this matter. You will cooperate with all investigation efforts, and you are not to leave the Temple without an escort."

I stand in silence, clenching my teeth to keep the words in. There is no arguing with a god. Autumn's eyes are dark, mere flickering embers, and a pang of something sharp and bitter twists in my chest through my link with him. His hands are clenched at his sides.

"Do you understand, Tirne of Autumn?"

I clear my throat, managing a simple, hoarse "Yes." My status, my training, all for nothing, stolen from me by some unseen blight. A sickness? Some other failing of mine?

Autumn nods. "Then fetch an acolyte's robe from the laundry. You may keep your room for now. While the investigation takes place, report anything unusual to Calder. He will also set your acolyte's tasks and leave a list in your room shortly. You are dismissed." He turns from me, my presence forgotten as he brushes a fingertip along the smooth surface of a Mirror shard.

I take one furtive glance at Calder. He watches me with shocked pity, his eyes too sharp, too bright, his fingers twitching at his side as if he's trying to grasp something invisible. An answer, maybe. I make my escape. Horror churns my stomach, and indignation. I *earned* my place. I bested six other applicants for the position. My ferrying of the dead has gone smoothly every single night for half a dozen years. I've been the picture-perfect Herald.

All gone now.

I'm clutching my hands so tightly my nails cut into my palms. I suppose I'll need to trim them now, given the same everyday menial tasks as any acolyte. It was vanity to keep them groomed long like a Scion's.

Like the rest of the Temple, the laundry bears a hushed, mournful quality. It lingers between the splash of water and the rustle of fabric, a harsh contrast to the usual cheerful banter and chatter. The high priest overseeing the laundry gives me a strange, perplexed gaze when I ask her for a russet acolyte's robe. She is one of Summer's children, dark of skin and hair, with honey-gold eyes and a merry, smiling mouth. But she does as requested, sizing me up and handing me a robe the color of pumpkin custard. The fabric feels stiff and scratchy, simple rough-spun linen rather than the soft brushed cotton of a Herald's robe.

A quick trip to my room sees my clothing swapped. I tug the robe into place. It's a passable fit, even if the hem is a bit short. I toss on the simple brown leather belt with a longing glance at the golden links of my old belt, draped over the bloodred robe on my bed.

My room is a comfortable place to gather my thoughts, at least. As the honored servant of a god, I have been given fine lodgings during my three months in the mortal realm. Lodgings I'll apparently be allowed to keep, for now. A large hearth rests along one wall to warm my bones as the land responds to Autumn's presence and grows colder. My blankets are thick and quilted. I even have my own privy.

When I returned here, a list already rested on the foot of my bed. An acolyte's chores, laid out in plain and simple ink with a sharp, jagged hand. The tasks are no more strenuous than they had been during my acolyte years, a morning duty and afternoon duty each day. Tending the garden, scrubbing floors, fetching Temple necessities from town. The last one piques my interest. I'll be in the company of other acolytes or a Scion supervisor, but at least I'll get to venture out. For today, I am spared any duties, but tomorrow I will report to the kitchen in the morning, then hang laundry to dry after the midday meal.

I want to confront Autumn, to ask why he lied for my sake, or protest my demotion, or beg for my title back. But I cannot approach a god without their request, and I certainly can't summon him to me.

Besides, I know where he will be right now. Laereda's rooms. The previous year was her last as Autumn's Consort, but the union was fruitful and she gave birth to her fifth child. He will be meeting with her now to greet his newest Scion, a future priest.

Like Jaed, all the gods' children automatically become priests, and they are the only ones allowed to hold that position. Some, though, reject the priesthood and leave the Temple to use their magic in a secular manner as sorcerers.

We need these Scions of the gods. Without them, our world would be devoid of magic. Healers would be limited to simple herbal medicines, and pest infestations would ravage crops without charms to ward them away. We need the fire-protectant spells that save the lives of smiths, or enchanted brooms that clean the homes of those who are unable to sweep for themselves. Charms to hang over cribs and ring an alarm bell when an infant stops breathing in the middle of the night.

Magic infuses our world, and it is the blood of the gods that carries it. They bestow us with their magic-bearing children, and in return, we worship them. We provide them every luxury during their months here while they absorb the vitality our world provides.

To give us those children, the gods each take a Consort such as Laereda. She's always been sharp to me, and I'm relieved that her fifteen-year service is at an end. She will retire and raise her children with the aid of the Temple's nurses, living out the rest of her life in comfort. She can enjoy her endless nosiness and gossip, as she always has.

This year, twelve hopefuls will be given the priest's blessing, granted temporary permission to touch a god. But only one will claim the mantle of Consort for the next fourteen years. When Autumn next returns, he will select one from those who have borne him a child and proven themselves fertile.

Maybe she'll be a sweet, wilting thing. Not another viper.

Still, my mind can't be distracted for long. It circles back to thoughts of my title stripped from me, to the Mirror in pieces, to everything that I've lost in the span of a single day. And finally I weep, in great, racking sobs, my hands fisted in the skirts of my new, rough-spun robe.

I'm too ashamed to leave my room, even for supper. Instead, I lie on my bed as twilight falls, my shutters open to the melody of the season's last evening cicadas in the futile hope it will calm me. The hearth remains dark and empty while summer's heat still lingers. A single candle flickers instead, casting dancing shadows.

My first evening as an acolyte once more. My fingertips brush Mother's necklace at my throat. Fine gold cast into autumn leaves with a single striped stone at the bottom. In the candlelight, the gemstone's striations shimmer in every shade of brown and gold and copper. *I'm so sorry, Mother.* I've lost the one thing she'd ever hoped for me.

The night deepens. My eyes stray toward my doorway, to the curtain of orange beads that acts as a door. Will Jaed even come tonight, after what happened?

I snort softly. Of course he will. And he'll murmur sweet lies, telling me it will all work out. But Lys knows I don't believe that, and I could use a distraction to quiet the cacophony in my head.

When the bell strung into the beaded curtain jangles, I leave my bed and push aside the strands to meet familiar pale eyes, like clear glass with a tiny bit of smoky gray mixed in. He looks me up and down, taking in my new robe, my face that must be red-nosed and bleary-eyed from weeping. "So. It's true, then."

I open my mouth, but no sound comes out. Jaed pulls me into his arms, making small soothing sounds as his hand strokes gentle circles on my back.

"The Tharem thinks I did it," I croak, and the admission burns.

"Oh, some of the theories I've heard are quite wild," Jaed says, resting his chin on my shoulder. "I particularly love the one where you're some sort of Kildara mimic pretending to be Tirne. But they'll sort this out."

What if they don't? But there's no use asking. We both already know it would spell disaster if the Mirror remains shattered, and panicking won't help.

He leans back and brushes a lock of my hair behind an ear. "The Tharem said—"

"I don't want to know what he said." Sudden fury sparks in my chest. The Tharem. He's always hated me, ever since I bested his nephew for the Herald's position. A spiteful man, he's as bad as Laereda. Worse, even. I'm sure he's relishing every moment of my shame.

But Jaed isn't. He's here, and he's warmth and comfort and more. He caresses my cheek, and shivery heat trickles down through my limbs, between my legs. My hands clutch at the front of Jaed's robe, pulling him farther into the room. "I don't want to think about the Tharem, or anyone else—anything else—for the rest of the night."

Despite my words, dread threatens to overwhelm me again, the apprehension that my livelihood and the thing I love both lie in pieces. That I might actually be at fault. It comes in waves. Fear, then anger at the senseless and unjustified loss of my entire life's work.

I drown all those dark, crawling emotions by kissing Jaed.

He may have a new lover, this Bix, but we have always held this agreement. I know of his other bed partners, and they know of me. Tonight, Jaed surrenders to my insistence, his arms tightening around me and his mouth parting for my tongue. With only the barest pause to close the heavier leather inner curtain on my door, we stumble to the bed. Soon my russet robe lies on the floor atop his white one, like autumn leaves scattered on snow.

Our first night is always intense. After nine months, I am all too eager for another's touch. Tonight, I desperately try to bury my sorrows in him, to quiet the chaos in my mind. He obliges, with warm and gentle hands that trail across my collarbone and down my stomach and tease between my legs until I reach the brink of pleasure, then topple over it, all other thoughts pushed from my mind.

Though I'm not his only partner, Jaed has visited my bedchamber for years. We'd been each other's firsts, in an evening of awkward fumbling and laughter and embarrassment.

We've both improved since then.

For a time, I do forget about the Mirror and the tragedy that hangs over us. I lose myself in the feeling of our limbs entwined, in the thrust of his hips, in the shuddering sound of his sighs. When his wave of pleasure ignites with a gasp and a soft moan, I let him spend himself inside me. It's safe; Scions are infertile and never suffer illness or disease. Not even a common cough. Just one of the side benefits of a god's magic in their blood.

Afterward, we lie in a satiated pile of limbs, hair plastered to our foreheads and necks. I let his magic shiver through me, like the giddiness of wine but better. The world grows brighter and the very air glitters. Every thread of my sheets presses into my skin. The pulse pounding in my ears sharpens to a steady drumbeat, a thrum I feel in my entire body.

Magic lingers in more than just a Scion's blood.

Jaed draws aimless patterns on my stomach with a silver-painted fingernail. He keeps them long, and it scrapes softly, tickling. With the magic still filling me, the sensation is even stronger. I shiver and laugh. "Stop that."

He obeys, his smile fading.

We remain silent for a time, until I ask, "What happens now?" I'm not talking about us.

He shakes his head. "They'll fix it."

"But—"

He silences my protests with another kiss, and I let him.

After Jaed leaves, I stare at the ceiling as my candle burns low, enjoying the tingle of magic trickling across my skin.

But Jaed's distraction does not linger, and my mind churns again. The Tharem's furious face lingers in my memory, jeering, snarling. The Mirror's jagged shards on that table haunt me, so obscene. I feel like I've lost a loved one.

A warm summer breeze swirls through my room, and I roll onto my side to look at my small desk. Three letters lie neatly folded and sealed on the corner of it. I know what they'll say. Aunt Ilna, once more reminding me that I can leave the Temple to join her in the city. Maybe she'll have added some bits about her shop, or other scraps of town news that is of little relevance to me. I never reply. I'm not the one who left. Someday, maybe I'll have the courage to toss them out unopened, but not yet. I'll read them tomorrow. Tonight, my mind is too full of the Mirror, of my demotion.

Wearily, I rise and don my new acolyte's robe. I should forsake this task, remain in my room rather than facing the truth. It's no longer my duty. But something draws me out to the courtyard anyway.

They're beautiful, the souls of the dead. There are dozens, hundreds. They create a sight no one has seen, save Autumn and his Herald. If anyone else were to look upon this scene, they would see me standing alone on the tile, illuminated only by the half-full moon.

I hear the dead, too, a sibilant chorus of distant whispers. The words are indistinct, the cadence of them worried, fretful, hushed, or panicked. My raised hand grazes a soul, and it chills my fingers as it passes. This one is green, the color of flame when copper shavings are tossed into the fire.

The Mirror's stone arch stands empty of all fragments, bare and black. The elaborate carvings along the frame gleam in the starlight, along with the etched symbols once hidden beneath the glass in the ancient tongue of the gods. I don't know what these words once said, before someone vandalized them. Another mystery, one only the divine can answer.

Resting my palm against the obsidian surface chills my skin. It's far colder than it should be while summer's muggy warmth lingers. Eyes closed, I search for that flicker of magic, the Mirror's power. It burns within me, but a hollow space echoes back. Even if I pierced my finger and summoned the magic in my blood, there would be nothing to link it to.

It truly is broken, the magic shattered as surely as the glass. So fragile, such power. I slump back against the stone, staring up at the sky. I don't know how long I stand there. I'm not surprised to hear my god approach eventually. The dry crackle of his cloak nearly drowns the soft cadence of his boots.

"Your Holiness." I greet him without turning. I realize belatedly that I should bow to him now, but he doesn't comment on my faux pas. Instead, Autumn stands beside me, tilting his head to peruse the heavens as I do. "They wait." He gestures to the souls.

I nod. "For something I can't give them."

We stand in tense silence for long minutes, until the pressure grows too strong and I blurt, "Why did you lie to the priests? About touching me?"

He hesitates. Then, "It was not your sin. I reached for you. But the Tharem would never accept that. He would still demand your exile. It is better for everyone to believe the lie."

I wonder if he's ever used his power on me, to make me believe something untrue. I'm not sure I want to know. Instead, I ask, "Why not just let them exile me?"

"Because we may need you to repair the Mirror. Until we know what happened, I'll have you here, near me."

Just business, straightforward and callous in his divinity. In some ways, I understand. Our mission and duties are of utmost importance here. Still, a part of me wonders if he possesses any scrap of pity for the one who's served him faithfully for so long, now bereft of her title. A trickle of emotion flickers along the thread of magic that connects us, something uneasy but indefinable.

My gaze drifts toward the pillar in the corner, the one covered in the names of past Heralds. His eyes follow.

Autumn says quietly, "If we can repair the Mirror and restore your connection with it, I will ensure the title returns to you."

"Why?" He could just as easily select another, as much as the thought leaves a sick twist in my stomach.

"Because your faith is more than lip service or force of habit. That means something to us—the gods. To me. You revere this duty more than many of my Heralds ever did."

I close my eyes. "How do you know that?"

"I've lived a very long time, and I've seen many Heralds come and go. Some, like Winter's current Herald, merely crave the status the title provides. But true, human passion, that's a gift. Something we cherish."

I hadn't known he'd noticed, or that he'd been looking at all. We've never talked of ourselves before, only our tasks. During his season in the human realm, he leads devotions and meets with Consorts. Our paths cross only at night to escort the dead, with few words spoken. But now everything is different, the status quo shattered in a single heartbeat.

Even stranger, it turns out that Autumn has been paying attention to me all along. My cheeks warm. I can't help but feel flattered and a little proud to receive a flicker of admiration from a deity. A small cough clears my throat, but my voice is still thick when I say, "I do love it. The Mirror, the duty. I like to think I'm a part of something important, something bigger than me."

"You are."

"Were." The word comes out bitter, stinging.

"For now. But we do not choose our Heralds lightly. I have never regretted my decision." A pause. "Not even today."

"So you don't think I broke it on purpose?"

"No." The answer comes without hesitation. "I don't think any power in the two realms could make you harm the Mirror or threaten your fellow people so."

Wait. A dark, creeping thought slips into my mind. "What if there was someone who would?"

"No mistake or misfortune, but sabotage." There's no surprise in his voice; the thought has already occurred to him.

"Who would—*could*—do such an awful thing?" Not many even have the ability to break such a powerful artifact.

Autumn's reply echoes my thoughts. "Sorcerers. High priests. Only they possess the magic needed."

Heart fluttering, I pace in front of the stone arch. "They wouldn't. No one would be stupid enough, cruel enough."

"Humans have done worse."

It feels like a rebuke, and I flinch, even as my mind races. Who would have a reason to trap Autumn here, to stretch out his season indefinitely? Maybe Laereda, trying to cling to her god. The Tharem, to shame and humiliate me. And others may have the skills and power to do this, priests I don't know well enough to guess their motives. Yet.

But I could. I will.

Laereda and the Tharem have no magic, though. They'd need help. Even if a regular human gets access to a Scion's blood, we can't use the magic contained within it. I force myself to stop pacing. Once more I press my hand to the chill stone, beside the carved, enigmatic letters. Two, three deep breaths later, I say feebly, "I never even thought it could break. It's just always been here."

Autumn's reply is a soft murmur. "Not always."

I nod, tracing a finger over one carved symbol, the scratches marring it. "It's strange, to think you were here when it was crafted. Is that what these letters say? Part of its magic?"

My god is silent long enough that I wonder if he'll reply at all. "No. Those words are older than the Mirror glass. Once, this was not a portal, but a barrier. This very spot is where Kild split the realms, the place where the fabric between them is now thinnest. He put this stone here and carved his own spell on it, like a piece of cork wedged in a leaking barrel."

"But Lys's love was stronger than Kild's jealousy."

"Yes."

It's a story all the faithful know. Lys's brother Kild was jealous of humankind's worship of the Seasons, Lys's children. Kild betrayed them all, sacrificing so many of the shadowy creatures that served him just to gain the power to sunder the world in two and lock the gods away. Then Lys spilled his own blood to create the Mirrors and reunite with his human beloved, Serrema.

If he did it once . . . "Can Lys do it again?" I ask. "Craft another Mirror from the other side?"

"He could. But last time, Serrema served as motivation." He stops just short of saying it. *He doesn't care enough, not anymore.* Lys is the coldest of the gods, the most incomprehensible. Even while living in Sylvus, I've never spoken to him. Only his children, the Seasons, do. It is strange to think that the gods had all once lived here, that they'd been as full of anger and jealousy and love as any human. I wonder, if Lys met Serrema now, could he still love her? Or would the emptiness of Sylvus fill his heart?

Hopelessness creeps up my spine. "So it's up to us. I'll help. Whatever it takes."

His flickering eyes turn to meet mine, an intensity in them I've never seen. "Do you swear it? Truly, whatever you must?"

I swallow. I can't deny a god. The faintest thread of his worry and despair slips through my connection with him, and everything in me aches to soothe it. He is my god. Autumn and the Mirror together lie at the center of my life, constant and unchanging. I'll do anything to restore that. And solving this problem means finding out what's wrong with me, why I can't touch the Mirror. If we undo that, we can fix it. I can become Herald again. Life will be normal again, the world safe and everything in its proper place.

I nod. "I promise, Your Holiness. Anything it takes."

Autumn's expression remains cool, collected, aloof as a god. At least for now, until our world starts seeping into him as the days stretch on. I can feel the first tremors of his humanity, a soft sigh of relief through our bond. By the end of the season, he'll be very nearly like a mortal, with our full range of emotions.

I'm speaking half to myself when I murmur, "If we don't fix it soon, what happens to a world that can't escape autumn?"

"Nothing good. You humans have always known exactly when autumn would end, and winter, and set aside the appropriate amount of food to last the cold months. If it takes too long to fix the Mirror, hunger will come for you all."

I swallow. If that happens, it threatens everything. Not only our food supply, but the Temple itself. The Empire and the Temple have always stood in alliance, but what if they blame us for their troubles? The balance between the Empire's secular rule and the gods' divine authority has always been tenuous at best, a stalemate. If things get ugly, they could spiral out of control in so many ways. The Emperor, the Temple, and the rogue sect of the Kildian religion all exist in such a delicate equilibrium.

And then there are the souls. I am the one Herald with an additional duty. Life is the dominion of Spring, but he does not create souls. His Herald does not bring new ones through the Mirror every day. No, the ability to generate new souls is a tiny bit of magic that humans possess, given so by the high god Lys.

But the dead . . . they are my responsibility. I usher them into the underworld when their time in the mortal realm is done, to find peace. And now these remain trapped, a sign of my failure. I caress a blue soul as it passes, its light flickering in agitation. "When the last Herald trained me, he said that escorting the souls was a serious duty. That they can turn vicious, hungry, and dangerous if they aren't taken to the well."

Autumn makes a small sound of affirmation. "They can."

"How long does that take?"

"I don't remember. It's been thousands of years since that has been a concern. It only happened once, not long after Kild split the worlds, before the Mirror was created."

I swallow, words failing me as the souls drift about, fretful but still harmless for now. Their threat presses on me, though, an hourglass spilling sand. "We have to fix it."

"We will." The utter assurance in his voice calms me. He is a god. If Autumn believes it will be fixed, it will. Silence falls for a time, and we stand our vigil illuminated by the eerie light of the souls.

Finally, my god speaks again. "Good night, Tirne." He walks away, fallen leaves scattering in his wake.

Before I follow him, I cast one last apologetic glance at the souls in the sky. "I'll make this right."

THREE

A familiar cascade of pain welcomes me back into the human world when I awaken the next morning, a sharp, relentless stabbing sensation behind my right ear, always in the same spot.

The first headache after my return is the most jarring. While gods absorb the mortality of our realm during their three months here, we Heralds draw a small measure of divine power while in Sylvus. It is a mere crumb of what a Scion possesses, but for me, it is enough to keep my frequent headaches at bay.

Here in my realm, I awaken to agony. The episodes, though erratic, will grow more frequent before I leave for Sylvus, if I ever get to return. Every moment here, the magic of the gods' realm leaks away from my bones, my flesh. But the first attack always strikes sharp and fast. If it begins during the day, I can sometimes prevent it by taking my medicine at the first sign: the first watering eye, the moment my nostril plugs. Not so if it strikes in my sleep, as this one has.

With slow caution, I ease myself up and gently massage the back of my head. I don't know why I still do that; it doesn't help. A disgruntled meow drifts up from the foot of my bed as I dislodge one of the Temple cats from her slumber.

"Sorry, Hilo." The sleek gray cat stretches and jumps to the floor. I fumble in my nightstand for my precious bottle of bittersweet, peppery goldroot extract and the small spoon I use to measure it. It burns my tongue, but I welcome the sensation. It's the taste of relief, though it will take perhaps half an hour to settle in. I glance at the other jar in the drawer, full of gritty black grains like bitter sand, but I decide against the kaoreh today. It can help the pain, but at the cost of elevated anxiety and a jittery energy I am in no mood for this morning.

Instead, a trip to the baths and a lungful of steam should help ease the ache. Gingerly, I slip out of bed and toss on my robe, slipping a small vial of goldroot into my pocket in case of a later emergency before I pad down the hall in simple leather sandals.

A scattering of other residents already populates the baths. The ceiling is high, with small vents that allow steam to drift out. Several pools take up the space, a large communal one and a handful of smaller ones for groups of two or three. Private baths hide behind curtains along the far wall.

Today I choose one of the smaller public pools currently empty of other bathers. A solitary bath is tempting, but curiosity lures me more strongly. I want to overhear the gossip, even though the chatter rattles through my aching head.

My robe and sandals are placed on a shelf near the door, and I sink into the steaming water of an unoccupied pool. Enchanted by the high priests to remain the perfect temperature, the scent today seems to be a spiced mix of cinnamon and sandalwood. I breathe it in deeply.

There are others in the baths. I'm not immune to their stares and hushed whispers. They look at me like I carry contagion.

Fire and shadow, does *everyone* think this is my fault? Impotent anger flares again. Though frustration fills me to the brim and that tender spot on the back of my skull throbs, I refuse to let myself cry. *This is normal*, I tell myself over and over. *You lived like this all the time, once.* The episodes started a little over two years after Mother died. When the first one struck, we thought it was a passing ailment. The second time it hit, only two months later, people began to mutter and wonder how I'd been unlucky enough to contract the same sickness twice. When my third attack came, I hid it. Any weakness could affect my eligibility to become Autumn's next Herald. At the time, the current Herald had been old, and it was understood that he would step down within the decade.

So instead of revealing my flaw, I'd gone to a physician in the farthest part of the city in secret, one of those who heal with herbs rather than magic. She'd seen my condition before, she said, but told me it had no cure. Reluctantly, I'd even visited the sorcerer Sidriel, the most renowned healer in the city and a Scion of Winter. Though he'd left the faith to practice his magic outside the Temple, it was still risky to visit someone with a connection—even a flimsy one—to the gods.

He'd poked and prodded and asked cold, clinical questions before dealing the final blow with a shake of his head. "This is something deeply woven into your blood, your very being. I'd wager a parent suffers from the same?"

"Maybe. I don't know my father."

Sidriel had offered me specialized treatment, tailored to my blood. But when I insisted I couldn't pay his exorbitant price, he shrugged and sent me away with my first bottle of plain goldroot extract instead. Even that cost a pretty chunk of my Temple allowance. I'd never returned to him, especially after I became Herald. At least he'd assured me it was neither life-threatening nor contagious. Small comfort on days when the pain flares so hot that I can barely get out of bed.

The god of Spring might be able to heal me, with his power over life and wellness. But if he refuses to help, I'd risk losing my title and rank. So I endure the pain.

Eyes closed, I soak in the bath until the piercing sensation in my skull lessens. Whether it's the medicine taking hold or the hot water, I don't know, and I little care. When my fingers and toes look like raisins, I take my leave, hauling myself out of the pool and patting myself dry with one of the soft towels on a shelf before dressing.

Next, I'll be on my way to the kitchens, available for whatever task the cooks set me. I wince at the thought of a day of labor and how it may kindle the fading headache back to life. My hand tightens around the vial in my pocket, the glass cool and reassuring. Jaed can fetch my medicine from town when I run low; I dare not ask to shop for it while I'm with others. And maybe, just maybe, I can pester Jaed for a scalp massage tomorrow. He knows only a few small spells, but the one that warms his fingertips eases the pain.

I loosen my grip on the medicine and withdraw my hand from the pocket as I near the kitchen, painfully aware of my acolyte's robe. This is my life now. Plain, simple, just one in a sea of faces. All my hard work unraveled, the last six years undone.

But I lived like this until my twentieth year. I can do it again.

I clutch the pendant of Mother's necklace. *You receive what you think you deserve.* Her voice echoes in my head, one of her favorite sayings. I'll find answers and regain my title once more. Whether it's some sickness or a curse, I'll solve this.

I swear it.

And yet, after two hours in the kitchens scraping pumpkins empty of seeds, the fierce throbbing in my head threatens once more. I dare not complain. I'd look lazy unless I confess my true ailment, and that is out of the question. The heat of the room may seem stifling to others, but I welcome it. Still, my work suffers. I'm slower than the other acolytes, and the one in charge of my group casts me weary, judgmental glances.

What happens next should not surprise me, but it does.

When I leave the kitchens, Calder waits for me in the hallway. "You're wanted in the Hart Room," he tells me.

Worry trickles through me. "Why?"

"I wasn't told. Autumn asked directly. It's not for me to question a god."

I nod. "I'll go."

Beads clack as I slip through the curtain of the Hart Room. I don't know what I expected in the small meeting chamber, but it wasn't a grim-faced physician wearing the black smock of his profession, his tools laid out on a pristine white cloth on the central table. A single chair sits ominously beside him while a handful of priests and sorcerers circle the opposite side of the table. Lamplight flickers in this inner room, no windows to let in the sunlight. Right now, it seems choking, the air thick and hot in my lungs.

Autumn stands beside the chair, his expression solemn. "Tirne." Command lies in the tone, but not his magical compulsion, not for me.

I swallow back the shivery, cold lump in my throat, my glance darting to the metal instruments. "Yes, Your Holiness?"

"The sorcerers and priests have requested your blood as part of their investigation, and I have chosen to grant it."

No choice is given to me. This is a demand from my god, one I cannot refuse no matter how a sick, slimy quiver has gripped my guts. The vials, the tubes, the needles, they wait patiently, greedily. They're lovingly polished, gleaming and immaculate, ready to pierce my flesh and steal my blood like hungry parasites. Cold metal leeches with shiny, sharp teeth.

Of course the sorcerers would ask such a thing. Blood is the conduit of all magic. If I am cursed, my blood will tell the story of it.

The chair bears makeshift straps, long bits of leather tied around the sculpted wooden armrests and legs. If I protest, I will be forced. Would Autumn use his power of compulsion on his own Herald, or would the sorcerers just manhandle me into the chair, struggling?

Instinctively, my hand lifts to again grasp Mother's necklace, a source of steadiness and strength as always. My voice rasps, "Understood." I will not be pinned down by the physician's wiry, gloved hands. He has a callous look to him, watery gray eyes watching the scene with disinterest. I am as little to him as a book to a scribe, a mere task to perform.

The walk to the chair seems endless, my head spinning and my breath sharp and shallow. The thought of those metal *things* piercing me, drawing out my blood, makes my stomach heave. It's one thing to puncture my own skin in service of the Mirror, but for someone else to do it leaves me shaking. Autumn stands straight and cold beside the chair. When I sit, I cast him a short glance. There. The smallest of furrows in his brow, a small downward curl at the corner of his lips.

And through our connection, I feel a twinge of relief. Had he thought I would refuse him?

The physician speaks not a word. With ruthless, quick efficiency, he ties a tight, wide ribbon around my upper arm and presses my wrist down onto the armrest. Cotton gauze swipes cold, pungent liquid on my skin. I can't tear my eyes from the contraption as he assembles it. Tubes and a bright silver needle, shining and oh so sharp, with a bulb attached to create the pressure vacuum that will steal my blood away.

"Breathe," Autumn's dry voice murmurs, and I realize I am not. I suck in a sharp lungful of air, let it out slowly. The physician squeezes tightly on the bulb, and the thick, hollow needle hovers over the thin skin at the inside of my elbow. I screw my eyes shut.

The pain is sharp, pinching, bruising. Then the strange, weightless sensation of my blood being pulled from my vein as he releases the bulb. Still, I refuse to cry out at such a small indignity. Scions drain their own blood to fuel their magic concoctions and conjurations. How could I do less?

It doesn't take long. My eyes remain tightly closed until the needle slides sickeningly from my flesh and rough gauze presses against the puncture. Another deep breath later, my eyes open. The physician wraps my arm in a neat bandage, then distributes the blood into six small vials. At the sight of it, my head feels light and dreamy, and my vision wavers.

The physician hands a vial to one of the sorcerers, someone all too familiar. Sidriel. The one who diagnosed my headaches a decade ago. Does he remember the young acolyte who came to him once, and does he realize it was me?

Sidriel swirls the vial in the lamplight and watches my blood swish in circles along the glass. He is Winter's offspring, Jaed's half-brother. Elder by a decade, but bearing the same icy complexion. He paints his lips black and lines his eyes with dark kohl. The effect is harsh, striking, like his smile, like his jagged stare.

"Tirne," Autumn says softly. "Sidriel has been assigned to study your blood and determine if there is any sort of dark magic lurking in it. He will be living at the Temple for the duration of this investigation."

To determine if I bear some flaw, or if I was cursed. And maybe, just maybe, to expose my headaches to all the world. Even if he doesn't remember me, will such a weakness be visible in my blood? I shiver.

Beside me, Autumn's hands clench into fists at his sides, then loosen.

As I stand, Sidriel catches my gaze with colorless, black-smudged eyes, his grin colder than his mother's. "Thank you."

A cough clears my throat. I stretch my arm out, then bend it gingerly. The pain is less than I expected. I wonder if they will bleed me again, if they don't get the answers they seek this time. A bitter smile touches my lips. "You're welcome."

As I leave, a light pressure at my shoulder makes me turn. My god pulls his hand away. My robe separated his fingertips and my skin, but still he looks a bit startled at his own gesture. "I . . . ," he says quietly, pitched low to avoid the earshot of the Scions chattering over my blood across the room. "Thank you." Softer than Sidriel's sharp gratitude, there's something haunted in Autumn's eyes. Worry. It flickers through our connection, and I nod weakly.

"Whatever you ask, Your Holiness. I made you a promise."

His smile is a delicate thing. He looks like he's about to say something else but shakes his head and walks away in a waft of apple-scented air.

Hunger gnaws at my stomach. I can't avoid the dining hall forever, but my mood sinks the moment I bump into other acolytes on my way. Their wide-eyed stares at my new robe leave me gritting my teeth and my cheeks burning hot. I do my best to ignore them, but as I enter the large room, conversation at the nearest table stops.

Somewhere nearby, a child blurts, "Is that her?" before being shushed by a parent.

The awkward silence falls again for several long seconds before the Temple's residents hunch together and whisper. "I told you," someone at a nearby table hisses. Their companion snickers.

Is that her? I told you. Do they know about yesterday's incident with the Mirror shard as well, or just the initial shattering and my demotion? I grimace and stare at the floor.

Trying my best to ignore the chatter that follows in my wake, curling away from me like steam from a teacup, I fetch a flat wooden plate and take my place in line at the long table. A hollowed-out squash stuffed with sausage and crumbly white cheese seems as good as anything, and I throw it onto the plate. Sliced potatoes baked in herbed cream follow, along with one small apple tart. The cinnamon smell of it sticks in my nostrils.

After selecting my meal, I scan the room. Jaed is nowhere to be seen. Of course. It's a wintersday, and he'll be teaching his lessons now, then dining later.

But two others wave me over cheerfully. Vanyse watches me with sympathy in their dark eyes, while Feryn scowls at any gawkers until they look away. She may look like a sculptor's dream, all reddish-blond curls and proud aquiline nose, but she has the glare of a lioness when she wants to.

Relief washes over me. At least these two still welcome me, though our friendship is newer than Jaed's. I'd met Feryn in Calder's mathematics tutoring group when we were eighteen. If I'd been content to stay an acolyte, I could have accepted less-than-stellar scores in the subject. But I needed every advantage when I applied for Herald, and I was determined to get a full commendation, even if numbers and calculations turned my mind into slush.

Vanyse had come later, one of my rivals for the Herald's title. After I'd earned it, we'd become friends. These two had hit it off, then stuck together like glue. Some might find it odd that I associate with a past rival, but Vanyse is like clean, flowing water, with no place for ill will to sit and fester.

Feryn greets me with her usual broad grin, rosy cheeks glowing. Vanyse is more restrained, their smile a small curve of closed lips, dark eyes in a bronze face watching the room as they murmur a quick hello. Their gaze flickers down to the bandage on my arm, a question in their eyes.

"The Scions are testing my blood," I say, my tone cutting off further questions. But as I take my seat across from Feryn, the new, white trim on her russet robe catches my eye. White marks a potential Consort, one of the twelve that will try to bear Autumn a child this year.

Feryn catches me staring and tugs at her collar with a shrug. "Yes, well . . . I figured, why not?" Feryn has been craving motherhood for a few years now, but I hadn't expected her to take this route for it. "And I'm tired of emptying chamber pots every other week." It is true that the life of a Consort would be a simpler one, with no more acolyte's duties. A Consort's only job is to bear and attend their children with the help of the Temple nurses. Any other stray time is their own. Her smile grows sly. "Besides, who wouldn't be curious about what it's like to share a bed with a god?"

I shake my head with a soft smile. Feryn has never been shy about her appetites between the sheets. Of course she would seize the chance to try something forbidden, rare.

"But," Feryn says, "my news isn't nearly as juicy as yours." She points to my orange robe. "What happened?"

I frown. "I was demoted. I'll tell you more later, but not here." Not in public, where anyone can overhear.

Although Feryn pouts, Vanyse pats her shoulder. "We'll talk about it tonight."

My second night back in the Temple is always reserved for these friends. Jaed gets the first, but tonight these two and I will talk until halfway to dawn. Feryn will eagerly share gossip I barely care about,

Temple relationship drama and other petty squabbles. But I will listen and nod along and gasp in dutiful shock because I love how much joy it brings her to tell me such things. Vanyse will inform me of the more important goings-on, the state of the Empire, how the council is getting along, and similar news.

I look forward to it gratefully. Amid all the chaos, I need a tiny bit of normalcy and peace.

As I leave, I drop my plate into the large wheeled crate with the other dirty ones. Tomorrow morning, I'll be scrubbing the soiled breakfast plates after the meal. But for now, my laundry tasks beckon.

Later that night, long after an eternal afternoon of hanging laundry, I greet Vanyse at my door. They're followed by a beaming Feryn, who quickly tugs me into an embrace. "Ah, I have so much to tell you!"

"First, tea." Vanyse points at the pot and cups on the table near my hearth as the two of them take seats there. I pull over my desk chair and sit while Feryn pours herself tea first. We've no need to follow host and guest propriety here, not between the three of us.

"So tell me everything," I ask after pouring my own cup and taking a sip of sweet cinnamon tea as Feryn launches into her flood of gossip. I let it wash over me, a comforting familiarity, nodding and making the appropriate sounds of shock at the more salacious bits.

"And, um." Feryn pauses. "I guess you should hear from us. Er, Rhinna got pledged. They've already adopted a pair of twins from town."

My hand shakes as I set my cup down. I take a long, jagged breath. "I see." It shouldn't sting like this. It's been six years. Rhinna, my first serious romance, a Scion of Spring with an infectious laugh and a vicious wit.

The look on her face when she said goodbye is seared into my memory, the resignation underneath the tears. I'd chosen the path of a Herald, and she'd decided that wasn't something she could bear, a relationship that only lasted a fraction of each year. A Herald couldn't be there for raising a child, something Rhinna had always wanted. Scions can't bear children, but those that want a family can adopt from orphanages in the city, if they want to.

I'd lost her, and it still hurt. I knew she'd found another since then; the Temple wasn't so large that our paths didn't cross. But things would always be brittle between us. I couldn't hate her, but the loss left an ache that will never truly go away.

Vanyse's hand comes to rest over mine, and they give it a small squeeze.

"I'm all right," I say, and my voice only cracks a little.

"Well, you still have us," Feryn breaks in, too brightly, then changes the subject.

Later, after Feryn's well of gossip has run dry, Vanyse tells me of broader news. The border skirmishes near the mountains have ended, the Empire brokering a treaty with the neighboring kingdom at long last. In the city, the latest fashion trend is for elaborately ruffled hats imported from the south, which make the wearers look like ridiculous crested birds.

"The Kildians are petitioning to have their holidays recognized by the Empire, too," they tell me with a sigh.

I frown. Even though the gods cast Kild down, his sect remains. They worship the strange shadowy creatures Kild once called his minions, the imaginary—or at the very least, extinct—beasts they hope to lure with altars of dried herbs and placate with offerings left on doorsteps.

"The Kildians are going to love this," I mutter. "The Mirror broken."

Feryn waves a hand dismissively. "They can say their incantations and praise their figments all they want. The Mirror will be fixed, and they'll go back to their shadows soon enough."

I stare into the depths of my mug, swirling the tea as unease bubbles up within me. "I really hope so."

CHAPTER

FOUR

idriel isn't the only new visitor to the Temple. Autumn had sent a message to the Emperor, who passed a decree to the general populace. Anyone of a god's bloodline is commanded to come to the Temple, no matter how far-flung in the Empire they may be.

Sorcerers from the nearby capital city trickle in first, and the flood will continue for many days as others travel from farther afield. They arrive in ones and twos, these Scions who left the service of the Temple to pursue their magic among the people. Each one bears the stamp of their lineage: Summer's easy smile and dark complexion, Spring's round features in shades of burnished bronze, Winter's thin lips and utter lack of color. Some are Autumn's children, pale and sharp-edged, with that peculiar coppery sheen to their midnight cascades of hair.

Most of the sorcerers that live in the city—within walking distance—will not reside at the Temple, instead attending the Mirror during the day and returning to their homes at night. Those who traveled farther are given lodgings. Some will dwell in various inns and boardinghouses across the city, but the most important are given chambers here. Even a few city dwellers will remain in the Temple. These include Sidriel and the alchemist Wren, a foremost expert on enchanted items. They will stay here, at Autumn's beck and call, until the Mirror is repaired.

Wren keeps to herself, sitting alone at meals rather than at tables with other sorcerers, uncharacteristically solemn for one of Summer's children. Still, she attends the daily interrogations I'm subjected to by sorcerers and high priests. The questioning is always the same. Did anything seem amiss before the Mirror broke? Had the Mirror felt different that day? Was anything unusual in the night or days before? And on and on and on.

There's a sinister note to the questions, though. Suspicion. Doubt. Just like the Tharem, some seem to think I did this deliberately. Their questions are not meant to investigate, but to trap me in a lie.

I tell no one of the sick lurch in my belly as I passed through the Mirror. Shame roils within me, but I refuse to draw even more suspicion over something I did not do and that I don't understand. If they've already convicted me in their minds, how can I trust them to believe me?

While they study my blood, I conduct my own research, spending spare hours in the Temple's library, poring through ancient scrolls and hefty tomes for details of the Mirror's creation and any mention of strangeness about it. Had any other Herald felt that sickening lurch and nausea on their passage through?

I jot any detail of note down in my journal. Every suspicion, every possible suspect. Some names are easy to cross off: those who disdain much of their magic, choosing to serve the priesthood in other ways. Like Jaed's music and his teaching.

Then there are those like Laereda and the Tharem, who possess no magic of their own but have a motive for ruining my reputation or for keeping Autumn here.

Still, many of the priests and all the sorcerers are the unknown element. Other than Jaed, I know few of the high priests personally. I suppose I know a little of Calder, but it is a tenuous link. He is an alchemist, though, which puts him on the list. I'm familiar with some priests in passing, but I don't know enough of their private lives to determine a reason they would do this.

There *has* to be a culprit. I refuse to believe otherwise. If the Mirror's sundering truly was my mistake, they'll banish me at the very least. But that's not what makes me pale at the concept. The thought of admitting I failed, of seeing the judgment and disappointment on the face of my god, is enough to leave my gut tangled in knots. The look on Autumn's face when he demoted me had been icy cold, and I cannot bear it again. So instead, I search for answers, all while enduring my daily interviews and my headache spells with as much grace as I can muster.

And every night, as I fall asleep, I worry about Sidriel, the sorcerer who studies my blood, and what he might discover there.

FIVE

Jaed stands with his back to us while his students look to him attentively from their benches. We stand nearby to watch the performance in this small amphitheater near the central town square. Once a month, Jaed's students come here to perform, rotating among various groups.

I tilt my head up to the sun. It's a clear day with a mild breeze. I'm allowed out of the Temple to watch this show, but only because Bix and Jaed act as my escort. Babysitters.

It's the first time I've met Jaed's new lover. I've been so wrapped up in my interrogations and duties that I feel like I've barely had a moment to breathe. All acolytes lack Temple chores on their gods' day, but my autumnsdays are often spent giving my blood and answering questions.

Today, though, I finally have a few hours to myself. Bix stands beside me, and I sneak another glance at him. Tall, broad-shouldered, with bronze skin a shade or two lighter than Vanyse's, smiling eyes, and a trim, dark beard. He'd greeted me warmly, even throwing an arm over my shoulder companionably as we walked, as if we'd known each other for years. "Tirne! Finally, we meet."

I grimace. "Sorry, it's been . . . busy."

He laughs. "That's one way to put it. But come on, you can forget those fussy sorcerers for a day."

So we find ourselves standing in the brilliant sunshine while one of Jaed's older, advanced classes prepares to perform. Their music is far more tolerable than his classes of young children who've barely picked up their instruments.

A lanky youth stands in front of the benches, tapping his foot, beet-red and holding his flute in a death grip. A soloist. Jaed gives him a nod, and the young musician pulls the flute to his lips. The melody is impeccable despite his obvious nervousness. The other instruments join in one by one, bells and strings and a single lonely drum.

Beside me, Bix hums along to the well-known tune, a lively ditty about an enchanted well that brought forth precious gems instead of water, but only for the pure of heart. Other onlookers gather around, though most are family or friends of the performers. A few casual pass-ersby stop to observe, the rest moving along on their business.

I overhear snippets of conversation as they pass behind us.

"—how much longer—"

"—costs ten whole gold falcons now, if you can even find it—"

"—wouldn't have happened if Kild were still here—"

At the last one, Bix's humming falters, his shoulders tensing. I turn to catch a glimpse of the speaker and her companion, only to see them walking away. But I don't miss the wide black cuffs on their left wrists. Kildians, those who still worship the imaginary shadow-beasts the fallen god once commanded. I don't know if the creatures died out when Kild did or if they never truly existed to begin with, but I've never seen one.

"What's wrong?" I ask Bix.

He, too, watches the Kildians retreating with an unexpected inten-sity. He shakes his head. "Just someone I used to know. It doesn't matter now." A darkness lingers in his stare, and I let it rest. I wipe at my right eye, suddenly watery. Oh no. A faint spike of pain strikes me in that all-too-familiar area of my skull, and I struggle not to groan. I can't take my medicine here in public, even if the comforting weight of my emergency vial rests heavily in my pocket. And if I leave in the middle of the short performance, Bix will become suspicious.

I inwardly curse as the headache grows stronger, knowing that even my goldroot won't ease the pain if it becomes too much. The concert finishes to a smattering of applause, the students standing to give their bows. Jaed bounds over to us, grinning. "What did you think of Kero? He's going to be something special." I wince at his exuberance but manage a smile.

"He's very good," Bix says, tugging Jaed into a quick kiss. "But he also has a talented teacher."

"Well, that goes without saying." Jaed turns to me. "The students are heading back up the hill to the Temple, but I think Bix and I are going to visit the orphanage to play some more songs." He taps the flute case strapped over one shoulder. "Come with us?"

I should go with them. Technically, they're my watchers today. The students have already dispersed, making their way back to the Temple for their afternoon lessons.

"I . . . I can't. I promised I'd help Feryn with tidying her room. It's almost as bad as yours." The lie comes out easily. Too easily. At least the part about Feryn's room being messy is true.

"We should walk you back," Bix says. "We agreed to escort you."

I wave a hand. "No, I'll catch up to the students. They didn't say my escort had to be an adult."

Bix gives me a disapproving glare, but Jaed just laughs and tugs on Bix's hand. "Come on, it'll be fine. She's not gallivanting around, just going back. Kero and the others will keep her company." He turns to me. "But you'd best hurry if you want to catch them."

"I will. Now go."

Bix still looks doubtful but allows Jaed to pull him along down the street.

I make good on my promise and hurry to catch up with Jaed's students. The soloist, Kero, is in the rear of the group. He smiles shyly. "You're Jaed's friend, right?"

"Yes. You played well today."

He flushes deeply and stammers a quiet thanks before I let him flee to the other side of the group. The rest of the students chatter among themselves, the worries and gossip of the young. I catch a few tidbits of interest, though.

"Ma says you can't even find good firewood anymore. Not even a month in, but people are already buying it all up."

"Why?"

"For when it gets colder. Case it lasts."

"Seems paranoid to me."

But I have to wonder if it truly is all that paranoid or if some are merely more prescient and self-preserving than others.

Every step, my head pounds more furiously. Even though it's grown too intense for medicine to help, I take a dose when I reach my room anyway, then curl up under blankets in the dimness. This is one of the foggy ones, the kind that fills my brain with fuzz and makes it impossible to do anything but let the pain wash over me. It feels like being stabbed with my slender Herald's knife, over and over, always in that same spot on the back of my skull.

When the time comes for my afternoon duty, I stumble to the kitchen and beg off my tasks. I give the same reason I usually do when this happens. It's my courses, I claim, the cramps leaving me nauseous and incapacitated. I try not to use the excuse too often. I must look atrocious, for the sympathetic cook gives me one worried glance, listens to my explanation, and shoos me away. "We'll be fine without you. Go rest."

I feel a little guilty for the lie, but there's no way I could focus well enough to handle a kitchen knife right now. Instead, I slink back to my room, stoke the fire for a burst of heat, and burrow under the blankets again.

I'm surprised that Bix comes to me first. I groan at the ring of the bell, but he slips in with a soft apology. "I'm sorry. I won't stay long. Jaed is in his lessons, but one of the others on kitchen duty told me you weren't feeling well. I brought you some herbal tea from the Temple healers."

He sets a steaming ceramic mug on the side table by my bed. "Sorry, that's all they gave me. It seems wrong, to have magical gods' blood and still just give out herbs."

"Takes a lot out of a Scion," I mumble through the pain. "To heal. Worth it to save a life or soothe a suffering child. Not so much worth the effort for something nonlethal that many suffer monthly."

"Then what good is all that magic?" His voice ramps up a notch, tight with frustration. "It's unfair. The gods and their children have such power but refuse to do anything with it."

"When it's important, they do."

"Do they?"

It borders on blasphemy, what he's saying. My head throbs in the face of his irritation, and a whimper slips from me.

Bix's expression softens back into a smile. "I'm sorry." He pats my shoulder gently. "I hope you feel better soon."

A sick, shivery feeling washes over me for lying. Still, I manage a feeble thanks as he slips away.

Jaed finds me later, of course. He doesn't even bother to ring my bell, just slipping through the curtain in a soft pattering of beads. "It's a headache, isn't it?" He sits beside me on the bed, stroking my hair.

I nod miserably. The pain hasn't so much as budged while I lay here and let Bix's useless gift of tea cool on the nightstand.

"Thought so. I went to Feryn and asked if she'd seen you, but she said she didn't have any plans with you today. Sharply, I might add. Then Bix told me the 'truth' when I got done with my classes."

"Sorry about Feryn." She and Jaed have never gotten along, not since they met. He's always found her flighty. They both share my friendship, but never at the same time.

"I'll survive," he says, "and so will she. And so will you, if you let yourself rest."

I groan and pull my blankets up under my chin. "I can't do this again, Jaed. I can't live every day just waiting for one of these to happen. I need that time in Sylvus. I have to get my title back."

He chews on his lip before asking, "What if you didn't, though? Do you really need to be Herald?"

Tears burn my eyes. "Yes, I do. You don't know what it's like."

"But . . . you don't truly need to endure this. Slinking around in secret, pretending you're fine when you're not, overworking yourself. Visiting five different apothecaries in the city so none of them know how much goldroot you're taking."

"What else am I supposed to do?"

"Get help. Sylvus isn't the only answer to your problems. If you stayed here, you could look for better treatment, let yourself rest on days you need it. You don't need to push yourself so hard."

"I do. I'm a Herald. That means something."

Jaed looks away from me, staring into the burning embers of my hearth. "Is it really worth feeling like this? You could stay in this realm and find more effective medicine. Sidriel told you all those years ago that he could tailor something to you."

"For an obscene cost."

"Damn him." Jaed's free hand tightens around a fistful of my blanket. "We'll make him lower it, or find a way to pay it, or—"

"I can't. I need this." I squeeze my eyes shut, tears slipping free. "You have your music, and I have my Herald's title. Would you give up your songs so easily?"

"It's not the same."

"It is to me."

He sighs, giving my hair one last caress. "My music isn't forcing me to keep a secret that causes me so much pain. Just . . . consider it, all right?"

I sigh. "I'll think on it." A lie, but it mollifies him for now.

"Thank you." He kisses me on the forehead. "Now rest."

Jaed's words haunt me. Would I be better off letting go of my dreams, if I didn't feel like this again? But that title is all I ever wanted. To be important, to leave a mark in history. For my name to grace that tablet in the courtyard, to declare, *I was here, I did something meaningful.*

He can't truly understand. In truth, I don't know if anyone can.

CHAPTER

SIX

T he following day, I mend laundry after breakfast. Sewing has never been my best skill, but I'm still left to pluck out the threads of a worn hem on a Spring acolyte robe, then trim it and sew it shorter. I'm slicing the stitches free with a tiny hooked blade when I smell a familiar fragrance of mint and lemon. It twists at my heart just as a gentle voice asks, "This seat taken?"

I'd know that voice anywhere. Rhinna. I look up to find her pointing at the chair beside me, the rest of my table empty. No one wants to sit next to the pariah.

"No." My voice cracks on the word. Seeing Rhinna is an ache, like prodding at a sore tooth with my tongue. Six years have passed, but she's still beautiful, with a round, welcoming face, Spring's rosy hair cropped short, and dancing eyes the color of new leaves. She sits, letting her own mending project flop onto the table, a pale blue Summer Scion robe. A spool of matching thread is set down next to it, and she tugs a length free. When she turns to me, her expression is gentle, sympathetic. "Are you holding up all right?"

I don't know what to say. We've crossed paths since she left me, but only briefly. For the most part, we've avoided one another. I just nod.

"I'm sorry," she says, threading her needle and beginning her work. I return to my own task as she adds, "It's not fair, what they've done to you. Making you an acolyte again."

Miserably I ask, "What else could they do?"

"I don't know. But you sacrificed so much for it." It's not an accusation, just a statement, but still I hear the unspoken part in my mind. *You sacrificed our relationship for it.*

"I'm sorry."

She shakes her head. "We were both adults, and we chose the paths we wanted."

"It still hurt."

"It did. But I'm happy now. I think you were, too, before all this."

"I was."

"You'll get it back. I know you too well. You'll move sky and earth to fix things and regain that title." Her familiar smile beams, and I can't help but grin back.

"I am pretty tenacious." And I made a promise to a god. Still, I change the subject. "I heard you and Selere adopted."

Her laugh is like bells, bright and silvery. "Yes. Twin boys. Three years old and absolute terrors, but I wouldn't change a thing."

"I'm really glad." I'm surprised to learn it's true. I would only have made her unhappy. But here, she glows.

"I see you haven't improved at sewing," she jests, pointing at my first few uneven stitches.

"Not something I've practiced much." I tug the thread tight. "So tell me about these boys of yours."

With another snort of laughter, she launches into a tale of toddler antics, and I smile even as I struggle through the needlework for the rest of my shift.

After supper, my argument with Jaed lingers in my mind, a nagging guilt. Our disagreement may have been a small one, but I don't like feeling at odds with him.

"Come in," he calls when I ring his curtain's bell.

He's not alone. Bix lounges at a small worktable, chin in his hand and legs stretched out before him. Jaed sits cross-legged on the bed, fiddling with the tuning screws on a many-stringed tiilar.

His room is the usual jumble. Discarded robes scatter in careless heaps, while a tangle of jewelry sprawls across a side table beside assorted cosmetics jars. And yet, along one wall, his collection of musical instruments gleams spotlessly on shelves. A set of crystal bells, a tiny harp, an array of flutes.

I flop onto the bed wearily.

"Long day?" Bix lifts an eyebrow.

"Long enough." Another day of stares, of whispers, of both feeling utterly alone at my duties and also center stage in some play, unaware of the script. It had been a nice morning with Rhinna, but the afternoon was another story. I chew on my lower lip, trying to decide how to apologize to Jaed without telling Bix about my headaches.

But Jaed knows me too well. He catches my eye and gives me a small nod. Forgiveness. "Here, relax. I'll play something."

Bix winks from his spot at the table. "He's been composing something with three parts but won't tell me what it's for. Very pretty. I think it's for us."

Jaed flushes, his snow-pale skin turning a faint pink hue particular to a Winter Scion. "Well. Um."

I roll over and pat his knee. "Play it. I want to hear."

He does, closing his eyes as his long, silver-lacquered nails pluck the notes from the strings.

I love watching him like this. There's a special calm that settles over Jaed when he's lost in the music, an utter lack of tension in his body. A quick glance at Bix shows him grinning, too, though he closes his eyes, and his fingers tap the table in rhythm.

It's a sweet, lilting song, with three interweaving melodies. How Jaed manages that with just ten fingers and an assortment of taut strings, I don't know.

Three. A song for all of us. I wonder which melody is mine.

When it ends, Bix and I applaud lightly. "It's beautiful," I say.

"Told you it was." Bix's smile is too infectious. I can't help but return it.

Jaed crosses to the shelf and replaces the tiilar lovingly on it, then returns to sit on the bed and lifts my head to rest in his lap. Bix leans back in his chair, then pulls a half-carved wooden figurine from his pocket, along with a small knife at his belt, and begins to shape it. It's some sort of bird, wings outspread. "Well," he says, "music is a good beginning, but I do regret that we didn't meet in happier times." He stumbles a bit on the next words. "I'm sorry . . . about losing your job like that. Jaed told me it means a lot to you."

I suck in a long, shuddering breath. It's the second time today someone's expressed sympathy over it, and I wonder if such reminders will ever stop feeling like a punch to the gut. "It did."

"What was it like?" Bix asks, leaving wood shavings all over Jaed's worktable. "Becoming Herald? When did you know you wanted it?"

Jaed's fingertips find the back of my skull, his skin warmed by one of the few spells he's mastered. Under the guise of caressing my hair, he eases the pain. It's mild today, but the reprieve is still welcome.

I answer Bix. "Always. My mother said it was a sign, that I was born the day before autumn began. That loyalty to Autumn was my birthright, like hers, and her mother's before that."

I close my eyes as the story unspools from my lips. Jaed knows it well—he lived it alongside me—but telling Bix is calming, somehow. I add in the important details, such as the rush of using the Mirror's magic for the first time, or the feeling of triumph when my name was chosen. "In the end, it came down to three of us: the Tharem's nephew, Vanyse, or me."

Bix looks up, startled. "Your friend Vanyse?"

I nod. "We became friends later, after Vanyse came to congratulate me on my win. I don't know if I'd have been as gracious in their position."

Jaed snorts. "Certainly not."

"Hey!" I smack his knee, and Bix laughs as he sweeps his wood scraps into a tiny pile on the table. The scrape of his knife is soothing, and I sigh. This is nice. My months in Sylvus are lonely things. There are three other Heralds, but Winter's is like a jagged block of stone. Spring's and Summer's both grow close to the end of their service, far older than I and more aloof after so many years spent in the god's realm. We share the camaraderie of soldiers at some remote outpost, but there is little true friendship between us. A Herald's duty is important, but it is lonely.

This, here . . . this is true comfort.

I will become Herald again. But even so, these months here at the Temple with Jaed and my other friends are precious things. With Jaed's hands brushing my hair, listening to Bix hum an unfamiliar melody as he works, I am at peace.

They started by assembling the outer edges, just like any puzzle. Those are the largest shards and the easiest to identify. Some of the pieces in the center are barely more than pebbles, piled to the side for now. Puzzle masters guide those clustered around the table, showing small tricks. There had been some debate about whether to allow common folk to touch the Mirror, but Autumn decreed that any aid is to be accepted.

A half-dozen high priests walk around the perimeter, keeping a watchful eye on the secular puzzle masters who have come to try their hand at the greatest challenge of their lives. The priests ensure no one palms a scrap of the Mirror to sell as a holy relic.

Three thieves have already been caught, escorted to the Emperor and given to his secular authority for endangering the realm. I don't know what sentence they've earned for such a crime, and I don't care. My only concern lies with the Mirror shard before me, on the very corner of the table. That's more important than anything else, fixing it, returning to normal. If people threaten that, they deserve what they get.

Autumn stands nearby, watching. His command that I avoid touching the Mirror has been temporarily rescinded, but only for these closely supervised tests.

Both Calder's and Wren's gazes often flit toward me and my experiments. Between their attention and Sidriel's, I feel like a strange curiosity.

Twenty days have passed since my first bloodletting, and there have been a few other sessions since that have left me woozy. Time seems to slip away too quickly. Humanity seeps into Autumn's soul with each hour in our realm, and more scraps of emotion now trickle through my bond with the god. A pang of worry here, a thread of agitation there, and even the rare spark of joy. Today, unease flickers back and forth between us.

Sidriel frowns at me with his thin, black-tinted lips. He is a painting in stark black and white, his long hair tied back in a single plait. Midnight-blue sorcerer's robes echo Wren's in cut, if not in color, with similar charm-laden belts. He holds out a hand, and I grit my teeth as I place mine in

*D*ays pass.

This afternoon, I am in the council chamber, wa lytes and Scions piece together the Mirror with ex slow success. The expert alchemist Wren attends the repairs every afternoon. She is petite, pretty, with Summer's deep plexion and amber eyes, and a few years older than I am. I in dozens of small braids, the whole tied back loosely at the neck. Her sorcerer's robes are sage green, decorated with se eled chain belts, silver charms dangling from them. They shifts her weight, and I wonder how many of them are encl

Calder works beside her, as the Temple's most experienc in alchemy. They murmur together, theories that I only half derstand even less. His nervous chatter is endless, animate ments sharp and quick, eyes bright. Briskly, Wren pricks h smears a line of blood across the crack between two aligne When she pulls her hand away, it is one seamless piece aga

An alchemist, indeed.

She looks up and her golden eyes meet mine. An undef hangs in them before she turns to the next piece.

his, palm up. Despite his cool demeanor, Sidriel's skin is warm and dry. His thumb brushes the center of my palm lightly, gently. It's an intimate touch, and coming from this stranger, it makes me shiver. By contrast, the needle prick on the pad of my middle finger is sharp, efficient.

He turns my hand over and squeezes my fingertip over the piece of gleaming ruby Mirror. The drop of blood seems to fall in slow motion. When it lands on the glass, the softest of cracking noises reaches my ears.

The sorcerer releases my hand with a grimace and a soft curse. "Definitely magic at play here." He traces a fingertip through the blood that wells up on my skin, then touches it to his tongue, testing. I recoil, but he watches me thoughtfully as he does it. His eyes narrow suspiciously, holding my gaze like a snake charming a mouse. "But what?"

Clutching my hand to my chest, I stare at the glass, broken into three fragments. "Why do you even need me here? You have plenty of vials of my blood."

"Because," he says, "when we use the blood in the vials on the Mirror, it does nothing." Warning lies in his tone. Suspicion. His winter-white eyes stare into mine, asking a question that makes my nerves jangle. "The Mirror only reacts to your freshly shed blood."

"Nothing? So all that blood is useless?"

He shrugs as he gestures for one of the alchemists to knit together the piece I shattered. "You tell me."

"Tirne." Autumn says my name softly this time. When I look up into his eyes, something close to apology rests in them. His regret echoes through me. "You're dismissed."

I take the bandage a nearby priest offers, tying it tightly around my finger. On the way out, I cast one more glance at those working so diligently to repair the Mirror. Priests and acolytes, along with one lone common puzzle master—Tellus, a quiet, stern carpenter. The man chews his lip as his callused hands quickly sort through potential matches. He's helped cobble together an impressive section of Mirror on his corner already.

As I stand by the door, staring, the curtain clacks and the tiny bell set among the beads chimes cheerfully. I ignore it until I smell her perfume. Sickly sweet, a blend of vanilla and rich, sharp rose.

I turn to face her. "Laereda."

Autumn's former Consort meets my eyes with stunning green ones the color of Telesian olives, wide and surrounded by thick, honey-brown lashes. Her brassy hair is plaited back today, leaving her delicate features on full display. Soft rouge brushes her cheeks, the palest hint of pink on her creamy skin.

Her expression is haughty, proud. "Herald," she greets me. "Oh, wait, I'm sorry. *Acolyte.*" Simpering and false, the pity in her eyes. It makes my teeth ache. "Poor thing. I heard what happened." Of course she did. Everyone has. And if the Temple has a queen of gossip, it's Laereda.

"I suppose you would understand what it's like to be dethroned," I snap.

Her lips flatten, and I leave without another word.

After supper, I pore over my notes in my room. I've circled Laereda's name, underlined it. But I have to admit it is only my personal dislike of the woman that makes me suspect her so. She's human, like me. If she did this, she'd need the help of a priest or sorcerer.

While I chew my lip and ponder who might have cursed me, the tiny bell at my beaded curtain rings once, gently. Cursing softly, I blot at the ink and close the book to hide the list, hoping the letters won't bleed. "Who is it?"

"May I come in?" The voice is unfamiliar, and I cross the room to part the curtain. Wren stands there, a pensive expression on her face, a small bag slung over one shoulder.

I try to quell the nervous shiver that rolls through me. I gesture her in, and she takes a seat in one of the two chairs near the hearth. "Herald."

The title grates on me. It could be a mockery, but no merriment lingers in the word. Her eyes spark with cunning, but one hand plucks at a stray thread on the upholstered arm of the chair while her other clenches into a tight fist. Her foot taps out a staccato rhythm on the polished wood floor.

I unroll the heavy leather curtain that hangs inside the arched door-way. It's the best I'll get for soundproofing. "Wren."

With jerky, abrupt motions, the woman draws a small book and a miniature quill pen from a pocket. She dabs the tip of the pen on her tongue, and it darkens with ink. Magic, undoubtedly the work of her own hands. Her fingers are stained in smears of rich orange and smudges of emerald that almost look like paint. However, the scent of green things wafts from her, like the herbs in a spice merchant's shop. It's not paint, but the residue of flowers and leaves, ingredients for her enchantments. She watches me with sharp eyes. "Can I ask you a few questions?"

As I take a seat opposite her, I frown. "I've already answered a hundred questions. You know everything by now." My heart beats fiercely, but I keep my face calm and my hands still on the armrest.

She sucks in a deep breath. "Are you lying?"

"What?" I swallow, then cover it with a small laugh. "Of course not."

"I've been at your interviews. But there's something missing." The sorcerer leans over her tiny book, pen hovering over a page. "See, I was there the day the Mirror shattered, among the crowd. And I saw your expression as you came through, how you held your stomach. I studied medicine before I switched to alchemy. I know what pain looks like . . . and the look that crosses someone's face the moment before they vomit."

I try not to blink, to look away. "Passage through the Mirror is always taxing." Not entirely a lie.

Her eyes narrow. "True. But I've witnessed the Changing of the Seasons my whole life. I've watched you come through that Mirror six times, and never have you reacted like that. Nor given a look of such vast relief a moment later."

"So you accuse me of sabotage because of a single sour look on my face, one small gesture?" Fear leaves my nerves tingling, but I let only indignation show. Or at least I try to, but the too-sharp edge in Wren's scrutiny leads me to believe I may be failing.

"I ask you this question in private, out of courtesy," she says, clearing her throat. She scribbles a note in her journal. "We've always set aside the supplies we need for winter, with precisely enough to last us until Spring's arrival. I also see how slowly the repairs on the Mirror are going. If the Mirror is not restored by what should be summer, food supplies will dwindle, livestock will die. And we all know some will scrounge and hoard and stockpile supplies that should be shared, making it even worse."

Autumn and I had skirted around that very worry, the first night in the courtyard. And there was that overheard conversation so many days ago, about firewood already becoming scarce. Wren doesn't even know about the threat of the trapped dead souls, either. I cover the worry with a scowl. "So you're a soothsayer now, too?"

"I'm a problem solver." Wren scratches another line of text, then looks up once more, her eyes not quite meeting mine. "If you know something, now is the time to share. What will happen to the gods in Sylvus, without refreshing their life force here in our world? How long will *your* god survive, as he slowly turns mortal?"

My mouth goes dry, coated in invisible dust. "Gods can't die."

"Can't they? This has never happened before. It's bigger than you, than your pride. If you made a mistake, we need to know."

"I told the priests everything already. I'm sorry that's not enough for you."

With a grimace, she snaps the book shut, and I wonder if she just blotted her inked notes into oblivion. "I'm disappointed." She lifts the bag at her side, and glass clinks as she spills the contents onto the table. Vials filled with thick, red liquid.

My stomach tightens. "Are those . . ."

"Your blood."

I lean forward and pick up a bottle, then count them. Thirteen. They've taken fifteen so far, which means . . .

"I used two of them," Wren admits, picking one up and swirling it in the firelight. "For my own tests."

"But . . ." I let the sentence die, suddenly speechless.

"I stole them." She shrugs. "Swapped them for my assistant's blood. Simple, human, harmless. There's a reason the other sorcerers found nothing of note with their spells and divinations."

"Why did you do this? Sidriel—"

"Is a snake who would never share his findings with us." The vehemence in her voice startles me. "I had to know for myself what curse clings to your blood."

Was the Mirror's sundering truly my fault after all? Tears sting, but I blink them away.

Worse . . . shadows take me. Sidriel knows. That's what he was implying earlier. He's all too aware that the samples don't match, and he thinks I'm up to something. My mouth has gone dry, a bitter taste on my tongue.

Either dismissing or ignoring my distress, Wren leans forward in her chair, elbows on her knees and head in her hands. "Want to know what I found in your blood, Herald? Magic. Two strains of it. One is the weave of Autumn's, your Mirror magic. But there's another. Something diluted, hidden, something insidious."

I can't breathe, my chest tight.

"Someone poisoned you," she continues. "But not with rakeleaf or bleeding mercy. With a curse. When you passed through that Mirror, you were a walking trap. Threads of dark sorcery are woven into your blood, set to resonate out of tune with the Mirror. Like a specific musical note shattering a crystal glass."

"So I was right. This wasn't a mistake."

"No mistake. You were a carrier, an unwitting messenger of a skillfully crafted spell." The manic light in her eyes brightens, and I recognize it now. Fascination. Eagerness to solve a riddle. "I still haven't been able to untangle it. Layers upon layers to it, the work of an artist. I suspect it was a two-part spell, half of it set into the Mirror itself, waiting to activate until you touched it." She taps her fingers on one of the vials, her nails clinking. "That would explain why the Mirror in Sylvus didn't explode when you went through the night before. Unfortunately, it also means that your half of the curse could have been set at any time. Even last autumn. It could linger dormant in your blood for years. Then the culprit enchanted the Mirror before you came through again."

My shoulders slump. "So it could still be anybody."

"Anyone, as long as they possess a cunning mind and magic enough to craft a spell that powerful. And had access to the Mirror that night or morning."

Again, back to the same suspect list. Sorcerers who live in the nearby city, priests in the Temple. "Why are you telling me all this?"

"Because," she said, "I can't trust anyone who might have created this spell. But you couldn't have."

"What if I was a willing participant?"

"If you were, you're a consummate actress to feign your distress so well. And a fool to bring the possibility up now." She rolls the vial around in her palm. "I don't think you're a fool."

My eyes squeeze shut and I lean back in my chair. "So now I know *what* sundered the Mirror, but I'm no closer to finding out *who*."

"Ah, but that's the key, isn't it? You know the Temple, the priests. I know the sorcerers, lot of bastards that they are. I'll keep your blood to unravel the layers of the spell. There might be a signature buried in there, a trace of magic, a trademark. Something I can use to identify the caster."

Discomfort twinges at that, but I suppose it's better in her hands than in the others'.

"What if they bleed me again?"

"Then I'll swap it again. Hestor can spare a little more."

"And in the meantime?"

"I'll keep digging at the spell and the sorcerers. You poke your nose around the priests." She hesitates and looks away. "If you can somehow manage to get their blood or their saliva . . . I can measure their magical signature against the spell."

"I can't just go around demanding they spit into a glass for me."

"Fire and shadow," she swears. "Be subtle. Steal used wine goblets or silverware. And you can keep an eye out for other clues, as well. Spy, eavesdrop, whatever you must do."

"I'll work on it."

She stands, gathering up the vials with a nod. "Good. Come to me if you get anything I can test, and I'll tell you if I find anything of note. Until then, farewell."

A pounding head greets me yet again the next morning, and once more I head to the baths after taking my medicines. Both the goldroot extract and the kaoreh today. I move gingerly, trying not to jostle my skull as I walk.

When I enter the baths, Feryn trots up behind me. "Tirne!" She bumps shoulders playfully. I wince at the volume of her greeting.

Vanyse shakes their head with a yawn. "I still don't know how you can be so perky before breakfast."

"Call it a gift." Feryn disrobes, shoving her clothing into one of the cubbies. She tucks her hair behind her ears and I can't help but notice a fresh mark on her shoulder, in the unmistakable shape of teeth. My stomach lurches. Consorts, even the temporary potentials like Feryn, are forbidden to bed anyone save their god or goddess. And that can't be anything but a love bite.

I've never had to face the visible reminders of my god's nighttime activities. Laereda has always taken private baths. It's too human, that mark. I'm ashamed to admit it changes things, scraping away the image of an unknowable, inhuman god and replacing it with something utterly mortal.

Foolish. I already know Autumn experiences human lust, at least as our realm imbues him with an array of emotions he doesn't experience in Sylvus. Hence the three-month limit. Living here renews the gods' life force, but at a cost. They absorb not only our vitality, but our mortality as well.

Feryn notices my stare and blushes, bringing out the scattering of freckles across her face, her arms. "Hm. Yes. Well." She stammers, then smooths her hair back over the marks of Autumn's teeth. "It was, er, a memorable night," she blurts sheepishly.

Discomfort roils in my stomach. I don't like knowing these things about my god, not in such detail. This season, I've already seen sides of him that I never have, aspects of Autumn that are all too human. I didn't know gods could worry so deeply, or feel fear. And I didn't want to know quite so precisely what he does between the sheets, either.

Too eager to change the subject, I clear my throat as Vanyse and I disrobe. The kaoreh is kicking in, a flush of bright, shimmery energy. The goldroot, too. Already the pain lessens. Soon it will be tolerable, leaving me weary but functional enough to do my acolyte duties later. "So," I say awkwardly, "how did you like that new dish at supper last night?" It seems the Emperor and Autumn both have come to the same conclusion as Wren. Within the Temple, the cooks have begun rationing and preserving certain foods to bolster our usual stockpiles. Their latest attempt at trying new recipes had been a strange turnip-and-vinegar porridge that no amount of pepper could save.

Feryn makes a face. "Ugh, I think I'll starve, thank you." Her laugh accompanies the comment, and I respond in kind. But I can only think of that mark on her shoulder, Autumn's teeth in her skin. A shiver trickles down my spine. It feels like forbidden knowledge, and as much as it chips away at my impression of Autumn's divinity, the mental image also feels like getting away with something I shouldn't. There's a tiny thrill to wondering what it would be like, to be with a god.

After my bath, I'm on spice duty, grinding cassia into fine powder.

The scent of spices is nigh to choking. It clogs my nostrils, dries out my lungs. I'd forgotten what this was like, making incense for the Temple. Beside me, Bix does the same for his batch of clove. I wonder if he, too, secretly suspects I'm guilty. He's always affable, but every now and then I catch him watching me a little too closely. What if he only hides suspicions for Jaed's sake?

My muscles cramp from bending over the mortar and pestle, though thankfully the medicine I took earlier seems to have helped my head. The pain is steady, but tolerable. The kaoreh's invigorating effects are abandoning me and I yawn again, but I consider it a price well paid.

Today, Calder oversees us with those canny, darting eyes. It can't be coincidence how often he is my supervisor at daily chores. I'm left to wonder if he chose the task, or if he has been assigned to keep an eye on me. And if so, by Autumn or by the Tharem?

"Yilset," Calder says gently to a young woman in Summer's pale golden robes, "please make sure the molds are full to the top."

"Mmm." She nods with a blush.

I return to my task while Bix chats away about a recent game of ten-stones in the side yard where he and Jaed trounced a pair of Spring acolytes. The account drifts in one ear and out the other as my mind once more returns to that mark on Feryn's neck. What is it like, being the lover of a deity? Is the magic coursing through Autumn's body twice as intoxicating as a Scion's?

I swallow and blink away the image, scratching at my rough acolyte's robes. It's been well over a month, and I should be used to them now. But I look at our overseer and envy the brushed cotton that matches the luxe fabric of my old, stolen Herald's garments. No longer mine, the gold belt of my station. A plain strip of undyed leather wraps my waist.

And regularly sorcerers shed more of my blood on the Mirror shards, always to the same result. Sidriel doses me with potions or swirls my blood with herbs before touching it to the pieces, but they never fail to crack.

How many times can I proclaim my innocence before my god replaces me permanently, damning me to an eternity as an acolyte here in the mortal world? I don't know which is worse, the weariness of always wondering when my next headache will fall, or facing an expression of fathomless disappointment on the face of the god I've devoted my life to.

I gave him my oath. Whatever it takes. I have to keep it. Which, right now, means swiping samples for Wren's tests when I can find them and digging for clues in old books and scrolls. At least until I come up with something better.

A gentle hand on my wrist jolts me from my thoughts. Bix. His bronze face crinkles in worry. He nods back to my hands, and I realize my cassia has been dust for some time. I dump it into a bowl and throw more chunks of bark into my mortar.

"You haven't heard a word I've said, have you?" Bix's question could be a rebuke, but his rakish grin remains. "I'm a bit insulted that you'd rather stare into empty space than at this beautiful face." He winks as the other acolytes chat among themselves, ignoring the pariah and her friend.

"I'm sorry."

He shrugs. "You've got a lot on your mind."

"Still." I shake my head. "Not an excuse to be rude. Go on."

"Nah." Another laugh as he wipes a bit of spice dust from the back of his hand. "Ugh, I'm going to need to bathe for a full fourday before I stop smelling like mulled cider."

I heave a wistful sigh. Cider, one of the first victims of rationing. More than the usual allotment of fresh cider has been stored in cellars to ferment. Fresh vegetables are dried, the last of summer's fruits preserved in jams and shrubs. Just in case.

How long does Autumn think this season will last? It worries me that so soon, our god is already planning for the worst. Wren's words haunt me. She wasn't wrong. I've heard the rumors, that in town the longer-lasting foods such as rice or dried corn are bought by those who can afford it, stockpiled in their homes. The pickled items and tough smoked jerky that once were the staples of poorer families have begun to fetch a high price as they line the cellars of the wealthy.

I wonder how Aunt Ilna fares. Maybe I should visit her. I fear she'd take no help from me, though, not while I still serve my god.

Bix grunts softly. "You've gone far away again."

"Sorry."

"Why don't you tell me a little more about you? We haven't had much time to talk, the two of us."

I smile softly. "With Jaed around, it's easy to fade into the background."

"Well, he's not here now. So tell me something."

"Like what? My favorite color? A food I hate? My ideal partner?" It's hard not to match his teasing with my own.

He points to the leaf necklace about my throat. Real gold, it is a lovely thing for a mere acolyte to possess. "How about that? You wear it every day."

My hand flits up to it, and I close my eyes. She's been gone twelve years now. You'd think the tightness in my chest would go away. "It belonged to my mother before she died. And her mother before that. They were both acolytes of Autumn. It was a gift to my grandmother from my grandfather, a jeweler."

Bix's usual playful cheer slips away, sympathy painting his features. "And your father?"

"A pilgrim, come to the Temple to meet his god, Summer. It was a pleasure match, not a love one. He left to return home before he or my mother even knew I existed."

"I'm sorry."

I shake my head, letting go of the necklace and returning to my work. "It doesn't matter. Mother was enough for two parents." I sigh. "She had high hopes for me. I was clever, and ambitious, and she encouraged it.

Sometimes too much." A sudden lance of pain in my skull startles me, and I drop the pestle into the mortar.

"Tirne?" Calder asks. "Are you all right?"

"Sorry, hand cramp."

"Take a few minutes," he says. "Rest a bit, massage those fingers."

"Thank you."

Bix watches the exchange. He lets the subject go, but a sharp gleam in his eyes tells me he doesn't fully believe me.

I clear my throat. "So I told you my history. What about you?"

There. A flicker of . . . something, deep in his gaze. If I hadn't already been looking, I'd have missed it. A shadow. But he smiles again. "My favorite color is orange. I hate grapes. And my ideal partner has a wicked sense of humor and is a beast in bed."

I glare.

"Fine." He goes back to grinding cloves. "What do you want to know?"

"Why did you become an acolyte?" I point at his goldenrod robes. "Why choose Summer?"

He shrugs. "My father died and left the smithy to my brother, who sold it rather than see it in my hands. I had nowhere else to go."

"Why didn't your brother want you to run the smithy?"

He snorts. "Because I fucked his wife."

I sputter a sudden cough.

"Might want to close your mouth before you swallow enough spices to flavor your meals for a month." Bix's eyes dance with humor. "They weren't even courting yet when I tumbled her, but he didn't find out until she confessed to him in their marriage bed. Never got over it."

"And you came to the Temple."

"Seemed a fair shake. Meals and a roof, all for some simple work like this." He gestures down to his bowl. "All I had to do was pledge an oath to a god."

"And you chose Summer."

"Seemed a good fit."

I finish massaging my fingers and gingerly pick up the pestle again. "But you passed the entrance interview. Not everyone does." Bix is right. It's a good life, servitude in the Temple. He's not the only one to seek shelter here after misfortune. But the Temple has only so many beds, so much food, and there is a selection process.

"Well, I am awfully charming," he agrees.

I roll my eyes.

"What? Worked on you and Jaed, didn't it?"

If I were a more cautious friend, I'd warn him away from playing Jaed, but my friend is under no risk of swooning. Long ago, Jaed confessed to me his lack of romantic attraction. Sexual attraction he has aplenty, and his friendship is unshakable. But he doesn't feel the pull some do, that particular tug between two hearts.

I wonder if he's had that conversation with Bix yet, but I don't pry. Cautiously, I steer the talk in another direction. "So about that game of ten-stones you mentioned earlier. Tell me all about it."

Bix nods. "Well you see, the other acolytes thought they had us . . ."

Deep into the night, I walk back to my room with weary footsteps after my courtyard vigil. Autumn was nowhere to be seen tonight, and I wonder if he loses faith in me. My sandaled feet echo softly in the midnight silence, heavy in the Temple halls.

As I pass the Mirror's chamber, my feet go still, a chill settling over me. There should be a guard here. Someone always stands watch over the doorway, night and day.

I should call for help. But what if the guard is merely inside, and I make a scene over nothing? Heart pounding, I slip through the beaded curtain.

A single figure stands at the table, clad in a fine sleeping gown, a night robe tossed over it for warmth. A beauty with tumbling brassy curls, sleep-tousled.

Startled, I blurt, "You're not supposed to be here."

Laereda looks up at me, one delicate fingertip sliding a shard of the Mirror into place. "Neither are you. You're even more forbidden than the rest of us." The scrape of the glass along the table's surface seems unbearably loud in the quiet.

"The guard was gone. I wanted to make sure everything was all right."

"She needed to visit the privy. She'll be back shortly." Sweet mockery drips from her voice. "So now you can rest easy. The Mirror is in good hands."

I bite my lip. "Is it?"

"Are you accusing me?" Her eyes narrow. "That's rich, coming from you."

"What's that supposed to mean?"

Her mouth curls into a smirk as she manages to slide two pieces together, then sets them aside for the alchemists later. "You can't fool me."

It's a struggle not to look down at the small, healing puncture wound at my inner elbow, the spot where the sorcerers continue to steal my blood for their tests. Has Sidriel spoken to her? He hasn't confronted me yet, but there's a perfunctory quality to his tests now, a disdain in his eyes. He definitely knows the blood in the vials isn't mine.

I cover my nerves with an accusation. "How did you get the guard to let you in?"

"Everyone has secrets."

I blink. Is she insinuating she blackmailed the guard? It is rumored that Laereda knows all the gossip from the Temple halls, even more than Feryn. But why would she threaten a guard just to pore over the Mirror's pieces?

"If you damage it—"

She laughs. "Hard to break it more than you already have."

"I'll tell Autumn." As soon as the words leave my lips, I wince. It sounds like a child threatening to tattle to the nursemaid.

"Go ahead. Tell him that the mother of his children stayed awake long after others were abed to help salvage the Mirror and save us all." Her eyes wander over the pieces, selecting another and trying it against the two she just assembled.

My fists clench at my sides. "Someday, Laereda, everyone will see your true colors."

Her expression turns bitter, brittle. "No. No one sees me. But I know what *you* are. And now so does everyone else." Her smile is even sharper than her stare.

My stomach twists. I have nothing to say to that, nothing she'll believe. I turn and slip through the doorway without a farewell, but her insinuations send a shiver down my spine.

Halfway down the hall, I cross paths with a Summer acolyte being harangued by the Tharem, heading toward the Mirror Chamber.

"I don't care if she's a Consort," he hisses at the woman. "You do not leave your post." Glancing up, he sees me, and his expression darkens. I pass him wordlessly, though I feel his stare following me.

My boots clack on the cobbles as I walk the main street of town, Jaed beside me. Normally I'd avoid going out today. It's Remembrance Day for those of the Kildian faith, and they honor their fallen god's "sacrifice" for humans, when he split the worlds. Garlands and wreaths of their sacred plants hang on doorways and windows, their fragrance wafting on the chilly breeze.

Today, the Kildians wear more than their wrist cuffs. Garbed in black and gold, a group of them have erected a large tent in the town square over a wide brazier. They kneel before it and burn offerings of dried herbs to the shadowy beasts they hold dear, breathing in the acrid smoke.

The Kildian believers are fewer in number than my faith, but there are enough sidelong glances at my russet robes to make me uncomfortable. Still, it is an autumnsday, my free day. Jaed and I make our way down the street as guilt gnaws at me for withholding information from him. I have yet to tell him what Wren found out, but our last disagreement haunts me. I fear if I tell him of the curse, he'll try to convince me to go to Autumn, or worse, the Tharem. Maybe he'd even do it himself, "for my own good."

So I keep my secrets and fall into step next to him. Jaed carries a small tote of the supplies he's purchased today, oil for his wooden instruments and a new set of strings for his tiilar. Even a pack of Bix's favorite honey pastries, though Jaed paid twice what they would have fetched before the Mirror broke.

I have a mission of my own, too. We pause at an apothecary shop, and I skim the shelves. Vanyse is abed with a cough, and while the Temple healers provide the usual tea and medicine, I'm on the hunt for my friend's favorite lozenges. Anytime they've fallen ill, Vanyse has devoured the things like candy.

I find a crisp label on a shelf's edge, but it stands before an empty spot. I curse softly, fingers brushing the dust where the medicine should be.

"Guess we'll try one more," Jaed offers. I nod wearily. This is the third shop, and I'm losing hope.

"You won't find riddlebark here, or anywhere, most likely," a cool voice says behind me, and I whirl to find Sidriel at the counter, exchanging coins with the shopkeeper over a bundle of herbs. He points to the blank space. "Shipments from the Northern Isles have slowed to a crawl, and they're holding tight to their herbs anyway. Sickness season's hit them harder than usual."

I sigh. Well, that settles that. Vanyse will just have to cope without.

Sidriel pockets his coins and smiles slyly. "Good thing I'm the one person in town who still has any in stock. You're looking for the honey and riddlebark lozenges, right?"

"How convenient," Jaed says, and I startle at the bitterness in his voice. He places a protective hand on my shoulder. "And how much will you wring out of us for them?"

Sidriel doesn't even glance at Jaed, only meeting my eyes. "For mere lozenges? Standard market value. Three copper sparrows a dozen."

Biting my lip, I nod. This man makes me uneasy, after Wren and I have been lying to him about my blood samples for weeks. The sharpness in his stare worries me. Still, we follow him to a tidy shop on Yarrow

Street, in an affluent part of town. Passersby here wear silk and fine Telesian wool, not plain linen. The sun is just beginning to set, the stores shutting their doors for the evening.

Sidriel unlocks his workshop and gestures me inside. It looks just as I remember it, from all those years ago. The place reeks of herbs, of cleansing vinegar, of potent alcohol and spice and magic. It's orderly and clean, everything in its place. A large wooden worktable stands in the back corner of the room, topped with a neat set of vials and flasks. Shelves of books and bottles and odd trinkets line the walls. A set of narrow stairs leads up to a balcony loft.

The transaction is quick, just business. Still, something about the way Sidriel watches me makes me feel like I've been turned inside out like a pocket, searched for anything buried at the bottom. For my secrets, for my lies. I wonder if Sidriel recognizes me now, the acolyte that came to him complaining of headaches.

If he does, he doesn't mention it.

As we leave, Jaed mutters, "At least he didn't gouge you this time."

I nod, but before I can say anything, a sudden cry breaks the silence. It's a woman's voice, a strangled, wordless shriek.

Both Jaed and I are moving within a moment, rushing toward the sound. A small crowd is gathering at the mouth of an alleyway, blocking my view. Someone is sobbing and muttering hysterically over the rising din of the growing onlookers.

Wait. I know that voice.

"Feryn?" I call, pushing my way forward. Jaed grabs my hand to avoid losing me as people press in closer.

"Tirne?" It's definitely Feryn, a wavering, thick sound. "Tirne!"

There's a gap in the crowd, and I catch sight of Feryn, looking up at me with terror in her eyes. Someone is holding her hands, their back to me. They speak calmly, like one would to a spooked dog or horse. "It's going to be all right."

But Feryn is looking only at me as I approach, Jaed in my wake. Her face is blotchy, glittering with tears. "Tirne," she sobs. "It's so awful. I *touched* it—him." She starts shaking and crying again.

The person holding her hands turns to me, and it's not a stranger. Aunt Ilna's eyes widen, the same dark eyes as Mother's, as mine. "Tirne."

For a long moment, we stare at one another wordlessly, until Jaed breaks the silence. "What's going on?" He steps up beside me.

Feryn flings herself at me, and I wrap her in my arms, even as she buries her face in my shoulder.

"The girl found him, I think." Ilna points behind her, a few steps into the alley. The narrow path is not empty. Someone kneels beside a body partially hidden behind a refuse bin. The corpse's eyes stare glassily forward, hands contorted into claws as if he died fighting off an attack. There's a strangeness to him, like a husk of a person, cheeks hollow, skin dry as paper. The kneeling man examines the corpse, though it's obvious life is long gone. I can't tear my eyes away. There is no blood, no torn clothing. I overhear someone offering to fetch the undertaker, then sprinting down the street.

Ilna shakes her head, voice sorrowful. "It happens sometimes. Those who have no homes, caught out of doors. Sometimes they fall ill or become a victim of violence. Your friend seems to be all right, but she's barely gotten a coherent word out."

Feryn sucks in a long, shuddering breath and slips from my arms, wiping her eyes. "I just went to take a shortcut back home, and I tripped over his foot. I didn't know—I shook him, and the way his head moved . . ." She bursts into tears again.

"It's still a long walk back to the Temple," Ilna remarks. She says "Temple" like it's an unsavory word. I can't help but stare at the black Kildian cuff around her wrist as she points back through the alley. "Gantry's got the poor dead soul taken care of now, and the undertaker will be here soon. Let the girl rest at my shop for a minute, calm down. I'll make tea."

I start to shake my head, but Feryn nods gratefully and says, "Yes, please."

Ilna pats her gently on the shoulder. "Come on, then."

As they walk away, Jaed's hand finds mine again. "You don't have to go."

"I do." Ilna would see Feryn safe on her own, but I feel protective anyway.

Soon, I find myself inside my aunt's cobbler shop for the first time. She unlocks the door and leads us into a small kitchen in the back. A smaller side door leads into another alley, and I'm grateful we didn't take Feryn through it. She's still shaking, rubbing her hands on her robe as if she can scrub them clean of an invisible contamination. Ilna gives her a basin and soap. Feryn breaks down crying again as she washes her hands, but waves me away when I approach.

Soon enough, Feryn is sipping on chamomile and lavender tea alongside Jaed at the tiny table. It seems their usual dislike of each other is set aside for the moment. He pats her shoulder and murmurs what must be a jest, because she breaks into a shaky laugh before taking a deep breath and staring into her cup.

I am too uncomfortable to sit. Ilna catches my eye from the small hearth as she refills the kettle and hangs it. I almost wonder if she'll say something. Jaed knows all too well who she is, but Ilna left years before I befriended Feryn. Shaken up so, it seems my friend hasn't noticed our resemblance, or connected this woman to my stories of an aunt she's never met.

Maybe I should pull Ilna aside. I could apologize or, more likely, demand an apology. I was a child; she was the adult who abandoned Mother and me. Right now, though, Feryn's shock and panic lie between us.

Ilna's shoulders sag. "I'll be in the front room. Stay here as long as you need. I'll lock up behind you when you leave."

"Thank you," Feryn says. "You're so kind to a stranger. To . . ." Her gaze lingers on the black leather cuff at Ilna's wrist. The rest remains unsaid. *To someone in an acolyte's robe.*

After Ilna leaves for the other room, the weight of it pulls me down, this thing between Ilna and me. Years of hurt and distance. As Feryn grows calmer and Jaed cheers her with distracting stories, I stand.

"I'll be back in a moment." In the front area of the shop, the counter and workbench and display racks rest. Ilna is sweeping the floor and looks up when I walk in.

"Tirne . . . ," she says, trailing off.

"Thank you. For helping Feryn."

"I would have done it for anyone."

"I know." I lean against the counter. "But she's my friend, a Temple acolyte, and you helped."

"Kildians don't hate you, you know." She finishes sweeping the dust into a pan, then dumps it into a bin behind the counter. "I wish you'd understand the truth, but I don't hate the faith."

I snort. "The truth. We all know the story," I remind her. "Lys and Serrema, Kild's betrayal. We have the proof of it, the Mirror."

Ilna puts away the broom and leans on the counter beside me, staring out into the street. "That's not the whole story."

I am staring at part of the proof right now as dusk deepens, the dead souls that flicker through the streets. "If it's a lie, where did the Mirror come from, or the gods?"

"Oh, it all happened. But it's the *why* that matters. Kild wasn't jealous. He was protecting us—humanity—from gods that sap the energy from our realm, that care only about themselves. Kild cared about humans more than his kin, and he was cast down for it."

"That's not true."

"And you have proof?"

"I have a god. I trust him."

"Why?"

Anger flickers. Before I can reply, Jaed's head pokes through the doorway. "Feryn is feeling better. I think we're ready to head back home." He makes his escape quickly back into the kitchen.

Coward.

I want to prove Ilna wrong, to make her see, but it's never going to happen. Instead, I shake my head and say, "Thank you. And goodbye."

"I'll lock up behind you."

CHAPTER

TEN

So far, I've managed to snag only a scant few items for Wren's tests. A stray fork swiped from a sorcerer's table after the end of their meal. An empty glass of wine from dining hall cleanup duty. None have been a match, and I feel the weight of the season stretching on.

Today, I'm once again at the mercy of Sidriel and the other sorcerers in the council chamber. By some unfortunate twist of fate, Laereda is assigned to working on the Mirror this shift. I haven't told anyone I saw her here that night. She was right, I'm even more forbidden to be here after dark than she is. Most concerning, though, it doesn't seem she has told anyone of my trespassing, either. I worry that she plots something, that someday she'll come to me with a threat, with blackmail.

The Tharem stands to the side in his brilliantly violet robes, watching for thieves with a hawk's gaze. Other acolytes and priests stand around the table, sliding pieces across the now-scuffed wood. The puzzle master Tellus's corner is far ahead of the other meager, assorted chunks that have been reassembled. Still, they try their best. Wren connects two shards pieced together by a Summer acolyte.

Laereda watches everything closely, standing opposite me. Her gaze darts back and forth between my face and Autumn beside me. At least today she keeps her distance despite her sharp scrutiny.

I stare at the fragments scattered across the table. So little of the Mirror re-created for the days upon days that have passed. More than a month and a half now, the season halfway gone. Though six to eight people are on the task daily, many are not skilled at matching the pieces. There are just so many, all straight edges. Jaed once confessed to me that he would often go a full shift without matching any.

At this rate, Wren's warning feels all too real. It truly may be months before it's restored.

A jolt of pain drags my attention back to my hand. Sidriel squeezes more drops of my blood onto crimson shards while an alchemist repairs them afterward. Today his attempts involve treating the Mirror's surface with various concoctions before my blood touches it, but to no avail.

His boredom is clear. He knows this is fruitless and walks through the motions only because an emperor and a god have told him to. But if he does know, I wonder why he hasn't confronted me yet, or confessed his suspicions to the Tharem.

Autumn stands on my other side. His scent washes over me, dry and crisp, apples and forest loam. Wordlessly, he presses a hand to a large shard. I wonder if he quests for a connection. Though we work feverishly to reassemble the Mirror, we still have no idea how to restore its magic. The sorcerers continue to turn up nothing, no scrap of magic hiding in its pieces or in the frame that stands in the courtyard. So they theorize and study old texts. Stories from the days of the Mirror's creation.

"It will take blood, of course," Sidriel murmured to one of the priests when asked how he thought it would be fixed. "And a lot of it." He didn't specify whose. The priest had shuddered and their mouth clicked shut before they made an expeditious retreat.

I fidget where I stand. Puzzles within puzzles. Fixing the Mirror. Finding out who broke it, and why. I must dive deeper into the Temple's secrets, the connections between people that could identify any possible conspiracy. When I was younger, there were the usual petty squabbles and dramas of adolescents, but I earned the Herald's position at the age of twenty. For the past six years I've drifted in and out of this world, living in the Temple for a quarter of the year, but never immersing myself in its currents.

That's changed, now that I'm trapped here indefinitely. I watch Laereda's eyes burn holes into Autumn, then into me. Tellus is oblivious, focused solely on the puzzle of the Mirror alone. Laereda could probably stab me, and he wouldn't even notice.

So many unseen threads tie the Temple residents in a tangle. Jaed and Bix. Feryn and Vanyse. Laereda. Sidriel. Calder. I've yet to successfully get a sample from the latter two, though I've watched them closely.

And as the days have stretched on, I've tried desperately to ignore my own bond with my god. He stares in silence at the Mirror, but I can feel the roil of frustration and worry inside him, and regret. His gaze darts down to my hand cradled in Sidriel's, the sorcerer's alabaster thumb tracing gentle lines across my knuckles. Something else bubbles inside Autumn, something that leaves my stomach in a knot. I fight the urge to pull my hand free.

Sidriel shakes his head, his voice a low rumble. "Your Holiness, I fear we may need to abandon our attempts with the Herald. Our efforts may be better spent on forging a new enchantment to restore the Mirror's magic." No sorrow or regret in the words, just stating a simple fact, all while his thumb still caresses my skin.

I yank my hand away. "No."

Sidriel's cold, cold gaze pins me. "These experiments waste our time." A soft curl touches the edge of his mouth, an eyebrow lifted slightly in a question.

Yes, he definitely knows the blood has been swapped. The softness of his grip on my hand, the hint of a threat in those eyes, they suddenly feel like poised daggers.

But he hasn't told anyone. Why?

Autumn hesitates. At least he gives me that. But he acquiesces with a nod. "Tirne, you are hereby forbidden from entering this room again." His voice is firm, but I feel a tremor through our bond. Guilt. Sorrow. And something even more poignant, sharper, something I can't define. "The sorcerers are to focus on restoring the Mirror rather than determining what sundered it."

Once more, my world is pulled out from under me. Still, my promise echoes in my head. *Whatever it takes.* I choke out the words "I understand."

"However, it is possible we may still need your blood, linked as you are to the Mirror. We will tell you if we require it. You are dismissed." It's only the smallest comfort, the twinge of regret I feel through our connection.

I pass Laereda on my way out. She must love this juicy tidbit to add to her hoard of gossip. But the look she casts me is indecipherable, not one I've seen on her face before.

If I didn't know better, I'd almost say it was pity.

Later that afternoon, melancholy still clings to me. But today it's my job to feed the goats in the yards behind the Temple, though we've less and less to give them these days. Mostly scraps, or the woodier weeds pulled from the garden, the kind humans can't eat. As I scoop tough corncobs into the trough, they clamber over one another, bleating. If autumn stretches on, I wonder how many of them will last the season. One comes up to the fence and I scratch between his horns.

"Go." I shoo him toward the food. "Eat." I lean against the railing as I set the bucket down and let them lick out the last bits. The sun shines today, and it is welcome. Though the air remains crisp, it's much preferred to the dreary days we've had of late.

When the goats have licked the bucket clean, I pick it up and take the path back to the kitchens through the garden. Most of the flowers are gone for the year, but some of the shrubs blaze in colors of flame. I have memories of what the garden looks like in spring or the height of summer, but that is no longer my world. I brush a crimson leaf as I pass, enjoying this mercifully headache-free afternoon.

I turn a corner and very nearly bump into my god, caught in an embrace with Feryn. Autumn's hand cups her cheek as they lean into one another, his cloak encircling them both. They look up at the sound of my footsteps.

For a moment, I just stare, my stomach curdling with embarrassment. Then remembering myself, I bow, suddenly painfully aware of holding an empty slop bucket. "Your Holiness. Feryn."

Autumn merely nods, though I feel a brief pang through our connection. They slip apart.

"Er, hello, Tirne," Feryn says, smoothing the front of her robe as she collects herself.

An awkward silence falls, until I blush and step aside. "I, uh, guess I should be going." Before they can say another word, I scurry away down the path, following the scattering of Autumn's leaves. I try to ignore my racing heart and burning cheeks. Or the unexpected, ugly thing that claws at my insides. I find a bench and slump into it, letting the bucket fall to the path with a crunch.

The sight is burned into my memory, my god's lips nearly brushing Feryn's.

And so? She's a potential Consort. That's her duty. When Laereda had been Autumn's Consort, I'd seen them in similar cozy poses from time to time, especially toward the end of the season when Autumn experienced deeper emotions.

So why do I feel queasy now? Because he stands vigil with me at night, sometimes? That's hardly a reason for this shiver of unease. Still, I wonder if he lets any of his Consorts see the flicker of worry in his eyes that I do, in the courtyard by the light of all those souls. I don't know if he's ever vulnerable around them, or if only I am allowed to hear the thread of fear in his voice.

I close my eyes. *No. I'm just embarrassed. It's different when it's my friend.*

"You look like you've just seen a garvish."

The comment breaks into my thoughts, and I startle.

Laereda takes a seat beside me. Her newborn rests against her breast, wrapped snugly in a sling and sound asleep. "So. Which one is it? Autumn or Feryn?" Her smile is cold, but part of it seems to turn inward, self-mocking.

"What?"

"Which one do you love? I know that look."

"I don't. I mean, neither." I shake my head. Yes, I've had a few blasphemous musings about Autumn's nighttime activities, but those are just involuntary stray thoughts. "I was just . . . startled."

Laereda's laugh is a brittle thing. "If you say so." She nudges one of Autumn's discarded leaves with her boot, a grimace twisting her features. "I suppose it's neither of them, anyway. It's that shattered piece of glass. I've seen how you stare at it."

I don't deny it. "I . . . You do love him, though, don't you? Autumn?"

She stares down at the tiny form nestled against her chest, only his face visible, dark lashes against pale, round cheeks. "That would be foolish."

"Love isn't foolish."

Another sharp bark of laughter. "Now I believe you. Spoken like someone who's never been in love."

It stings. I immediately think of Rhinna and swallow back a cold lump in my throat. I stand to leave, retrieving my bucket, but I can't resist one parting shot. "You don't have to be so cruel, you know."

"Maybe I wouldn't be so cruel if you weren't so perfect." She looks me up and down. "But I suppose now you're just a fuckup like the rest of us. You and I both know what it's like to lose everything, don't we?"

The words slide into my gut like a blade. In some ways, it hurts worse that she understands what Jaed does not. Part of me wonders if she would orchestrate all of this just to step on me, or to keep her god here. Does she think she can win him back?

My knuckles ache as I grip the bucket's handle and flee without a goodbye.

⁂

That night, my foot taps nervously against the floor as I sift through the papers and books at my desk, trying to find any clue about a spell that could shatter the Mirror. I'm stacking books into piles—useful, useless, or uncertain which one—when a faint, warm sensation spreads in my stomach.

Oh no.

Not tonight. Not while the conversation with Laereda still burns in my mind, after seeing my god with Feryn earlier. I recognize this feeling all too well. Desire. And it is not my own.

It sings along my connection with Autumn.

He spends tonight with one of his new Consorts, and from the growing heat between my legs, they must know what they're doing. I don't feel his precise physical sensations, thank Lys, only his emotions. Still, it's enough to stoke my own flames.

I wonder if it's my friend he took to bed tonight, or another. For a brief, flickering moment, I picture it, his pale limbs entwined with Feryn's as he leans over her. I shudder, and shame coats the thought. I should not imagine such things of a god, or of my friend. We need the Scions, the conduit and source of magic for humankind. Creating them is a holy duty, nothing more and nothing less. If my god or his partner find pleasure in the task, that is none of my business.

Still, it grows difficult to concentrate as the tingling in my abdomen spreads, making my breath hitch. My gaze drifts to my bed. I should settle the matter myself quickly and be done with it. Or Jaed's room is only a hallway over.

Still, it feels like an intrusion, to act on an emotion I've stolen from my god. So instead, I shiver and bury myself in letters and books until it passes. By then, the hearth burns low, but sleep eludes me. I stand and retrieve my cloak. I could ignore the souls that gather, but I can't fully abandon them, even with the Mirror shattered, even with my title stripped.

In the courtyard, the dead cluster so thickly they cast as much light as an overcast day. They hover overhead, a few occasionally drifting low enough to touch. They extend out over the walls now, and I wonder how far they spread. How soon will the city streets spill over with them, unseen and weaving among the living?

I shiver, standing my silent watch and mourning the Mirror. Someday, I expect the hollow grief to lessen, but it has not. I hadn't realized how its presence filled a small space in my breast, not until it was gone. Restless, I turn from it and walk to the pillar in one corner of the courtyard, a litany of carved names covering half of it.

I trace my finger over the last. *Iniriah of Autumn*, the Herald before me. Retired six years ago, his name added to this record. He'd passed away last year, and I'd shepherded him to the underworld with the rest of that day's souls.

My hand flattens against the empty space beneath his name, the place where mine would have gone. No. Where it *will* go, once I prove my innocence. If we find the culprit, we'll know how it was done. Then we can cure my curse. We have to.

The rustle of leaves interrupts my musings. I'm surprised. Though the echoes of tonight's lust have long since faded, I expected Autumn to bask in the afterglow with his potential Consort.

Then again, it is not for me to wonder how their lovemaking plays out.

As before, we stand in silence. His eyes trace the names, dozens of them. All the lifetimes he's witnessed, the Heralds that have found their way to his underworld. Sorrow clings to him, washing over me in a somber wave.

"You don't need to stand vigil," he says, but it is too gentle to be a rebuke. "The souls are no longer your duty."

My gut twists. A sharp knife, those words. I look away and change the subject to banish the tears that threaten. "Can they actually fix it? Not just piecing it back together, but the magic that makes it work?"

This finally garners an answer. He shakes his head. "They don't know."

"But you were there when it was created."

A nod. "But Lys didn't tell us how he harnessed that magic. I watched, but I did not craft it myself."

Frustration flares. "So you don't know, and the sorcerers don't know, either. The best magical minds in the Empire, and they come up completely blank? They can't have found *nothing*." My hands shake, clenched into angry fists. I nearly reveal Wren's findings, but then he'd know we lied to the Tharem, to the other sorcerers.

He turns to me, the fiery glow in his eyes reflecting the hollow lights of the souls. In the ghostly violet-and-green illumination, he seems even more unearthly, his hair tossing back jewel-toned glints. His lean face takes on an eerie, skeletal quality. The souls flit around us, agitated, restless, their sibilant whispers echoing in my mind. They plead for guidance I can no longer provide.

The Lord of Death stands helpless before his subjects, and I am the lone witness to his failure. Not just an observer, but the cause of his impotence. Guilt claws at me. Words fail. Nothing I say can fix this.

Except. "I'm . . . investigating. Looking for clues, maybe ferreting out suspects." I still don't mention my plans with Wren, afraid to tell my god of my lies.

Autumn breathes deeply. "Those are muddy waters to wade. Can you play such a game?"

Squinting up at the souls' light, I let out my own sigh. "I gave my oath. I intend to keep it."

ELEVEN

I frown at Wren. "Nothing? It's not enough."

"These tests are all I have," she admits. "So unless you can think of another way to flush out the culprit, I'm out of ideas."

I need to do more, to squeeze secrets and clues from this place. And one person in the Temple holds the most secrets. More than Jaed, more than Feryn. Laereda. If there are scraps of gossip to be had that might lead me in the right direction, she holds them.

I don't know if she'll even speak with me, but I have to try.

She answers my gentle ring of her door's bell after supper. The orange beads part to reveal her sweet face, her hair in perfect golden-brown waves. Puzzlement creases her brow. "Tirne?"

I sniffle. It had not been difficult to conjure the tears; they seem always close to the surface now, my emotions raw and bleeding. My nose runs, and I'm certain my cheeks are a blotchy mess. A pretty crier I am not.

But this hook is baited with intrigue, not beauty. "I know you hate me. You were right. I was too proud. I'm sorry."

She stares suspiciously. "Why are you apologizing now?"

"Because. You said it. We both know what it's like to lose it all. You . . . You're the only one who understands."

With a sigh, she lets me in and encourages me to sit down while she bustles about nervously making tea. It is a friendly, inviting space, with a small, enchanted plate to heat her teapot on a side table. Rare globes of ethereal light illuminate a small but opulent chandelier hung from the ceiling. Warmth suffuses the space despite the lack of a hearth, almost stiflingly so. Her bed is visible through a door, her sleep and sitting rooms separate. Curtains of ivory velvet drape her mattress, and a pile of pastel-colored pillows spill out like rice from a torn sack.

I marvel at how casually she's made use of magic. How many high priests spilled their blood for this room? I wonder where Laereda will reside next year, when Autumn's new Consort takes over these luxurious rooms.

A small crib rests beside the bed, the pale form of her baby swaddled in soft pink blankets. The tea table where I sit is white, with floral patterns twining up the legs and along the sides, matching the general theme of roses and daisies and carnations that covers her room. An embroidered butterfly on the upholstered arm of her chair even flaps its wings gently.

My eyes settle on a small, lacquered box in ebony black atop her desk, glossy and filigreed with silver. It stands out harshly among all the pastels and motif of pale flowers.

Laereda follows my gaze and frowns before she settles into the opposite chair, the tea steeping in the pot. "So." The word is sharp, pulling my attention from the box. "Of all things, I didn't expect an apology."

"I'm starting to see a lot of things differently now." That part isn't a lie, at least.

Sympathy fills her gaze, but a shadow of doubt lingers.

"It's just that . . . with Autumn and the new potential Consorts, I thought you'd understand."

"I do." She pours a mug of tea and presses it into my hands.

"Will it get better?"

Her fingers pluck at a bit of lint on her sleeve. Her robe is plain orange now, like mine, but it bears a mossy-green trim, the sign of a retired Consort. "I don't know."

I breathe in the steam to clear my congested nose before blowing on the reddish liquid, then take a cautious sip. Too tart. My mouth purses and I set it aside.

"Skirtblossom hips," Laereda says. "Southern tea is so hard to get now, after all. These are heavenly with a bit of honey to smooth the sharpness, but that's in high demand these days, too." She uncovers a bowl of thick, dark brown liquid. "Sorghum. Not quite the same, but we all make do now. Even this is precious."

The enameled handle of a small silver spoon sticks out of the syrup, and I dutifully drop some into my tea. True to her word, the sweetness does cut the sour flavor of the flower hips. It tingles pleasantly on my tongue, like mint.

Mint. How I miss it. The dried stores have yet to run empty, but like many summer herbs, such things are hoarded now, precious commodities brought out for festivals and celebrations. A flush of warmth suffuses me, and I take a deep breath, setting the tea aside. Normally I would welcome the heat, but in here it's nearly suffocating, as if the air is thicker in Laereda's room.

"Are you all right?" Laereda leans forward and places a gentle hand on the back of mine. It feels clammy against my flushed skin.

"Just a bit warm," I say, rolling up the sleeves of my undershirt. I tug the neckline of my robe, fanning my face. Am I coming down with that cough Vanyse had? Others have caught it since. Such illness is not uncommon in the cooler months, but it feels more sinister this year, alongside all our other troubles.

"Sorry," Laereda apologizes, crossing to her window, throwing it wide. "I keep it warm for Sy." Her babe. "Sometimes I forget my room is a bit stuffy to others."

The breeze flows in, swirling through the room with the damp scent of impending rain. It fills my nose, my mouth, my lungs, a cool balm to the dizzy flush in my cheeks.

"Better?" Laereda's brow furrows with concern.

I nod. "Much." So strange, that I'd welcome the cold. My head doesn't throb at the sudden chill, though I do feel a bit giddy. Maybe I am coming down with a fever after all. I lift the teacup to my lips and drink deeply. The taste rolls over my tongue, dancing, bright, sweet.

"You can talk to me," she murmurs as she fusses herself into her seat again. "If it helps. I'm sorry they pushed you out of there."

My vision wobbles, and I blink. "What?"

"The council chamber. The Mirror. That they won't let you in anymore."

"Oh." My brain feels cottony. The window didn't help after all. "It doesn't matter."

"No?"

I shake my head. "That wasn't going to work. They—" *This isn't right.* The thought flickers through my mind as if someone else is speaking. Another wave of light-headedness makes the room spin. My teacup clatters against the saucer as I set it down. "I'm sorry," I mumble. "I don't feel well. I need to excuse myself."

"Oh no," Laereda murmurs. "Maybe just sit for a few moments, have some more tea, let the cool air clear your head?"

Then I catch it. A look in her eye, a tiny curl of her mouth. Something that isn't concerned at all, but triumphant.

Fire and shadow, the tea. I stand so abruptly I stumble as vertigo rocks the room beneath my feet. "I'm sorry, another time. Thank you for your kindness." I don't know how I manage the words, but I make my wobbly way out of the room and through the halls. Everything feels distant, like the floor is farther away, as if I've been stretched thin like flatbread dough, pulled into twists to bake into spice-covered holiday treats. The hall sprawls before me, winding in unfamiliar ways.

Mrorw. The sound comes from my feet, and I look down just in time to avoid tripping over one of the cats. Sinzi, the round-faced black cat with wide, pleading eyes of buttercup yellow. She paws at my leg, yowling again, more demanding. I circle past her and continue onward. Her meow seems to follow me, rattling around my head, bouncing off the walls.

I don't know how I find the green beaded curtain of Wren's room. I stumble across it more by accident than design. Nausea wrenches my stomach into queasy knots. I ring the bell, a light tap at first, then a more insistent jangle.

The beads rattle, painfully loud, as Wren's head pokes out. "Tirne?" She takes me in as I sway unsteadily, one long sweeping glance. Her scowl could light fires. "Are you drunk?"

"I don't know." My eyes are gummy, sandy. I blink them hard. "I think I was poisoned."

Her dark eyes widen, and she ushers me in. "Sit down."

Gratefully, I do. "Tea. I think it was in the tea."

"What tea?"

"Laereda. Gave me this tea, something about dresses? Skirts? Skirt flower?"

"Skirtblossom." Wren shakes her head. "Benign. Good for digestion, but harmless. It might cover the taste of something else, though." She holds her candle close to my face. "Open your mouth." I do, and she peers inside, murmuring, "No visible staining." Without asking, she lifts one of my eyelids and leans in close, shifting the candle so the flame dances slowly left, then right. "Follow the light with your eyes."

I try, but immediately become dizzy again, and close them.

"It's definitely something. Your reflexes are way off. I know a bit about poisons, but we don't have enough information to determine exactly what you took." She gnaws on her lip again, tugging on the end of one of her braids. "There's only one thing for it, but you're not going to like it."

"What?"

Wren stands and makes her way over to her assortment of vials, then begins mixing things on her small, rickety table. "An emetic."

"That doesn't sound good."

"No, it's not. I'd appreciate it if you hastened back to your own room and your personal privy before you drink it."

"I . . . oh."

The sorcerer's motions are sure, deft, as she mixes in a powder with a thick liquid, then pierces a thumb to add a drop of blood. She grimaces. "Although, I suppose I'll have to attend you, to make sure you don't dehydrate."

I scowl. "Sorry to be a burden." The words come out blurry, thick.

"You're not." Wren adds a drop of something shimmering and silver to her concoction, and a puff of dirty orange smoke drifts upward. The smell of burning hair fills the room. I gag, but Wren just shrugs and swirls the vial once more before stoppering it and slipping it into one of the pockets on her sage-colored robe.

"Come on." She hauls me up by the arm, and I'm forced to steady myself against her shoulder or stumble. Together, we make our way through the halls. I'm so used to scurrying about in the dark of night that it feels surreal to be seen with Wren while the slanting orange light of dusk filters through windows.

We garner a few suspicious glances, but I little care. My sole focus is on putting one unsteady foot before the other and keeping my stomach from heaving up its contents. From the sound of it, that's Wren's end goal anyway, but I'd prefer to do it in my privy closet rather than soil the colorful tile floor of the Temple hallway.

I nearly stumble into Sidriel as we turn a corner. I reel away, dizziness rocking me. Wren hisses in a breath and stumbles back while Sidriel gracefully sidesteps. The corner of his lip curls upward ever so slightly as he takes in my companion. I get the impression he's about to say something, but Wren yanks on my arm and drags me around him.

I glance back to see him watching us with narrowed, pale eyes.

"What's your problem with him anyway?" I mumble as we approach my room.

"If you don't have a problem with Sidriel, it means he doesn't find you a threat. Consider yourself lucky and keep your head down."

I blink blearily and replay her words in my head. This is so much worse than my occasional brain fog. It's like her words dart away from me, bright and shiny fish in a stream dodging my awkward, grasping fingertips. "What is that supposed to mean?"

"It doesn't matter." We make it to my room and she pushes me through the curtain, fumbling the vial into my clumsy hands. "Drink that, and quickly." I struggle with the stopper until Wren pulls it loose for me and pours it down my throat.

It tastes like milk gone sour. I cough and splutter, but the liquid is already down.

Wren crosses quickly to the ewer on my desk, lifting it and giving it a cautious sniff. "Is this fresh?"

My eyes water and I can barely rasp the word between coughs. "Yes."

"Good. You'll want to get to the privy soon, but you'll need water after."

"How bad is this—" I don't even get to finish the sentence before my stomach gurgles alarmingly. I make a mad dash for the privy and spend long, miserable minutes of retching until my abdomen hurts.

I emerge later, and Wren presses a cup of water into my grasp, urging that I drink it slowly. I ignore her, gulp it down, then promptly return to the privy to vomit it back up. The second time, I heed her warning and take cautious, small sips.

It takes three rounds of that before I feel empty, gutted. I shake with a chill, my teeth chattering. Wren tucks me into bed, placing a fresh cup of water on the nightstand. I huddle beneath my blankets, curling into a ball and luxuriating in the soft warmth of their thick layers. At some point while I was heaving my guts out, Wren kindled my hearth to life.

Now that the worst of it is over, a low ache settles into my limbs, my bones.

"Thank you," I murmur.

Her response is an angry scowl. Something thunks onto my bedside table. A bottle, blue glass, sloshing as she slams it down. My medicine. "You didn't tell me you were taking this."

"I—" But my tongue sticks to the roof of my mouth, my heartbeat a dull roar in my ears. No. She can't know my secret. My weakness.

"This reeks of goldroot," she snaps, the words flung like a sharp-edged stone.

I should keep my mouth shut, roll over, feign a slide into unconsciousness. And yet the words spill out of me, the confession bursting forth like a pierced boil. "It's for my pain. I don't take it every day."

"Of course it's for pain," she says, then shakes her head and takes a long, deep breath through her nose, huffing it back out again. "What pains?"

I hesitate, but her stare is unyielding. "Headaches."

The sorcerer's brow furrows, and she sits on the bed. "How long have you had them?"

"Ten years. It goes away when I'm in Sylvus."

Wren swirls the bottle of my medicine in her hand, staring at it. "I know what you were given today. And why it hit you so hard. To most, it would merely be like having a glass or two of wine, loosening the tongue. But when combined with some other medicines, it causes this. Dizziness, nausea, a mental fog."

I yawn. My eyelids are heavy weights, and her words bounce around inside my skull. "Why would Laereda poison me?"

"She didn't. Well, at least I don't think she meant this." Wren palms my medicine and slips it into her pocket. I start to protest, but she cuts me off. "Come to me in the morning, and I'll return it. But if you take it tonight, you could make yourself sick all over again."

My stomach turns at the thought. Sleep drags at me. I've given up on my eyes, leaving them closed. I mumble but lose track of what I intend to say.

Distantly, I hear Wren heave another sigh. "I'll see you in the morning, when you come back for your medicine." Footsteps thump across my rug, followed by the clicking song of my beaded curtain, like a child's wooden blocks toppling to the floor. Then nothing, and darkness.

"You can't tell anyone," I demand of Wren the next morning when I come to her door.

"Good morning," she says with an eye roll, but ushers me in.

My medicine sits on her shelf at eye level. I clutch at it, savoring the reassuring feel of the smooth glass bottle in my palm. Cool, comforting. When I'd woken to a tight knot of pain on the rear side of my skull, I'd instinctively fumbled in my nightstand drawer before I remembered Wren's promise. Panic had scrabbled at me, but it settles now with the medicine in my hands.

"Did you do anything to it?" I squint at her suspiciously.

"No." Her reply is terse. "But I'd like to know more about these headaches."

After a brief hesitation, I insist again. "You have to keep it secret."

"Why? Wouldn't it be easier if you had help? It's not a crime to ask for it, you know."

"If anyone found out, I could lose it all, forever." I ask again. "Please promise me you won't tell anyone."

"What if I don't make that promise?" There's a deeper implication in the question, and I'm forced to wonder how far I would go to keep my secret. After a moment of heavy silence, she adds softly, "I won't tell. But if you won't let anyone else help you, let me. Tell me about these headaches."

"I already saw a physician about it. I . . . I even went to Sidriel when they started. I don't think he realizes now that it was me. He said it was permanent. But he wanted a fortune for custom medicine, so goldroot it is."

"I could help. With your blood, I can tailor something better for you." The same offer Sidriel made years ago.

I stare down at the bottle, at the dark liquid that sloshes within. I don't realize I'm crying until a tear drips onto my hand. I wonder why, until I realize it's anger. I'm angry that she gives me hope. "For how much?"

"Nothing."

No. I can't believe that. There's always a price. And besides . . . "Then what happens when the Mirror is repaired? When you don't need me anymore? Then will I go back to the goldroot, knowing that it could be better?" I don't speak my worst fear aloud. That the Mirror will be fixed, and that I won't be. A new Herald would take my place, leaving me here to suffer.

"I wouldn't do that."

"How am I supposed to know that?" My temper snaps. "Do you have *any* idea what it's like, to always live in dread of the bad days? Even on the good days, I'm so tired. All the time. It never stops, even when it does." I've stepped closer, Wren shrinking back.

Her eyes are wide, her nostrils flared. Her chest rises and falls rapidly, a startled rabbit. She clutches at her breast before fumbling past me, shoving aside bottles and tins in a flurry. With a sound of relief, she tugs out a small, flat brick that looks like compressed herbs, a deep green. Breaking off a piece the size of her thumbnail, Wren shoves it in her mouth and chews, breathing through her nose as she clutches the shelf for support. I watch, frozen and uncertain.

After a long, silent minute, the sorcerer turns. She places a slim brown hand flat against her robe, right over her left breast. "No. Maybe I don't know what your experience is like, not precisely. But don't think you have a monopoly on pain. You're not the only one hurting, or the only one who's been betrayed by her own body."

"What was that?"

She hesitates.

"You know my secret," I remind her.

Wren turns back to the shelf, nudging an empty bottle back and forth. Just as I'm about to give up and leave, she speaks. "It's my heart. It lurches, like missing a step in the dark, except it's a wrenching, sudden *wrongness* in my chest. I've developed my own treatment to keep it functioning properly. So yes, I do know what it's like to be at the mercy of medicine."

My mouth goes dry.

"Rest assured, Herald." I sense no mockery in her use of the word. It's almost an honorific, an acknowledgment that I was stripped from it wrongfully. "I will share your condition with no other. But I do hope you'll let me help you."

I swallow, ashamed of the hope that leaps in my chest. "I . . . I'm sorry. You really think you could?"

"I'm not a full healer," she admits, "but I studied it once, before alchemy. Sidriel may be a snake, but he knows his business. If he told you it's incurable, he's right. Otherwise he'd have offered to do so, for an even more obscene price than the medicine he suggested. But I do think I can make you a treatment that works at least as well as your medicine, with fewer side effects. You'll have to lay off the kaoreh entirely, though."

My mouth curls into a frown. "You saw that, too?"

"And go easy on the valerian. I won't begrudge you that one from time to time, but if you stop using the ground kaoreh to stay awake, I think you won't need it to sleep. You'll rest easier and your mind will be clearer. If you're willing to try a potion I make, it could ease the headaches without fogging your mind as badly as the goldroot, or the jitters of kaoreh."

"Why would you do this?" I ask.

She blinks at me, as if she doesn't understand the question. "Why wouldn't I?"

"I . . . thank you."

As I go to my morning duty of sweeping the main corridors, I still wonder if I can play Laereda at her own game, somehow. At least I know one way she collects so much gossip now. I'm glad I didn't tell her anything, that I stopped when I did.

As I dutifully sweep the tile, exhausted from my long night, Laereda finds me. Her brow crinkles as she places a comforting hand on my shoulder. "Are you feeling better? You gave me quite the fright."

It is a challenge just to smile gently and nod. "Must have been something I ate, I suppose."

"Indeed. I'm glad you're back to yourself," she purrs. "My room remains open, if you ever need a sympathetic ear."

Sympathetic as a fat magpie sitting on a shiny pile of secrets. I wonder what she wanted to pry from me. If she helped with the Mirror, was she prying to see how much I know? Or did she seek a confession of my own guilt from me?

Whatever it was, she's an element I can't afford to anger or ruffle feathers, not now. I nod again. "Thank you. I'll keep it in mind."

And still, the days pass. Wren's potion does exactly as she promises. It helps the pain a little better than the goldroot did, most days, and it leaves my mind clearer. Wren was right about one more thing, too. With the new medicine, I use the kaoreh less. I didn't realize how bad the fluttering anxiety in my chest had been until it was gone.

Today is mercifully free of pain, and I take lunch with Feryn and Vanyse for the first time in days. I feel stretched so thin, between my research and snooping around for Wren's samples and my daily tasks. Though Wren's medicine tames the headaches better, it doesn't eliminate them entirely. There's an exhaustion that comes with incessant pain, even at low levels, a tiredness that I had forgotten.

Even when I was here for past autumn seasons, I'd return to Sylvus briefly every night to escort souls. I didn't realize how much that helped. Some days—rarer, now, but not gone—even the new medicine can't touch the worst of the pain. Instead of taking a meal, I'll lie in my bed, a cloth over my eyes. If I'm lucky, I can manage a brief nap.

Between the pain and the rest and my other tasks, juggling time with my friends is where I falter most.

"Oh, did you hear?" Feryn says conspiratorially, leaning forward.

"Laereda went to the Tharem and asked for an extension on her service. She protested that she still remains fertile, and has found a way to remain so longer than most. She says she shouldn't be demoted just for—and I quote—'some upstart to swoop in.'"

Vanyse takes a bite of some grainy potato flatbread. "That's not going to work. No healer or physician has managed to do that for any past Consort. No one would now, not without the discovery being news."

"She's just desperate," Feryn says. "I feel bad for her. She had her title and job taken away—" She stops, mouth closing as she gives me a guilty look. "Um, I mean . . ." The words trail into helpless silence.

My food turns to tasteless glue in my mouth. I swallow it down and stand before she can say more. "Sorry, I have to go. I'm on dishwashing duty after lunch." My cheeks burning, I make my way stiffly to the bins where the trays and silverware are dropped.

The Scion in front of me is one of Summer's children, and one of the minor alchemists helping with the Mirror. I can't recall his name, but I watched him stitch together enough pieces beside Wren and Calder to recognize his face. He sets his tray in the bin, a single spoon resting in the middle of it.

Quickly and as surreptitiously as possible, I pick up the spoon and drop it into my pocket. I turn, only to find Sidriel sitting at a table halfway across the room, watching me with narrowed eyes. His stare darts to my pocket and back up.

Oh no.

Maybe he didn't see. Or maybe he'll just think I'm selling the silver for extra coin. I wonder what it means, that thievery is the lesser accusation, these days. I swallow, then hurry away.

Still, I can only steal so many spoons, and I grow desperate. There's a line I've yet to cross, but today something breaks inside me.

Jaed had asked me to visit the hospital in town with him this afternoon. I declined, blaming my aching knees from weeding gardens the day before. A lie. After delivering the spoon to Wren, I stand in front of the curtain to a high priest's room. Ceilis, a priestess of Spring and another minor alchemist. Probably not strong enough to break the Mirror, but I'll leave no stone unturned. According to Wren, she's on the duty roster for the Mirror tonight.

I tap on Ceilis's bell first, lightly. When there's no answer, I part the pink beaded strands and slip in, breath held, waiting for someone inside to cry out. But it's empty.

Heart pounding, I sort through the papers on her desk, taking special care to put them back where I found them. There isn't much, just notes on herbs and charms for the usual things: to ward off fatigue, to rid livestock of fleas.

I find one interesting tidbit. A vial of translucent crimson liquid with a shard of glass in it. Tilting the vial shows that the shard is silvered, not scarlet. No stolen piece of the Mirror, then, but some other experiment. An attempt at repair, or a test how to break it? I don't know, but I can't take it with me. I'll tell Wren later and let her make sense of it.

I make my escape soon after, heart racing. I try to suppress the guilt at violating someone's privacy like that, but my nerves still jangle fiercely. To settle my head, I seek a place of calm, silence.

Outside the main buildings of the Temple, but within its surrounding walls, a gathering of trees unlike any other sprawls. Oaks drop acorns beside crimson-leafed maples, while cherry trees flower in pale pink petals. Winter's pines hold stalwart against the dying season, their boughs thick with fragrant needles. In the fog of another gray autumn evening, it feels like a place outside time, the sparkling pressure of magic suffusing the air.

I lean against a papery birch and breathe until the restless, anxious energy settles. A few others seek their own solace here, but as the evening grows colder, they make their way indoors. Dusk falls, and I am alone as the souls of the dead appear in the fading light, bobbing toward the courtyard and the Mirror's empty arch.

I don't know if others can feel them the way I do, at least in some small unseen part of their soul. Maybe that's why so few people linger out of doors as night falls. A handful of the dead cluster around me, silently pleading. Needy. Frustrated. And hungry.

I wonder again how much longer until they become a true danger. I brush one apologetically. Its touch is icy, stinging my fingertips. "We'll solve this, I promise."

A crunch of leaves makes me turn, and I flinch at the sight of Sidriel approaching. With his wintry skin, dark eyes and lips, and midnight-blue robes that swallow light, he looks like a strange, dark echo of Jaed. He smiles, but it is a cold thing. "If someone catches you talking to yourself out here, they might think the former Herald's mind has finally broken."

I swallow. *Danger.* It's an instinctive reaction, an alarm ringing in my mind. But he merely takes a spot across from me at a nearby aspen, leaning against it. He catches a falling leaf, twirling it in his fingers.

"I'm not," I protest. "Talking to myself, that is."

"I know. You still see the dead, don't you? Autumn's magic still courses through your blood."

Wren's warning echoes in my mind. *If you don't have a problem with Sidriel, it means he doesn't find you a threat.* Instead, I clear my throat. "Why are you out here?"

Again, that cold smile flickers across his lips. "Can I not merely enjoy the grove, same as you?"

I fix him with a flat stare until he barks a single laugh.

He points the dead leaf at me. "Well, you have me. I came here looking for you. Someone told me they saw you walking this way."

"Why?"

Pale, pale eyes lock onto mine. "I know what you do with Wren."

A shiver of fear trickles through my chest, my belly. *Play ignorant.* "What?"

"Don't treat me like an idiot," he says, low and warning. "I deal in the body, in blood and all its secrets. And the vials I tested were not yours. A human woman, yes, but no trace of Autumn's magic." He crushes the leaf in his hand, opening it to sprinkle the bits into the breeze. "I don't like being played for a fool."

I want to flee, but he stands between me and the path back to safety. Still, he's made no move closer.

He continues. "I know why you did it, and only one person with access to those vials would have come up with such a plan. Wren." He spits the name like an epithet. "But she's not as skilled in the magic of the blood as I am. If you give me your blood—the real thing—I can find who did this to you."

"I—"

"Doubtless that's the same offer she made you. But I saw you slipping spoons into your pockets. Wren found something, didn't she? But she isn't good enough to locate the answer with your blood alone; she needs to find its match." This time he does move, but only to take a single step away from the tree.

I flinch.

"I'm not here to harm you," he assures me. "I'm here to make you an offer. Give me your blood, and I can find out who did this without needing to hunt for a match. Or at least, I can narrow it down. I can tell you which god they sprang from, and other various traits hidden in their blood. Clues you can use, like their general appearance."

"Why? Why would you do this?"

He blinks. "We all want to fix the Mirror."

"But why not go to the Tharem with my secrets?"

Another icy grin. "The same reason I'm sure you haven't. He hides something, that one, with all his bluster and anger. I know the type."

The Tharem. I can't test him. Human, he has no magic of his own. But again I wonder, what if he had an accomplice?

Sidriel pulls a spoon from his pocket. Slowly, deliberately, he licks it, tongue flicking out from between his dark lips. He holds it out to me. "Test this. Tell Wren you took it from my table in the dining hall. I swear

I didn't curse you, and I will help you. But if you tell Wren of this, I will not hesitate to go directly to your god and tell him what you've done."

I take the spoon cautiously. "You—"

"I will not work alongside her. And I daresay she holds the same sentiment. The offer stands. You can steal cutlery from every magic-user in this place, or you can come to me." His smile turns sly. "And you will. Eventually."

He says no more, and I watch him go, belly churning.

I'm afraid he's right.

THIRTEEN

I sigh, shaking out cramping fingers. I should have been done with this an hour ago, but here I am kneeling in the vegetable garden. One would think the cool weather would kill pests, but an infestation of tiny red beetles crawls over every plant, devouring gaping holes in the leaves. A handful of sorcerers and priests crafted the potion I now use, harmless to the plants and to people, but deadly for the insects.

I dip my bristly brush into the small bucket once more and scrape my hand across it, flinging tiny droplets at the frilly leaves of a carrot, then scoot over to do the next one.

When I finish and stand, my knees ache. I stretch, pick up my brush and the bucket, and head back toward the Temple just as late afternoon darkens. I might have missed supper, but no food is wasted anymore. Rations are tight, but if anything was left over, it will be stored in the magically cooled cellar and reworked into tomorrow's lunch. After I drop off my bucket and brush, I can go beg for something to eat.

I yawn, weary and unsteady on my feet. I slept little last night, racked by one of the nasty headaches, the kind even Wren's potion only softens partially. The world seems foggy, fuzzy around the edges. Maybe I'll turn in early tonight.

On my way back, my growling stomach is interrupted by a familiar voice drifting around a corner. Bix's low rumble. What's he doing in this odd, secluded part of the Temple, so close to dusk? To make things stranger, he speaks a language I've never heard. Something sinuous and sibilant. I circle the corner, to find Bix facing the wall, talking to his own shadow. He whirls to face me, the startled look on his face quickly smoothed over with a sheepish smile. "Tirne?"

My brow furrows. "What are you doing out here?"

"Oh. Um." He blushes. "I'm practicing a Pseran poem for Jaed. I want to recite it to him as part of a gift for starting a new cycle of lessons. It's an old poem, in the ancient version of the language, and it's taking some practice to get it right."

Pseran. I've never heard it spoken aloud before. Time blurs these days. I hadn't even realized it was the beginning of a new teaching cycle. I should have noticed, if I hadn't been neglecting them both. I spend all too much time tarrying with gods and sorcerers. I've even missed our usual lunches lately as I sneak into rooms and scour people's belongings. This is the first time I've said a word to Bix in a dozen days. Guilt wrenches me. Jaed and Bix have this connection, and I'm not a part of it, even as welcome as I am. All because my mission and my frequent pain has kept me from them.

"We miss you, you know," Bix says, as if reading my thoughts.

"I'm sorry."

"Are you all right?" Worry crosses his face. "You look tired."

"Just exhausted from garden duty," I lie, then yawn. "I'll see you at lunch tomorrow. I promise."

I can feel his eyes following me all the way down the path.

Later, long after night has settled in, I once more return to the courtyard. Everything is falling apart. Bix's words haunt me. I haven't spoken to Jaed in over a fourday, a rarity. Same with Feryn and Vanyse. Our last talk was that brief lunch session, days ago.

Fine mist drizzles down from clouds that obscure the stars. We've had nearly two whole fourdays of wet weather, and I grow weary of rain and wind and cold. An aching chill settles into my bones as the souls swirl around me. One unspoken rule limits the dead; they cannot enter a place where the living reside, inside closed doors. It's one reason the courtyard lies open to the sky, with the Temple gates thrown open even in the dead of night.

They are restless tonight, frustrated, swirling about. Even when erratic, they are hypnotic. I don't know if I'll ever become used to the faces that grow clearer every night. Their expressions vary, but only between anger, fear, and frustration. I yawn as a tiny shard of pain begins on the back of my skull. These late-night vigils take their toll, and I'm so, so tired. The souls brush my skin with their chill touch, and I shiver.

Fatigue drags at me. My eyes drift closed, just for a second. For a single, long moment . . .

I awaken to a snug sensation, my cloak wrapped tightly about me, bobbing gently like a ship on ocean waves. A pair of arms cradles me. I'm being carried, and the scent gives away my rescuer. Crisp rain and apple, hay and cinnamon and a crackling fireplace. Autumn.

I'm soaked to the bone, and cold. Agony lances through my head, burning, throbbing, stabbing. My teeth chatter as I try to speak, and my god shushes me softly. "Stay still."

I want to reply, but exhaustion drags me back down under the pain into oblivion once more.

This time when I regain consciousness, my cloak is gone. Warmth surrounds me, and I sigh as everything comes into focus. The scent of lavender and lemon, the steamy air, the fact that I'm immersed in hot water, my robes sodden and drifting in the slow, artificial current.

The baths.

I blink and stir, just as my foggy brain connects the dots and realizes Autumn is holding me up.

Flailing, I push away from him, careful to touch only his chest, safely covered by his shirt. When I get my feet under me and stand, I see his leafy cloak on the tile near the bath, tossed aside without care. Mine is heaped beside it.

Luckily, we are alone, the baths empty at this late hour.

"Sit," he commands me gently, as if he hadn't just been committing a crime.

"I—" I splutter. He can't have touched me. Not skin to skin. "You didn't . . . did you?"

The corner of his mouth curves softly. "No."

Relief washes over me, and my shoulders ease. But I realize how chilled I still am, how painfully my body clenches, and I obey him, sinking gratefully back into the water. This time I sit on the submerged bench opposite him. We're in one of the smaller public baths designed for two or three. Autumn reclines, water up to his chest, the ends of his dark hair floating around him.

Though his cloak remains several feet away, the peculiar gusts of wind that follow him have blown leaves across the floor, into the bath. I pluck one up. A bloody red, spiky. Maple. Twirling it by the stem, I collect my thoughts.

The souls. The dead sapped my energy, leaving me unconscious in the icy rain. Autumn found me and brought me here. My body still throbs, but the warmth is helping.

I can't even bear to look at my god without a twinge of shame. Everything aches, and it's not just my usual screaming skull. There's a deeper pain, something intangible but ever-present. My guilt, a splinter that festers.

Autumn frowns. His eyes search mine, and I feel a sharp spike of something through our bond. Doubt.

I crumble the leaf in my hand, then wash the pieces away in the water. My hands clench into fists along the hem of my robe as it tries to float upward. I should tell him. My shoulders stiffen. A deep breath, then a confession. "I'm . . . I'm working with Wren in secret. To find out who did this."

"The sorcerers are already analyzing your blood."

"And they've found nothing." I bite my lip, staring down at fingertips that trace lines through the water. "Because she's the only one who has my true blood. The rest is false, switched out." Sidriel's offer still tempts me, a bright and shiny lure.

Autumn's eyes flash bright orange, a spark of flame. "What?"

"I don't trust them," I blurt in protest. "The others. Any one—or more—of them could have done this."

He glares, imperious. "And yet you trust Wren?"

"Yes, I do."

Autumn's voice is low, a warning. "You defy my decree."

"You never said anything about the blood after I was bled. Only that I must let it be taken."

His eyes widen, then close. Autumn shakes his head. "I would never have thought you capable of such deceit."

"I told you I would go as far as it takes to fix the Mirror, and I am. You have to trust me with this."

He searches my face, a furrow forming between his brows. "Don't get caught."

It's as close to endorsement as I'll get. With a slow nod of understanding, I find another leaf, this one longer, a dull leathery brown, with rounded, undulating edges. Oak. I watch it for a few moments, dragging it back and forth across the surface of the water. "Thank you," I finally manage to say, daring to peek up from the leaf. "For saving me tonight."

"You are welcome." His face is calm, but I sense a frisson of worry through our connection. For the first time, I wonder what it would be like without this bond, to see him as others do. Cool, impassive, distant. But only I know he frets. About me. Dizzyingly, I realize I am the only living soul to understand him so. Not even his Consorts know these things about him.

And here I see him unguarded, soaking in water up to his chest. To my knowledge, he's never been to the public baths. Gods have their own luxurious tubs in their private chambers, tended by the few priests allowed to enter their demesne for cleaning.

I try not to notice how the water turns his pale shirt to translucence, revealing the shape of the form beneath. I bite my lip. My robe drifts again, and I tug its edge back down. Hoping Autumn will ignore my unruly clothing, I say, "It was the souls, wasn't it?"

A nod. Another tremor of concern. "The souls are drawn to you, connected to you. You're to end your vigils."

"What about the city, people outside at night?"

"They are not connected to the Mirror, to me. We've some time yet before they're in danger." He stares down at his hand, tracing patterns through the water's surface. "I . . . I would prefer you remain safe."

Because he needs me to fix the Mirror, or because of this tremulous thing I sense along the thread that links us? I don't ask, but he's right. Venturing out into that courtyard at night is a death wish now. The silence is weighted, heavy, a rope coiling about our throats. I break it with a cough and stand. "I think I'm warm now, at least enough to go to my room and drown myself in blankets."

He smiles at that. Just the tiniest twitch of his lips, but I know it for the grin it is. "Very well. Good night, my Herald." He stands, water cascading from his hair, dripping from his clothing. His shirt clings to him, outlining every curve of trim muscle. I avert my eyes again with a blush. If he notices, he says nothing, collecting his cloak and exiting among a cascade of dead leaves.

I close my eyes, inwardly curse at myself, and drip across the floor. I wonder what the other acolytes will make of the leaves that litter the baths in the morning.

FOURTEEN

J aed tightens a string on the tiilar and tests it, then loosens it again ever so slightly. I sit on the bed, across from the chair and table where he tunes the instrument. It is a rare moment of calm, this time with him.

"So," I ask, tucking my legs up under me, "how is the new lesson cycle going?" I ask partly out of guilt, after my conversation with Bix recently. Also, I'm eager to talk about something—anything—that doesn't involve the Mirror or the long season or my blood's curse.

"Well, later today I'm introducing a dozen eight-year-olds to the lark-whistle. I'll be hearing the screeching in my nightmares for days."

"You know you love it."

"I do." Plucking the final string and nodding at what he hears, Jaed skirts around his ever-present pile of discarded robes, past a crate of broken instruments he's collected from junk shops to repair. The tiilar is replaced in its usual spot of honor on the center shelf.

"I can't believe that thing still works," I say. It was the first instrument he owned himself, rather than borrowing battered ones from the Temple's collection. I'd saved up my Temple allowance for months to buy it for him. Even then it had been used, scuffed and worn.

"Instruments can last a very long time, if maintained well."

I point to his most recent project, the disassembled pieces of some elaborate flute on a lower shelf. "What about that one?"

Jaed doesn't answer. Instead, his gaze comes to rest on my extended arm, bandaged from another official bloodletting. I'm still forbidden from the Mirror's room, but they take my blood all the same. And Wren keeps swapping it out.

I still haven't told Jaed about Wren's experiments or Sidriel's offer. I know I should, but anytime I mention the curse or my title at all, he stiffens up and frowns. I get so little time with him lately, I don't want to poison what we do have. Even now, just seeing the results of the sorcerers' research makes him prickly.

I cover the bandage with my other hand.

"I hate that they do that to you. The sorcerers. Sidriel, especially. I can't forget that he refused to help you. He only shares his magic with the wealthy, and people like you suffer. Scavenger. Feeding on corpses and growing rich with it. And now he pretends altruism, as if he hasn't stepped on those beneath him all along."

He's right. The price Sidriel had asked for his medicine was far more than a Temple acolyte could pay, and he'd known that. Yet still I protest. "It doesn't matter now, not for the Mirror."

"I can still hate him for leaving you in the cold."

He can, and I don't argue.

"Well." He collects a pair of empty baskets by the door. He sighs, and I can see him shake off his troubled expression. "I suppose it's time we headed out."

"Thank you for offering to be my escort." Again.

He smiles softly, irritation gone. "You're welcome. Come on, let's go."

An hour later, mud squelches under my boots as I shift my weight, shuffling my basket of candles to the opposite arm. My shoulders throb from the burden, but though I curse my body, I do it in silence. Jaed, too, carries a heavy basket, and he doesn't complain.

Someone jostles me from behind, almost shoving me into Jaed. I turn to glare, but the culprit is already lost in the market crowd, one in a sea of cloaked figures half-hidden by a drizzling mist. I worry about cutpurses, then remember I don't hold any money. Jaed carries our coin today. It's cold, and dreary, and my throat rattles, scratchy from the wet, chill air.

In front of me, Jaed is still haggling with a wine seller. "A cask of this same vintage was only three falcons last month."

The old woman scoffs before the sound turns into a long, wet cough. She recovers after several tense moments. Grizzled, but her back straight as a post, she waves a dismissive hand. "Last month, we still hoped the Mirror would be back up soon. But winter's supposed to be here in a few days, and rumor is that Mirror ain't even halfway fixed yet. Shipments not comin' in like they used to, either. So now I got panicked restaurants and pleasure halls worried we ain't gonna get a spring. So they stock their cellars, but there ain't enough casks to fill 'em. So it's eight falcons."

He sighs. "I guess it'll be the five-falcon Jeti Red instead. But I'm only buying three casks."

The wine seller shrugs. "Suits me just fine. I'll sell the rest soon enough."

As Jaed looks down to count out his payment, the old woman's eyes meet mine. They narrow, and I wonder if she's trying to place my face. I duck my head, investigating my boots with sudden interest as a cough of my own bubbles up. Though I never spent all that much time in town during my three months here, if this woman visited the Temple or watched the Changing of the Seasons, she might recognize me even in the orange robes of an acolyte. And I don't want to bear even more scorn out here. There's enough of that in the Temple. Although, perhaps this particular woman might actually thank me for her new profits.

Money changes hands, and the merchant assures us she'll send a cart up to the Temple with the wine casks by evening.

Jaed sweeps a drip of rain from his brow as he turns. The rain smears the brush of dusty purple across his eyelids, but he doesn't seem to care.

He sighs. "At this rate, we'll return to the Temple with only half my shopping list."

It takes hours before we manage to bargain for everything. By the time we're done, my coughs have taken on a damp, rattling quality. I worry. I'm not alone. Coughs are common among the chatter of townsfolk now. Jaed is forced to exchange small magical favors for some items, the few scant, simple bits of magic he knows. Minor spells for a few days of good luck or to ward mites away from a scraggly vegetable garden.

With each passing minute, the damp and chill seeps into my skin, my bones, my skull. It carries with it one of my headaches. I fumble my basket and nearly drop it, my movements sluggish. I barely hear half of what Jaed says, nodding numbly at the rest.

"We have to get you back," he says. "It's another headache, isn't it?"

Even though no other faithful are nearby, I still glance around nervously. "I'm fine."

"You're not. Let's go."

Pain makes me sharp, prickly. "I don't need your pity."

"This isn't pity, it's common sense. We have enough of the list, and I'm cold and wet and ready to be home." There's an edge to his voice, too.

"Fine." I stomp back up the path to the Temple. I hate this. I hate being a liability, that sometimes I can't even do the simplest of tasks. I miss the soothing balm of Sylvus. And I hate the way Jaed looks at me like I'm a wounded animal.

In my room, I toss aside my wet cloak and sink into a chair. Here, I let myself weep. The pain is worse now, and the chill that makes my teeth chatter doesn't help. Not winter's frost, but cold enough. The hearth burns in glowing embers, but even prodding it to life is not enough to warm me.

A tiny scrap of white fluff stands up at the foot of my bed and stretches, her feline mouth opening in a wide yawn. Daisy.

"At least you look cozy," I sigh as she approaches. Stabs of pain lance through my skull as I bend over to unlace my boots and strip off sodden socks. I flex my icy feet gently. Daisy trills a sound that is half-mew, half-purr and bats at my wriggling big toe.

I shiver. Cold. Too cold. I should be grateful that at least it's not as frigid as winter. Some days are even passably warm, when the sun shines and clouds are sparse. But the slushy, gray days like this are harder to bear.

Later, after I've warmed myself and fully changed into fresh clothing, it's time for supper. A spoonful of kaoreh along with a double dose of Wren's medicine means I'll sleep poorly tonight, but it's a trade I'm willing to make right now. I promised to join Jaed and Bix today, and I don't want them checking up on me later if I don't show.

Unease bubbles up as I approach their table. My sniping with Jaed wasn't quite an argument, but it was still unpleasant. After collecting my food, I take my seat with another cough. Fire and shadow, those trips to town are miserable things on a day like this. Maybe I'll visit the baths before bed, clear my lungs from the chill.

"Jaed . . . ," I say as I sit, but he waves aside my apology before I can make it.

"Don't worry. I'm used to what the cold does to your shining personality." A grin softens the teasing. "Finally get warm?" But the question in his eyes isn't about warmth. It's code. *Is the headache better?*

"Somewhat."

"It is pretty disgusting out there," Bix says. "Glad I was on floor-scrubbing duty indoors today."

I scowl at him, but only in jest. "Lucky."

"Not going to complain."

Jaed turns to give Bix a light kiss on the cheek. "Well, I'll expect you to warm me up later." As his hair swishes with the movement, I catch a sparkle among the curls.

"New earrings?" He wasn't wearing them earlier, and I don't recognize them.

"Opals from Psere," he confirms, tucking his hair behind an ear to show them off. I yawn, rubbing my eyes, and only realize a moment later that I've lost track of what Jaed was saying.

"I'm sorry," I apologize. "What?"

Jaed frowns in concern, and his voice is gentle as he repeats himself. He knows all too well how my mind blurs sometimes. "They were a gift."

Oh. I remember. The poem. "Right. Good taste," I say to Bix.

He tosses me his rakish grin, reaching across the table to ruffle my hair. "I think the cold froze both your brains today."

I devour a forkful of roasted carrots and gira root soaking in heavy spices. More vegetables. Our meals have been lean on meat lately, as they hoard the livestock for eggs and milk. But even the animals have to eat. Cabbages and some other crops have been tolerating the cold well enough, but it's a dreary prospect to eat the same food over and over. Some seasonings grow scarce, while others remain plentiful, leading to a surplus of cinnamon-infused sauces lately.

I'm not a farmer, or one who studies such things. I don't know how much longer we can last with the scant assortment of crops we can keep growing. Or how people will suffer on such a diet. Worry flickers through me, but I shove it down deep. Not for now, those thoughts.

Today I should be here, stealing one of these now-rare moments with my friends. Not harried by my fears.

Jaed grimaces at his stew, letting it drip from his fork into the bowl. "How I yearn for fat chicken thighs drowning in herbed butter." His sigh is deep, dramatic.

"Join the Temple, they said," Bix mutters. "Three square meals, they said."

I snort. "They said 'square,' not delicious."

He laughs. "I suppose they did."

espite all our fears and all our hopes, the fateful day arrives. Winter's arrival. Or it would be, if the Mirror weren't still a wreck.

They've managed to assemble a third of it now. The smaller pieces in the middle are a greater challenge, though. Tiny slivers, many of them seemingly identical. But the alchemists' magic can seal together only two proper pieces, and so much time is wasted trying incorrect fits.

Too slow.

Even so, no one works at the Mirror today. No one does anything. The whole Temple is silent and still, even the kitchen staff mourning as we all fast in grief. I should be returning to Sylvus right now. Fumbling, I quest for that spark of magic inside me, but nothing stirs. Only a deep and infinite sorrow that does not belong to me, but my god. I've been told he sequesters himself in his rooms.

I, too, mourn until the despair grows so great that I can bear it no longer. I've spent the day in my room poring through notes, but I can't focus with this void of ennui coiling in my gut. On a normal day, it would be nearing supper time. My stomach growls, and I take a sip of my now-cooled tea in an attempt to appease it.

It doesn't work. But I can do something about this other feeling that twists my belly into knots. I close my journal, tuck my notes away in a desk drawer, and smooth out my robes. When I glance into my mirror, I do not see the Tirne my god once knew. This woman is leaner, with thin cheeks from the increasingly invariable diet of rations and my worries. Dark hollows rest beneath my eyes. An ache settles in my chest, a longing for a time now gone, an innocence I cannot reclaim. There was a time when my life and purpose were clear, when all looked upon me and saw someone—something—special.

With heavy steps, I make my way to his rooms. Only the gods have true doors in the Temple. Heavy wood, with solid locks. Autumn's is made of pale birch, intricately carved with a silhouette of a tree. The leaves are painted in his fiery hues, the trunk gilded.

I knock.

When he answers, Autumn's eyes spark with surprise. Perhaps he expected one of the potential Consorts seeking the comfort of his embrace. Whatever he thought he'd find, I was obviously not it.

Most unsettlingly, his usual finery is lacking. Oh, his shirt is fine cotton, his trousers perfectly tailored in vibrant bloodred, but his feet are only in pale socks and he wears no vest or jacket. He'd look like one of us mere mortals if it weren't for the glow in his eyes, the strange shimmer to his hair.

"Your Holiness." I quash my unease and bow, as I must do now. A mere acolyte, paying deference.

"Tirne." His voice is rough, rusty from a lack of speaking today. No one has seen him since last evening's devotions, and the nervous gossip flies. I alone know for certain that he is too overwhelmed with mourning to pretend it will all be okay.

His expression shows none of his grief, but I can see it in the small changes to his demeanor, the subtle slump of his shoulders and the way his hand grips the door frame too tightly. His surprise vanishes quickly, and his usual cool demeanor falls over his face. "Why are you here?"

"It's time to stop moping," I say, not caring about my impertinence. He's already stripped me of my position, and I hate to feel his depression swirling in my head. "Let's go." I'm not welcome in the room of a god. Only a select few priests are allowed in to maintain his rooms, and of course his potential Consorts.

"Where?"

"Anywhere. The grove," I blurt out. I haven't been there since I spoke with Sidriel. I took his sample to Wren, and it turned up a mismatch. He was telling the truth; Sidriel did not curse me. Still, he leaves me uneasy, and I have not gone to him to accept his offer.

Autumn frowns. "A day of mourning has been declared. No one is to leave the Temple's main building."

"Can't a god do what he wants?"

At that, his lip quirks. "I suppose so." He collects his cloak of leaves from a hook near the door, and it's unsettling how very human that seems as he quickly dons boots and gloves. He gestures for me to lead the way. I concentrate on the link between us, questing for his reaction. His sorrow is lightened, and it lifts my own heart.

I lead the way to the grove, listening to the crinkle of his leaves behind me. We walk in silence, passing a few other acolytes and even one high priest of Summer, who gapes openly at my brashness to walk before a god. I don't know what he sees on Autumn's face behind me, but the priest glances away quickly and scurries off on whatever business he has.

When we pass the Tharem's chambers, I overhear a single sentence.

"You can, and you will." The Tharem, sharp and firm.

"But—" A female voice.

"Do you want everyone to know?"

A pause, then nearly inaudible, "I can't."

I want to stop, to listen, but when my footsteps falter, Autumn casts me an odd look. Either he was too distracted to notice or he does not care about petty mortal squabbles. I swallow and move on, the Tharem's response lost.

The Tharem. I have yet to fully explore him as a suspect. As bitter and furious as he can be, I find it hard to imagine him shattering the whole world just to demote me. Why not just poison the water in my room when I'm out and be done with me?

Still, Sidriel's warning echoes in my head. *He hides something, that one.*

My thoughts circle like vultures. Outside, the cold buffets me, and pain flares at the back of my skull. I wrap my cloak tighter around me, not nearly as warm as my luxurious Herald's cloak had been. Even my thick leggings and the long-sleeved undershirt beneath my robe aren't enough to keep the chill out entirely. Boots and woolen socks do their best, but my toes soon feel like tiny icicles.

And yet, water from today's rainfall drips from bare branches of the ornamental trees that line the path. The steady *pat-pat-pat* of water falling on the paving stones is clear sign enough. Cold it may be, but these are still the dying throes of autumn, not the first of winter's frost. Never icy, never snowing. Not until Winter enters this realm.

The damp air makes me wheeze, and I wonder if I'm coming down with the Red Cough, as it's been named. It's spreading in the city now, too. Fever, and a hacking, wet cough that can turn bloody and deadly if unchecked.

There have been no deaths in the Temple, though. Not with our healers.

I tamp down my morbid thoughts as we enter the grove, and the air instantly feels a bit warmer, not even the faintest breath of a breeze stirring the space. A steady flow of lazy leaves flutters down from one elm, never losing its endless supply, the same magic that maintains Autumn's cloak. I lift a hand to snatch one of the leaves from the air. My first attempt misses awkwardly, and a small puff of sound erupts behind me.

Was that a laugh? From the Lord of Death?

I manage to catch a leaf in my second attempt and twirl it by its stem. An almond shape, serrated, in a yellow so brilliant it puts marigolds to shame.

Autumn stands in the center of the circle of trees. They shed their leaves upon him like flower petals tossed at a baby's naming ceremony. Elm, oak, maple.

Our eyes meet, and a merriment dances in the firelight flickers of his gaze. I didn't imagine the laugh, then. He smiles. Actually smiles. It's a gentle one, to be sure, not Jaed's or Feryn's broad, unabashed grin. This is a rare treasure, a secret. Something I've seen only a few times in my long service. And never with that strange warmth behind it.

I swallow. "What?"

"Thank you. You were wise to pull me from my rooms. No one else would have dared do so." Autumn lifts a gloved hand, and his leather-clad fingertips pluck another leaf from my shoulder, this one the fiery heart shape of an aspen. "And now that you've managed to pull me from my melancholy," he says, "what would you do?"

I stare at the leaf between my fingers. "I don't know, Your Holiness. I just couldn't bear feeling it anymore. Your sorrow."

A silence falls, heavy and thick. It drowns me like syrup, like Laereda's sweet sorghum. Swallowing hard, I glance up to find him staring at me with a gaze so sharp it stings. "What did you say?"

"I, um, couldn't stand feeling your sadness anymore?" Uncertainty makes it a question.

"You can sense it."

"Er, yes."

"And can you feel . . . other things?"

My voice cracks. "Yes. Ever since I took your blood, since I became a Herald." I hesitate. "Is that wrong?"

Autumn sighs, turning aside to stare up at the canopy above. His profile is a sharp silhouette in the cool light of early evening. Pale as bone, thin and wan. This close, I can see the weariness hanging over him like a physical weight.

"Wrong? No. Uncommon, yes. I've had a dozen Heralds since one had such an ability."

Shame washes over me. All this time, I thought he knew. I'd never spoken of it with the other Heralds; we talked little of our jobs, to be honest. Or at all, really. There was little friendship shared between us, and our duties were sacred, simple. When we spoke at all, we discussed commonplace things such as the scents and tastes and people we missed in the human realm.

It was not much, this bit of connection, but now it feels like an intrusion, a crime. Should I have told him before now? But when would I? We never spoke of such things before this season. But now he's growing more human than he's ever been, and I'm no longer his Herald. I don't know what I am. A confidant? If I am, I'm one who crossed a boundary I never should have.

And yet Autumn watches me not with condemnation, but a cautious hope.

"I'm sorry," I say.

The expression on his face is indecipherable, but the thing I feel through that bond is not. A gentleness stirs in him, a warmth. "You did no wrong."

I can't help but feel like I have. I let the leaf drop, staring down at the loamy ground. I stand at the center of the four quadrants. One scattered with fall leaves, one littered with pine needles, a third coated in pink and white flower petals, the fourth covered only in lush, knee-high grass gone to seed.

And I belong in none of them. Not only am I a disgrace now, this whole time I've peered into something I never should have, a child creeping into the sweets jar unwelcome.

I was a fool to do this. What did I expect would happen? This isn't a merry twilight jaunt with Jaed. The two of us would have danced here, a cheerful, whirling jig, then fallen laughing to the ground, scattering leaves.

Instead, I'm standing here before the Lord of Autumn and confessing that I know secrets about him that I shouldn't.

"I'm sorry," I apologize again, and turn to leave.

When fingertips catch mine, the world pauses for a moment, like a stutter, a blink. I turn to find he has snagged my hand in his, just a brush of fingers.

Even gloved, this feels like a sin.

Words fail me. He looks as uncertain as I am, a puzzled furrow creasing his brow before he drops my hand. Silence envelops us both, suffocating, unbearable. I wait longer than I should, holding my breath.

Finally, he says, "You know."

I don't understand. "Know what?"

"What these things mean. These human emotions. You feel them, you understand them."

I nod.

"Sometimes, when I think about the future, about the Mirror . . . there's this cold sensation, like ice in my chest."

That one I know well. I've felt it humming through our connection all too often lately. "Fear."

He watches me intently. "Fear. An unbecoming thing for a god, is it not?" When I don't respond, he shakes his head. "It haunts me, when I wonder what it will take to repair the Mirror. I'll shed my blood for it, but we may need everything I have to muster enough magic for such a spell. It nearly destroyed Lys to create it the first time."

"Can you?" I ask the question Wren posed long ago when this whole mess had just started. "Can a god die? Is that even possible?"

Autumn says softly, "Yes. It happened once. The split between our worlds was new, and we did not yet know that your realm saps our immortality so. She . . ." He pauses. "She grew too mortal."

"What? Who?" I pace now.

"After the Mirror's creation, the gods walked freely between the realms, their Heralds at their constant beck and call. The seasons did not turn as they do now. Weather patterns changed based on which gods were here, and how long. The crops and creatures . . . they were very different back then.

"Sometimes, we spent months upon months here. Summer especially. She loved this world. But there was a slip, a careless fall, and her life spilled out on the floor before we realized what was happening. Serrema was closest, kneeling beside her. And when Summer's breath left her body, the power moved to Serrema."

I stop moving, settling against the rough bark of an oak. My voice comes out a whisper. "Lys's beloved is now *Summer*?"

He steps closer. A slow nod. "Only the gods know. It's why Lys never leaves Sylvus. But he could never forbid his love from her home, this world she cherishes dearly. So, like the rest of us, she takes her turn here every year."

My throat is dry. The words taste like dust on my tongue. "How long does it take? To become mortal?"

"I don't know. Perhaps I already am. In a normal year, I'd be in Sylvus now." I feel it then, the sharp electric tang of dread, a slow panic spreading through him. He laughs bitterly. "An irony that I fear death. I, who am master of its domain." A shake of his head. "But I suppose if anyone were to know that of me, I'm not unhappy it is you."

I shouldn't ask, but my lips form the word anyway. "Why?"

He snatches a falling leaf, then tucks it behind one of my ears, fingertips brushing my cheek. "If there is a human who can be trusted here, I think it would be you. Which, I suppose, is a proper enough introduction to the next request I make of you, my Herald."

It stings to hear the title once more, but I sense no cruelty in it. I don't know if my god is even capable of mockery. I swallow. "And what is that?"

His smile is a sad thing. "If I die, my powers will pass to the nearest human. There must always be an Autumn. When I bleed to restore the Mirror, you will choose who stands beside me, in case. Someone must decide, and I want it to be you."

"Why me?"

"This place is too full of secrets and scheming, so many petty mortal squabbles. I don't know these humans well enough. My Consorts, they come to my chamber for one thing only. Some are kind, but I don't know their hearts, not truly. Nightly, for six years, I've seen the light in your eyes when you bring me souls, your joy when we pass through the Mirror. No matter what other concerns you have, you are loyal to the faith. You care about this world and this Temple as much as I do. You will choose someone worthy."

I'm a secret-keeper, a schemer, and a squabbler, too. Still, the earnestness in his expression disarms me. He extends a hand, hesitating just shy of my face. A turmoil rests in those eyes, gleaming like torches in the distance. "I put my faith in you. Will you do this?"

The trust of a god is a heady thing. Part of me fears he shouldn't believe in me, but I lean into his caress as his gloved fingertips stroke my cheek, the leather velvety against my skin. "Yes." Something flutters in my chest. Something fragile and sweet and warm. I don't know if the feeling is mine or his. "Why?" I ask. "Why did you pick me as Herald? Three of us passed all the tests, the interviews. The others jumped through the same hoops. So in the end, why me over the Tharem's nephew, over Vanyse?"

"You wanted it more than they did. More than you wanted anything."

I blink, a stinging tear squeezing its way out. "I did." *I do. And I lost it all.*

"Even now, after all of this, you have . . . a spark. A tenacity that belongs only to mortals. And that's why you'll choose my successor well." His words are as soft as his touch. "I hate it, this fear. How do you humans live with it, day after day?" His hand withdraws, my cheek burning where his palm rested.

It takes a gentle cough to clear my throat before I can reply. "We don't have a choice. But they'll find another way to fix the Mirror. You'll return to Sylvus, and all these human things will fade."

He closes his eyes. "You lie so beautifully."

I swallow. "It's not a lie. It's hope."

"Another mortal thing. I admire it, but that particular emotion still seems to elude me."

"You'll get the hang of it." But the words sound hollow.

"Thank you. For everything." He exits among a swirl of dry leaves, and for long minutes, I stand in the cold, alone.

I don't know what just happened. Our dynamic was always clear, a professional distance. Now, he's touched me thrice. Once a sin, the other two skirting it. I've felt the depths of a god's despair, and I hate it.

Winter should be here, and I just want everything to be normal again. I've just been tasked with choosing a new god, if it comes to that, and I can't even solve my own problems. Wren's plan and my snooping have turned up nothing. Months of effort, all wasted.

I need to know who did this, then force them to undo it. I made Autumn a promise. If I can't give my god his privacy back, I can at least fulfill that oath. Finding out more about my curse, learning how the Mirror was shattered, uncovering a way to restore the Mirror's magic. *Whatever it takes.*

I need answers, and I know who can help me.

When Sidriel responds to my ring at his bell, his smile is sly, smug. "Tirne."

"Don't gloat." I frown. "Or I'll leave."

"Will you?" He steps aside to let me in. "If you're finally desperate enough to come to me, I have to assume a little smile won't drive you away." Too knowing, that grin. The kohl around his eyes remains, along with his black lip stain. Cautiously, I enter the spider's lair. Sidriel occupies one of the Temple's guest rooms, nicer than Wren's. It's a comfortable chamber, if smaller than mine. No hearth, just a pair of flickering sconces. Tapestries and a heavy rug ward off some of autumn's chill, but still I shiver, goose pimples prickling my arms.

My gaze latches on to something else on the shelf. A shiny black box, filigreed in silver, one I've seen before. It, or its twin, rested in Laereda's room, so conspicuously out of place. To my knowledge, Sidriel and the former Consort have spoken only in passing. So why do they have matching boxes, or the same one?

Though Wren tested Sidriel's sample and found nothing, that doesn't absolve him entirely of guilt, just of casting the spell himself.

"Sit." He gestures to a chair at a small table.

Unease ripples through me, but I need this. *Whatever it takes.* I do as he bids. Sidriel is efficient, I'll give him that. The sorcerer quickly sets up the vials and implements he'll need on the table in the corner. It's sturdier and newer than the rickety one in Wren's shabby room. On it, a small knife reflects the lamplight next to a green glass vial, a stopper, and a scrap of pristine white cloth. He holds out a hand.

I shake my head. "No. First you tell me why *you* need this. See, I've thought about your offer. It's more than the Mirror. If that were the case, you'd just go directly to Autumn. But you want this to be a secret. So tell me why you truly want my blood, and I will give it to you."

Sidriel stares at me carefully, and I watch him weigh the options. Finally, he nods. "Your blood contains traces of Autumn's magic. I wish to study it."

I bite my lip. "Why not get that from a Scion? Why me?"

"The closer I get to the source, the better. A Scion's blood is mingled, a new concoction. Like yellow and blue fabric dye, mixed to make green. But you are human, Autumn's blood an addition. You, my dear Herald, are like blue fabric stitched with yellow thread. And if I'm careful, I can pluck it free."

"It's forbidden to handle the blood of the gods." I say this like he doesn't already know it.

"It is." His cold stare is challenging. "But you just made a promise. Your hand, please."

My heart hammers. What I do now is heresy. I could deny him despite my promise, run to Autumn or the Tharem and confess Sidriel's plan.

Sidriel's voice is low, soft. "Do you want your answers? To find out who cursed you? To get your title back?"

The weight of the decision settles on me, suffocating. I make my choice and lift my hand. "Hurry up and get it over with, so I can be done with you."

"Oh, you'll be back. Like draws to like," he murmurs, cupping my hand in his. It's a gentle touch. His thumb traces a circle in my palm.

"I'm nothing like you."

"Liar." Sidriel laughs. He positions the point of the blade and presses it into my flesh, slicing a thin line along the pad of my fingertip, a flick of the wrist that's light as a feather. It still stings. A soft hiss slips from me as he speaks again. "You may have everyone else fooled, but not me. You're a far cry from the good girl you pretend to be."

I open my mouth to protest as he guides my hand to the vial. "I am. Good, that is." But it tastes like a lie on my lips. I've been trespassing, stealing, lying to almost everyone I know in some way or another. A thin trickle of blood slides down my finger into the bottle.

Another laugh. Sidriel releases my hand but traces a tickling line along the back of it with his fingertip. "No. You're ambitious. Ruthless. I respect that. You know what you want, and you make it happen. Being pious and hardworking got you the title you always wanted. But once it was lost? You betray your very god to get it back. And you come to me to do it." His lips curl into a smile. "Someone like you deserves better than my brother." Jaed. I haven't seen him in a fourday. Again. And though my friend has been clear about his dislike of Sidriel, I didn't even know the healer knew Jaed. They are a decade apart in age, with different fathers.

"Someone better? What, you?"

No mockery lies in his tone or his expression as he draws another aimless pattern along the back of my hand, dragging his fingertip up the back of my wrist. "You could do worse." A frown. "You already do, with him."

"Why do you say that?"

"People like Jaed . . . they hold back people like us. So morally superior."

"That's not how it is."

"Isn't it?" When I don't flinch away from his touch, Sidriel's fingertips trail up my arm, my shoulder, then twine a lock of my hair around his index finger. A shiver ripples through me, but I keep my hand still over the bottle as the other clenches into a fist.

"But you," he says. "You're more like me than you are any of them. You know what you want, and you'll do whatever it takes to get it. Determined. I admire that."

A sick, shivery feeling settles in my stomach, the suspicion that he's right.

"When you're ready, when you admit that to yourself . . . then you'll come to me. For more than blood."

I could bat his hand away. Tell him he speaks lies.

I should.

But I don't.

CHAPTER

SIXTEEN

I shouldn't be doing this. I don't know what punishment I'll earn if I'm caught, but it's the Festival of the Dead, and I'll be damned if I spend it locked up in the Temple.

I could have asked one of my friends to come with me, but they have their own dead to honor. And this is special, private. It's been half a dozen years since I was in this realm during winter. I circle Poplar Street and Ilna's shop. Will she be at Mother's mausoleum? I doubt it. The Kildians don't observe this festival.

This year, it feels obscene to celebrate the memory of the dead while their souls crowd the sky and the streets, unseen to all but me. They flicker into sight as dusk begins to fall, orbs of jewel-toned flame. They weave about the living, a macabre parade. The city streetlamps pale in comparison to their brilliant fire. The light gleams off living, smiling faces. Garish, ghastly.

After they already sapped my energy once, I am taking a risk being outside after nightfall. But it's Mother. And I can hurry.

The townsfolk dance in the streets, wearing the garb of the Festival of the Dead, covered in drapes of crimson cloth and simple white half-masks designed to resemble skulls. Tambourines and bells ring out along with cheerful voices in songs to celebrate lives well-lived. People dance with dolls made of old clothes stuffed with straw, to represent those long gone. Despite the lively melody, one elderly man cradles his mannequin close, swaying slowly to a different song only he can hear.

Celebrants place their deceased loved ones' favorite things on porches and stoops, atop beautiful trays of painted wood or even silver, if the family is wealthy enough. Bowls of precious cream and wine sit beside sweet spice-flecked breads, treasured heirloom hairpins, old handmade toys. One tray holds nothing but an assortment of seashells from the faraway coast, polished to a gleaming shine.

The dead, for their part, act as agitated and impotent witnesses to the revelry of the living. Their murmuring, indecipherable voices echo in my ears, a discordant counterpoint to the merry music. They dart about, eager to leave this world far behind, this place where they no longer belong. Do some of them flit past their former loved ones? If I look closely, I can see faces inside the glow. The sharp angle of a chin, the hollow of tired eyes, the curve of a nose.

It is me they cluster about most thickly, lured to the faint spark of magic I still carry. Like moths to a candle flame, or like wild game to water.

The shadows they cast flicker and dance, stretched into eerie shapes. For a moment, I imagine I see a jagged mouth full of sharp teeth, a set of claws extended from a long-fingered hand. Like the creatures my aunt used to tell me about, the Kildara. Once servants of the exiled god Kild, the kexas and garvishes and other unholy beings haunted my nightmares as a child. But as I blink, the streetlamps flicker and the shadows blend back into their normal shapes.

Those loyal to Kild do not celebrate tonight, not as those of my faith do. They burn their dead and believe it causes the soul to return to the earth as ash, to the darkness of the sky as smoke. I can't truly say they're wrong. Maybe the souls that follow me belong only to those who worship the Seasons.

It's been the better part of a month since I was last in town. Coughs echo back and forth, wet, sickly sounds, as gaunt-faced figures plod along on their business. Sour faces stare back at me, grim and hollow. One person walking past has a forehead gleaming with sweat despite the evening's coolness, pallid with dark circles beneath their eyes. They cough into a hand, then wipe a smear of red from their lips. I give them a wide berth, as do others.

Fire and shadow, how did it get so bad?

But I know the answer. Autumn grows mortal, his powers dwindling. The Cough sweeps through a populace demoralized. Winter should be here by now, and even those who'd once been optimistic begin to lose hope.

The sorcerers haven't puzzled out a new enchantment, either. The Mirror still lies beautiful and dormant, a glittering corpse in pieces. It can't be fixed too soon.

My own time to cure my curse is running out, hour by hour. I still await Sidriel's findings, but all my other efforts are fruitless. I haven't even had the chance to poke through Calder's things. He spends most of his time holed up in his room these days, tasked with testing ways to re-enchant the Mirror. As one of the few exempt from a full shift assembling pieces, he scurries back and forth from his chambers to briefly visit the Mirror. I've yet to find a time he will be safely absent.

Another path still lies open to me, to uncover the Temple's deepest, dirtiest secrets. Laereda. I'll admit she makes me nervous, after she poisoned me. Still, she's my best bet at ferreting out scraps of information. I'll need to draw her closer, and soon.

Simmering in these thoughts, I make my way through the streets, surrounded by the dead. I already feel my mind fogging, a lethargy seeping in. I increase my pace. If I can get to the graveyard, I'll be safe.

Even cloaked, I'm anxious about using paths commonly taken by Temple residents. The route I take leads me through parts of town I normally avoid. Still, passersby veer around me as much as they do those who cough loudly, avoiding my cloud of worry. A mental fog and my frustration make my vision go blurry, the shadows dancing at the edge of my sight.

Then I catch a flash of brilliant violet from the corner of my eye, robes in a color worn by only one person. The Tharem.

What is he doing in this shabby part of town? I stop beside the corner of a building, peeking around it. He pauses at the door to an apothecary's shop with a beaten, faded sign that reads *Remedies and Tinctures*, then glances around. I duck behind the corner, and when I dare to look again, he is gone.

I clutch my cloak tightly to hide as much of my russet robe as possible. For once, I'm glad for the threadbare, plain cloak, rather than my old one in every autumn hue. I argue with myself for a few moments, then grow bold. Still, I remind myself to act casual. Just a nameless nobody on an errand, nothing more.

The storefront isn't promising. It's not particularly dirty, but it could certainly use a new coat of paint. The shop may have been able to afford that once, but certainly not now. No one can manage such luxuries these days, at least not in this part of the city. It bears a single window, but no glass. Just an open hole with plain wooden shutters thrown wide. Inside, out of reach of passersby, rest racks of bottles.

I'm surprised it's open after dark, but I suppose shops that sell more discreet items would be. I creep through the door, hood up. There are a few other shoppers, and the cold blows in through the open window, so my cloak isn't too conspicuous. The shopkeeper glances up to give me an unenthusiastic grunt in greeting before returning to his conversation with the Tharem.

One shopper lifts bottles one by one and swirls them against the candlelight. Another digs through a bin of tiny tea tins. Behind me, the souls hover in the entryway at the edge of the window frame. I breathe in relief. The dead do not follow into dwellings of the living. Like many, this apothecary must live above the shop. My strength slowly returns while I do my snooping.

The Tharem is at the front counter, speaking in hushed tones. I can't make out the words, just an irritation in both voices. Finally, they seem to agree, and the shopkeeper gives the Tharem a few coins in exchange for a bag of clinking bottles. The Tharem leaves quickly, not even casting me a sideways glance.

Slowly I scan the racks and shelves. Just browsing. At least everything is labeled clearly, but nothing out of the ordinary jumps out at me. Just the usual teas and tisanes and tinctures.

Now the shopkeeper addresses me. "Whatcha need?"

I lie. "I'm looking for a stomach-soothing tea?"

But then I stop short as the shopkeeper pulls one of the bottles from the Tharem's bag to place it among matching ones on the counter nearby. They're clear glass with a liquid inside, shimmering in a very peculiar shade of lavender. All five of the bottles are labeled *Miracle Cure-All*. I'd have scoffed and laughed, but I recognize the liquid within. It's water from the fountain in the gods' palace in Sylvus.

Forbidden, and only accessible through the Mirror.

"Ah." The shopkeeper sees me staring at the water and smiles a weasel's grin. "That's the good stuff, much better than tea. Will heal a sour stomach and anything else that ails you. Even the Cough. Only twelve eagles a bottle." It might as well be a king's ransom for such a tiny vial. It's an entire year's allowance at the Temple. Maybe he notices my grimace. "The price is fair. These are the last bottles till the spring, after the Mirror's fixed."

Spring.

Oh no.

I know why the Tharem comes to this shop. If he sold this water closer to the Temple or along the main roads, places where a Herald may visit, he'd be caught. He could get this only from a god or a Herald, and

I can't see any of the gods caring about money. No, they'd be furious at this.

I shake my head at the shopkeeper and hope my voice is steady. "Out of my budget, but I'll take the tea, if you have it."

He leads me to a corner of the shop and presses a small packet into my hand. "Two sparrows."

That, I do have. I give him the money and leave, my thoughts swirling as I pick up my pace toward the graveyard. Spring, he said.

Which means only one person could have brought this here. Spring's Herald. The Tharem has hated me since I bested his nephew for Herald, and now I know why. He knew I'd never help him with this. Fire and shadow, if the Tharem had access to Autumn's Herald, he could get a delivery whenever he wanted. Only I am allowed to travel between realms nightly. Or I was, when the Mirror was whole.

But it doesn't add up. The Tharem would want to keep the Mirror open. Unless . . . unless he was in danger of being caught and wanted to trap his conspirator in Sylvus. It would be dangerously petty to burn the world down for it, but he's a petty man.

I push my worries aside for now as I approach the cemetery. These are thoughts for later, to consider in quiet. A shiver ripples through me as I walk through the gates. Here I enter a place of the dead, and some tiny part of my magic recognizes that, deep inside. The souls, too, slough away from me, waiting outside these gates. I don't know why they don't enter here. Perhaps they do not like to be so close to their mortal remains.

Others walk the graveyard, of course, paying their own respects. Some celebrate in their homes or in the streets, but I'm not the only one who wants to visit the resting place of a loved one, not tonight.

It's calm and still, as if the breeze is afraid to gust here. I fight back a tickling cough, along with the worry that comes alongside it, and make my way to the section for the faithful, to the mausoleum that houses

Mother's sarcophagus. Her beloved aster flowers have long since died, and the candied walnuts and honey cakes she so favored are an expensive rarity. So I set a delicate handkerchief on the tray instead. It's embroidered with a pattern of ravens. "They're smarter than many a human I've known," she'd told me once. "But not as smart as my clever little girl."

A part of me will never stop missing her. Sometimes, I feel like I hear her voice calling to me, murmuring encouragement. Or I'll catch a whiff of someone else's jasmine perfume and it's like her arms are around me once more.

Gone, but never ever forgotten.

At least until I die. Then there will be no one left to remember her. She'll just be another body in this graveyard, another set of crumbling bones with no one left to visit. Not Aunt Ilna, certainly. If she didn't come tonight, she must surely have washed her hands of us entirely.

Inside these stone walls, the floor is dry. I sit beside Mother's bones and tell her everything that's happened. All my worries, and how I'm terrified to let her down if I fail. I always imagined how proud she would have been when I'd won my title. I'd fulfilled the potential she'd always hoped for me.

"I had it, Mother. Everything we'd ever wanted. But it's gone now, and I still don't know why, or who did it. What if I never find out?"

Eventually, I stand and brush dust and dirt from my robe. As I make my way back through the cemetery, a chorus of murmured prayers and hymns to the dead weaves through the air. But just as I'm leaving Autumn's section of the graveyard, I hear a familiar voice, a low raspy purr, and halt in my steps.

Sidriel. What is he doing here?

The words are too quiet for me to make them out, but I recognize the cadence. A prayer, half-speech and half-song, the lilting rhythm of Autumn's litanies. A memoriam.

Slowly I walk closer. A quick peek around the corner of a mausoleum reveals him. Sidriel stands not before a common grave marker. No, he kneels before a pillar with an etched likeness of a woman. It is part of a spiral of waist-high stones spreading outward from a central tiled circle, at the end of the line. The very end, in fact.

Even in the moonlight, it's clear that the memorial's stone robes are painted the color of spiced pumpkin custard, trimmed in white along the edge. A Consort. *Autumn's* Consort. The last, before Laereda.

Why is Sidriel praying before her stone? But before I ponder too deeply, another idea strikes me. Sidriel is here, in the graveyard. The memoriam he chants is a long one. Which means he won't be back to his rooms for a time.

That black, ornate box. The one I saw in Laereda's rooms and also in his.

I turn and creep away until I'm out of his sight line, then hurry through the cemetery. When my feet hit the town's cobblestones, I rush toward the Temple. It's difficult, my legs feeling like they move through water as the souls chill me with their phantom touch, buzzing around me like wasps. Celebrants give me sidelong glances, but I keep my hood down and walk as quickly as I can without breaking into a full run and drawing even more attention.

By the time I make it back, I'm panting, out of breath, my lungs burning and my legs screeching at me. A growing pressure in my head is unbearable. I should go to my room, should lie down. Unless . . . My hand slips into my pocket, caressing the smooth glass of the medicine vial. Tiny, just a single dose. I've already taken one today. I shouldn't double up like this. But the pain lances through me, paralyzing. I withdraw the bottle, tug out the cork, and gulp the medicine. The vial goes back in my pocket, and I wait for the blissful numbness to ease the ache.

My breathing slowly returns to normal, though my heartbeat refuses to slow. I pass other acolytes, some of whom cast odd glances at my flushed, sweating face. I ignore them and keep walking.

There. Sidriel's room.

I suck in a deep breath and walk toward it, trying to appear casual. I'm merely visiting to ask the sorcerer a question, you see. Sorry, didn't know he was out.

But as I approach the curtain, the hallway is empty. I slip through the beads and step inside. The box rests on his desk. My trembling fingertips stretch out and brush the lacquered wood of the lid. Cool, smooth. I reach for the latch.

Pain racks me. It is worse than the headaches, than searing fire. Despite grasping at the desk for support, I collapse to the floor. My muscles clench and cramp, my hands curling into agonized claws as my back arches. I don't know how long I manage to fight it before the blissfulness of oblivion drags me under.

I awaken to a foot nudging me in the ribs. I roll over.

Sidriel stands above me, cold as winter frost in his indigo robes and sharp contrasting features. Those eyes are like piercing needles, his dark-painted lips in a frown.

"Awake, I see."

I groan.

"You're not in any position to complain, my dear former Herald. I believe I'm the one catching *you* slinking into my room. Were you ready to accept my other offer? Although I suppose if that were the case, I'd have found you draped across my bed like a feast day gift. No, instead I find you on my floor, curled up and trembling, unconscious. And only one thing in this room would do that."

I manage to scramble to my feet, first kneeling, then grasping the desk to stand. My legs tremble beneath me, ready to give way at any moment.

"Oh, do have a seat," he purrs. "I intend to ask you a few questions, and I'd rather you not fall and bash your head against the corner of my desk while I do."

I bare my teeth in a snarl, but I sink onto the corner of his bed. He's right. My knees feel ready to buckle.

"So." He steps closer, my eyes at a level with his chest. His fingers grip my chin, forcing me to look up and meet those icy eyes. "Tell me—"

"Who was she?" I square my shoulders. I will not let him cow me.

"What?"

"The woman on the gravestone in the cemetery. Who was she to you?"

For the first time ever, I see him stricken. It makes him look younger, and so unlike the Sidriel I know. His eyes widen, his mouth parts, and pain rolls through his eyes. It passes quickly, but neither of us can pretend I didn't see it.

"I'm not the one under questioning," Sidriel hisses.

"Tell me who she is, and I'll tell you what I came here for."

I watch the debate play out across his face. "I could make you tell me."

"You could try."

Another pause. He watches me, head tilted like a hawk. "You confess first. You came here looking for something. What?"

"I . . . I came to take my blood back." It's not the best lie, but it's the only believable reason that comes to mind without telling him I know about Laereda and the box. "I thought maybe it was in the box. Then I was on the floor."

For a long moment, he stares at me. Judging. But it seems my half-truth has paid off. Sidriel sits on the other corner of the bed. "Her name was Oluryn. Autumn's Consort before Laereda."

"That much I gathered. Why were you singing a litany at her grave?"

He hesitates. I can see him weighing the answer in his head.

"You promised the truth."

His lips thin into a flat line. "I loved her."

I flinch. Love? It's not a word I'd ever have expected from his lips. "But she was—"

"The Consort of a god?" A bit of his prickly demeanor returns. "Yes, she was. I was a young fool who loved her, and your god killed her." So chill, those words, deathly cold.

I remember now, how she died giving birth to one of Autumn's children. Even the Temple's healers can't always save a life that flees too quickly. I'd attended her funeral, holding my mother's hand. I'd been only eleven at the time, with a child's simpler understanding of such things.

"I'm sorry," I say. Condolences given years too late.

Now I know why he left the Temple.

He turns toward me, caressing the spot on my jaw where he gripped it. "My apologies for that."

I almost murmur a placation, a simple "It's all right" or "No harm done." Old habit, left over from the days when I was the top of the class, the obedient Herald. But that woman died when my title was stripped from me, or at least has been dying a slow death ever since. I lift my chin and glare at him, touching my skin gingerly.

There. Gone almost before I see it, a flash of something in Sidriel's eyes, something that might be guilt. "Perhaps next time you'll think before poking around where you shouldn't be." He lifts a finger and tucks back a lock of my hair, trailing the edge of my ear with one gentle fingertip. "You make a poor thief."

Pulling away, I change the subject. "Did you check my blood yet?"

"Yes."

"And?"

"I need more."

I shake my head. "No."

"I was able to find the curse," he says, "but the results are . . . unclear."

"You just want more to run your own experiments on Autumn's blood."

He smiles. "That, too."

I hesitate. My head pounds too fiercely to think this through. *Whatever it takes.* "One more."

"Good." Sidriel stands, plucking several items from a shelf. A thin, gleaming blade, a vial, a pale gray towel.

I choke back the nerves and take a deep breath as I stand. I won't do this sitting on his bed. "Only if I get to make the cut this time."

Sidriel hands me the knife, small but shining. I pierce the meat of my thumb, and the blade sinks deep. A gasp bursts from me and my eyes water, but Sidriel holds the vial under my hand. The blood flows easily, too freely. Two drops splat onto the floor before the vial is in place. When it is nearly full, Sidriel nods and I curl my hand, cupping it with the thumb pressing into my palm. Though the sorcerer first places the container on a shelf, he turns to me with an outstretched hand, palm up.

After a moment's hesitation, I place mine in his. He pats the wound dry with the towel, then takes the blade from my right hand. "Messy," he says, peering at the wound.

"It was sharper than I expected."

Sidriel pierces his own fingertip, much shallower than the cut I made. Before I can protest, he presses our wounds together. My thumb tingles, the shiver of magic. When he pulls his hand away, I wipe the blood clean with the towel to reveal unbroken flesh. Sidriel takes the cloth and does the same. His wound is also closed.

I'd known he was a healer, but it is unnerving to feel the tingle of it in my own skin. I shake my hand to clear the pins-and-needles sensation.

A single question now screams in my mind. I want to ask it desperately. *Can you cure my headaches?* He'd told me long ago that he couldn't, but what if something has changed? New discoveries are made all the time, in magic and medicine.

But that would mean revealing my condition to this man I do not trust. No. If he doesn't remember me, I won't remind him.

Instead, I rub my thumb against my forefinger. It doesn't twinge at all. While I do so, Sidriel lifts the vial, swirling it in the light of the sconces. "I'll let you know what I find," he says brusquely. "I'll need a longer series of tests this time."

"If we're done?" I ask, pointing at the door.

He turns, his winter-pale eyes watching me closely. "For now."

SEVENTEEN

The next morning, I fall ill. One of my headaches grips me, along with a sore throat and a thirst I can't seem to slake. I shiver and sweat, alternately freezing or feverish.

I beg off my morning duties to lie in the quiet. In a feverish haze, thoughts dart around my brain like frantic dragonflies. They circle back again and again to the Tharem's betrayal. What do I do? Tell Autumn? He would be forced to exile the man, or worse. And if the Tharem was complicit in my curse, that might destroy the only chance of finding the key, the cure, a way to undo it all and fix the Mirror.

No. I could confront the Tharem, but I'm surprised to find how much I fear him, now that I know how far he's willing to sink.

I toss and turn, sweating in my bed, unable to think clearly enough for a solution and incapable of thinking about anything else. I miss my afternoon duties as well, guilt swallowing me over forsaking my chores. What will people think of me?

That evening, I start to cough. Wren visits to drop off potions, but the next day I'm shaking in bed anyway, downing her remedies to soothe my raw throat. Vanyse even stops by with the rest of their favorite lozenges.

I haven't seen them in days, either, and a twinge of remorse fills me, but they wave away my apology.

"I know you've been having a rough time of it. I understand." I wonder if it's a lie, but they, too, leave me in peace.

Jaed does not leave me to wallow. He visits me that night, doling out chamomile and peppermint tea to help augment Wren's remedies. "You need to rest."

"I have to get better," I mumble. "To get back to my duties."

"I assure you," he says, "the Temple will not collapse without you."

"But—"

"Don't worry about it." He hands me a steaming mug. "I'm more concerned about you than I am about anyone else."

"I'll be fine." But I still accept the tea as I sit in my bed draped in blankets. Worry shines in Jaed's colorless eyes, his usual smile replaced by a furrowed brow. He perches on the side of my bed, watching me like I will keel over at any moment. He'd come to my chamber when the hymns of nightly devotions echoed down the halls, across the tile mosaics, through my beaded curtain. "Shush," he tells me now. "I'm not about to abandon you when you've caught the Red Cough." He places the back of his hand against my forehead. It's icy-cold against my flushed skin, and I bat it away while trying not to spill steaming tea all over my lap. The illness makes my headache worse, even through the haze of a double dose of my usual medicine.

I blow on the tea and take a cautious sip. "You Scions get so fussy about these things. Must be nice to never fall ill."

A hint of his typical grin ghosts across his face. "I'm not complaining."

"Well, I've been sick before. I've got Wren's potions to help, and the Temple healers gave me some herbs compressed into little tablets. Now stop being a mother hen. Don't you have students to teach in the morning? Lessons to plan? Bix to keep you company?"

His reply is clipped. "Bix is worn out from pulling weeds all day." But something flickers in his eyes.

"Jaed . . . is everything all right with you and Bix?"

"It's fine." He smiles, but I can tell it's forced.

"Tell me."

He chews his lip, then sighs. "I don't know. He's been tetchy lately. Then again, so have I. Maybe I'm rubbing off on him."

"What's wrong?"

"You." I flinch, and he frowns. "I didn't mean it to come out like that. But you're turning into a skeleton of yourself, hiding away, obsessed with this curse and pushing yourself too far. You haven't even been around to talk to us, but don't think I don't see you anyway. Hauling books from the library down the hall, missing meals I know you should be at. Growing thin and pale and tired. You're making yourself sick, with or without the Cough."

And he doesn't even know about Wren, about Sidriel. "Jaed . . ." *We've been over this.* "It's important."

"Not as important as everything else that's happening. The Cough, the rations, and the hoarding. The Kildians ballooning in number over everyone's anger at the lack of progress on the Mirror. And you don't know about any of it, because you just care about getting your job back." His words are harsh, but his tone is gentle. "Please, let it go."

I shake my head, even as I'm racked with a fit of coughing that splashes some of the tea onto my lap.

Jaed frowns. "I'm sorry. We'll talk about this later," he says. "For tonight I'm your caretaker whether you like it or not."

Welcoming the change of subject, I breathe a sigh and give a tentative smile. "At least get off the bed." I nudge his hip with a knee, and he obliges.

He still scoots a chair to my bedside, pulling a notebook from his pocket and flipping it open, then scribbling in it with a paper-wrapped bit of charcoal. I know that journal, the one he writes all his music in.

I slurp the tea as fast as its temperature will allow. A luxury now, these herbs and spices, given only to the ill. Clove, chamomile, mint, and even a precious dollop of honey. "You don't have to stay."

"I do. Just keeping an eye on a friend who's a little too stubborn for her own good. Now finish your tea, then eat your soup."

"You're worse than the healers, you know that?"

He doesn't look up from his book. "So I've been told."

I lapse into silence as I drink down the tea. I don't want the soup, but he's thwarted me. If I refuse, it will just prove his point about being too bullheaded. With a grimace, I pick up the bowl. Chicken bone broth with a few finely chopped vegetables in it. Dried, then dropped into the soup to rehydrate.

We still have our usual stores to get us through the months that would have been the cold season. But I know how much of the Mirror needs to be repaired, and so does Autumn. These vegetables are carefully rationed, even the desiccated ones.

The thought sobers any levity Jaed tries to bring. What will we do when the last of our food stores run out? When there are no more seeds to plant? With an autumn that extends months and months? Or years?

I succumb to another fit of coughing and set the broth aside. Jaed stands and fusses over me some more as I lie down, tucking me into the blankets.

"But I'm burning alive," I complain, throwing them aside the second he stops.

He huffs. "I told you, too stubborn."

"You love it," I mutter, immediately feeling a shivery chill and yanking the quilt up over me again.

"Maybe." He brushes a lock of hair from my temple, damp and stuck to my skin with sweat. But he doesn't flinch or grimace, just tucks it aside as he leans over me. "Go to sleep, Tirne. Rest will do you good."

I yawn, realizing just how exhausted I am. A weak cough or two later, Jaed presses a kiss to my forehead as I drift to sleep.

I awaken to the scent of crisp apples and brittle leaves.

Half-delirious, I roll over and the world sways. Sweat soaks me, and I shiver.

"What's that smell?" I mumble as I crack my eyes open. The instant before his silhouette comes into focus, I recognize it. If I hadn't been addled with fever, I'd have known it instantly.

Autumn sits by my bedside, in the same chair Jaed occupied when I drifted off.

The fire in my hearth dwindles to embers, casting sharp orange shadows on his narrow features. He'd been staring across the room at those dying coals, but he turns at the sound of my voice, dark hair swishing around his face like a dancer's skirts.

I blink again, my eyes crusted with sleep and my throat sore. "Where's Jaed?" I struggle into a sitting position.

"I asked him to leave."

"Asked, or told?"

Pensive orange eyes meet mine. "Are they not the same from the lips of a god?"

He has a point. "Why are you here?"

Autumn frowns, opening his mouth, then closing it again. A shake of his head. "Am I not allowed to check in on my H . . ."—he skips over the word—"an acolyte if she is ill?"

I suck in a sharp breath at the almost-title, which turns into more coughs. A new cup of tea rests on my bedside table, and I reach for it in desperation. Not hot, but not truly cold yet, either. I sip it. When I can speak again, I say, "I know the Lord of Autumn can do whatever he wants. What I want to know is why?" Why, when we haven't shared a word since the day Winter should have fallen.

Autumn's lips thin, and he stares into the dimness of the room. "A good question."

"You don't seem happy to be here."

He shifts in his seat, clasping his hands in his lap, then placing them back on the arms of the chair. His eyes meet mine once more, and a conflict lingers in them. "I don't like it."

"Like what?"

"Sickness. You're such fragile things, humans."

"You're the God of Death. You should be used to this."

"I should be." A pause. "Right now, I'm not."

I shiver as I gulp down more tea. He's already confessed to me he fears his own death. It's not a far stretch to realize illness would unnerve him as well. I cough again. "Right now, I wish you had Spring's powers." The God of Vitality can heal with a gesture. Autumn holds only the power to snuff out a life.

"I suppose I could end your misery," he says softly. A small smile graces the edges of his mouth, and merriment dances in those fire-colored eyes.

My heartbeat skips and stutters. I swallow hard. "Did you just make a jest?"

"It appears becoming more human has many effects."

"Oh."

Autumn leans forward and lifts a hand. Gloved again, in snug black leather. I wonder if he's worn them just to visit me, then curse my own foolishness. Of course not.

Still, he makes the same motion Jaed did hours before, plucking a lock of sweaty hair away from my forehead and tucking it back. His leather-clad fingertips are tender, like the brush of a feather, and I shudder. *Stupid, stupid Tirne*, I curse myself. When my best friend had done this, I felt only irritation and affection. Now my heart speeds into a sprint, my breath catching in my throat. I shiver from more than just the fever.

Maybe I truly am sick, and not just with a cold.

When his hand draws away from my skin, do I imagine that it does so reluctantly? Or the faint flicker of something dark and pained in his eyes?

Of course you did, you idiot.

"I don't have Spring's abilities," he says. "But I do have something to offer." Gently he takes the tea from my hands. Setting it on the table, he tugs off one glove. With the other, he picks up a letter opener left there.

"No," I whisper just as he pierces a thumb with it. A small puncture, but a wound nonetheless.

He squeezes a single drop of blood into the tea and replaces his glove. "Take it."

My hands curl around the teacup even as they tremble. I've had a small vial of Autumn's blood once before, when I'd been consecrated as his Herald.

"I can't."

Autumn's eyes meet mine, and that shadow of a smile touches his mouth once more. "Do you defy your god?"

My eyes narrow. "You play dirty. Anyone ever tell you that?"

"I'm the God of Death, my dear." His voice lowers to a purr. "Only Winter plays dirtier than I do."

My breath freezes. There is an inflection in those words that I dare not question too deeply. My thoughts spin. I remember what he'd looked like in the baths, his shirt soaked into translucence, water dripping from his hair. The strange, haunted look in his eyes that day in the grove, what should have been the beginning of winter. The soft rasp of his voice when he said he trusted me.

What would happen if I lean over and kiss him right now?

I bark out a laugh. The fever really has burned my brain. Here I am, daydreaming about heresy. Delirium grips me, the world going sparkly around the edges as I break into spasms of laughter and great, hacking coughs.

Autumn watches me in puzzlement until the fit subsides. The unspoken question hangs in his eyes.

"Never mind. It's not that funny." I flush even hotter than the burning fever.

He nods at the cup. "Drink it."

Cautiously I lift it to my lips. This is not technically forbidden. A god can gift anyone they wish with the blessing of their blood. But it's not a thing that ever *really* happens aside from appointing a new Herald.

I take a careful sip. The honey and spice drown out any odd flavor, but the moment I swallow, the edges of the room soften in my vision. The spinning in my head eases, but everything feels muted, wrapped in cotton.

Sleep suddenly drags at me. I barely feel it when Autumn coaxes the teacup from my grasp.

"Rest, Tirne. My Herald." The cup clacks softly on the tabletop. I'm too groggy to correct his use of the title, though it stings. As I lie down and curl up into the blankets, his last words drift to me. "I'll be here."

Chapter

EIGHTEEN

For three more days, I shiver and sweat, fretting over the work I'm missing. Do they think me lazy, or that I'm faking this? Every day, I'm letting someone down, some other acolyte who must cover my share of the work.

On the fourth day, the fever passes, though the cough still lingers and I find myself dizzy sometimes. I can't bear to lie abed any longer, though, so I force myself up and to my duties, slogging through them in a foggy daze.

But my search for answers presses on me still, and even fatigued, I can't pass up an opportunity that comes. I creep through the halls this evening, preparing to slip into Calder's chamber. Wren told me she'd sent him into town for spell supplies this afternoon.

His curtain rattles as I pass through, the bell tied onto it a small alarm. But I've long since set aside my worry for such things, after prying into other rooms in this quest.

Once inside, I quietly shuffle through his belongings. Disorganized piles of papers, books, and scrolls fill his shelves and cover his desk. Just notes containing mathematical formulas. I may not be an expert, but I know enough to guess they don't look like spells, only numbers and notations, the work of his lessons. Mundane, harmless. Until one drawer gives me a nasty surprise. I barely brush the handle before a painful sting burns my fingertips.

I yank my hand away and massage it gingerly. This enchantment is too much like the one on Sidriel's box, though weaker. What does he hide here?

But time is short, and I have no solution for that trap. I return to the rest of his belongings. Papers and books and more papers. Other than his mathematics lessons, some seem like plans for inventions to help with various everyday tasks. Teakettles, something that resembles a shovel.

Then I find it, peeking out of the pages of a book. A crude sketch. The symbols that rest on the Mirror's frame, once hidden beneath its surface, now marred. The ink is clear, new, unlike the faded, walnut-colored inks of some of the older tomes I peruse in the library.

Tucked in with it are a handful of other notes jotted in the same hand. Numbers, formulas, but on each page, one of the Mirror's symbols in the center, the notations circling it like water swirling down a drain.

One scrap of paper leaves my breath frozen, my hands trembling.

My name, written beneath several of the symbols. Lines connect the letters of my name to one symbol or another, with numbers beneath each. Computations add them together in a messy scrawl.

I consider stealing this so Wren can analyze it. But no, Calder may notice it missing. Instead, I snatch a loose page from a careless stack on one corner of the desk, in the shadow of a tower of books that looks ready to topple at any moment. Using a nearby pen and ink bottle, I copy the page carefully, then replace everything exactly where I found it and blow on the ink.

Once I'm certain the page is dry, I fold it and clutch it tightly, then make my retreat. I'm shaken, neglecting to listen for footsteps before I exit, and I nearly bump into a figure in white.

"Tirne?"

"Jaed!" My cheeks warm.

"What are you—?" Jaed peers into Calder's room through the beads, seeing it empty. "Wait." His eyes dart to the paper in my hand. "Are you spying? What's that?"

I straighten my shoulders. "It's a clue. To the curse, maybe. Listen, I can explain."

"Tirne . . ." Warning and worry make his voice deeper, rough. "We need to talk. Your room?"

It's closer than his. I nod. That withering look of disappointment turns my stomach inside out. As soon as we enter my room, I close the leather flap. "Jaed, you don't underst—"

But he doesn't let me finish. "This has gone too far. You're creeping into people's rooms and pawing through their things now?"

"It's already winter. We need to find who did this."

"So you can get your job back."

"So we can fix it!"

"You tell yourself that, but if you really cared about people affected by this, you'd go with me out into the city when I volunteer. Help me carry water to those sick with the Cough, take what sweets we can manage to the orphanage. It would help ease so many hearts if you went out there with us, if the Herald assured people it's going to be all right. But instead you're burying yourself under books, and apparently rummaging through people's rooms on this useless mission of yours."

My chest is tight, my face burning. "It's not useless. If we know who did this, we can undo it."

"They'll enchant the Mirror again, with or without that information."

"I can help!"

"This isn't about helping. This is about you destroying yourself over this. And I can't watch you do it anymore."

Guilt wraps around me, strangling, then burns into frustration. "You don't know what this is like! Everything is gone. If I can get it back—"

"I'm not gone." The words are low, quiet. "But apparently I don't compare with that damn Mirror. With that fancy title you love so much.

You're so focused on this stupid *job* that you don't even care about people. Not me, not your other friends, not the ones you violate with your burglary. How many have there been?"

I'm trembling now, with fury and with pain. "It's not—"

"They aren't pawns in your game, Tirne."

"I know that!"

His voice is small, mournful. "I don't think you do. You don't even see what you're becoming. I . . ." He pauses, then shakes his head. "Maybe too much time in Sylvus has changed you."

"I haven't. Just . . . you don't know how much it hurts when something you love so much is just suddenly gone."

He stares at me for a long, heartbreaking moment, agony in those pale eyes. "Actually, I do."

I swallow. I don't know what to say through the broken glass in my chest.

Jaed sucks in a long breath. "You're not coming back from this, are you?"

The look on his face hurts. Oh gods, does it hurt. "I'm still me."

"You're not. You're holding the evidence of that in your hands. You're losing yourself, all for nothing."

In my hands. The paper. Wait. I unfold it and show it to him. "This isn't 'nothing.' Maybe I broke some rules to get it . . . but it's important. He wrote my *name*, Jaed, along with the Mirror frame's symbols."

He sucks in a breath as I wave the paper in his face, then snatches it from my hands. "Tirne . . . you have to take this to Autumn."

"If Autumn makes this public and Calder did it, he'll be exiled. He may never—" I stop.

Jaed finishes for me. "May never remove your curse." He shoves the paper back at me, and I take it. "I won't turn you in. You have to make this choice yourself. But if you don't tell Autumn, I . . . I can't watch you do this. I can't be friends with whatever you're becoming. Something hard. Something ruthless."

I can't breathe. All the air is gone from the room. "Don't say that."

"Then make the right choice. Until then . . . I can't be around you." Sorrow bleeds into his eyes, and he walks away. The beads of my curtain clack, my bell jangling. It feels like thorns wrapped around my heart.

I tuck the note in my journal, then crawl into my bed. Jaed doesn't mean it. He can't. I curl on my side and stare at my wrist, at the bracelet he gave me so many years ago. It feels like I've lived a lifetime since we slipped the last amber bead onto it.

It seems like a rebuke, a guilty reminder. I unclasp it and toss it onto a side table, where it clatters loudly.

I lie like that for a very long time as the light dims around the slats of my window and turns to dusk. I've missed supper, but I don't care.

How could he? His words rattle around my brain. *Something ruthless.*

He's not the first to call me that. Maybe he's right. Maybe they're both right. And only one of them won't judge me for it.

I can't be alone, not right now.

Sidriel answers the ring of his bell. "I won't have your new results until tomo—"

"That's not why I'm here."

He lets me in as his eyes drink in my expression, the resolve that must be plain on my face. I wonder what he sees: fear, desire, both. Whatever it is, it pleases him. He smiles and tilts my head up with a fingertip on my chin. His lips press to mine, coaxing, insistent, his tongue sweeping into my mouth. When he draws away, the curl of his lips is mocking.

I swallow. "This isn't—"

"I know exactly what this is," he says. "And what it isn't. For tonight, I promise that whatever troubles you will be the last thing on your mind."

For a heartbeat, I take in his dilated eyes, the flare of his nostrils, breathing in the scent I dabbed on this morning. Sidriel's hand circles to the nape of my neck, then tangles in my hair to hold my head in place, and I'm embarrassed at the sudden flush of heat between my legs. This is so unlike Jaed's sweetness. My heart hammers.

Sidriel's other hand wanders, caressing my bare shoulder, my hip, trailing up to cup my breast through my robe. I cry out softly. He smiles and kisses me again, excruciatingly gentle. Teasing.

Sidriel starts slow, pressing me to sit upon the bed with kisses and nips on tender skin as he strips me of my robe. Warm, deft hands tease everywhere save the place between my legs, until I give in and plead breathlessly. I lose myself in the wanting, the satisfaction of it. No more thinking, no more worries. My mind is blissfully empty of all but this moment.

It is not lovemaking, what we do. It is the craving of bodies alone and nothing more. Fierce, desperate, savage. And yet it feels like a part of me needed this. My frustration and anger bleeds out of my fingertips as they dig into the flesh of his back. The violence of it is a release of its own, something I've needed without knowing it.

Much later, I lie shivering and panting from the aftershocks. His magic sings through my veins, stronger than Jaed's. I writhe against his silken sheets and revel in their cool slickness, like running water on my skin.

"Come to me again tomorrow," he says, his hand stroking a teasing line between my breasts, then withdrawing.

I should go. As if echoing my thoughts, Sidriel sits up and stretches, then crosses the room to fetch a cup of water on a shelf. A single cup, nothing offered to me. The silent dismissal hangs in the air.

I know exactly what this is. And what it isn't.

Throwing my robe over my head and hastily tying my belt, I leave without a reply.

"It's nonsense." Wren plucks at her eyebrow and chews her lip as she analyzes the scrap of paper I've brought her. I bathed thoroughly this morning, hoping I could scrub away any hint of Sidriel before I showed up at Wren's door. I don't know why she hates him quite so deeply, but the withering looks they cast one another when they're in the same room are enough to make me avoid mentioning him in her presence. She scowls again. "Are you absolutely sure you wrote it down correctly?"

"Yes. I compared it three times."

"It just doesn't add up," she admits. "I can see the arithmetic he's trying to do, but not the purpose. Then again, numerology and symbolic magic were never my strong suits." She pulls the page closer. Her brow furrows before she sighs and smacks it down onto the desk in her room. "I can't make any sense of it."

I settle back in my chair, rubbing my weary eyes with my hands.

"I wouldn't think Calder could do this," I admit. "He's smart enough to put together a spell like that, I suppose, but he's a human dandelion puff. Still, that trapped drawer . . ."

"That sort of jolt is not an easy enchantment, and it's expensive. It definitely means he wants to hide something, and badly. That's incriminating enough."

And the spell on Sidriel's box was worse. I chew on my lip. "What if it's just money? Or an important heirloom?"

"Could be, but it's worth looking into."

"Can you break the spell?"

"Maybe, but you need to destroy a ruby to do it. A large one. And he'd know someone tampered with it."

I swear. "Then we're stuck." I fiddle with the corner of that piece of paper, rolling it between my thumb and forefinger. "Wren . . . he has my *name*. This isn't just some random thing. It's me, specifically, and the Mirror."

"I know. Did you at least manage to get a sample from his room?"

"No." I grimace. "I was so shaken by the paper that I forgot."

"Well, get one. He's now at the top of our list. I'll keep at this code and these numbers. Maybe some research will turn something up."

I don't know how I'm going to do that. Calder is so rarely away from his rooms anymore. He doesn't supervise me at daily tasks because he's holed up working on the Mirror's puzzle. He even takes meals there.

Frustrated, I shove my chair away, the legs scraping loudly on the floor. I struggle for words, then give up. With only a simple "Good night," I turn and walk out of the room, the beaded curtain clacking behind me.

s I pass Jaed's table at the morning meal, he meets my eyes briefly before frowning and staring down at his plate. Bix glares, too, and I wonder what Jaed has told him.

It would normally be one of the rare days I eat at their table, but not now. I seek out Feryn and Vanyse instead. When I sit, Feryn glances back and forth between Jaed and me, puzzlement plain on her face.

Vanyse's eyes narrow. Feryn's expression asks a dozen questions before she blurts, "Lovers' quarrel?"

"We had a fight." I don't elaborate.

Feryn shifts in her seat, unruly curls bouncing. "His loss. We miss you, you know. It's been days, and I haven't even had the chance to ask you about the autumnsday after next and going into town for—" She stops abruptly with a wince, and I suspect from Vanyse's small grimace that they may have kicked Feryn under the table.

I frown, but Vanyse smooths things over before I have to say no. "We can always talk about that later," they say. "For now, I'm sorry about you and Jaed, though."

Feryn shakes her head. "I'm sure you'll patch it up. You've been friends since forever." Her grin turns sly. "But until he comes to his senses . . . I know just the trick. A good tumble will clear your head. Something mindless, the world-rocking kind where you forget your own name for a while."

I sigh. Of course that's Feryn's answer. One-track mind as always. I almost tell her that's what I already did, but I find myself reluctant to admit what happened with Sidriel. "Maybe."

"I can help with some therapy that's a bit less impulsive," Vanyse offers, their voice gentle, though they smile teasingly at Feryn. "Come to my room tonight after supper. We'll have a night in." They glance at Feryn questioningly.

Feryn shakes her head. "Can't. It's my night as Consort."

I almost miss it, the flicker of sorrow that crosses Vanyse's features. "Tirne, guess it's just you and me, then," they say.

I don't really have a reason to say no. "I . . . All right."

Later, when I enter Vanyse's room, a basket of various paints and creams and powders rests at their table, along with an assortment of fine brushes. A polished silver mirror sits propped up on a stand.

"What you need," Vanyse says, "is a little indulgence. Pure and simple." A slim hand tugs something out from behind the basket, a small packet of brown paper. When unwrapped, it reveals four tiny spheres, golden brown. Sweets. Balls of honey and ground rice with cinnamon and cardamom. Precious, these days. Vanyse nudges them closer to me. "Here."

Awestruck, I pluck one off the paper and pop it into my mouth. The burst of sweetness and spice has me closing my eyes and making a small sound of appreciation.

"See?" Vanyse asks. "A little better already. Now sit and let me pamper you."

And they do. "You have such great cheekbones," they murmur as they brush a pale powder along the ridges of my cheeks.

"Thank you for this." Vanyse doesn't even know about my worst worries. All they know is that I'm trying to forget a painful fight with a friend.

"I'm glad to help." They wipe off a brush on a damp cloth, then set it neatly beside the others. A gentle shrug hides a glimmer of sorrow hanging in their eyes.

I chew on my lip, debating, but the words slip from me anyway. "Are you all right?"

Vanyse's reply is guarded. "What do you mean?"

"You seem . . . I don't know, subdued. When Feryn said no earlier . . ."

"She has her duties now. She'll have them forever, if she becomes Consort." Once they start speaking, the words rush out. "And even if she isn't, Feryn has chosen motherhood as her future. Adoption instead, maybe."

"She's not leaving. She'll still be here," I say gently as they move to stand behind me and comb my hair, splitting it into sections for plaiting.

"No," Vanyse agrees. "But she may as well be gone. Children are just too . . . *much*. Too loud, too messy, too chaotic. It's overwhelming. I can't." Their voice cracks. "We've known each other so long. Eventually it was inevitable our paths would diverge."

I swallow the lump in my throat. Even things I thought were stable are changing.

"I think," Vanyse says softly, "once this is all over, I'm going to leave the Temple."

"What?"

"You found your purpose. Feryn found hers. Even Jaed has his students, his music. I don't know what I have. I thought once I could be Herald, but even I have to admit you're a better choice."

I close my eyes. "I'm sorry."

Their hands are gentle, weaving my hair and pinning braids into some sort of extravagant masterpiece. "That wasn't a barb. Just a simple statement. But the fact remains that I feel rudderless here. Maybe out there I'll find something more. A calling."

It hurts. I could ask them not to go, but who am I to tell Vanyse not to pursue their happiness, wherever that may be? Still, tears sting my eyes, and my breath hitches. "I'll miss you," I say instead. "But I understand. Have you told Feryn?"

"Not yet. She's all wrapped up in the warm fuzziness and excitement of being a possible Consort, of having a babe of her own. I don't want to step on that, not yet. Not until everything is back to normal."

Neither of us admits what we're afraid to say. That "normal" may never be the same again. The Mirror will be fixed, I have to believe that. But the marks of this long season will last for years, decades maybe.

"I won't tell her," I reassure Vanyse as they place the last pin and circle to admire their work.

A sad warmth lights their eyes. "Thank you."

After I leave Vanyse's room, it's well past dark. I find myself too restless to sleep, wandering the corridors aimlessly and breathing in the incense that lingers. Spice and smoke, it is a scent of comfort, but there is no longer any true solace to be had. The world fades in a dying season, everything in tatters. I'm hiding things from everyone. Secrets within secrets, a tapestry of intrigues, and I'm still no closer to breaking my curse or finding who placed it.

For the first time, I truly wonder if I ever will.

The next morning, I lie in bed and stare at the ceiling.

I already miss Jaed. Fire and shadow, it hurts.

I have Feryn and Vanyse, but it's not the same. Jaed has been by my side since we were toddlers.

Memories flit through my mind in an endless loop of grief. The snow-ball fight in the courtyard where a face full of snow and a laugh had turned into our first heart-pounding kiss. The way he'd stayed up all night with me when Mother died, rubbing my back as I sobbed help-lessly. How his face had beamed with joy when I gave him that first tiilar. The birthday bracelet that now rests in a drawer, tucked away because I can't bear to look at it.

I can't be friends with whatever you're becoming.

It's an echo of what Vanyse said. *We've known each other so long. Eventually it was inevitable our paths would diverge.*

I drown myself in busywork, seeking out additional chores each day I can.

The nights are harder, trapped inside the walls alone. I find a book on numerology in the library and try to unravel Calder's mathematical riddle, but I've simply no mind for numbers.

The deadline is past for Sidriel's results on the new blood sample, but I've been too ashamed to face him since that night.

I know exactly what this is, and what it isn't.

Still, I need answers. Briefly I consider showing him Calder's notes but decide against it. No. I certainly don't trust him that far.

As I leave my room, my footsteps are indescribably loud in the hollow silence. Likewise, the ring of Sidriel's bell and the clatter of the beaded curtain echoes off the Temple walls. He greets me with a nod, gesturing me into his room, and I enter.

"Tirne. How is the headache today?" His stare is sharp, canny.

My mind stutters for the barest second. "I don't know what you're talking about." Too late. I didn't cover my spike of fear quickly enough, and I know it.

His smile widens as he steps closer. "Did you think I wouldn't find traces of medicine in your blood? Or the reason for it?"

I swallow and keep silent, my mind racing, searching for a lie.

"Medicine and illness are my trade," he says. "I'd be a poor excuse for a healer if I didn't detect your headaches in your sample. And then I remembered a young acolyte who came to me so long ago, complaining of the same ailment. You."

Watching him closely, I try to keep my voice steady. "And what will you do with this information?"

"Right now, nothing. But I need more of your blood. A sample every fourday." He doesn't speak the threat aloud, but it's there, hidden between his words.

"So you can study the gods' magic."

He nods.

Fury burns. I resist the urge to give ground when he moves closer. "You're vile."

"You've known that. And yet you came to me that night. Not my brother, not anyone else. You're here now, committing a sin."

"I'm just here for my answers."

He frowns. "I have them, but you won't like it. The signature doesn't match a Scion's, of any god."

"That doesn't make sense."

"No, it doesn't. But I am confident in my findings. With another sample, I might be able to determine more in a few days."

"And if I don't give you one, you'll tell everyone about my headaches."

He stares at me with those pale eyes. "This is bigger than you or me. I will do what is needed. I've never hidden what I am from you."

Reluctantly, I give him the blood sample. Quick and perfunctory.

Returning to my own room, I weigh my options. The threat of Sidriel revealing my illness hangs heavy over me. I sink into a chair, rubbing my face with my hands as if that will make me think more clearly.

It doesn't.

***

The next time I meet Feryn and Vanyse for lunch, the Emperor's newest law is the latest gossip.

"My cousin told me the Emperor demanded each farm give half of their seed cache over as tax, to hoard for when spring comes and they can be planted under the guidance of the Empire," Vanyse told us. "The farmers are furious. They're already stretched so thin."

"Won't they just get more seeds from their current crop?" Feryn asks.

"Without summer sun, most plants aren't flowering. The berries went first, then the gourds. Some vegetables still grow, but for the farmers, those seeds are the key to their livelihood when spring comes again. My cousin was livid. They've spent generations cultivating those pepper strains."

I try not to think on it, but it's difficult. Jaed was right about one thing. I have neglected the bigger picture. There were signs on my trips to town, but I dismissed them too easily, so focused on my goal.

Still, I don't know what I can do to help those in the city. I don't have

Jaed's gift of music to lighten hearts, or the money to help anyone. I've always spent my allowance on my medicine, and I have precious little coin at the moment.

Those worries haunt me all day, and guilt drives me to devotions. I've been skipping those lately, too. I sit in the worship hall, trying my hardest to find a little peace, lulled by the simple melody of a common hymn. It tells of Lys's reunion with Serrema, a tale of sacrifice, of a love so deep Lys would bend the world itself to his will.

Only I know that it is a lie. Or at least, that there's a part of the tale we were never told.

What else do the gods keep from us? The Kildians believe their god was wronged. What if they're right, and the story has merely been prettied up by the victors? Resentment blooms, that Autumn would foster such doubts in my mind. I hate this new uncertainty in my chest.

I take a deep, steadying breath. There is still a simple comfort in this familiar song, one I've heard a thousand times. I remember my mother singing it to me when I was a child, to help me fall asleep. So I close my eyes and think of happier times, of days when my whole future was planned out, my ambitions secure.

When the gods were still infallible.

TWENTY-ONE

oday's first duty is hanging laundry up to dry, after an overnight soak and a quick rinse this morning. It is blissfully sunny outdoors, though the damp on my fingers and arms leaves a chill. At least Wren's potion keeps my headaches at bay this morning.

Still, it's not a completely worry-free day. Though I ate breakfast, my stomach growls, and I count the hours until lunch.

Worse, I'm paired with Bix today. I don't know what Jaed has told him of our argument, so we both work in stony, tense silence for an hour. Thrice, I open my mouth to speak, to apologize, to say something—anything. But each time, words fail me, and I fall back to my task in silence.

Bix casts me sidelong glances but keeps his mouth shut, too. His shoulders are tense, jaw clenched. Only the rustle and slap of damp fabric breaks the quiet, along with a few lonely birdcalls.

When we've hung the last bits of laundry up to dry, I turn to go.

"Wait." Bix stands with a hand halfway outstretched toward me. His usual rakish grin has turned wry, bitter. "Come back."

"I . . . I can't." Shame washes over me at the memory of Jaed's judgmental gaze.

"What happened?"

I shake my head.

Darkness flickers over his face. Anger. Something I haven't seen on Bix before, startling in its intensity. "Jaed won't tell me, either, but you've been friends since you were children. How can one squabble have ruined that?"

"It doesn't matter."

"He misses you."

"Then he can apologize."

"You miss him, too, don't you? You could apologize first." Bix searches my face, but I keep my cold mask up.

"It's not that simple." Bitterness leaks into my voice as I add, "Besides, you have each other." Bix and Jaed, drawing closer, when I've been pushing everyone farther away.

"Except I don't really, do I?" There's a hopelessness in his eyes that makes me wonder if he's feeling more for Jaed than he pretends. I would never have expected to see the smiling, confident Bix wounded like this. "Not when there's a Tirne-shaped hole in him. I . . . Please. If you came to his room tonight, I don't think he'd turn you away. You can talk through it."

If Bix doesn't know the cause of the problem, it means he's unaware it can't be fixed with a simple apology. "I can't."

Bix stares, then frowns. "Suit yourself." He pushes past me and back to the Temple.

I let him go and head to the midday meal. For most of it, I'm silent. Maybe it's my anger, or my guilt, but I devour my food while barely pausing to chew. At the end of it, I point at the small remaining bit of flatbread on Vanyse's plate. "Are you going to finish that?" They stopped prodding at their dish a few minutes ago, and I already polished off the bits of sweet potato Feryn had picked out of her stew.

They shake their head and push the bread toward me. "I know we're all on rations, but . . . are you all right?"

I tear off a piece of bread and shovel it into my mouth, even as my stomach clenches. "I don't know. I'm just so hungry."

Feryn gives me a sly look and a pointed stare at my belly. "Are you sure it's not . . ."

"No. I just finished my cycle." And the only bed I've been in lately is Sidriel's, as infertile as any other Scion. Not that I'd admit that to anyone.

My stomach growls again, despite the amount of food I've stuffed into it. I don't know what's wrong with me. The steadily gnawing hunger has been worsening since yesterday.

"Maybe you should see a physician," Vanyse suggests.

"I feel fine." I shake my head. "Just ravenous."

Realization hits me. The bit of flatbread turns to glue in my mouth, a flavorless paste. It's not my own hunger I'm feeling. This isn't my own belly twisting itself into starving knots.

It's Autumn's.

Gods don't feel hunger, but I'm certain. I know the signs. A strange, weightless tug at the other end of the sensation, something almost impossible to describe.

I finish the bread and excuse myself. I can't take more food from the large serving table that runs the length of the room, not under the watchful eye of a Scion sentry. I can slip out to the gardens and filch a carrot before dusk falls, though. I will be punished if I'm caught stealing it, but it'll be enough to confirm or disprove my theory. After a quick trip to my own room to wash the carrot, I slip it into a pocket and venture to Autumn's chambers.

He answers, cloak on. "Tirne?"

I bow. "Your Holiness. I bring a gift." The carrot feels all too plain and simple in my hand, a meager offering for a god.

His brow furrows. "A carrot?"

"That wrench in your gut, the discomfort you've been feeling?"

His eyes narrow, suspicious. "What of it?"

"That's hunger."

"Only mortals need food."

"And yet." I bite my lip at the audacity of my words. "I wish I didn't feel what you did, truly. But it's driving me mad. Please eat." He already looks even leaner, the hollows beneath his eyes deeper. If I'd been attending devotions more often or paying attention lately, I'd have seen it.

"I . . . Thank you." He takes the carrot from me, careful not to brush my fingertips with his own.

"If . . . if it helps, maybe you could get the Tharem to bring you meals, in secret?" I hate suggesting it, but he's the only one who could sneak additional food without being questioned or punished.

Autumn nods, somber. "I'll think on it."

On my way back to my room, I pass Bix and Jaed, walking hand in hand. They halt when they see me, and my earlier argument with Bix flickers through my mind. He glowers, his fingers tightening around Jaed's.

The look in my friend's eyes knocks the wind out of me. Wounded, yes, but also cold. A callous iciness I've never seen in Jaed before. His lips press together, as if to hold back words he shouldn't say. He tugs on Bix's hand, and they turn down another hallway with only a single dark backward glance.

That coldness, that anger, I did that to him. To the compassionate, smiling musician. I stole part of his warmth away, because I wouldn't choose him over everything else I'd always wanted. Guilt wars with anger, and I don't know which wins the fight.

I stand frozen, hands clenched into fists. Everything is slipping from me. I've corrupted him. Like a poison. Like the curse that lingers in my blood.

Maybe Sidriel was right. Maybe at my core, I've never been a good person. And it took a stranger to see it, someone I'd never fooled into thinking otherwise. Feryn and Vanyse don't know all my dark secrets, only seeing the shiny veneer I paint over them. Jaed is the only one who has ever seen all the pieces of me, and he rejected me for it.

What if he was right? What if my time in Sylvus truly has drained my softer humanity away? Perhaps I am cold. Wicked. And perhaps I truly deserve only the company of scoundrels.

Good thing I know one, then.

The choice I make this time is deliberate. Not to donate my blood, not an impulsive bout of lonely self-pity. Right now, I seek the only place I am truly seen in all my sinfulness and poison and accepted anyway.

It's only late afternoon, but Sidriel answers the ring of his bell.

"Tirne?"

I push past him into the room. As he turns in surprise, I clutch at the front of his robes and pull him in for a kiss. He makes a low, small sound, and his lips part for my tongue.

After a moment, he pulls back but only enough to ask, "Why—"

"No questions, sorcerer." I don't want to tell him why. I just want someone—even this villain—to welcome me.

And he does. He follows my command and asks no more. Instead, his lips find my jaw, my throat, as we make our way to the bed with desperate hands and greedy kisses.

"This doesn't mean anything," I say as he unfastens my belt and tosses it aside.

"Liar," he murmurs against my skin. He slides my robe from my shoulders, his mouth wandering lower.

"I hate you," I tell him as the kisses drift down my belly, now-gentle fingertips coaxing my legs apart. My own hands tangle in his hair, grasping tighter as I shudder a sigh.

"Hate me all you want," he says, just before his tongue finds me and pushes all other thought from my mind. I'm nothing but the rush of heat in my stomach, the pressure building between my legs. And blissfully, I remain so, until the pleasure swells and crashes over me. I don't know how much later I return to my senses, sprawled across his bed, Sidriel lying beside me and scattering kisses on my shoulder.

His voice is husky when he says carefully, "So. You said no questions."

"I did."

"But I think I've earned a single answer. What made you loathe yourself enough to crawl into my bed again?"

"It doesn't matter." I roll out of the bed, throwing on my robes and belting them. For a long moment, I stare at that glossy black box on his table, wondering if I can pry those secrets from him between his sheets. But he's too savvy for that.

If I tell Sidriel of Calder's notes, could he make sense of them? No. Sidriel only offered to test my blood because I had something he wanted. He threatened to blackmail me.

Raking my hand through my hair, I wince as a tangle snags. As I cross Sidriel's room, the soft rumble of his voice follows me.

"Next time, Herald, it will be my turn."

"There won't be a next time."

As I slip through the doorway, his soft laugh echoes in my ears.

F eryn cradles an infant in her arms, face strained.

I can see what Vanyse meant about the noise now. The child cries, a piercing and heart-wrenching sound. We sit in the nursery. It is one of Feryn's duties as a potential Consort. She aids the Temple nurses in caring for children left here while their parents are at other chores or tasks. Nearby, another potential Consort dutifully stacks blocks, only for a toddler to knock them over and giggle. The Consort gasps in mock surprise and laughs, then starts building again.

"He won't stop," Feryn frets, shifting the babe to her chest. Her voice is taut, her eyes pleading. "He's been fed, I've checked his napkin, he won't sleep. It's just screaming and screaming and screaming."

"Here." The voice behind me is familiar, and I startle. Laereda leans over to take the child. "Naru here doesn't like his arms and legs wiggling about. I'll show you how to swaddle him."

Feryn looks up at her gratefully as they head to a table covered with soft blankets. Laereda settles the child on a small one. "You fold here, then here, then roll it here." Her movements are steady, sure. As soon as the blanket is snug around his body, Naru ceases crying, murmuring a babe's gibberish.

Laereda hands him gently back to Feryn. "Next time, you can try it yourself. I practiced on a pillow until I had the folds right."

A new babble comes from a crib in the corner, and Laereda's eyes light with recognition. "Excuse me." She crosses the room to collect her own awakening child.

Feryn smiles, but the expression is tense. Her eyes glisten with unshed tears. "I don't think I can do this," she admits, voice breaking. "It's all I wanted, but it's so much. So hard. And this one isn't even my child."

I bump my shoulder gently against hers. "I'm pretty sure all new parents feel the same way. That's why you're here now, so it's not as scary when it's your own."

She nods weakly but doesn't seem mollified.

"You'll get it."

"I don't know anymore." Her breath hitches. "And in some way it feels wrong to bring a child into a world like this. Everything is crashing down. No Mirror, food rations, hopelessness. A plague. You know they've been finding more bodies in town? It's the Red Cough, they say, but I don't know. The man I saw in that alley, his skin looked gray, like a dry, dead rose." She shudders. "It didn't look right. I wonder . . . what if it's the Kildara, finally come to take revenge? What if the Kildians were at least partly right?"

"You were in shock, maybe you didn't get a good look." But my mouth has gone dry, my skin clammy. Pieces are falling into place. I know what it was, and it wasn't the Kildara. Or illness or starvation or any of a dozen other natural causes.

The hungry souls of the dead are claiming victims.

"I need to talk to you," I murmur, keeping my voice low. It's two days after Feryn told me of the dead bodies, but this is the first time I've been able to catch my god alone, approaching him in the hall after devotions.

It had been awkward to sit through them while the Tharem exuded platitudes and Autumn granted his blessing to supplicants. People who were already scrounging for sustenance came to offer their coin in tithe, hoping for some good fortune in return. There are fewer of them now, and I wonder just how much resentment grows for the faith that left the world withering.

If I still bore a Herald's robe, I would eschew it when I went to town anyway, out of caution and fear. Most do not recognize me there now, just a nameless acolyte. A nobody.

As I look up into Autumn's eyes now, I wonder if he sees a nobody, or the Herald I once was to him. Then again, he asked me to choose a god. Maybe to him, I will always be someone special.

"Yes?" His expression is calm as ever, a still pond.

"Er, privately," I mutter. "My room?" We're not far from it.

He nods and leads the way. Once I've closed the leather flap, I blurt, "People are dying in town, and not from the Cough. The bodies are gray, dried out, unnatural. I . . . I think it's the souls."

Autumn's calm expression doesn't falter.

Realization settles in my gut. "You knew."

A nod.

"And you did nothing?"

"If I acknowledge it, I give the threat weight. It would only incite panic."

"So you let people die? You're a *god*. Your word is law. Make a curfew."

His frown deepens.

Again, understanding strikes, hard and fast. "You're afraid they wouldn't obey."

"It would give them one more thing to blame on the gods." He loses his grip on his own followers with every day that passes. Even I've noticed more black leather cuffs around wrists on my rare trips to the city. The people's hope wavers. Autumn is powerless now, save the belief of his dwindling faithful.

It sparks a memory in me, one I've always held close, one that also leaves me uneasy. "Do you remember the first time you spoke to me?"

A pause. "There was a bird."

"Yes. I was twelve. I found a bird, gravely injured. You passed by, and in a child's earnestness, I asked you to help. Do you remember what you said?"

"That life was Spring's dominion. Mine is death."

"You told me you could end its suffering. You touched it, and I was left holding a bundle of bone and feathers, its life gone. I carried it to another part of the grove and buried it." I blink up at Autumn. "It was the first time I realized the gods are not omnipotent. That you have limitations."

He sighs, the softest of sounds. "You cannot tell others what you know about the souls. I forbid it."

I bite my lip and bow my head. "As you command, Your Holiness." But when I look up, I suspect my anger is written all over my face. Autumn's impassive expression slips for the barest of moments, and a glimmer of guilt trickles through our connection.

Still, he nods, his decree made, and leaves me in my room alone.

I turn to my desk, to my research, and my heart stumbles, a stutter. My breath freezes. The book I'd been reading last night is at the bottom of the stack, not the top.

It seems I'm not the only one who's resorted to poring through others' things.

Shadows take me, Calder's notes. I shuffle through the papers to find them in the middle of a sheaf of other sheets, tucked into a book on numerology. Was this where I left them? I don't know.

A cold shiver trickles down my spine as I stare down at the letters. Who else has seen these now?

TWENTY-THREE

I straighten my shoulders as I approach Laereda's room. It's time to stop avoiding her possible trove of clues. All I need to do is decline her tea, and my rift with Jaed gives me the perfect excuse to visit her for the comfort she once offered.

Yet as I near her room, lowered voices make me pause. The leather flap is closed, but I can just barely make out the words.

"This is blackmail," Laereda hisses.

"Such an ugly word." The Tharem. My teeth clench.

Wait. Was Laereda the one I heard the Tharem threatening before, the day Winter should have arrived?

He continues. "The fact remains. Get it back, or I'll tell your beloved god what you've done."

Get what back?

I think I might know. The box. The one in Sidriel's room that I first saw in Laereda's. The one that struck me to the floor in a spell eerily similar to the one on Calder's desk. Stronger, yes, but the same jolt.

Fire and shadow, what if all these pieces are linked? Laereda, Sidriel, Calder, the Tharem. They could be connected in a spider's web with threads I cannot see, and I need to know which of them sits at the center.

What if it's Sidriel, if it's been his master plan all along? I feel sick, thinking I might have bedded the man who did this to me, to everyone. Wren said his sample didn't match, but that doesn't mean he played no part. I wonder if his baffling test results are merely lies.

And I still haven't gotten a sample from Calder.

"I need time." Laereda, pleading.

The Tharem speaks again. "You have one month. After that, I go to Autumn, and you'll never see him again. I'll be back here the day after Serrema's Eve."

Laereda's reply is choked, tearful. "Get out."

I scramble backward down the hall until I hear the rustle of the leather flap. I pinch my nose to make sure it's nice and pink, scrubbing my eyes to mimic the redness of weeping. As soon as the beads rattle, I walk forward again. Hopefully I'm far enough away that he won't know I was eavesdropping.

The Tharem pauses in the hallway at the sight of me, and I give a small, hiccuping sob to sell my distress as I fake a startle. "Your Eminence?"

"Tirne." His voice is cold, but his eyes burn. He brushes past me without another word, and I bite back my sigh of relief as he rounds the corner at the end of the hall.

A ring at Laereda's curtain brings forth a harsh "What now?"

"Um, it's Tirne."

"Oh!" She lifts the beads and gestures me in. "Sorry, I thought you were someone else."

She'd know I was too close to miss the Tharem, so I go for the blunt approach. "I saw the Tharem leaving. Did he upset you?"

She scowls. "I asked for my Consort position back again. He denied me."

Laereda's a good liar, I'll give her that. If I hadn't overheard their conversation, I'd have bought it.

She continues. "I know you all laugh at me, that everyone knows

I've begged for it back. But . . . well, you understand what it's like to lose something. You've lost your title, and I've heard rumors about your friend, that Winter Scion."

It's the perfect opening, and the fresh tears aren't feigned. Shadows take me, it hurts.

"I'll make tea," she offers, and I shiver.

"No thank you, I won't be long. I . . . I'm in no shape to talk tonight. But I thought maybe . . . maybe I could join you tomorrow at lunch?" The dining hall is the perfect place, far from her supply of poisonous tea.

She gives me a sympathetic nod. "Tomorrow, then. Come find me at my table."

"Thank you."

※

That afternoon, I'm back in the city, once again in a priest's care. I don't know her well, an ill-tempered Scion of Autumn named Mallen. She watches me like I'm going to steal something, her expression dour. The weather is cold and clear, the sky a watery blue without a single cloud in sight. The breeze is brisk, but not freezing. Never freezing. We've had no snow, no frost, only rain and occasional drizzle. And until Winter arrives, there will be no ice, no slush, no cold snap.

We pass under ornamental trees in the city plaza, bare of leaves now. The world is stuck in the final weeks of autumn, holding its breath as it awaits the arrival of a goddess who has not come.

It's nearly the end of Winter now, or it should be. Six months since I lost my title. My life has become little more than my research and a familiar slog of menial tasks, of plainness, unremarkable as any other acolyte. Though a heaviness hangs in my heart, the sharp edges of my humiliation have been worn smooth, like bits of rock polished in a riverbed. My dull orange robes no longer seem ill-fitting and rough.

It feels as if time has been turned backward, the hourglass going in reverse. Back to my life before I was chosen as Autumn's Herald. But even then, in those days so many years ago, I prepared for something greater.

You get what you believe you deserve, my mother had always told me. She'd taught me to work hard, that I was capable of so many things. What would she think now, to see me tugging a cart full of wares behind Mallen, panting like a hardworking goat, all her encouragement and training undone by some still-unknown assailant?

The headache today is excruciating. The cold drives a spike into my skull, and Wren's medicine this morning only lessened it slightly. It's an effort just to place one foot in front of the other without bursting into tears. The wagon is laden with vegetables, an endless parade of the same ones we've been eating. I miss summer's fruits so dearly.

"Last remaining gourds are running thin, too," a chatty vendor tells us. "How long till we're left with only the cold-weather vegetables, what little milk we can get from ill-fed goats, and eggs from scrawny hens? There's little enough grain left to give the chickens, just the scraps we can't eat, or else they can find the bugs that still crawl about. I've heard stories some flocks have even turned on each other, attacking the weakest and eatin' them, like falcons."

Mallen grunts and hands over two small coins for a stack of candles. Tallow, of course. The bees have gone dormant, and there is no more beeswax to be had. Even the tallow is precious now.

The vendor continues as he loads the candles into our cart. "Even those that once helped everybody have gotten tightfisted. Heard about a family down the street boiling old shoes to eat," he opined sadly. "We've got goat's milk for now, but even the animals have to eat, and ol' Hanie is getting stingy with her milk on so few scraps." Unease ripples through me. The Temple gardens provide most of our food, but we've always supplemented it with supplies from town.

By the time the cart is mostly full, I've tuned out even Mallen's incessant grumbling about going back short again. I sigh and adjust my grip on the cart's handles.

Halfway back to the Temple, Mallen stops and turns to me. "I can't do this anymore. I have to ask. Did you really help with it?"

"With what?"

"The Mirror."

I reel back. "Of course not."

She barks a humorless laugh. "Maybe not. I've heard the rumors, you know, the rumblings of the Kildians. That we faithful reap what we sow, choosing gods that don't truly care about humans, only what they can get from us." Her last words are hopeless, weak. "What if they're right, and the gods just decided to start over? To wipe the slate clean of us?"

I swallow. "You really think Autumn did this? He's your own father."

"Do you have proof he didn't? And it's not like he bounced me on his knee as a child."

It's true. Only Summer really takes a hand in raising her children, and to a lesser extent, Spring. When they spend much of their time away, then half their time here slowly becoming human, there's not much empathy for them to give.

Doubt claws at me. Autumn could have done this. Sidriel's tests showed no Scion's magic in the curse. What if it wasn't a Scion, but a god?

A moment later, I'm ashamed of myself for the thought. Autumn is as heartbroken over the Mirror as anyone. That grief I felt the day Winter should have fallen, that wasn't feigned. I shake my head. "The gods didn't do this. Besides—"

Then I see Mother, standing on the edge of the street. Her messy mahogany knot of hair is darker than mine, her eyes just as black. Thin lips set in a firm line, strong jaw. But she's not wearing her acolyte's robes. No, she wears a heavier knitted shirt in a dreary gray wool, over leggings that must once have been black but have faded to a sort of uniform charcoal hue. The sleeves of the shirt are rolled up to the elbow even in the cold, baring wiry arms, hands knotted with labor.

Not Mother. Aunt Ilna.

The shape of her name passes my lips without sound, our eyes locked. I could have gone to her again, sometime after that night with Feryn, but I haven't. There's no ground to give on either side. She gnaws on her lip, clutching a burlap sack more tightly as she turns away.

And still something twists in my stomach. I'm once again the heartbroken child, bereft of her beloved aunt.

The memory still stings.

"I can't keep living like this," she'd told Mother in a strangled voice. I'd peered at her from beneath the covers where I pretended to be asleep. Ilna had shoved her belongings into a knapsack. The painted ceramic pot I saved my tiny allowance for weeks to buy her as a harvest-day gift last year. Her journal. A glass-beaded necklace my grandmama had given her when I was too little to remember, before Grandmama passed. A sack of money she must have been saving for years.

She was crying, something I'd seen her do only once, when her favorite Temple cat had died. "You're killing the world, the old world. I've *seen* them, Raijeen. The old ones. The gray ones." The shadows. The Kildara. "They're real. Garvishes, flower spirits, the thregas that clear a house of mice and pests. I see them."

"Please don't say that." Mother's voice was strained. What Ilna speaks is blasphemy to the faithful. "I've never seen such things."

Ilna hiccuped a sob. "Not here. In town. They don't like the blood of the gods, or their children. It's poison."

"You don't mean that."

I'd huddled deeper in my blankets as something painful and brittle cracked open inside of me. Aunt Ilna was leaving. And with her, the merriment that balanced Mother's stern nature. Gone would be the vibrant stories of the creatures of old folklore. The fey ones. No more ribbons strung into braids as she wove my hair into fanciful confections. I closed my eyes, squeezing the tears out, but I dared not sniffle. A thin stream of snot dripped onto my pillow.

"Don't do this." Mother's voice cracked.

"Come with me," Ilna offered instead. "We can go anywhere, be anything."

"And what about Tirne?"

"She can come with us, learn a trade. We could have a little cottage somewhere, maybe a shop or a farm." Desperation made her voice tight.

I could hear the soft pad of her feet as Mother backed away, closer to me. "No, we belong here, and so do you."

"No. I never really did. I'm sorry you couldn't see that. Goodbye, Rai." Her voice went low, a whisper. "Goodbye, Tirne, my little rabbit." Spoken to herself, not to me.

Now on the city street in the cold fifteen years later, I watch her walk away from me once more. In the bright sunlight and on the uneven cobbles, shadows seem to waver oddly in her wake.

But the memory makes me wonder if I've been looking in the wrong place this whole time? The Kildians and the Temple have always existed in a tense truce. Maybe, just maybe, they wanted to end that peace.

M y lunch appointment with Laereda arrives the next day, and thankfully my headache has eased into something manageable. She sits with her babe and a pair of her younger children. The older two enjoy the company of their peers at meals.

For the first time, I realize Laereda rarely keeps other mealtime companions. I wonder if she truly has any friends, or if Autumn and her children are her whole world. Today, she avoids speaking of our god entirely.

The conversation starts awkwardly. Small talk. The usual worries over the long season and weather and similar minor chatter of folk who don't know each other terribly well, often interrupted by coaxing her six-year-old child not to climb out of his chair, or urging the three-year-old to eat her potatoes.

When she steers the subject toward Jaed, I defer. "Can we just talk about other things for a bit? I'm . . . I had a long day in town, and I'm too weary to cry right now."

She watches me closely but returns to aimless topics, which shift to her ample supply of gossip.

"It seems Geven can't keep a leash on her eldest anymore. He's leaving to join the Kildians. Not the first, and doubt he'll be the last."

I nod absentmindedly, but I'm only barely listening as she chatters and rocks Sy in his basket beside her. Sidriel has caught my gaze from across the room and smiles slyly at me. Tonight I'm due for another blood sample, and we both know where that will lead. Where it has led the last few times, a sweaty tangle of desperate limbs.

I don't know why I find myself seeking the mindlessness of Sidriel's passion again and again. Maybe because everything else is falling apart, and his bed is the one place I can forget. Every autumnsday, I return to his room and give him a traitorous sample of my blood. And he proves just how wrong I was when I told him I would never bed him again. I fall into him, time after time. For precious minutes, I can bury all my fears and guilt and worries in him.

I wonder what he hides in me.

I know exactly what this is. And what it isn't.

I hate myself for it.

And yet.

Across the room, a familiar laugh catches my attention. Jaed, hand over his mouth, his shoulders shaking at something Bix has said. He seems to feel my stare on him and turns to meet my gaze. I look down.

"What's wrong, dear?" Laereda asks. "You look positively green."

I shove my plate away. "Just getting tired of turnips."

She laughs. "Aren't we all?" Lifting her fork in a mock toast, she spears a bit of boiled turnip on her fork and pops it into her mouth. "What I wouldn't give for honeyed bread again. And peaches. I miss them so dearly."

My mouth waters at the thought.

We continue to talk, and I lure the viper ever closer, though I'm still unsure how to unravel her connection to Sidriel and that box. Or to find a sample from Calder. He's focused entirely on the Mirror repair, practically a hermit now.

I'd hoped Laereda's gossipy nature might lend me some additional clues in my mission, but all I have are an assortment of mundane scandals filling my head. Lunch goes by, as do my floor-scrubbing duties in the afternoon. Before supper, I join Feryn and Vanyse in the game room for a round of Spinner.

"So," Feryn asks me as she picks through her hand of cards, "Laereda? I thought you hated each other."

I knew she'd ask. I chew on my lip, ready to give the answer I rehearsed, but Vanyse speaks first.

"It's about Bix, isn't it?" they ask as they lay out their cards. "I've seen her and Bix a bit chummy lately. You're looking for word about Jaed."

It's as good an answer as any. I nod.

Feryn sighs and plays her own hand. "You've got to move on."

"I know. I'm trying."

"She's known him since they could walk," Vanyse says.

"I get it," Feryn replies, scooping up the cards she won. "But it's gone on long enough. Either you two need to talk and apologize or realize you've grown apart."

Vanyse flinches, but I don't think Feryn sees.

I protest. "We haven't grown apart."

"Then one of you needs to say you're sorry. If you truly are still friends, you'll forgive each other."

I sigh. "It's not that easy."

"Of course it is. Stop being so stubborn."

"I'm not—"

"Hush, both of you," Vanyse says, though the reprimand is gentle, their eyes sad. "It's going to hurt for a while, no matter what you do. Love—of all kinds—can be a violent sport."

Their words make me think of Sidriel, of the viciousness that flavors our own . . . what? Certainly not a romance. Just bodies entwined in anger and loathing and lust.

"Fine." Feryn's response jolts me out of my thoughts. "Truce?"

I'm all too happy to put it behind us. "Truce."

"Good." She throws down her cards with a grin. "Because I'm about to kick your ass in Spinner."

CHAPTER

TWENTY-FIVE

When the hour arrives to meet Sidriel long after dusk, anticipation leaves me jittery. I hate that I've come to expect this, to welcome it.

"Tirne," Sidriel purrs as I slip through the beaded curtain and close the leather flap. He stands before me in his indigo robes, haughty and beautiful. His hair falls like the sweep of a snowdrift over his shoulders. He hasn't even removed his belt, the chain laden with enchanted charms. No, he expects me to do that.

"Sidriel."

We require no further greeting than that, not anymore. Our lips meet. I unfasten his belt, the metal jangling as I toss it aside. The hook that holds his robe closed is next. He smiles and urges me back toward the bed.

I go without a word.

Afterward, Sidriel lies beside me as I bask in the shivery warmth of his magic. He twirls a lock of my hair around a finger, then unwinds it. My eyes land on that glossy box on his table. It taunts me. Laereda was a fountain of unrelated, unhelpful gossip, but no true clues.

I sit up. Pain lances through my skull, and I wince, hand darting to the back of my head.

"Here." Sidriel slides out of the bed and crosses to his tools. Before I realize what he's doing, he presses a sharp needle into the pad of his finger, then stands in front of me once more. "Where does it hurt?"

I glare.

"Don't be stubborn," he says, unexpectedly gentle. This is the healer I've never seen before. It shocks me into silence and stillness.

Tentatively, Sidriel reaches toward me. When I don't push him away, his bloodied fingertip presses to the back of my skull, where my own hand rested a few seconds ago. Where the pain drives a spike deep.

A heartbeat later, the throbbing recedes, replaced with the cool tingle of his magic. A relieved sigh slips from me as he draws away, then wipes his finger with a handkerchief from the side table.

"There. Better?"

I nod. "Can you—"

"Cure them? No. I never lied about that. This is temporary."

I'm certain my disappointment is painted plain on my face, but he doesn't comment on it. Instead he asks, "Why, if you hate it so, do you keep coming back to me?"

"Because you threatened to expose my headaches if I don't give you my blood."

He smiles. "Sex was never a part of that bargain. But here we are. And I know why." He finishes his cleaning and sets it aside.

I snort. "Oh, you do?"

"You don't care what I think of you, so you show me the ugliest side of yourself, the one you think would disgust your friends." When he approaches the bed and sits beside me once more, I hate the way my heartbeat races. I don't know if I want to lean closer or inch away.

He presses a kiss to my shoulder. "You come here because I don't pretend to see you for anything other than what you really are."

My throat is dry. I clear it. "And what's that?"

His arm slides around my waist. I don't pull away. His free hand brushes through my hair, tucking it back and away from my face as he meets my gaze. "A lioness, hiding in a kitten's skin." No hint of mockery lies buried in any of it, no snide curl of a lip or sneer in the words. Instead, there's a soft light in his pale eyes, something almost akin to . . . admiration?

I swallow. No. Whatever this is, I don't like it. "I need to go." I point to the table where I bleed for him every fourday. "Let's get this over with."

"Not yet. Stay here."

I blink. "What?"

"Stay with me. For a while."

"Why?" I search his face, seeking the taunt, the ploy. It terrifies me that there might not be one. So instead I bark a laugh and jest. "Are you falling for me, sorcerer?"

He leans in and nuzzles my throat. There's a single, long breath before his response, one that leaves a nervous flutter in my gut. "Do you truly think I'm that weak? The night is young yet, and we've both nowhere else to be."

This has to be some sort of game. Sidriel isn't a tender sort of lover. But I had seen softness on his face once before, when I asked about that memorial in the cemetery. *I loved her,* he'd said, an aching sadness in the words.

I clear my throat. "You fell once before, though, didn't you? The woman in the graveyard. Autumn's Consort."

His hand curls into a fist against my back, and his breathing stills against my neck. "Oluryn." He says her name like it wounds him.

I whisper, "Tell me about her."

"No."

"You said you loved her. But she became a Consort. Did you fall for her before or after?"

He's silent for a very long time, his hands unmoving. "Before."

I bite my lip, afraid to ask the next question. But it slips out anyway. "Did you ever tell her?"

Another pause. "No." His teeth nip lightly at my skin, a warning. "Why are you so curious? Shall I ask you about my brother?"

Thoughts of Jaed are like a stabbing pain. My voice cracks on the reply. "There was no romance between us."

"But you shared a bed."

"Yes."

"And you were close."

"Yes. But not in love. Not that way."

"Ah. My dear Herald." A hint of his sharp teasing is back in the mockery of a title. "And have you ever been in love?"

A question Laereda asked me once before.

Unbidden, my mind flickers to the look in Autumn's eyes that night he'd told me his worst fears. How he'd sat watch by my bedside when I had the Cough, or the strange wrenching sensation in my stomach whenever he touches me with gloved hands. A sickness and elation all at once, uncomfortable and glorious and agonizing.

And heresy.

It's only after that first, traitorous thought that I think of Rhinna, of so many nights spent laughing at the most ridiculous things until the candle burned low, of our first hesitant kiss, the way my chest fluttered when she smiled at me.

Was that love, or youthful infatuation? How does one know the difference?

Have you ever been in love? I shake my head. "No."

"Liar."

"We're both liars," I say softly.

He tugs me closer, his lips scattering a line of kisses along my throat. "I'm many things, not all of them good. But I have never lied to you."

I don't know what to say to that. Instead, I meet his lips with my own and sink back onto the bed, letting my mind drain of such uneasy thoughts.

Much deeper into the night, we finally do take our leave of his bed, the world glittery with the magic that courses through me in the afterglow. I don't even bother sitting down for the bloodletting as he pricks my finger and drips blood into the vial. That cursed box rests on the table just within my reach, gleaming. Emboldened by the magic shivering through me, I ask, "What's in it? That box."

"It's private." Sidriel drops my hand after smoothing over my wound with his magic.

"Does it have to do with the Mirror?" A shaky breath, and I blurt, "Did you help with it?"

His expression goes flat, and if I didn't know better, I'd say he looked truly wounded. If he lies, he does it so smoothly that even I believe it. "I did not break the Mirror, nor did I aid anyone else in doing so."

"Swear it on Oluryn's grave."

He flinches as if struck, then glares. "I swear on my beloved's memory and all that I hold dear, I had nothing to do with the Mirror's destruction."

Shadows take me, I think I actually believe him.

After a ragged breath, he says, "Please leave."

"I'm sorry . . ." I massage my tingling finger, where I'd bled.

"I told you," he says softly, "I've never lied to you. About anything."

"I know." He's always been clear about what he wants, and why. I struck a nerve asking about the box. I wonder if it's a keepsake from his past with Oluryn. But then why would the Tharem want it? Unless he and Laereda spoke of something else, leaving me back at the start of this puzzle.

I exit Sidriel's room quickly. I don't even bother with my belt, tying the knot of my robe and letting the strip of leather dangle from one hand. It's not terribly far to my room, and it's closer to dawn than dusk. I doubt I'll run into anyone, and even if I do, there's no shame in having had some sort of tryst tonight. I won't be the first to make that sort of trek through the halls, and I won't be the last.

However, I don't expect the person I encounter to be Feryn, just as I slip out of Sidriel's curtain.

We stop, taking each other in. Dreamy eyed and hair mussed, she practically glows. There's no denying where she's been, or who she's been with. I'm certain I look just as rumpled, and my belt dangling from one hand is evidence enough.

Feryn breaks into a wide grin as she approaches, glancing at Sidriel's curtain. She whispers, "You didn't." But there's less condemnation in her words than there is admiration.

I shake my head, trying to come up with an explanation. But there's only one reason I'd be leaving his room in this state. "Please don't tell anyone," I plead. I can't let word get back to Wren about this.

My friend makes a small motion, a pantomime of pinching her lips together with one hand. "Your secret's safe with me. Now go to bed. Looks like we could both use some rest." She laughs and pushes me lightly down the hall as she turns a corner.

As I reach the end of the corridor, I hear the soft ring of a curtain's bell behind me. I glance back, and the figure I see standing at Sidriel's doorway makes my stomach clench.

Calder. He doesn't turn to see me, his eyes focused down on his fidgeting hands. One foot taps nervously on the tile.

Why is Calder visiting Sidriel in the dead of night? The matching spells on that black box and Calder's drawer already haunt me. If it had been the middle of the day, perhaps it could be Mirror business. But when it's not yet dawn?

Unease settles on me like a heavy weight, but I go back to my room, thoughts all in a jumble.

TWENTY-SIX

A ring at my curtain awakens me the next morning. I groan. The pale light of dawn seeps through the shutters. Burrowing deeper into my blankets, I silently hope my visitor will give up and leave me be.

"Tirne." The voice is Wren's.

"It's too early. Come back later."

Instead, she sweeps into my room in a clack of beads. "Morning!" she chirps, unusually cheerful. But there's a bite in the words. "Did you have a nice evening?"

I roll over, away from her. "Whatever you want, it can wait until after breakfast."

"Why?" Her next question is low, sharp. "Maybe because you're recovering from a night with *him*?"

Oh no. "Wren—"

"No." She stands by my bedside, glaring, her hands clenched into fists.

"I didn't—"

"Don't lie to me. I overheard your two friends whispering about it in the hall. Is it true?"

Feryn. I should have known she couldn't stay quiet, especially not to Vanyse. Not even a full day and she's already spilling the secret.

Wren paces. "I tried to warn you. I can't believe you didn't listen."

I glare as I slip out of bed, draping a blanket over my shoulders and crossing to the hearth to poke it to life. "You don't get to decide who I share beds with."

"But I do gift you with doses of my medicinal tonic every fourday. A gift I could stop bestowing at any time."

A trickle of dread coils in my gut. "You wouldn't."

No uncertainty shows in her hard golden eyes. "You need to stay away from Sidriel."

"Why? You keep warning me he's dangerous, but you refuse to give a reason."

She doesn't answer my question. "My ultimatum is simple. Give me your oath that you will break it off with him today, and I will continue to provide you with medicine. Speak to him again or return to his bed, and I refuse. And I'll work on the curse alone from now on."

I snort. "Not that it's done much anyway. We've tested most of the Scions in the building, and you can't make any more sense of Calder's notes than I can."

She shakes her head, quaking with anger until she sucks in a sharp breath, steadying herself against the table before pulling a small ball of compressed herbs from her pocket. She chews it quickly before falling into the chair at my table.

One of her attacks, her heart. It deflates my anger, guilt pricking at me. "Are you—"

"I'll be fine." She sounds exhausted, but her tone warns against discussing that further.

I understand. Sometimes, the last thing I want to talk about is my headaches. Instead, I ask, "Please tell me. Why do you hate Sidriel so much?" What if I find out I've been bedding a monster? Not just a man who's ambitious, but someone truly evil?

"I . . ." Wren swallows, staring down at her hands on the table. "I was his apprentice, when I studied medicine."

"Did you—"

A sharp laugh. "No. Nothing like that. But I was still awestruck. He has a brilliant mind, able to see and detect maladies in blood that I never could. To formulate cures and potions no one else had discovered. Of course, he kept those recipes to himself. Even his apprentices didn't know his most valuable formulas. And it wasn't just remedies. He's a master of poison, as well."

"He sells poison?"

"Not sells. Experiments with." Her stare goes far away, seeing some past tragedy. "On volunteers. His fawning apprentices, or people willing to risk their health for coin. He had theories that one could use poisons to heal, if manipulated correctly."

I swallow but stay silent.

"This thing with my heart, stuttering and lurching? That's what Sidriel did to me in the name of medicine, what he did to a young fool who worshipped his brilliance and stupidly volunteered for his experiments." She closes her eyes, her fist tightening where it lies on the table.

I feel cold, a numb tingling in my fingers and toes. He did this to her. From the sound of it, to others, too. "Wren . . . why didn't you tell anyone?"

"He's powerful. Members of government and other sorcerers admire him, respect him. Rely on him for their intoxicants, and medicine for ailments. They'd turn on me. One does not tattle on a master of poisons or run afoul of such powerful people."

"You could—"

"Do what? Get him arrested by the city guard, half of them addicted to his tonics for boosting strength, their sharpness of mind?"

I bite my tongue. She's right.

"So," she says, "I left. I switched my focus to alchemy. The other sorcerers see me as a failure, someone who couldn't cut it in medicine and took an easier path. And I let them, because I have no alternative." She picks at a stray splinter at the corner of my table and looks up at me.

I hesitate, then make a decision. "He's helping me look for answers. I need to take every chance to fix this. Even with him."

"He's using you, and he'll drop you the moment it benefits him."

He might. Sidriel has never promised me loyalty, just honesty. Yet I remember the strange softness in his eyes when he asked me to stay with him last night, and a cold knot settles in my stomach.

Wren stares at me, her eyes like knives. "Promise me you won't see him again."

"But—"

"I'll give you no more medicine until you break it off with Sidriel and swear to me on your god that you will not go back to him."

I glance at the nearly empty bottle on my nightstand. I've only a single dose left. "It's nearly Serrema's Eve," I say feebly. The realization is a cold one, that a part of me had looked forward to experiencing the holiday with Sidriel.

"All the better." No sympathy lies in Wren's tone. "My ultimatum stands. If you want to keep receiving my medicine, you won't see him again."

It hurts, this bitter threat. I'd thought Wren a friend, but a friend wouldn't wield the promise of my medicine like a weapon. She holds my headaches to my throat like a dagger. A betrayal of the trust I'd foolishly placed in her.

My reply is dry, hoarse. "Get out."

She hesitates, as if she's about to say more, but leaves.

Just like Jaed, Wren tries to make me into what she wants. She'd rather see me in pain than have me go against her wishes. However, she's not the only one who can give me relief. Sidriel has never pretended to be a friend, or faked kindness, but he'll give me the medicine for cold, simple coin. Right now, brutal honesty stings far less than Wren's betrayal.

I don't often seek out Sidriel in broad daylight. Only a short time remains before breakfast, but I won't be able to eat until this is settled. The thought of running out of potions leaves a churning storm in my chest. I can't get goldroot now, either. Jaed was my supplier, and I can't shop for it while I'm chaperoned by anyone else.

Sidriel answers the ring at his door in a sleep shirt, pale legs bare nearly to the thigh. His hair falls in mussed tangles, his eyes still hooded with sleep. "Yes?"

"May I come in?"

He steps back and gestures me through the doorway, his supercilious smile creeping onto his lips. "Back for more so soon?"

So. "I suppose I'm forgiven for last night's accusation?"

A hesitation, then a sigh and a nod. "Everyone is a frayed rope these days. Is my pardon so important that you had to rush to see me? I'm flattered."

I ignore his jest. "Can you still make a potion that helps soothe my headaches? A daily one? Without the fuzziness of goldroot?"

He blinks. "Of course I can. But I assumed Wren did that."

I sit on the corner of his bed. "She did. Until today."

"Wren's not the type to abandon someone. Another bleeding heart, that one."

"Except when it comes to you." A deep breath. "Wren gave me a choice. Her, or you."

I almost miss it, the strange look that crosses his face. He masks it quickly. "You chose me?"

"She's the one who gave me an ultimatum. Not you. She feigned friendship, but it's a lie. Or at least she loathes you more than she cares about me. She told me why she hates you, too."

He grimaces, falling into a chair. "So. You know. It was an accident, not that she believed that. Neither of us handled it well, afterward."

"Do you regret it?"

". . . Yes. And no. Sometimes to save many, to advance medicine, someone gets hurt. She volunteered, and I told her the risks."

Strangely enough, I believe him. He's been ruthlessly pragmatic and blackmailed me about the headaches, but he has always been straightforward in his callousness. Unlike Wren, who pretended kindness, only to take it away when it suited her.

I take a deep, shaky breath. "So what would I need to give you for a potion like hers? You already have my blood." And my body. "I have little coin."

He hesitates. "Nothing."

"Nothing?"

"Well, you'll have to cover the cost of the basic supplies, but it's no more than you'd have spent on your goldroot extract. It's mostly my magic, and that I will donate."

I blink. "You really don't want anything for it? Years ago, you asked an obscene price."

"I can't help everyone. I only have so much blood in my body, and the price reflected that. But right now, your blood is helping me with my research." He stands and sorts through a shelf of bottles. When he turns to look at me, there's something indecipherable in his expression. He clears his throat, then blinks, and it's gone. "We'll consider it a fair trade."

"Thank you."

I almost think he won't reply, but after a moment he murmurs, "My pleasure."

TWENTY-SEVEN

It seems a mockery to celebrate a holiday when the world is falling apart. Worse, to honor the very thing that lies in pieces. But tradition makes demands of us all.

I stand at the edge of the worship hall, draped in a gown of thin, garnet-hued silk, holding a wineglass. Like the Mirror itself, the wine is a deep red, rich and sweet and smoky on my tongue. It's a special vintage, holy, crafted specifically for Serrema's Eve and bottled over a year ago, when the world was stable. Outside these walls, wine prices have soared, but even so, we kept this safe.

I take another precious sip and watch the revelers collected in the grand hall for Serrema's Eve. Moonlight streams through the stained glass ceiling, scattering colored lights over the celebrants. The usual solemnity of Temple hymns is replaced by a trio of drummers, a flutist, and the indistinct chatter of a crowd.

Autumn sits in his throne on the dais, with his chosen escort for the evening standing at his side. Feryn, her red-gold curls gleaming. Her hand rests atop Autumn's, his expression indecipherable. No glove needed, not for her. They look beautiful, otherworldly. A god and his maiden, gracing our mortal lives with their presence.

Autumn looks my way. His lips curve into a hint of a smile and he nods. Feryn's grip on his hand tightens, and he turns to her, the moment broken. Then I feel it, the tiniest tendril of his affection. Soft, tender.

My gut twists, and I turn aside. Of course he and Feryn would get swept up in the mood of the evening. Tonight we celebrate Serrema, Lys's long-lost human partner, and their deep love that created the Mirrors.

Among the mortals here, only I know that she never perished a human death.

I haven't attended Serrema's Eve for the past six years, trapped in Sylvus during spring. The crowd seems thinner than I remember, and I wonder if Jaed and Laereda were right about the faithful leaving the Temple.

Still, those who remain celebrate with enthusiasm. The gaiety of the evening swirls around me, a festival celebrating all forms of love, of affections both romantic and physical, as well as deep, abiding friendships. A pang plucks my belly. Jaed. My eyes wander, searching revelers for a familiar head of snowy curls. I find him grinning, twirling Bix in a dizzy spin to the merry tune and pulsing drums.

Does Jaed notice the warmth kindling in Bix's eyes? They laugh and dance as I take another sharp swallow of wine.

I wander, taking a few dance partners but mostly studying, watching, keeping my ears open for any bit of gossip that might tumble from wine-loosened lips. The chatter only grows more salacious as the night stretches on. I learn altogether too much about who's fucking whom, and which of the puzzle masters loathe one another in their rivalry to piece together the largest chunk of the Mirror. Apparently, the priests caught a sixth commoner trying to palm a piece of it today.

The most frequent topic of conversation, however, is the Red Cough. It should have run its course by now, but it lingers, always spreading. Some mutter in hushed tones about how even the Temple's food supply is threatened now, with the farms failing. One acolyte wonders if the

Emperor will go so far as to requisition our stores, ending the peace between the faith and the state.

I share an amicable dance with Rhinna, and another with her partner Selere. I'm surprised to find the ache healing. It's hard to feel upset when I see how Rhinna beams at Selere and tosses her head back in a laugh. How can I begrudge someone who makes her so happy, when I made my own choices?

"A dance?" a familiar voice purrs at my side. I whirl to meet Sidriel's colorless eyes, his lashes darkened as usual. His robes are replaced with dark trousers and a long, fitted jacket of bloodred, making his skin all the paler in comparison. His hair is loose tonight, falling about his shoulders like drapes of white silk. I tilt my head, scanning his face. Thin lips twist into a knowing grin, and a dark merriment dances in his stare. A challenge.

"Why?"

"That is what one does on Serrema's Eve, is it not?" His voice dips low, nearly a whisper. "And don't you want to know if I'm as good at dancing as I am at fucking?"

Lust sparks, sending a shudder through my belly. I chew on my lip, then cover the motion with another sip of wine. What is his game? Sidriel has never approached me in public before. In fact, he never approaches me at all, always waiting for me to seek him instead.

Well, if he is playing games, there's one way to find out. "Very well." I toss back the dregs of wine and hand it to a passing young acolyte serving the party.

Sidriel grasps my hand and twirls me onto the floor. True to his word, he's as commanding here as he is in the bedroom. Hands wander. His fingertips rest at my hip, skate over the curve of my back, grip my shoulder as he guides where I will go. "How fares the medicine?"

"Well, thank you." Wren hadn't exaggerated his skill. Sidriel's potion eases even more of the pain than hers did, leaving me blissfully headache-free tonight.

"Good." His smile isn't his usual mocking one, more open, more . . .

something. I'm not sure how I feel about that, and I scan the crowd as we dance, noting whose eyes linger on the two of us. A wicked grin on Feryn's face, thoughtful contemplation on Vanyse's. Jaed's eyes are wide, wounded. Bix murmurs something in Jaed's ear, turning him away from the sight of me and into a gentle kiss on the cheek.

The song ends. He leans in close to whisper, "I want you to think of me while you dance with the others, imagining everything we'll do together when this night is over." When he leaves me there, I weave my way through the dancers to the wall.

"What in the name of shadows was that?"

I turn to greet the speaker with a grimace. Wren scowls at me.

"That," I hiss, "was a dance."

"It was half a step shy of rutting right there on the floor. I told you what he did to me. To others."

"Did you volunteer? He said you knew the risks. Is that a lie?"

She pauses, teeth gritted, shaking her head. Something ugly crosses her face. "No."

"It was an accident. You're the one who made me choose, who threatened to leave me in pain, after telling me you wouldn't." I walk away, and she lets me go.

As it turns out, Sidriel is right. No matter who partners me on the floor, I can only think of what will happen later: his hands gripping my hips, burying himself in me.

Hungry gazes make it difficult to wander through the crowd unnoticed to eavesdrop. Sidriel's boldness has attracted too much attention. He threw down a declaration to all assembled, choosing me as his partner tonight, this night we celebrate love and lust. Few will return to cold sheets unless they wish it so. The entire party is a dance of offers, of coy flirtation, like brilliant birds displaying mating plumage.

And now that I've been chosen, I'm all the sweeter a prize. I participate in more dances than I've ever had before while acolytes and priests alike bat eyelashes at me.

Once or twice, my gaze snags on Laereda, her ample form draped in swaths of azure silk. Tonight, most discard our robes of station, wearing whichever color strikes our fancy. The blue of a summer sky brings out the honey color of her hair, elegantly coiffed.

I notice she does not linger long with many, but drifts about like I do, listening, watching. Collecting her secrets.

I need to crack her.

Eyeing how deeply she drinks of the wine, I wonder if I can manage both Sidriel's bed first, then go to her room to dig for secrets before she passes out. When I approach her, I dip into a curtsy. "Laereda."

"Tirne!" She greets me warmly, planting a small kiss on both cheeks, holding her wineglass aside to do so.

"Heard any interesting news lately?"

She shook her head. "Far be it from me to gossip." Her eyes sparkle.

"But . . . ?" I lift a brow.

With a single furtive glance about, she leans in closer. "I *have* heard some deliciously dirty rumors about you," she says conspiratorially. "Tell me, are you really bedding Jaed's brother just to win him back?"

A lump forms in my throat. I should have known others would make that assumption. I neither confirm nor deny. "I seek pleasure where pleasure is to be found."

A guffaw bursts from her throat. "Fair enough. Especially tonight, it being a celebration of love and lust, after all. I'll wager there are many seeking your bed this eve." She fans herself with one hand, taking a sip of wine with the other.

"Are you offering?" I grin.

She swats at me playfully. "I fear I'd not even be a contender tonight, not with those Scions of Winter panting after you. But after their heat and flame has settled, you come knocking on my door for something a little sweeter, eh?"

It's my turn to laugh. "I'll keep that in mind."

I turn aside from her to meet the eyes of another sorcerer, one whose name I do not know. A Scion of Summer, his dark hair cropped close to his head, skin shining rich brown in the moonlight. He holds out his hand for a dance, and I accept. Behind him, Sidriel watches me, the hint of a smug smile dancing around his lips.

When did I become this strange new thing, an object of desire? I could chalk it up to the evening, to the atmosphere of this celebration, dancing pairs sharing deep kisses between twirls, innuendos flowing more freely than the wine. But I know it was that show with Sidriel.

Autumn's current potential Consorts—save Feryn, of course—linger at the corner of the room in a cluster. Forbidden from sharing their bodies with any other, some of this evening's luxuries are denied them. I feel a moment's pity, until I remember they may go to empty beds this evening, but in nights to come, they will bask in the attentions of a god. Three of them are already showing the signs of their pregnancies, over half a year into Autumn's stay here.

Sidriel does not approach me again. Once or twice he catches my eye, his tongue darting out to lick dark lips, a promise hanging in his heavy stare.

Then I notice it. Almost hidden, a faint shimmer of emotion. Something dark, something sharp. And it isn't from me.

I turn to find Autumn staring at me, eyes glinting orange as sparks from a smith's anvil. Something all too human twists his features. Subtle, but it's in the small frown, in the white-knuckled grip of his hand on the armrest of his throne.

Jealousy.

I blink, and the emotion fizzles away. Did I just imagine that? Surely so. I've been Autumn's Herald for six years, and never once has he looked upon me with desire. Except . . . there was that night in the grove, when he held my hand and stared at me with something new, something terrifyingly fragile in his expression.

How he'd gifted me with his magical blood to soothe my illness.

The way he'd cradled me gently to his chest in the baths the night he saved me.

I swallow. No. It's silly to think he'd want me, with his coterie of potential Consorts. It must have been something else, a stray scrap of unrelated emotion. Taking a deep breath, I turn back to my mingling, my spying.

Only one thing of note happens during the dancing, and it leaves me burning for answers. At one point, my eyes are again scanning the crowd for Winter's Scions, searching for one in particular. And I find him in strange company.

Sidriel stands in the far corner, nearly in shadow, and facing him is Laereda. Her eyes well with tears, but on her face is angry determination. She leans in and says something, to which Sidriel frowns. He sneers at Laereda and she nods weakly, then flees. I want to follow her, but the bells cry nine. Too late. It's time for me to take the stage.

The floor empties, the crowd circling the edges of the room. Autumn stands, leading Feryn to the center of the dance floor through the parted celebrants. The music slows, a deep, melodic tune that has been played at every Serrema's Eve since the first. Feryn gazes up at Autumn, flirtatious, her eyes sparkling.

For his part, my god is as distant and unknowable as ever. To all except me. I feel the roil of conflict in his belly, doubt and confusion and a subtle fear. Lys knows, he has enough to worry about, but he keeps his face neutral as they dance.

This should be Spring's dance with his Consort. But we make do with the god we have. It's a lovely number, sweet and delicate and perfectly executed. But my own gut bubbles at what comes next.

Serrema's Eve celebrates Lys's reunion with his beloved after the creation of the Mirrors, the connection forged between Sylvus and the human realm. At this ceremony, Feryn stands in for Serrema, but the Herald is the one who takes the role of the Mirror in this drama. As a replacement has not been selected, the task falls to me.

I take a breath, squaring my shoulders. It's a simple enough part. A dance, nothing more. So why does it make my heart pound and my belly quiver? Because right now his eyes should be on Feryn, but they keep darting up to meet mine? Or because I fear that the slurry of emotion I feel from him is not over the broken Mirror?

The music strikes an uncomfortable chord, and Feryn twirls away into the crowd. Lys's beloved, lost when the realms separated.

My turn.

I step forward. While others choose their own garb this evening, the Consort and the Herald wear the traditional costumes. Feryn wears Serrema's golden gown and matching crown dotted with topaz gems, while I'm draped in bloodred satin and bangles.

Autumn plucks a pair of gloves from his belt and dons them before taking my hand. His movements are precise, perfect, the same dance I've done for years. Everyone knows the steps, even if I did need to brush up on them after six years away. Feryn and Vanyse had enjoyed refreshing my memory as we practiced in their rooms on one of our rare nights together.

But on this dance floor, I'd always partnered with Jaed or some other acolyte in these steps. Never a god. Autumn's fingers grip mine just a little bit tighter than Jaed's ever did, and a strange brightness dances behind the flames of his eyes. Something terribly taboo flickers within me. Desire.

As Autumn grasps my hand, leading me into a steady turn, I wonder what it would be like to tumble into his bed, to feel his teeth grazing my shoulder. What would a god's magic feel like coursing through me?

These are forbidden thoughts, the gravest of sins. I swallow hard as my cheeks burn hot.

Autumn's hand twitches, and I recognize the emotion that flutters down our bond, the kindling of heat low in his belly.

No.

It can't be. Not while he looks at me.

I stumble, and a few small gasps come from the crowd. Quickly I recollect myself and slip back into step despite titters at my gaffe. For the rest of the dance, I carefully watch his collarbone, never meeting his eyes. Another acolyte joins us, wearing the gray mask and attached crown that represent Kild, Father of Shadows. The routine ends with me twirling him aside, away from Autumn, symbolizing Kild's exile into the human realm. As I do, I tear off his crowned mask, throwing it to the floor. His divinity stripped from him. The acolyte kneels, head bowed, and the dance ends with Feryn returning to Autumn's arms.

As quickly as I can without drawing undue attention, I flee the floor and collect myself against a wall. Deep breaths. Then I plunge back into the crowd to forget what just happened. The evening continues in a swirl of wine and merriment and desire. Dance partners grow bold, hands wandering, and I let them. Daydreams of Sidriel's passion mingle with sordid thoughts of Autumn, and I lose myself in anyone who will partner me.

At one point, Sidriel catches my gaze, holding a deep and intense stare for several long moments. He stands by the doorway and gives me a single nod before he slips out.

Part of me aches to go to him immediately. But no, I am not a dog to be called. I will seek him when I am ready. So I dance. I whirl into the crowd and find myself matched with Calder. This dance is chaste, innocent, a welcome respite. When I asked him to dance, he'd stammered and flushed. His hand in mine is trembling, clammy.

I find that the wine seems to have loosened my tongue. "Why are you so nervous?"

"I'm not." When I fix him with a wry stare, he sighs. "You're . . . well, *you*. Eyes are on you tonight, and I'd rather they not be on me."

I could read more into that. Why does he avoid scrutiny? Mere shyness, or guilt? I want to know why he was at Sidriel's door in the middle of the night, but I don't know how to ask him that. We dance, and the song ends. Calder fades back into the crowd. Too late, I realize this could have been my chance to poke around more in Calder's rooms, to steal his sample. But Wren is no longer working with me, anyway. And if Sidriel *has* been telling the truth, it was not a Spring Scion that broke the Mirror.

Laereda still twirls around the dance floor, laughing and giddy and flushed with wine. I have time. Sidriel's earlier promise has stoked a fire and a craving that I can't deny. I leave, making my way through the halls. Laughter and moans echo through the Temple, through doorways with their leather flaps carelessly left open.

When I slip through the beaded curtain into Sidriel's room, he smiles his usual wry grin as his hand finds mine and pulls me close. For a time, my other cares vanish amid our usual pleasures.

Afterward, we drink water from his side table and rest, sweat cooling on our bodies. I sit on the edge of the bed and watch him cross the room to pour another glass of water, heedless of his nudity. My eyes skate over his skin, so winter-pale, the lean shape of his calves, the curve of his shoulder blades in the candlelight.

He hands me a glass and sits beside me while we catch our breath, sipping the water. I should go, should find Laereda. This is my best chance to peel her secrets from her.

But just a little longer.

I glance around Sidriel's room as I bask in the shivery magic that tingles across my skin. It even makes the water taste sweet. My gaze lingers on the mysterious box for a few long heartbeats before it lands on the vial on the corner of one shelf. My blood, from yesterday's collection.

He follows my stare and grimaces. "Still nothing. I've never seen the kind of magic that cursed you. Are you sure you don't have any other clues?" There's something pointed in his question, something that makes me bristle.

"No. I've told you that."

"And you're certain there's nothing you've forgotten to tell me?"

I don't like his leading tone, the implication that I'm lying. I set my glass aside on an end table, my reply sharp and sour. "Of course I'm certain. I want this fixed more than anyone."

Sidriel returns the empty glasses to the table, then stands before me, caressing my cheek. "I swear I'll get to the bottom of this and fix the Mirror. Whatever it takes."

I shiver at the echo of my words to Autumn. There's something dark in Sidriel's words. A threat, a promise. Just how far will he go for this? And will I join him?

But all of that is forgotten when he leans in for a kiss. No. Just for tonight, for this holiday, the Mirror is a worry that I will push aside.

Our fires banked low this time, the second session is a slow thing, gentler, full of quiet desperation as he murmurs my name. We cling to one another in the dark of this night, long past when spring should have fallen, and try not to wonder how much longer this will last. How much longer we have to enjoy each other. It's quiet and intense, the way we move together, as if this is our last chance.

We lie tangled together afterward as he strokes my hair gently. I don't understand him. First he tears my clothing off, then later he cradles my hand and plants light kisses on my fingertips.

"I'm sorry," he says softly.

"For what?"

Something deeply pained haunts his eyes, but he just shakes his head. "I . . ." He sucks in a rattling breath. "Never mind."

But there's still that look on his face, something terribly open, something that feels like missing a step in the dark. No. Part of me worries that his apology almost preceded a confession I'm not ready to face. "It's late. I should go." I slip from the bed, get dressed, and leave. He watches me with haunted eyes but says nothing.

I should sleep this off, if I were wise. But it nears two bells, and I have one more appointment. Laereda must have found her own rooms by now, dizzy with wine. The Tharem had given her an ultimatum ending tomorrow, yet the box still rests in Sidriel's room. If, after all, that's what it meant.

And I intend to find out.

TWENTY-EIGHT

*Y*ou've been to his room tonight, haven't you?" No uncertainty lies in Laereda's tone as she gestures me in, though the words slur a little.

"Yes." No use in lying. I'm certain I reek of him, his bergamot and herb scent. His magic flows through me, leaving me bubbly as sparkling wine.

She sighs and pinches the bridge of her nose as she paces. Her steps are uneven, wobbly.

I stand in the middle of her bright, cheery room while dread squirms through me. "What were you two arguing about, earlier tonight?"

"Shadows take me," she swears. "You saw that?"

I nod.

Laereda slumps onto her bed, hanging her head in her hands. "Um . . . I . . . I've done something terrible." Her voice is a miserable whimper. "And the Tharem knows. And now it's all going to fall apart. I'll be exiled, and I'll never see him again."

I don't need to ask who she means.

"What happened?" This is it. The secret she and Sidriel have kept. That damnable box. I keep my voice steady, sympathetic. Sitting beside her, I cautiously take her hand in mine. Fire and shadow, Sidriel's magic is strong tonight. Even this small touch is intense, my skin so sensitive I can almost feel the ridges in her fingerprints. "It's okay. You can tell me."

"No. Not if you're in bed with *him*," she hisses.

"If it has to do with the Mirror, that's more important to me than anything. Please. If you know something, help me fix it."

Her hand tightens in mine, and her breath is ragged. "I gave him something. Something I took. Well, I guess it was given to me, not stolen, but only because I knew an awful secret."

My voice cracks. "What was it?"

"A bottle of Spring's blood."

"What?" I can't keep the shock from my face or my voice. "Where did you even get that?"

"From Spring's room."

"But only his Consort has the key to that."

". . . Yes."

"Fire and shadow."

She nods miserably. "I blackmailed her. I found out she dallied with another and used that against her. Spring is the most fertile god, the god of life. Sidriel promised me he could use the blood to make me bear children longer."

The pieces click together. Her previous requests and pleas to the Tharem. "You could become a Consort again."

She nods.

My mind scrambles to add the pieces together. Sidriel gave me a different story for Autumn's blood. Did he tell me the truth, or lie to me, too?

Does he have Summer's blood? Winter's?

The story spills from Laereda in a rush. "The Tharem found out what I'd done—I don't know how, maybe Spring's Consort told him. He said that if I couldn't get the blood back, he'd tell Autumn everything. Tonight I told Sidriel I'd made a mistake, that I needed it back. He refused.

I threatened to go to Autumn himself, but Sidriel laughed in my face. He told me to go ahead and write my own sentence. He's right. I'm doomed."

I squeeze her hand. There are no reassurances I can give her. No matter what she does now, her treason will be discovered, and she will be excommunicated from the Temple.

She whimpers. "What am I going to do?"

"I don't know."

Silence falls. Heavy, thick, choking.

"I should leave. I doubt you want my company."

Laereda leans her head on my shoulder. "No. The opposite. I can't be alone with my thoughts, and . . . there's no one else."

Unease bubbles within me, but I pause, then sigh. "All right, I won't go."

She lies on the bed, curling up on her side and tugging me down beside her. It's a gentle position, comforting, her head on my shoulder.

We hold each other close as my mind whirls over Sidriel's plots. What is he truly planning? He'd insisted he never lied to me, but now I wonder if it's the opposite, all while I spent nights upon nights in his bed.

"You know . . . ," Laereda says, "I wasn't lying earlier. When I invited you here." It's a small motion, a brush of her lips against my cheek.

For one moment, I am weak. I let her kiss me, but after a heartbeat I come to my senses and pull away. "No. You've had too much to drink."

I expect her to argue, but her eyelids already droop. "I think you're right. But still stay?"

That much, I can do. "All right. We'll figure out something in the morning."

I know she is dead the moment I open my eyes.

Laereda's skin is pale, waxy, grayish. A blue tint coats her lips.

No.

In my blurry state, I shake her. Her skin is cold, but I call her name anyway. It starts as a whisper, then escalates until I'm screaming. Her body is heavy, limp, her head flopping in a way that makes my skin crawl. My chest is tight, and my vision wavers black.

Her name, uttered over and over, shifts to cries for help. I stand, lurching toward the doorway. Footsteps approach, hurried, and two priests surge into the room, lifting the leather flap and pinning it up. They take one look at my trembling form, arms wrapped tight around my middle, holding in the panic that threatens to overwhelm me at any moment.

Their words are an incoherent buzzing in my head. A question, I think. One of them sees Laereda, and I am forgotten. They rush to her, checking for a pulse, urging her to awaken. Useless.

Soon, the room is full of priests, acolytes, until someone has the presence of mind to force them all out. The Tharem arrives with a physician, both groggy-eyed before dawn. The physician—the same one that always bled me—confirms what we already know.

"She's gone." He lifts one of Laereda's hands, the fingertips purple as a bruise. "Bleeding mercy," he names the cause of death. Poison.

All eyes turn to me, the accusation clear. I don't remember sitting down in a chair in the corner. "I didn't do this."

The Tharem glowers.

My voice ramps up a notch as I repeat myself. "I didn't kill her!"

"You were the last person to see her alive. When did you come here?"

"Around one and a half bells? Two bells?"

The physician adds, "Bleeding mercy isn't immediate. Once I determine time of death, we'll know when she was poisoned."

"Tirne," the Tharem says, voice low and shoulders hunched. His bald head beads with sweat in the light of Laereda's enchanted sconces. "You are to be confined to your room while this is investigated."

I shake my head in denial, but the damage is done. The Tharem's word is law in the Temple. Only the gods rank higher. Shadows take me . . . the gods. What will Autumn think? The thought leaves a bitter taste on my tongue.

One of the priests speaks up. "What if the Herald was poisoned, too? Just hasn't shown up yet?"

The physician nods toward me. "There's no antidote for bleeding mercy. Make her vomit and hope for the best."

Numbness has set in. I barely shudder at the thought of being poisoned. I don't protest when the Tharem grabs my upper arm and drags me to my room.

"Two priests on watch at the doorway and two at the window at all times until this is resolved," the Tharem commands.

I shuffle into my room. No one followed the physician's recommendation to give me any sort of emetic, but I flee to my privy and shove my finger down my throat until the contents of my stomach spill into the chamber pot. Only a bit of wine, deep purple and bitter on my tongue. I do it again and again until only bile heaves up. Afterward, I gulp greedily at water straight from the pitcher on the sideboard.

Shaking, I throw on a nightdress and kindle a fire in the hearth, then fall into my bed, yanking the blankets over me. My hands tremble too fiercely, my teeth chattering. Bleeding mercy, or just shock?

I don't know how long I stare at the wall, thoughts clattering through my head.

Poison.

Someone must have tampered with Laereda's wine at the party. It's the only answer that makes sense.

Eventually, a familiar rusty voice murmurs outside my doorway, and the priests reply. With a deep breath, I slide out of bed and stand to face him. The curtain rattles, and Autumn slips into my room. The flickering light of my fireplace casts his face in orange, the hollow angles of his cheeks even more pronounced as the scent of pumpkin and hay fills my chamber.

"Tirne." Judgment lies in the utterance of my name. "A woman lies dead." His former Consort. Did he love her? Does he grieve?

I clear my throat and risk a single question. "Have you come to condemn or absolve me?"

His eyes search mine, something conflicted and too frighteningly human flickering in them. We're long past the time he should have left our world. How much more before he begins to grow old, like any mortal? Will his ageless face wrinkle and sag?

No. The world will run out of food long before then.

The thought sinks my spirits even further, but Autumn speaks. "The physician and a sorcerer are currently determining the time of death. Their findings will convict or exonerate you. I am here to look into your eyes and ask."

I swallow and lift my chin. "I didn't kill Laereda."

For the briefest moment, he glances at the door and back. His voice lowers, even as a sigh of relief sings along our bond. "Do you know who did?"

The tension leaves my shoulders. He still trusts me. I respond in a similar whisper. "Anyone. Laereda is gone, and all of her secrets with her. Any one of those secrets' owners could have wanted her dead." I want to mention the Tharem, but I can't tell him what Sidriel has been doing without admitting I've been lying to my god, too.

Autumn looks past me. Finally, he says, "If you tell the truth, if Laereda was poisoned at the holiday celebration, the sorcerers and the physician will know."

"You could make them free me with a mere word."

A twist of something tugs at my stomach, one of his emotional echoes. Remorse? "When their findings corroborate your claim, then you will be free." For one haunted moment, it feels like he will say something else. But he walks out the door without another word.

I'm left in my room. Acolytes bring me meals, eaten in the solitude of my chambers. I'm allowed no visitors, other than that one brief contact with Autumn. Once, I hear voices raised outside.

"Let me in!" Jaed. My stomach twists. After all this is over, I'll go to him. I'll meet his ultimatum. This quest to cure my curse has only led to misery.

The guards turn Jaed away, though he spits a few uncharacteristic curses first.

I wonder how long it will take to prove Laereda was poisoned at the party. Until then, I wait.

TWENTY-NINE

I know it's bad news when the Tharem himself comes to escort me. The knock wakes me in the coldest hours before dawn, accompanied by the Tharem's voice. "Tirne of Autumn, you are summoned."

Even Sidriel's medicine doesn't touch the headache that pierces me today. Still, I throw on my robe and part my doorway's curtain.

A gloating sneer decorates the Tharem's broad face. "I assume we can do this in a dignified manner?" Autumn is nowhere to be seen, but I can sense his unease.

My lips press together. I swallow and nod.

They escort me down the corridor, and my heart sinks. We're heading toward the worship hall. It will be empty now, hours before the first service, but the formality of it worries me.

The Tharem ushers me in and closes the doors behind me. Only a few people stand in the hall. The benches are back in place, and light spills through the tinted windows, the first blush of dawn. But I barely cast it a single glance. The Tharem's smugness wafts from him like heat from a furnace. At the base of Autumn's dais stand a few high priests. Sidriel stands there as well, his face emotionless and cold as a serpent.

Dread settles over me as pieces click into place. No. This isn't happening.

But it is. Sidriel always told me he was ruthless. Wren was right all along. I feel like a fool, that some part of my soul thought I was exempt from his ambition. Even now, a tiny scrap of hope lingers, that his icy expression hides something else, something other than what I fear.

Autumn sits in full regalia, a thick litter of leaves at his feet attesting to some time spent here. How long had he sat upon his throne, deciding my fate? Dark waves of emotion roil within him, buffeting me. Anger, despair, pain. Betrayal.

I approach his throne and kneel. My heart thuds fiercely in my chest, my skull a painful echo with every beat. The tiled floor is hard, unforgiving, pressing against my knees like a knife.

"Tirne of Autumn. Stand." My god's command is flat, and I obey. "Laereda of Autumn ingested poison around two bells, on Serrema's Eve. You admit to entering her room between one and two bells." He gestures to the foot of his dais. "Sidriel, repeat your claim against Tirne."

The sorcerer clears his throat. "I maintain a few vials of poison in my chambers, to aid me in the creation of remedies and cures. And the morning Laereda was found dead, I noticed one of my bottles was missing. Bleeding mercy. After Tirne had spent part of the evening in my chambers."

I truly was a fool. He didn't even lie about his nature, and I still fell for it. My body goes numb, my fingers tingling and my heart in my throat. My hands tighten into shaking fists. I have to unclench my teeth to snarl, "You filthy liar."

All of it was a ploy. *I'm sorry.* He wasn't making a confession, he was saying goodbye before he framed me for Laereda's murder. That bold dance was just a part of the plan, so all would believe I went to him after the celebration.

And I know why. Murder to protect the secret of that little box, of Spring's blood, to keep Laereda from telling Autumn.

He doesn't know the Tharem already knows. Well, let him hang for that, when the Tharem brings it to light.

Sidriel watches me closely. "Laereda was poisoned while you were in her room. The physician confirmed the timeline, and the high priests checked my chamber. Their magic proved your presence there that night. If you didn't kill her, then how did she die?"

A tremor starts in my belly, spreading outward until I shake all over. "I don't know. But I didn't do this." My eyes meet Autumn's, and something sick and uncomfortable shivers through our bond.

My god watches me with a vast emptiness in his eyes. "The evidence speaks for itself. Yet one question lingers. Why? Why would you do this?" A dozen things echo across our connection, a slurry of agony and grief.

"I'm not lying." But as I stare at Sidriel, I realize I've lost. The sorcerer played me like a flute. I fell into his bed, his charms. How he poisoned Laereda, I don't know. But I'm certain he did it. He needed to silence her, and someone to blame for it.

But why me?

The answer seems simple. To tie up one more loose end to whatever plot he hatches, whatever he needs the gods' blood for. He'd told me he was merciless, and I hadn't listened. Maybe it was sheer coincidence, the fact that Laereda invited me to her rooms, and he merely seized the opportunity.

My head pounds. "You did this," I growl at Sidriel, then look back to Autumn with a plea. "He killed her. He—" I stop. I could tell them he has Spring's blood. But then he'd reveal my own betrayal, my own sin in giving him my blood—Autumn's blood—for more than just fixing the Mirror. He'd tell them I knew of his forbidden experiments and participated anyway. I already teeter on the precipice of exile or a death sentence for the murder; committing treason against my god would only seal the deal.

The Tharem knows of that box. Let him reveal it to Autumn. Later, Sidriel will be just as doomed.

"I was never in Laereda's room," Sidriel says coolly. "The priests confirmed that. But you were."

Everyone stares, disgust on their faces. They've already convicted me.

My god clears his throat and speaks. "In light of that evidence, you have been found guilty of the murder of Laereda of Autumn."

I swallow. If he declares death, I'll spill all the secrets I know before I go, taking Sidriel and the Tharem with me. Then I'll die in disgrace, interred in the grave of a commoner without a marker, not beside my mother in her mausoleum. I'll never be known as anything more than a murderer, the saboteur who destroyed the Mirror and killed an innocent woman.

Autumn says, "Due to your faithful lifetime of service until now, including six years as Herald, your sentence will be exile, and you are never to set foot inside the Temple again. Nor is any one of the faithful to contact you, on pain of their own exile. You will be allowed to take a simple set of clothing and any personal effects that do not belong to the Temple, if they are small enough to wear or fit in a pack." His eyes flit down to my throat, to Mother's necklace.

I blink, tears spilling. I own precious few personal possessions. Mother's necklace. My journal. My medicine. Jaed's bracelet, still tucked in a drawer. Shadows take me, I'll never see him again, never get the chance to apologize. Our argument seems so pointless now. I'm losing my home, my life, my friends. What will Feryn and Vanyse think of me?

Autumn watches with an expressionless face and distant eyes. But the sting of it sings across our bond, the shock of betrayal.

I kneel before him, no more than an acolyte. No, not even that anymore. A commoner, not even one of his supplicants.

My god continues. "My blood—and your connection to the Mirror—will be stripped from you."

Sidriel steps forward.

No.

Surely they won't let him do it, my accuser. But who else is better suited than the man most skilled in the magic of the body, of blood?

He looks down at me, in his robes the color of the darkest sapphires, his kohl-rimmed eyes vicious. "Stand."

I bare my teeth, but I do as he says. I don't want the priests at the base of the dais to haul me up and hold me. No, I'll face this on my own feet.

Reaching forward, Sidriel traces the edge of my jaw. I flinch away.

I accuse him in an angry whisper. "Murderer. Liar."

A deep and endless cold lies in his stare. "I told you. I've never lied to you. I wish you could say the same to me."

Before I can ask what he means, he places one hand flat against my collarbone. The tingle of magic thrums through me, little more than a prickle at first, like a limb that has fallen asleep. Soon it turns to a sting, then a burn like a thousand tiny, red-hot needles piercing my skin.

I grit my teeth. I don't know how long we lock eyes as the sensation grows stronger, then worse still. Eventually, even I can't contain the scream anymore, and it bursts from me as my knees buckle.

This time the priests do step forward to hold me up, one of my arms draped over each of their shoulders. And still Sidriel's palm presses to my skin, still the fire courses through me.

A drop of warm liquid rolls down my temple, my cheek. I'm sweating. Then I glance down at my chest and see the tiny splatter. Red. I stare at my arm. Like tiny rubies, drops of blood well forth from my skin. Autumn's blood. Sidriel is stealing it from me, along with the magic that ties me to my god. Though the pain makes me scream, it's this thought that hurts the most.

Every moment gets harder. It is so much stronger than my usual headaches. Every nerve in my body lights up with agony. When my vision wavers black, the pain finally vanishes and the priests let me go. I collapse to the floor, an undignified puddle of anguish. A sob bursts from me and I curl into a ball. Eventually, I manage to stand on trembling legs, straightening my spine.

My god speaks. "You are dismissed." Not even a fleck of warmth kindles in Autumn's eyes, but his hands clench into fists and there's the tiniest crack in his voice. "We shall not meet again."

I choke back any reply I might have made. What would I have said? Goodbye? Pleading for clemency, to take it all back? None of it would do any good. Without a word, I turn away from Autumn and leave him behind.

It takes little time to wash the blood from my skin, to change into the simple clothing they give me and stuff the pockets of the pack with my scant personal possessions. I clutch Jaed's bracelet tightly before clasping it back on my wrist. It's a reminder of what I've lost, but also of what I once had.

The Tharem watches the whole process, even keeping a sharp eye on me while I dress, to ensure I steal nothing that belongs to the Temple. I find it hard to care. He grimaces at my medicine, and even eyes my valerian tea closely, giving it a sniff.

I almost leave Sidriel's pain-relief potion behind. I want no part of him or his poison. But I've few enough coins, and something makes me shove it in my pack anyway, despite the Tharem's scrutiny.

Emptiness consumes me as I walk through the halls, a dizzy fog in my head. I feel as if I stand outside my own body. Perhaps it is all a nightmare, and I'll wake up to another day in the Temple.

But no, that is a child's daydream. This is real. I have no idea what to do outside these walls. They shove me out the door with a bit of dried food, although it is not as much as it once would have been, with the rationing. I've no home, no roof over my head.

I walk into the city, my boots crunching on damp gravel. Soon, the pebbles give way to cobblestones. This is the nicer part of town, and I know I will never find someone kind enough to take in a disgraced former acolyte on charity alone. Instead, I make my way to Poplar Street, a place of dirt-packed roads turned to slush with the recent rain.

To the one haven I might still have left.

I clutch my pack tightly. The sky is clear after a recent rain, a pale watery blue, sun shining, mocking my misery. It's still cool, though, and I shiver. The Temple gave me an old set of plain clothes from the laundry, and they were kind enough at least to include a cloak, but it's a threadbare thing. The trousers are ill-fitting, too short, baring my ankles to the chill air over my low boots.

I have only a few coins to my name. I never expected to need excess money, and most of my allowance had gone to my medicines. The few silver hawks in my bag wouldn't be enough to keep me at a boarding-house for long.

There's only one place to go.

A cheery bell chimes as I enter Ilna's cobbler's shop. There are no other customers. She is bent over her work, threading a heavy, curved needle. "One moment." She tugs it straight, poking it into a boot held in a vise of some sort. I stare at the black leather cuff on her left wrist, a sign of her Kildian faith.

Only then does she look up. She stares at me with Mother's dark eyes, though her cheeks are hollower, her arms thinner than when I last bumped into her.

Silence holds. Her eyes take in the worn shirt and trousers, the dull beige cloak. Gone are all trappings of the Temple, save Mother's necklace. She sucks in a hissing breath, hand flying to her mouth in eager surprise. "You left."

"I was forced out, but yes."

Ilna blinks, and I realize her eyes are welling with tears. "You're free." She doesn't seem to care at all that my "freedom" was unwilling. "Come." She crosses to the door in hurried motions, twisting the latch and turning the sign to the red *Closed* side.

I follow her through the back room, past racks of foot-shaped wooden molds and leather and large spools of sinew. Boxes line a lower shelf, crammed up beneath.

Ilna nods at them. "Beads and ribbon for embellishing fine ladies' shoes. Not much use for those now. Even the rich have tightened their purse strings."

Even the Temple. I had thought our trials irritating. The lack of luxuries like fresh cider, the endless supply of turnips and dried stores of beans. But at least we'd had food at all. Guilt gnaws at me as I take in Ilna's thin appearance.

She leads me into the small kitchen at the back of the shop, where she'd once served a shaken Feryn tea. My bag thumps to the floor as I sit at the small dining table. The space is simple, but comfortable. Cozy wood floors and brick walls, a small stove in the corner. She pokes at the coals and adds some wood scraps, the fire flaring to life before she fills a kettle and swings it into the fire on an iron hook. My chest tightens watching her, and I realize just how much I missed her and her silly stories lulling me to sleep at night.

"I don't have much for tea anymore," she apologizes. "But something hot in your belly is better than nothing."

I nod numbly, and I wonder if being forced from my life, my friends, left me broken. A hive of bees buzzes in my head.

She sits while the water warms and places a callused hand over mine on the tabletop. "What happened?"

"I don't want to talk about it."

"Well," she says softly, "you have a home here. I . . . I missed you."

Not enough to come back. But I don't say it out loud. Instead, I merely nod once more.

We sit in silence until the kettle whistles and she pours the water into a teapot, tossing in some nettles and other leaves I don't recognize. "I didn't want to leave you, or Raijeen," she blurts out as it steeps.

"Then why did you?"

"I couldn't bear it. Once you see that the gods are broken, just as fallible and horrible as the rest of us, you can't unsee it."

I think of Autumn's gloved hand in mine, how fear changed his voice. I remember the deep, unrelenting sorrow that echoed across our connection, so many times. The lie of Serrema as Summer. "They're not horrible." Broken, maybe. Even fallible. But not horrible.

She leans forward and pats my hand again. "We can talk more about that later." Pouring a cup of tea, she pushes it at me. "I never stopped caring about you, or thinking about you. I sent you letters. Even if you didn't reply, I at least thought you were happy."

"I was." And that's what makes the dam break. The sobs that rack me are sharp, jagged things. Ilna abandons her tea to kneel by my chair and pat my back, murmuring soothing nonsense.

But nothing will make this better.

I don't know how long I sit there, crying over my tea. Long enough for it to become tepid. Still, I gulp it down, hunger from my missed breakfast starting to gnaw at me.

"Come," Ilna says gently. "Let me show you upstairs. I had an apprentice, but . . ." Her eyes darken and her breath hitches. "Well, he's gone now. You can have his quarters. It's not much, but it's yours."

We emerge at the top of the narrow stairs and stand in a small hallway with two doors, lit only by the light streaming through a shuttered window at the end. Ilna points to the first door. "That one's my room."

Garlands of dried garlic and rosemary hang over each door. They're ancient, the garlic withered and the rosemary missing most of its leaves. I suppose those were too costly to replace.

She catches me looking at them. "Keeps out the kexas," she says belligerently, as if expecting me to protest.

But I've no room to complain, not anymore. I'm no longer of the faithful. Might as well join the Kildians. But even I don't believe my own bitter thoughts. I could never truly forsake my god. He believes me a murderer; it's no wonder he exiled me.

My aunt leads the way to the second door and opens it. "Your room." I have to squeeze my way past her. The room is small, painfully so. It bears little more than a narrow bed with a straw-stuffed mattress and a chest at the foot of it. Not even any sort of desk or table. But there is a window with wooden shutters.

"It's a bit musty, but we'll get it all aired out and cleaned tomorrow," she apologizes from the doorway.

It's strange to realize I'll be sleeping in a room with a door, closing myself off from the world. I thought I was done crying, but suddenly the space feels too close, too tight, and I can't breathe. I drop my pack and run downstairs, ignoring the way my head pounds as I find the base of the steps and sit, taking deep breaths.

Ilna finds me there, head in my hands as I try to calm my nerves.

"I know it's not much," she stammers, "but—"

"I just . . . I need a minute."

Silently, she steps past me and back out to the shop. I can feel her hurt poking at me, and I want to call her back, to apologize. But I don't. I stare around at the trappings of my aunt's trade, and my heart fills with sorrow. This is my life now. Gone are the soothing hymns, the purr of a Temple cat curled up by my side in bed at night. The scent of the grove, cherry blossom and dying leaf and astringent fir. Or the smell of incense wafting through the worship hall.

Gone are my friends. Jaed. Feryn. Vanyse. Even Bix. They're as forbidden from coming to see me as I am from reentering the Temple. I'll never even get to apologize to Jaed.

Everything my life was . . . it's been erased from memory like it never existed. Not only will my name never appear on that memorial tablet in the Temple courtyard, but I also won't be interred in the Temple's section of the cemetery. They might even have me burned as the Kildians do, on an open-air pyre.

I sniff and wipe my nose on a sleeve like a child. Even my handkerchiefs belonged to the Temple.

And then I see it. A flicker of motion against the wall, like the shadow of a tree branch swaying in the wind. I blink, but there's nothing there. Only my own long shadow. The figment of a mind scraped raw, seeing monsters where there are none.

Taking a long, steadying breath, I creak back up the stairs.

THIRTY-ONE

My first day as a cobbler, I practice my stitches on a tiny piece of scrap leather, a small triangle of mis-dyed suede. My work is clunky and uneven, but Ilna says I'll get better with enough practice. Worse, it is one of the irritable days before my courses start, and my loneliness and grief are accompanied by cramping guts. Every frustration seems insurmountable. I grit my teeth and draw deep breaths to steady myself.

Ilna sings softly as she works beside me. The notes are strange without the cadence or key of Jaed's music or Temple hymns.

It grates on me, the annoyance building until I break. My thread tangles and I shove the shoe away. "Can you please stop that?"

"What?"

"The singing."

She clucks her tongue. "Are you saying my voice is not lovely?" Mock affront flavors the words, her eyes sparkling with teasing humor.

"It's not your voice, it's the song."

Her smile loses a bit of its luster. "This melody soothes and pleases the herren. So they'll bless us."

It grates on me, this insistence on such make-believe childishness. I stare at the black Kildian cuff on her arm, and my frustration snaps. "What blessings? These figments of yours, why do you cling to them so?"

"They're not figments," she insists simply, her own needle flying in deft, practiced motions. "They just won't show themselves to you until you lose the scent of the Temple, of the gods' magic. It'll wear off eventually."

"Why?" I ask. Maybe it's all just stories, but if I understand her reasons, I can talk her out of them.

"They hate the gods. Lys in particular, but his children as well. They love only Kild, their father. They lost their way when Lys cast Kild out, stripping his godhood. Now back to your stitches." She clucks her tongue and points at the leather before me.

I scowl, but I pick it up. If I'm to earn my keep, I'll have to improve no matter how much the twisted, knotted thread infuriates me. But I can't let her lies about my gods stand. "That's not how it happened. Kild betrayed Lys, and he was rightfully punished for it."

But doubt tugs at the corner of my mind. Autumn's confession about Serrema planted a seed, one that slowly grows. Suspicion.

I hate it.

Ilna just shrugs calmly. "Were you there? Two sides to every story. Who are you to say which one is true?"

"And how do you know, either? Autumn wouldn't lie about such things," I insist, just as the needle stabs my finger for the umpteenth time. "Fire and shadow!"

Even now, her advice is softly said. "I told you, if you wear the leather gloves, you won't stab yourself like that."

"I can't feel what I'm doing when I wear them," I grumble, but grudgingly slip one on.

Ilna ties off her own stitch and snips the end of the thread. "And why do you trust your god so much?"

I'm reluctant to admit to her that I felt my god's sorrow, his joy, his regret. It is too personal. "I just know."

She shakes her head. "You'll learn. Once the Kildara grow familiar with you, they'll show themselves. They might even speak to you as they do me. Then you'll hear their truth."

My jaw clenches. There's no swaying her. Not now, maybe not ever. I wonder if her mind has broken, seeing hallucinations of her own. I weary of arguing, and bite back my retort. Instead, I jab my thread through the holes punched in the leather. I can sense her disappointment in my belligerence.

We work in dreary silence for the rest of the afternoon.

My life takes on a new routine. Ilna teaches me her craft, and I help her run the shop during the day. Instead of rising to a murmuring chorus of morning devotions echoing down the hall, I awaken to silence. The scent of whatever Ilna has managed to cobble together for breakfast wafts up the stairs, rather than the fragrance of holy incense.

I miss the cats, too, the warmth of a soft form draped across my pillow in my sleep, or a furry companion weaving between my feet as I walked down the hall.

On my regular ventures to sell our shoes, I wander the city streets. It's nearly the end of what should be spring. I'm shocked to see how many stores have hung handwritten *Closed* signs or just lie hollowed out, the door hanging open and the shelves vacant. Lost souls huddle inside the empty ones sometimes, their belongings in threadbare bags nearby. Some merchants still ply their wares, but fully half are just . . . gone. Coughs rattle through the streets, among people gaunt and skeletal.

But not everyone is quite as dire and weary. One day, I pass a trio of men in clothing a bit worn but still fine, their cheeks full and pink. A woman ahead of me complains to another. "Rich bastards." She spits in their direction, but the men are already past. "More food than they can ever eat, and do they share? No."

Watching the men go, guilt overwhelms me. That was me until a month ago, living in comfort, ignoring this disaster. Jaed had tried to tell me, and I didn't listen.

But the gods didn't, either. Does Autumn know how bad it truly is out here? Does he care? I'll never know. I'll never see him again to ask, or to plead that he help somehow.

And I have greater worries. Now I understand true hunger for the first time in my life. I'd thought I'd known before what it was like to be hungry, but I was wrong. This is more than simple craving. My stomach wrenches itself into queasy knots. I'm nauseated, dizzy, exhausted. My temper frays, and I grow sharp-tongued.

It boils over eventually, on a day that would normally have been a joy. It's the first holiday of the faith that I've missed since leaving. Today, back home in the Temple, they celebrate the birth of the first Scion, Darrow of Summer. On any other year, there would be a great feast and games. I don't know what they're eating now, with the shortages, but it's certainly better than my current diet.

My belly grumbles, made worse by the row of cured sausage links in front of me at the butcher's shop, sausages we cannot afford. Still, Ilna uses two precious coins to buy stripped bones, even the marrow already hollowed out.

"What do you need dry, empty bones for?" I snap as the butcher hands over a sack, my arms already full with a basket of well-wrapped, gristly goat meat. Not the parts I once would have eaten, either, but the head and the feet, the bits that are mostly bone. "They're not even good for broth."

"They're for the thregas." There's a touch of defensiveness in her tone.

"Thregas?" My temper flares. "We can barely afford these chunks of chewy old goat, and you waste money on one of your imaginary creatures?"

"It protects the shop from ill will and keeps bats from roosting in the eaves," she says, as if explaining something obvious to a child. "Bats that carry disease. And it's my store, my money." Her point made, she clutches the bag of old bones and stalks quickly back to the shop.

My belly growling miserably, I follow a distance behind. When I arrive, the bones litter the alley by the side door, along with an assortment of glass beads tossed to scatter among the cobbles, gleaming every rainbow hue. Useless for slippers now, left as an offering to another of her fictitious monsters.

That night, I'm still awake well past the time I would normally be abed. I sit at the counter in the front room, the shades drawn and a single precious candle flickering. The scent of tallow tickles my nostrils. No beeswax for us. Possibly no beeswax for anyone, save a few tapers some may have hoarded long ago.

I squint as I once again practice my sewing on tiny bits of waste leather. I've already punched the holes in this piece with an awl; that part is easy. But my thread always seems to tangle and twist. I'm determined to master it, though. I was Autumn's Herald, damn it. I won't be outdone by a bit of sinew.

Biting my lip, I untwist the needle once more.

Then I see it. Light, spilling through the tiny gap in the curtains. But not just any light. Wavering, in shades of blue and violet and green.

Souls.

No. I shake my head. My magic is gone. Sidriel stole it from me. I shouldn't be able to see the dead. I blink, but the light remains, scattered across the floorboards in a sliver of jewel tones.

Hands shaking, I set aside my sewing practice and approach the curtain, then slide it back in one sharp motion.

I nearly scream, but I bite my tongue and choke on the sound.

These aren't the gentle bobbing lights I remember. The dead look almost human, stretched into skeletal shapes made of ghastly light. In place of fingers, their glow illuminates long, tapering claws. And they have faces, grotesque mockeries of human skulls with hollow black eyes and noses, their teeth long and sharp like a cat's.

One throws itself at the window, and the glass shudders. I jump back, a sour taste in my throat, a buzzing in my ears. Its claws screech down the windowpane.

This can't be happening. How can I see them? And is this what they become, after months in the human realm? Some of the usual gentle souls bob behind the monstrosities. Those must be the newly dead, but the older, horrible creatures scratch at the windows with their claws, scrabbling to get in. Not that they could. The homes of the living are safe, aren't they?

The glass rattles, and I slide the curtains closed quickly, as if that will protect me.

While the light of the dead stretches across the floor, a shadow crosses it. Not mine. Something big. I whirl to see what new horror has entered. A hulking form lurches through the room, like a figure made of black smoke. It passes by me, ignoring my presence entirely, and approaches the window.

A thregas. Shadows take me, they're real.

Once the Kildara grow familiar with you, they'll show themselves.

It shies away as it slinks around me, a beast of smoke and darkness, ghostly claws gleaming and two eyes burning bright as coals. I dart away from it, scurrying behind the counter. But I don't run to the back room, or up the stairs. Something about the thregas commands my attention, and I watch it with rapt eyes. The shadow-beast makes it to the window and passes through. I can hear a sound like thunder far in the distance, a rumble that shakes the floorboards.

Then the souls' light disappears, and I'm once again caught only in the yellow illumination of my single candle. The thregas reappears on this side of the glass. A shape that might be its head lifts, as if it's looking at me. Then it sinks into the floor and is gone, save a ripple in one of the shadows on the floor.

Trying to breathe steadily, I put away my practice and scramble up the steps. This time, I'm grateful to close the door and shut myself away in that tiny cell of a room, far from unholy creatures, be they friend or no.

I long for the simple chores of an acolyte again. Those duties barely hold a candle to the nonstop grind of learning a cobbler's trade and trudging the streets trying to sell our wares. It's even taxing to prepare our own food each day, scraping every shred of meat from a bone, boiling the handfuls of lentils and shelling the few nuts we can afford. Not for us, the meaty, sweet, easy-to-crack virnuts. No, we're stuck with kers nuts, unhusked and unshelled, with only a tiny bit of bitter sustenance hidden in their mazelike shells.

Also, I had only three doses of Sidriel's medicine when I left, and I ran out nearly a month ago. All that remains is a little goldroot, which I hoard desperately. Aside from the near-constant pain in the back of my skull, my hands ache, thumbs bruised from the needle.

I'd thought someday I'd get used to the tightness in my stomach, the gurgle and knots of hunger, but I haven't.

Twice a week I wander through the marketplace, scrounging up what bargains I can for food. Offal and scraps are cheaper, or bones with a few bits still clinging to them if I'm lucky. But even those cost more than they did months ago. Summer should be only a few days away by now, and everything grows dearer in cost. Only a few types of vegetables yield anything edible anymore. The weather is always close enough to freezing that not many crops still thrive.

The berries and apples and other sweet fruits have long since gone away, save what people were able to dry or preserve, and jars of pickled cherries are far out of our price range. Chickens subsist on insects and table scraps or devour each other. Goats eat the thorny weeds that still manage to grow in this weather, or chew off tree bark. What meat I can find is stringy, sinewy, good for soup and not much else.

We're far from the only ones suffering. The Red Cough endlessly rattles through the city. Townsfolk grow lean, and moods are caustic when they muster any energy at all. Hollows hang beneath tired eyes, cheeks sunken.

Acolytes and priests venture into town as always, and now I notice how their hair is a bit glossier, their skin less sallow. Even they don't look quite as vibrant as they once did, but compared to the townsfolk, they're practically glowing. Some come to provide aid, to donate food or pass out medicine, but most are merely on their errands.

I never see Jaed, and I wonder if we merely have not crossed paths, or if he avoids the city now. Because of me? Or do they watch him, afraid he'll visit me if they let him out of their sight?

What do they expect him to do, if he did?

The Temple folk I do see avoid me, of course. Occasionally I'll catch one's eyes before recognition dawns on their face. Then their expression goes cold, embarrassed as they look away. I'm a true pariah now, anathema. To talk to me would risk their exile from the Temple as well, so they flow around me like a stone in a river's current, pretending they can't see me.

To them, I am a ghost.

Only I understand how deadly the true ghosts are.

I see them at night, outside the windows of the shop. Distorted, unholy things, creatures of shadow and eerie blue flame. Their teeth and claws grow sharp, their empty eyes ravenous. I don't know how I can still see them; that magic should have been taken from me along with Autumn's blood. Perhaps it's a new curse, punishment for such a miserable failure, to watch their misery.

And their hunger.

Now no one left out of doors at night will make it until morning. I found one once, a withered husk that used to be a person, huddled in the alley behind our shop. A bottle still lay clutched in their grasp with only a few drops of spirits left in the bottom. Most still believe such deaths are a result of the Cough. The Kildians claim it's the fault of the Temple faithful, that those found dead are being punished by the Kildara for their misplaced faith in the gods. They're not entirely wrong. It is the Mirror's shattering that did this, and Autumn's failure to fix it.

My failure.

Kildian numbers swell as more of the faithful abandon the gods. Stores and homes are deserted by the day, eerie monuments to those now gone. Those buildings now overflow with those who have nowhere else to go. By day, they cluster at the edges of the marketplace, desperate for any aid. At night, they seek cold shelter within the walls of shops long since left behind. Whether the owners died or left the city to seek greener pastures elsewhere, I'll never know.

What I do know is that there are no greener pastures. The whole of the continent is blanketed in this endless autumn.

I pity those without homes of their own, those even worse off than us. If not for Ilna, I'd be one of them now. When I lived in the Temple, I'd known such people existed, but either I was ignorant of their numbers or it's gotten worse. These are the people Jaed wanted me to see, to help. Now our lot is only a step better, and there is no aid I can give. We donate old boots to warm their feet sometimes. It's not like they're selling, anyway. No one wants new shoes anymore, especially the fancy beaded and embroidered kind that would once have filled Ilna's coffers.

It is not all misery, though. Ilna introduces me to the neighbors that still remain, her Kildian community. I attend the twelfth birthday celebration of the baker's nephew. Ilna made him a fanciful leather belt, tooled with patterns of swallows. Even in this time when we struggle to put food in our bellies, one of the boys' mothers sings loudly and a little off-key while everyone else takes turns leading the child in dances. He is shy around me, the one newcomer to their circle, but laughs gleefully when his mother twirls him in a reel.

It's a small thing, but those moments are the faint bit of hope that helps on the bad days.

Today, I visit the scraggly market. In the past, the first market day of the month would have been an event. Farmers would travel from outside the city, some that could only make the journey once a month, or even once a season. Honey from beehives would sit in fat pots on colorful tablecloths beside dipped beeswax tapers. Another stall would serve balls of spiced, peppery bread on skewers, fried fresh to order. Performers gave puppet shows or minstrels chose a corner to play for stray donations. Even Ilna sometimes had a table full of beribboned slippers and hardy leather sandals.

Some here still cling to that. One musician plays a wooden flute nearby, and she even has a few copper coins in the plate at her feet. Weavers still hawk colorful blankets and shawls. The fried bread stall is gone, though, and the beekeepers.

I thank the glowering merchant who sells me a bag of small, hard potatoes, and turn to head home. These should keep us both for a couple of fourdays, along with the precious dried beans we managed to trade a few of our scarce remaining candles for.

Longingly, I eye the stand where a hunter sells his wares. He sees me and gestures. "Best prices on hare in the city," he says. Those who can hunt or forage come to town from the grasslands outside the city, selling strips of smoked rabbit or turtle meat at exorbitant prices. Most of them were once farmers, now using the skills they'd honed protecting their crops to catch the pests for food instead. Someday, the rabbits and squirrels will run out, too.

I shake my head, lifting the bag of potatoes. "This is it for me today, sorry."

He watches me with eyes full of pity. Once, that would have filled me with indignant rage, but now all I feel is hope that perhaps it will tempt him to some act of charity.

It doesn't. He frowns and turns away to shill his wares to someone with a bit of coin instead.

At a nearby table, one of the city's pest-catchers displays a row of rat carcasses tied up with string for those who can't afford the hunters' rabbit, those desperate souls willing to pay a smaller fee and risk the disease such vermin carries.

How long until I am one of them?

I trudge home with my small treasures. Later, I'm reorganizing the back room's lower shelves when the bell rings. "I'll be right with you," I call, standing and dusting my hands on my apron as my back and knees creak. My head gives a warning throb when I stand. I've got only two doses left of the less-effective goldroot, now that Sidriel's potion is long gone. I don't know what I'll do when even the goldroot runs dry. Even that plain, herbal medicine is far out of my reach now.

"How . . . rustic." The voice behind me sends a shiver through my bones. A deep rasp I'd know anywhere.

"Sidriel," I hiss as I turn. He's sauntered into the back room like he owns the place. I shove at him in an attempt to force him back into the front shop area, but he stands his ground.

His eyes widen as he scans my body, up and down. I know what he sees, a shadow of the woman he once took to bed. Ilna has no mirrors in her home, but I can see my own hands growing knobby and skeletal. I wonder if the dark hollows beneath my eyes match Ilna's by now.

His voice softens. "Tirne . . ."

My hand moves of its own volition, slapping him hard. I don't even realize I'm going to do it until it's over, my palm stinging and Sidriel's cheek already reddening, a painful pink against his snowy white skin.

He frowns. "I suppose I deserved that."

"Murderer. You *framed* me!" My whole body shakes. I want to slap him again, to strangle the life from him. I've never felt such vicious fury. My chest heaves, and my rib cage hurts just looking at his face. "How did you even know I'd go to Laereda that night?"

"I wasn't certain. But I overheard her proposition you at the party, and I knew you'd seen us talking."

"How? How did you do it?"

"I had enough of your blood to tune a magical poison that would harm another, but not you. All I had to do was get you to drink it."

"But I didn't—" No. I did drink something that night in his room. A simple glass of water to refresh myself between our trysts. Fire and shadow. I *was* the weapon that killed Laereda. My teeth grind together, and I blink at the angry tears that threaten. What if I'd gone to someone else? To Jaed, to apologize? "Wren said you were a snake, and I didn't believe her. I should have. Did it bother you at all to betray me?"

He steps closer. "I have to wonder . . . what answer do you hope for? That I am racked with guilt, so you can forgive me? Or that I relished it, so you can despise me all the more fiercely? Which would bring you comfort at night?"

I stand wordlessly, shaking with fury.

Sidriel rubs his cheek where it still reddens. "I suppose it little matters. I'm here to offer a deal, and either you'll take it or you won't."

"About what? You've already won. You got me exiled, you have your vials of blood. Has the Tharem come to you yet, to get Spring's blood back?"

"He has. But men like that are easy to handle. I merely gave him enough money to keep his mouth shut."

Money. Sidriel has enough to feed me and Ilna for months. I wonder if I'll beg him for it. How far am I willing to go to ease the ceaseless knot in my belly? In Ilna's?

Sidriel sighs. "I need more of your blood. I am willing to compensate you for it, both in coin and in medicine. Goldroot grows scarce. I doubt you can afford it on your own now, and my potion is even better."

I glare, but I don't say no. Not yet. "Why do you even need my blood? Autumn's magic is gone."

He tilts his head. "Tell me, Herald. Do you still see the dead?"

And it sinks in. I curse under my breath. "You didn't take my magic."

"Not all of it, anyway. I left just a bit, the tiniest thread. Why would I sabotage my one reliable source of Autumn's blood? I knew once you were desperate, you'd give it to me once more."

My hand flits up to touch my chest. It's still within me, my magic. *Autumn's* magic.

"And we are still working on the Mirror. Are you ready to undo it yet, now that you see the true aftermath of what you've done?"

"What I've done?"

His stare could burn holes in me. "Breaking the Mirror."

"I didn't . . . I thought you believed me."

"Liar." This time, it's not a term of endearment. "I'd thought you were better than this. Do I need to leave for another month, let you grow even more desperate?"

"You're vile."

Any softness has drained from him, a cruel sneer touching his lips. "And yet I'll wager sometimes you still think about the things we did together and shiver, alone in your rickety cot at night."

I want to stab him, to choke him, to claw at his skin. I swallow hard. "I don't."

Again, his smile is cold, mocking.

I hate him.

But he's the only fragment of my old life to find me in this new one, and I miss the Temple with an ache so deep it cuts inside, like I've swallowed some of Ilna's hobnails. His sorcerer's robes are a velvet echo of the ones I used to wear. And he looks too much like an older version of Jaed. I miss my friend so fiercely that even this wicked reflection of him is enough to bring tears to my eyes.

My cheeks burn. No. I won't cry in front of Sidriel.

If I take his offer, he'll have more of my blood to do whatever he plots with it. I know now what a spider he is, weaving a web I don't quite see. He lies to get what he wants, and I don't know how much harm he'd do with my blood. As much as hunger chews at my guts, I can't let him. It pains me to say it, but I squeeze out a simple "No."

The sorcerer leans close, and I quash the urge to pull away as his lips touch my cheek. Gentle, a mockery.

He disgusts me.

His words are a low murmur. "You'll find no other aid. The Temple has guards now, you know. Your friends are as good as imprisoned, for fear they will come here to you. I'm your only refuge, and you will run out of coin someday, cobbler. I'll be back, and we'll see if your answer has changed."

THIRTY-THREE

S idriel was right. Less than a month after his visit, I'm forced to use my last dose of goldroot on a brutal headache that leaves me unable to keep my eyes open. The options are to take the gold-root or lie abed, and we can't afford that. I must venture into the city each day, knocking on doors to sell our shoes. We even barter our stores of silk and ribbon and beads, though only the wealthy take us up on those, or seamstresses who cater to the upper class.

The leather that has gotten too old and dry and cracked for shoes because we can't afford to oil it all anymore, that I sell to the poorer folk, those made desperate enough from the bite of hunger to cut up the leather and boil it into soups.

The hunger is bad enough, but the lack of medicine haunts me. What happens the next time I can't function through the pain? The next dozen times?

How long until we, too, boil bits and pieces of old leather for some-thing to fill our bellies? Sidriel's offer dangles before me, a carrot on a string. A rotten, worm-eaten carrot.

I just sold a spool of blue silk ribbon to a seamstress and managed to get more than we'd planned for it. These luxuries go to those who can afford to ignore what's happening. It's just a couple of spare copper sparrows, but it might be enough to buy me a small bottle of goldroot, from the right seller. My thoughts wander to the rundown shop with the Sylvus water, what seems like an eternity ago. I remember where it was, in a part of town I rarely venture into, at least not alone. But that sort of place might have what I need at the price I can afford. It'll be the cheap stuff, gritty and even more bitter for the lack of sugar. It'll dull the pain, though, and that's all I need.

A glance at the sky makes me shiver. It's nearly dusk, with just enough time to cut through the seedier part of town and stop by that shop before the souls emerge in the darkness. More have died in the streets at night, collected by the guard and tossed into unmarked communal graves at the edge of the cemetery. If the dead catch me out of doors after dusk, I won't last long.

I hurry, my pack light with the few things we could not sell. Mostly a few small tins of glass beads and our last half-used spool of crimson ribbon.

The shopkeeper doesn't seem to recognize me, and why should he? I was just a Temple acolyte come to visit one time, now some nameless cobbler. Here, even his shop grows barren, whole shelves empty.

Still, I find what I'm looking for, clearly labeled despite the shop's shabbiness. *Goldroot extract*, the price listed beside it. Four copper sparrows.

I point. "Would you take two sparrows? Or do you have a smaller bottle?"

He shakes his head. "Prices firm. That's all I got."

I could dip into the other money I have, tell Ilna that I got less for the ribbon and silk than I'd hoped. Or I could just tell her truth, but then she'd scold me for it. She, like most Kildians, distrusts medicinal herbs and potions. No, they prefer to use their herbs to entreat their heretical creatures for aid instead. Burned, or dried and hung on walls and doorways, but not consumed.

I shake my head. "Sorry, I can't. But thank you."

He shrugs, and I leave, rushing home before the dark catches me.

Sidriel's words rattle in my mind. *You will run out of coin someday, cobbler. I'll be back, and we'll see if your answer has changed.*

At the time I'd been defiant, but now I'm no longer so sure. I return to our shop with my pack and meager bag of coin. Ilna is sitting at the table, nose red and eyes puffy, cheeks damp.

I drop the bags on the table. "What's wrong?"

She shakes her head and wipes her face dry. "I suppose you stopped counting the days."

I stand beside her, putting a comforting hand on her shoulder while I take stock of the time. Fire and shadow, it'd be nearly a month into summer.

Tomorrow will be the anniversary of Mother's death.

I lift a hand to my collarbone, to the pendant of Mother's necklace. I still wear it, even though I've lost everything she wanted for me. It's my only connection to her.

Ilna's eyes follow the gesture, and I take a seat on the other side of the small table. Her words are soft, barely above a murmur. "It hurt so much to leave her, you know. To leave you." Ilna chews her lip, then stands to boil water for tea, although now it's mostly just woody chora root shavings. For a few moments, I think she won't talk, but then she clears her throat. "I always thought—hoped—that she'd follow me. That one day I'd hear that bell ring and she'd step through that door, hand in hand with you. Then . . . then she was gone."

"And only days after that, you tried to talk me out of the Temple." It was the last time I'd spoken to her, until this season. I was fourteen, and grieving. This aunt who'd abandoned us and didn't even attend Mother's memorial came to me, insisting I should become a cobbler. She wanted me to leave the only life I'd ever known, the peace of the Temple, and the god I'd devoted my life to.

I said no. Not gracefully. And she'd left.

"I know you still don't believe me." The kettle whistles and she takes it from the stove, pouring a pot to steep. "But the gods poison our world.

Before the Seasons were created, when it was just Lys and Kild, there was harmony. The Kildara lived in peace with us."

"Even the garvishes and kexas?" I don't mean my reply to come out as sharp as it does.

"Yes, even them. They turned when their god was taken from them. They blamed humans for our failure to protect their father and for believing the gods' lies."

I chew on my lower lip. Autumn's confession about Serrema haunts me.

Ilna continues as she pours us both tea into wooden cups. "Kild wanted peace for us, for humans and shadows and gods. But Lys was selfish and made the Seasons, each given a portion of Lys's power. But only a scrap of it. They were incomplete, lacking. Cold, inhuman. So they need to leech human energy to feel, to live. Kild saw how this affected humans, and split the world in two. But while he was weakened, Lys created the Mirrors, and the gods cast Kild down. But then the gods learned that if too many of them remained in our new realm at once, humans grow weak. It's like having too many cats in a barn. They eat all the mice and have nothing left to live on. So the Seasons take their turns devouring us slowly."

"That's not true," I say weakly. "Kild was jealous. The gods saved us from his tyranny." But if Autumn and the others lied about Serrema, about the fact that they could die and transfer their power, what else might they be keeping from us?

I can't believe it, though. My entire faith can't have been a lie.

This time, Ilna lets the matter rest, going silent again. The only sound is the thunk of the cups on the table, the slosh of the tea.

When she breaks the quiet, Ilna just says softly, "I miss her."

"I do, too."

"I . . . I'd like to visit her. If you'll go with me."

A nod. "Have you, before?"

"No. I was ashamed. But now I think I can."

"When?"

She finishes off her tea. "Let's go tomorrow at dawn, before we open the shop."

Again, I nod.

The next morning, we leave while the sunrise still paints the sky gold. The souls have drifted away, banished by morning's light. I lead Ilna to Mother's mausoleum, my steps heavy. We have nothing to give her in offering, no flowers or candied nuts or funeral bread. But I know she wouldn't care. Mother never said it, but I knew she missed Ilna deeply. Sometimes she'd start humming a song that Ilna used to sing, then she'd go very quiet for a while.

The graveyard had always seemed a peaceful place to me, but as we approach, we're passed by a wide cart drawn by a heavy-footed mule and led by a man in black. A large tarp covers the mound atop the cart.

Corpses.

A chill washes over me. Are they the victims of ravenous souls or the Cough or hunger? Does it even matter anymore?

We watch the cart pass in silence. The collector of the dead leads the mule through the gates, down the wide path along the center of the cemetery, toward the back places where those who cannot afford a proper funeral are buried in mass graves.

Somber, we turn aside and take the path leading to Mother's resting place. We don't speak of the cart, silence heavy between us. When we arrive at the mausoleum, Ilna takes a deep, shuddering breath. "Do you mind if I . . . if we're alone for a bit?"

"Go on."

Ilna stays inside for a long time. I wait, leaning against the cool stone. When she emerges, her face is pink again, eyes swollen. I don't remark on it, but we share a nod as I enter. To Mother, I say my greeting, my goodbye. I reassure her that I'll be all right, even if I don't truly believe it.

Ilna and I don't speak after I come out into the morning sunlight, blinking. But as we head home, Ilna's hand finds mine.

THIRTY-FOUR

As days pass, Sidriel's offer continues to haunt me. Every time I'm stirring our thin soups, I think of him, of the money he offered just for more of my blood. And I think of how much food I could have bought with it, how Ilna and I could rest, or at least afford to burn wood to heat the home rather than the small amount we use only for cooking. The weather never quite freezes, but the deepest parts of the night are just bitter enough that I pile blankets atop myself and still shiver.

I don't tell Ilna that I turned down an offer of help. Would she accept it from a Scion of a god, even one that left the faith?

Instead, we get to know one another as the adults we have become. She was younger than I am now when she left the Temple, and I haven't seen her since I was still playing make-believe games with Jaed in the gardens between our lessons.

She'd always been humming something back then, no matter what task occupied her hands. Now, though they're often her atonal, wandering Kildian hymns, she also sings more familiar songs in a lilting voice. Never Temple hymns, but folk songs and lullabies and even a few bawdy tavern ditties that leave me in stitches.

As long as I'm not disparaging her faith, Ilna's humor sparkles in small moments. The odd jest or gibe is a breath of fresh air. I no longer mock her belief in the Kildara, now that I've seen the thregas myself.

And not just that one. Others now creep out of corners, flickering shapes half-seen from the corner of my eye. One, the herren, sometimes ventures to slink near me but always darts away.

"They say they can still smell the Temple on you," Ilna tells me as we shell nuts at the kitchen table with a hammer. I crack them, then slide them over to her so she can pick the meats out. The shells are tossed beneath the table, an offering for the herren, who skitters back and forth across the floor. It looks like a smoky echo of a ferret or weasel, as best I can tell from glimpses. I can barely keep all her sacrifices to these Kildara straight. Bones for the thregas, glass beads and other shiny trinkets for the illip, nut shells for the herren to bring us prosperity. I don't know why she bothers with that one anymore, but I keep my mouth shut.

"I've been gone from the Temple for months," I say, though I know why the Kildara still shun me. I still possess the last traces of Autumn's blood.

Sidriel hasn't returned yet, and I don't know how long he will wait. If he showed up today, I fear I'd take him up on his offer. My head pounds with every blow of the hammer on the worn tabletop, my stomach endlessly clenched and queasy.

"I . . . I made you something that might help," Ilna says cautiously. She pushes back her chair and leaves the kitchen, returning with something in one hand. A curved rectangle of black leather, with a simple buckle to hold it together.

A Kildian cuff.

My heartbeat stutters. No. I know the Kildara are real now, but they are not mine. Autumn is still my god.

Is he? I was cast out, no longer welcome. I'm adrift.

Ilna sets the cuff on the table. "You don't need to decide right now. I know how hard it is to leave everything behind. But I think the Kildara would accept you if you bore a symbol of your faith in them."

She's so certain I'll turn my back on everything I've known.

But what's left to turn aside from? My old life is already gone. I won't ever return to it.

With shaking fingers, I reach out to brush the leather, supple and well-oiled and dyed the deepest black. Autumn rejected me, left me out in the cold. His pain when he thought me a murderer leaves me wondering what I'd once meant to him. I never got to learn the meaning behind those wounded stares, or his gloved caress against my cheek. It was ripped from me so suddenly, that tie severed cleanly.

Well, maybe not cleanly. Messy and painful and lingering.

Perhaps this is the answer. A full break, a symbol that I have left that life behind and begun a new one.

Before I can overthink it, I nod. "Yes."

Ilna grins widely, holding the cuff open. I place my wrist on it, and she fastens the buckle. It feels like a manacle, and panic washes over me. I suck in a deep breath. No. I'm not betraying my faith, my god. I can't betray something that is no longer mine.

Still, the snug leather feels heavy on my wrist, even as Ilna's eyes well with happy tears.

"Do you want me to come to your services now, too?" The Kildians don't have a set house of worship, not like the Temple, but I know Ilna goes to worship with others in their homes, sometimes, to make offerings to the Kildara and sing their songs. I wonder if it's more about having a community than anything. That's a part of the Temple I miss dearly, the familiarity of being around others like me.

"Only if you want to," she says.

My reply is interrupted by a delicate scratching on the side door, like tree branches against window shutters. With a glance at Ilna, I stand to check it.

No one is there, save a smoky form roughly the size and shape of a hawk. Ephemeral wings open and flap once, twice, and it launches into the sky, an elongated shadow along the alley wall. Where it sat, two fat pigeon carcasses rest instead.

"The illip," Ilna says softly behind me, her hand resting on my shoulder. "It's welcoming you. Well, that, and bringing gifts in exchange for more beads and baubles."

The two dead birds are cold, such a light weight in my hands as I bring them inside.

It's been so long since I had squab, or even chicken or other poultry, but I spent my share of hours preparing them in the kitchen at the Temple. Ilna and I quickly set to readying the birds for plucking. Once, this would have been a meager bit of meat. Now it's a feast. We'll stew them, of course. Can't waste anything, not even the tiny hearts and livers.

As I scoop the nuts aside to prepare the birds, the ferret-like herren hops up on the table, a shadow on the silvery wood. I reach out and brush the spot where its head would be, and I can almost feel it thrum in pleasure like a cat's purr.

I twist the cuff on my wrist. It binds tightly, a weight, an accusation of my treachery. But I stare down at the pigeon before me, and my eyes brim with tears.

Sidriel had told me I'd find no other aid, no other shelter. He was wrong.

All it took was abandoning everything I'd ever known.

THIRTY-FIVE

Summer is halfway through—or it should be—when my aunt first coughs. The sudden fit consumes her, leaving her leaning against the countertop.

"Ilna." I stand to help her, but she waves me off.

"I'm fine," she rasps. But I know she isn't. I experienced that cough, wet and hacking. She won't listen to my protests, my insistence at rest. Instead, Ilna goes about her day as normal, no matter how her breathing rattles.

The next morning, she's not in the kitchen when I awaken. Fear slices through me, and I dart back up the stairs, knocking on her door. "Ilna!"

At her faint reply, I open the door to find her curled on her side in bed, her hair plastered to her scalp with sweat. Even as I watch, another cough seizes her.

Kneeling beside her, I press my hand to her forehead. This can't be happening. *She'll be all right.* But deep down, I fear. I survived the Red Cough, but I was well-fed and under the care of high priests with their magical remedies. I also had Autumn's blood.

Ilna is frail, weaker than I was, malnourished and without medicine.

But I know someone who can help, if I can get a message to her.

Wren. I squeeze my aunt's hand. Leaving a glass of water by her bedside, I venture out into the breezy autumn weather, locking the shop behind me.

I could send a message to Sidriel instead, offer him more of my blood to heal Ilna. But Wren will help a suffering soul without asking for payment, I know that much. Sidriel might just wait to see if my aunt dies, leaving me destitute and even more needy.

No. Wren it is.

The sight of the guards standing by the Temple gates unsettles me. I'm even more concerned by the knives they wear at their belts. I lift my head, pull my cloak hood tighter, and make to stride through the doors as if I belong there. Just another worshipper from the city here for morning prayer.

"Hold," one of the priests says, and I recognize him. One of Autumn's high priests, older than me by a decade or so. We did not know each other well, but well enough that he recognizes my face, grabbing me by the arm and yanking me aside. "Tirne of Au—" he bites off the word. "Tirne. You are forbidden from the Temple. We're not even supposed to exchange words with you."

"I just need to get a message to someone," I plead. I reach into my pocket to withdraw the hasty note I'd scribbled. "Can you get this to Wren? She's one of the sorcerers here?"

He glances down at the note, then back up at my face, his jaw clenched.

"Please," I whisper, my voice breaking. "My aunt is sick, and Wren could save her. Sorcerer Wren is not of the faithful, not forbidden from talking to me. Please," I repeat.

He snatches the paper from my hands and nods sharply. "Go."

It's not a promise, but it's the best I can hope for.

Though I know it will be fruitless, I ask around for a simple, nonmagical physician. They've been unable to stop the spread of the Cough, but I need to do something, *anything*. But when I do manage to find one whose shop remains open, she laughs bitterly.

"There's no medicine left," she says. "The herbs we needed are all gone, spring flowers. What little help they could give can't be found anymore."

I return to the shop empty-handed and panicking. My breaths are rapid, quick. My usual headache burns. Still, after checking on Ilna to find her in much the same position and urging her to drink some water, I sit on the floor beside her bed, staring at the ceiling, wincing at her every cough.

The shop remains closed that day. I boil soup with the last batch of goat's bones for the third time, knowing that this broth is little more than hot water with a few dried beans thrown into it. Still, I force Ilna to drink it. Nothing I can do will help her breathe easier, though, or stop the rattle that has settled into her lungs.

Wren will get my note. The priest at the door will give it to her. He wouldn't be so callous as to let an innocent woman die, would he?

A full day passes, and I have my answer. Wren never got the letter, or she couldn't escape the Temple. I don't believe the alternative, that she would abandon my aunt to the Cough.

The next afternoon, I find myself standing before a shop much finer than my aunt's. I've avoided even walking by Sidriel's apothecary since leaving the Temple. The building is made of solid brick rather than wood, and the sign is painted with elaborate care, obviously done by a hired artist. *Potions and Remedies*, it reads in lovely script.

It doesn't say anything about poisons.

I come prepared to pay any price he demanded, warm his bed for a year or bleed into a hundred vials, but it's shuttered, closed. No one remains here while he stays at the Temple. I collapse onto the doorstep, my back against the door, squeezing my eyes shut as the tears fall.

"Miss?" The voice is hesitant, almost frightened.

I look up to see a youth, maybe sixteen or so. His rosy-gold hair gives him away as a child of Spring, but he does not wear the bright green of a Spring priest. No, his robe mimics Sidriel's in deep midnight blue.

I swear at myself. "Shadows take me, of course he has apprentices."

I don't realize I spoke aloud until the boy steps back cautiously. "Um, are you all right?"

Standing, I ask him, "You're Sidriel's apprentice, aren't you? Can you take him a message, up in the Temple? It's . . . it's urgent."

The boy's eyes widen as he stares at my face. "Fire and shadow . . . you're *her.*"

No use denying it. I nod. "Go to him immediately. Tell him my aunt is ill, and I'll do whatever he asks if he can save her. He knows where to find me."

The apprentice hesitates, chewing on a lip. I wonder how much Sidriel has told him of whatever he plots. Does this child know secrets I don't?

Whatever he knows, he makes a decision. "I'll go."

Heavy silence hangs in the shop when I return. Panic claws at me, and I bolt to Ilna's room.

Too late.

Her skin already has the waxy look of death, and her raspy breathing has gone still. Shadows writhe over her form, the anguished spirits of the house. Still I shake her as tears burn my eyes. No. This can't be happening. She was all I had left.

It's a gruesome echo of that morning I woke up next to Laereda's body. All my cries and denials do no good here, either.

She's gone.

I hug my knees to my chin on her bedroom floor and give in to the despair, my sobs harsh and spiky things. We just found each other again. How cruel is fate, to rip her life from her now?

I don't know how long I spend there, but I'm jolted into awareness by a loud pounding on the front door. At first, I hope they'll just give up and go away. But the knocking continues, incessant.

With leaden feet, I plod down the stairs to tell them the shop is closed. Will always be closed. I don't know how to run it. I'll have to sell it and make another path for myself.

When I open the door, Sidriel doesn't mince words. "Where is she?"

I choke on my fury. "You're too late." A rasping, keening sound seeps from me.

His eyes go wide. "No. Let me see her. She might be—"

I'm embarrassed by the flare of ridiculous hope in my chest. Even Autumn can't bring back the dead. Not even Spring. Sidriel certainly can't. Still, I can barely hold myself together, let alone stop him from striding through the door carrying a large bag. A few steady breaths later, I follow.

I find him kneeling by Ilna's bedside. He glances up at me, and his eyes say it all. "I'm sorry."

"You're only sorry you lost a bargaining chip. I don't care anymore. Let me starve. I won't ever help you."

"I—"

"Go!" I scream the word, yanking him out of the room and shoving him down the hall, down the stairs.

With one last, indecipherable look, he goes. The bell over the door chimes merrily on his way out.

The rest of the day passes in a hazy blur. I find the undertaker, and he comes for the body. I can't afford a memorial stone or proper burial for her. She'll go into that unmarked common grave in the easternmost part of the cemetery.

And I'm left to decide what to do next.

The next day, I spread word that the shop is for sale, whole cloth. I want no part of anything within it.

Ilna's friends and fellow Kildians stop by to offer sympathy, but even they have little charity left to give. A few woody vegetables, some dried nettles for tea. One gives me a woolen shawl, a bit worn but once a lovely shade of green.

Their charity might help for a few days, but all too soon I'll be out of food entirely.

I go to market and sell Jaed's beaded bracelet and Mother's necklace. Both pieces sell for a fraction of what they once would. No one wants gold anymore. "Can't eat it or burn it," the jeweler grumbles.

It's irrational to feel so broken by the loss of simple stones and a bit of metal, but it feels like tearing out a piece of me to hand it over to this stranger, just for a bit of food that will be gone all too quickly. In some ways, it's like discarding the last tiny scrap of hope that I would ever see my old life again. But I suppose I gave that up when I donned the black cuff around my wrist. It's not worth my life, not worth starving, and these meager coins will keep me fed for a little longer.

Hopefully the shop will sell by then. If not, I don't know what I'll do next.

That evening, a faint knock comes on the side door by the kitchen. For a moment, I almost imagine a twinge of sadness and sympathy that isn't mine, a shadow of what I once felt from my god. When I open the door, a package rests on the ground, a small parcel wrapped in plain brown paper. With a confused glance up and down the alley, I pick it up and carry it inside.

My eyes burn after unwrapping it, my vision blurring with tears.

It's a small loaf of dark bread, made with precious rye. The scent of it is rosemary and herbs, wafting upward. Creases mark three separate pieces, ready to be pulled apart.

Funeral bread. This is a gift only given to those in mourning, a comfort to feed them so they may take three days to rest and grieve.

Who left this? Jaed? Wren? How did they sneak it out of the Temple?

But when I lift the bread, something else lies beneath the loaf. A single, brilliantly orange leaf as big as my hand.

No.

It was truly Autumn's sorrow I felt, then. My god has defied his own decree to bring me this charity. How human it is, such hypocrisy. How mortal.

It terrifies me, even as I pick up the leaf and twirl it in my fingers. It could merely be a symbol of my former devotion, a gift from anyone. It could be a mockery, part of a cruel joke. But I lift the leaf to my nose, and it smells of my god. Every scent of autumn, pumpkin and hay and apple.

My breath is stilted, my heart beating fast as I set the leaf next to the bread. I tug at the cuff on my left wrist, a glaring reminder that I betrayed Autumn. But still, my stomach grumbles at the smell, and I tear off a piece. There's no sense in letting the gift go to waste, even if it did come from a man who was once a god, now mortal enough to feel human sympathy.

I manage to stretch the bread and other charity to last six days. Sometimes, I remember what it was like to live each day without worrying where my next meal would come from. And every night, the dead mock me, their eerie glow dancing outside the windows, scratching at the shutters of the shop I cannot sell.

A fourday after that, I have only a single copper sparrow left to my name.

I dig out my old journal, unused since I left the Temple, and flip to the last page. It bears a list of suspects, including ones I never cleared, like Calder. Ironically, Sidriel's name stares up at me, crossed out, eliminated as a possible culprit before I truly knew how far his deception and cruelty could go.

Tearing out one of the pages, I pull out a bottle of ink, mostly dry. A few drops of water sloshed into the bottle make it usable once more. With quick, jerky motions, I pen a simple note.

I know about the water. You know where to find me, and what I want. Come tomorrow, or I will make it known.

—Tirne

Simple and to the point. I learned my lesson with my note to Wren, and don't take the letter to the Temple doors. I roll it up and stitch it inside a tube of scrap leather, so the sinew will need to be cut to read it. Then I take it to a courier service, who agrees to run a message to the Temple and the Tharem for a copper. The man gives me a puzzled glance, likely wondering why I don't just take it myself. The Temple is only on the city's outskirts. Still, he takes my money and agrees to deliver the letter. I go home to live among Ilna's Kildara, and I wait. Without a buyer for the shop, I've resorted to blackmail, and I can't even bring myself to feel guilty about it.

The next afternoon, the knock comes from the kitchen side door. It's not the Tharem that awaits me, but Bix's worried face. His scent clogs my nostrils, clove and sandalwood. He must have been at incense duty this morning.

"I need to talk to you."

"About what?"

"Jaed."

Alarm flickers through me. "Is he safe?"

Bix chews his lip and looks down the alley. "Can we talk inside?"

I step aside, and he enters. "What's wro—" Before I can finish the sentence, someone slips in behind him.

The Tharem. "Hello, Tirne." His grin is vicious, and he shuts the door, locking it.

Panic floods through me, and confusion. "Bix—" But Bix's hand darts out and grips my throat. He tosses me into the kitchen chair. I scramble to get up, to run, but Bix says a word in a language I don't know and makes a small gesture.

A shadow rises up beside him, one I've seen before. The thregas. The one that protects this home.

Yes. It will save me, just as it fought the souls away that night.

But instead, the creature lunges, slipping through me in a blast of cold. It looms at my back as I try to stand. Ghostly claws slide down my arms and pin my wrists to the table. I struggle, but it holds me fast. It looks like sooty smoke but is solid as stone. Its presence at my back is icy, heavy.

"What—"

Bix snaps, "Quiet." The word is harsh, a command. This is a version of the man I've never seen. His gaze flickers down to my wrist, to my Kildian cuff, and he laughs. It's a harsh, mocking sound, something I never thought I'd hear from him.

"Bix," I plead as the Tharem comes to stand beside him. "What's going on?"

"You made a threat," Bix says calmly. "One we can't let stand."

Shadows take me. *Bix* is working with the Tharem. Someone whose name never graced my journal's notes. But why? How? And how is he controlling the thregas?

I splutter, "What are you—"

The Tharem interrupts. "You don't ask the questions." But he looks at Bix after he says it, as if for approval.

Bix stands silent, but more shadows gather around him—the herren, and something with flapping wings, barely visible. They writhe around him in smoky swirls. He lifts a hand to caress one, the same way I used to do with the dead souls. And he murmurs soft words to them in that strange, sibilant language I heard him speaking before.

At the time, he'd said it was Pseran. But it's not. He speaks their language, and they obey.

"The shadow on the wall that day you claimed to rehearse a poem, it wasn't a trick of my mind. It was a Kildara."

He nods grimly.

"How? They hate the Temple."

"They like me more."

It makes no sense, but the Tharem interrupts before I can ask another question. "We should just kill her. Then no one will know."

Ice slithers down my spine. I try to yank free of the thregas's grasp, but I might as well fight steel manacles.

A shake of Bix's head. "Even though we were careful, it is possible we were seen. I refuse to leave a trail for others to follow, evidence they could link to us. Especially now that we're so close."

I ask, "Close to what?"

He ignores me. Bix says more words in that strange language, and another creature shimmers to life in the air between us, a flickering darkness in a serpent shape. Two glowing eyes form in the misty black, a pale luminescent yellow. Another word from Bix and the creature darts toward my face.

I feel it in my nostrils, my throat, a cold that feels like drowning. I gasp, but the sudden pain inside my skull is worse than any headache.

Bix says something else to the shadow creature crawling around in my brain, and the agony is too much to bear. I wonder if this is what dying is like. Then the darkness claims me.

I awaken with a jolt. I don't remember going to bed last night. In fact, the whole evening is a hazy blur. I ache all over, like my whole body is bruised. I wonder what I did in my latest mental fog. Fire and shadow, just how bad have my headaches and poor memory become? It's worrying to know that I somehow overexerted myself and still don't remember any of it.

The pain in my head today is particularly sharp. It leaves me wanting to lie abed, but if I intend to have breakfast tomorrow, I need to find something else to barter and head to the market.

I smell the ghost of spice and incense halfway down the stairs. That tiny whiff brings back a slurry of emotions. It's our same plain cobbler's shop, but it smells like the Temple, like home, the scent of morning devotions. But where did it come from? I check the kitchen's side door and find it unlocked. A panicked search through the place reveals that nothing else was disturbed. The chair is pushed out from the table, rather than tucked in as usual, but I've been careless before in the throes of a headache.

Perhaps I truly am going mad. But there's little enough I can do on that, except gather up another roll of ribbon and try to hawk it in exchange for something to fill my belly for another day or two.

THIRTY-SEVEN

I've grown to loathe that bell over the shop door, its tinny sound a cheerful taunt. It rattles around my throbbing head, a special sort of torment. I could rip it from the door frame, but I need it as much as I hate it, at least while the shop remains for sale.

Today, I haul myself from the kitchen when I hear the bell's call, where I'm boiling some chicken's feet left by the illip. I have no idea what happened to the rest of the chicken. They're tossed in with a few scraggly cabbages and the scraps of a worm-ridden beetroot. Sometimes I wonder if I really remember what pepper tasted like, or mint, or fresh succulent pork stewed in butter. Are those just figments, dreams of a life that never existed?

The headaches are relentless now, a constant ebb and flow of agony, but it is just more background noise among the other miseries. I suppose a person can get used to anything.

I stop short in the doorway. A pale, indigo-robed figure stands in the front of the shop.

"What are you doing here?" I tremble. Anger, frustration, and maybe a little fear that Sidriel, too, bears yet more bad news. "Checking to see if I'm still alive? To see if you can drain my corpse of blood like a slaughtered pig?" I can't control the tide of fury and despair that washes over me. Everything is too close to the surface.

In the face of my anger, Sidriel holds his distance. "I just wanted . . ." He hesitates.

"To watch me on my knees? To laugh?" My hands clutch the hem of my shirt, balling into fists. My breathing is ragged, the words crackling and brittle.

He flinches. "I came to make an offer on the shop."

That makes me freeze. "What?"

"I was told it was for sale. I have the money."

I scan his face for the jeer, the lie. "What game is this?"

"No game," he says quietly, this time taking a cautious step to stand beside a counter that once held a display of shoes, now empty. "A simple exchange. Money for the store. Nothing more."

"Why?"

A pause. He stares at my collarbone, not meeting my eyes.

"Sidriel." His gaze flicks up to mine as I ask, "What are you plotting? Just tell me."

He shakes his head. "If you don't want to take the offer, don't." He turns to go.

"Wait."

He pauses.

"You aren't even going to ask for my blood?"

A bitter laugh. "Why ask when I already know your answer?"

"You said it yourself. You have money."

"Would you even take payment for blood, if you won't take an honest sale for the shop?"

No, but I expected him to try. "Why did you need it, really? Autumn's blood. You told me a different story than Laereda."

"I did."

I meet his conflicted stare, determined not to blink.

He speaks first. "How did you break the Mirror?"

"I didn't. I've told you that, again and again."

"And you're a liar. Why do you think I framed you? I saw the notes of the curse in your room, in your own handwriting. One that involved the Mirror and your name. Even I haven't managed to untangle it fully."

I swear. That night I found my books and notes disturbed. "It was you who went through my things?"

"You crept into my room first and went straight to the box with Spring's blood. I had to make sure you were what you seemed. Later, when I found that spell among your belongings, what else could I surmise but that you were complicit?"

A desperate, fractured sound bubbles from me, and it could only barely be called a laugh. "I found that spell in Calder's room and copied it. It was a *clue*, you idiot."

"On Serrema's Eve, I asked you if there was anything else you had forgotten to share. I gave you the chance to tell me."

He had. And I'd said no. "I didn't trust you, either."

"Well, trust me now. There's a very obvious reason I want the blood of the gods." He clears his throat. "How was the Mirror created in the first place?"

"With Lys's blood." Everyone knows that.

"The father of the Seasons. The ones who bear his bloodline. Yes."

Realization settles over me. "Shadows take me, you actually *have* been trying to restore the Mirror this whole time?"

His smile is wry. "I told you I never lied to you. And I haven't. To Laereda, yes. You? Never."

"But you still didn't tell me everything."

"No, I didn't. For the same reason you kept your secrets."

"But you murdered Laereda."

"She threatened to bring everything crashing down. If she told Autumn that I had Spring's stolen blood, I'd have been forbidden from the Temple at the very least. And I needed to be close to the Mirror. She could have doomed us all."

"You *killed* her."

"I swore I'd fix the Mirror, whatever it takes. One life or millions? Not everyone has the luxury of such high morals."

Deep breaths. This entire time, Sidriel was working toward the same goal I was, depraved as his methods were. "Do you have the blood of the other two gods?"

"Not yet."

"Why not just tell Autumn you need the blood?"

"Autumn has become . . . unstable. He's grown morose, his moods erratic. He wanders the halls in a daze, when he even leaves his room. I fear he's grown too human. With all a human's faults, and potential for lies and deception."

But one piece still lies outside the puzzle. "Calder had an enchanted drawer in his desk. When I touched it, the latch gave me the same jolt as your box. How? You're not an alchemist. And I saw him coming to your room once."

Sidriel snorts. "He enchanted the box of Spring's blood without knowing what was in it, in exchange for medicine. Well, a drug. The man's addicted to a particular stimulant. Strong. Not strictly legal."

Calder's constant fidgeting, his too-bright eyes. It all fits.

"And you just give it to him?"

"If I don't, he'll seek it out elsewhere, and get an impure batch laced with fillers that poison him. I've been slowly lowering the amount of stimulant, diluting it a little each time with another one that's less addictive and harmful. He doesn't know that."

Sidriel is actually *helping* Calder? In his weird, twisted way?

His voice drops. "You said the spell notes were in Calder's room?" There's cold steel in the question, and it makes my stomach turn.

Have I just sentenced another man to death at the hands of this cruel healer? "Will you hurt him?" I still find it hard to believe the blushing, nervous Calder could do this.

"I make no promises. And if you won't sell the shop, we're done here."

I want to take his offer. I need it. I've less than a month before I'm boiling old shoe leather for food and burning my own furniture to cook it. But I shake my head. "Not from you. Not from a killer."

Sidriel dips a hand into his robe's pocket and sets something on the nearby counter. A bottle, green as a beetle's wing, sloshing with dark liquid. It thunks on the wood.

Medicine.

While I stand there, speechless, he leaves. Long after he's gone, I cross the room and pick up the bottle, swirling it.

Do I trust him? What if this whole thing—the dropping of walls, the sharing of information—was all another ploy?

Then I notice the two gold falcons lying underneath the bottle. I curse Sidriel for the gesture, but I clutch them tightly in my palm. This much can feed me for days upon days, if I'm careful.

I tuck them away, my pride keeping me from rushing out to buy food immediately. However, I manage to last only two days before I'm miserable enough to try his potion. When I awaken and every scrap of light is a dagger behind my eyes, I swallow a spoonful. If he's decided to poison me, Sidriel has chosen a roundabout way to do it.

The pain fades within minutes, and I curl up in bed, weeping in relief. I feel like someone awakened from sleepwalking, but my current reality is its own nightmare.

My mind replays that visit from Sidriel over and over. Why did he want to buy the shop? What is his plan?

A deep, uneasy part of me fears there isn't one, but that's even more terrifying. What if, instead of some nefarious scheme, Sidriel had come to make his offer out of true pity?

I'm not sure which is worse.

THIRTY-EIGHT

A numbness settles over me. Today, in a moment of weakness, I splurged on smoked hare from a traveling hunter. Even though I chose not to spend extra for spices, it feels like a delicacy. Sidriel's charity has kept me alive for another half a month so far, with coin still left to spare, but even this decadence can't truly lift my spirits. It should be the end of summer. In a normal year, I'd be in Sylvus right now, preparing for my arrival a few days hence. It's hard to believe I've been in this realm a full twelve months.

After the first few bites of rabbit, my stomach turns, and soon I'm heaving up the precious meat into the alleyway. It seems my stomach is so used to emptiness and thin soup that even the richness of this lean game is enough to make me sick. Instead, I reluctantly shred the meat into a pot for still more soup, hoping that diluting it in broth won't make me sick again.

As I sit back at the table, a shadow flickers across my floor. I sigh and let my hand hang down from the edge of the chair like I once would have for a Temple cat. The darkness slithers over and wraps my hand, cool like a breeze. I can almost see its shape, long-bodied and short-legged like a weasel. The herren.

"Should I be thanking you for those coins?" I murmur at it. Ilna had always said they brought wealth. Maybe it was the herren's luck that touched Sidriel's heart with sympathy.

He hasn't been back, though. It seems he truly has given up on my blood.

And me.

The herren swirls around my hand, its coldness brushing the black cuff on my wrist.

I finish my cup of cooling tea and stand to rinse my wooden plate in the corner bucket. At least the nearby well still provides clean water, and it's time to go fetch more. As I pick up the bucket, the herren skitters away.

I throw on my cloak and lock the shop behind me as I trudge up the streets. The sky is clear, but cold. Another twilight in-between day, trapped in that space between autumn and winter when it's not quite freezing, but brisk. Only days away from a full year since autumn fell, and I've no idea how much of the Mirror is assembled. If Sidriel is still working on a plan to restore the magic, I wonder how much longer it will take.

Pain lances through my skull with every footstep, and I hurry to the well. Afterward, I'll return to the shop, take a tiny, precious dose of Sidriel's medicine, and sleep this off. But when I get to market, there's a strange, crackling energy among the crowd. Excited whispers flitter back and forth, and people are smiling. Laughing, even.

I stop at a pig-monger's stall, selling a few thin and ill-looking hogs he can't afford to feed. "What's going on?"

"You haven't heard? They're fixing the Mirror next autumnsday. This season will finally be over."

A ringing begins in my ears.

Fixing the Mirror. In three days.

A queasy mix of emotions churns within me. Relief. Joy. Bitterness. Grief. Soon things will return to normal. Winter will come, and with it even more death until Spring arrives. But Ilna will still be gone, and I still have nowhere to turn.

Autumn once told me that fixing the Mirror might take all the blood in his body. Did he give someone else the task of choosing his possible successor?

My heart twists in my chest. I remember that loaf of funeral bread that was dropped on my step, a single autumn leaf wrapped up beneath it. He banished me. I shouldn't still feel this way about my god.

But I do.

The thought of losing him forever is like breathing glass. My whole life has spun around him. At least it did, once.

I suck in a jagged breath and dazedly make my way to the well.

The next morning, I'm boxing away the last of the cobbler's tools. If I need to, I'll start selling these off one-by-one. Soon I'll have to get more money for kindling or use the furniture to keep the stove burning for meals.

I don't know how I'm going to make it through three bitterly cold months of winter unless someone buys the shop. But for now, I can only exist day-to-day.

The doorbell rings as someone enters, and I look up. It's an acolyte of Autumn. Not one I know well, but she wears the unmistakable russet robes. She ducks her head in a nod. "Tirne of Autumn."

"Not anymore."

She ignores that. "You are summoned, by edict of Autumn and the Emperor. Your exile is rescinded for one day only, this upcoming autumnsday. You are to arrive in the courtyard at ten bells in the morning."

I hate the way my heart leaps at the announcement, even if it's for a single day. Commanded not just by my god, but the Emperor himself. "Why?"

"As the one who was originally cursed to break it, your blood is needed to undo the spell and restore the Mirror."

I swallow. "How much of it?"

"I was not informed of that."

Would it take everything in me? Will they kill me to bring it back?

"I was told to obtain your promise you will come. If you are not there on time, the Emperor will send guards to fetch you, willing or not."

A grimace tugs on my mouth. "I understand."

"Farewell, then."

The door chimes behind her, and I sink into a chair, head spinning. They're fixing it. And they need me to do it. For one precious morning, I'll be home again. Maybe my last morning ever. But if I'm going to die, I'd rather do it on those courtyard tiles than starving to death here in misery.

The herren nuzzles my hand with its ephemeral snout, and I take what comfort it can give.

THIRTY-NINE

When twilight falls, I lie in bed, haunted by too many thoughts. Tomorrow should be the first day of Autumn, but instead, it will be the dawn of a new Winter. Sidriel must have succeeded. He got the blood of all four gods.

All he needs is me.

I've just rearranged the blankets for the dozenth time when a sound echoes from the front door. A steady rap, neither insistent nor tentative.

Why am I consistently plagued by visitors every time I seek a little peace? And who would come to my door at dusk, when even the most strident of unbelievers fears to venture out after dark anymore? "We're closed," I grumble as I yank open the door.

I don't expect to see Autumn on the other side.

And I particularly hadn't imagined him in a simple robe, roughly belted at the waist. His cloak of leaves is absent. A plain, brown one replaces it, the hood drawn up to shade his features. "Can I come in?"

My tongue freezes. Not only is he standing here on Ilna's stoop, disheveled, he's making a request. Not a command. Numbly I nod and step back.

He shuts the door behind him, and I find my tongue. "What are you doing here?"

"Tirne." Autumn's voice is strained, my name uttered as if it pains him. He looks me up and down, and the shock shows plain on his face. Now that he's this close again, I can feel his horror jolt through our connection. Then guilt. How thin have I become? Only my flimsy sleeping gown drapes me, and I cross my arms over my chest.

"What?" My eyes skate over him, the robe hastily tied, hair mussed. It's his final night in the human realm. Why isn't he spending it alone, or at least in bed with one of his potential Consorts? My mind is still wrapping itself around his presence. A god, in this plain cobbler's shop. "What are you doing here?"

"I . . ." Autumn clears his throat. "I needed to see you." His face twists in irritation.

"You'll see me in the morning."

"I know. But that is public. The ceremony. And . . . I worry. About tomorrow."

He'd told me once about his fear of death. And now he comes to me with panic and anguish roiling within him. It mingles in my chest with my own confusing emotions. "You shouldn't be here. Your Consorts can provide comfort."

His gaze wanders over my face, lingering on my lips. "I don't want any of them."

A dizzy nausea grips me. No. "I'm not your Herald anymore. Not even your acolyte. I'm nothing. You convicted me of a murder I didn't commit." My breath comes in great, heaving gasps, my head spinning. "Leave. Please."

He flinches, then straightens. "The Lord of Autumn does not take orders from a human."

I bite my lip, hoping the pain will stop the tears from spilling. I don't want him to see me like this. Starved, desperate, broken. Still, he sent me that bread, when I was grieving and so desperate for food. Somehow, he knows what I've been through anyway.

His frown turns into a faint, bittersweet smile. "I haven't slept properly since you left. I can't eat. It gnaws at me. Guilt. Such a mortal, human thing. My potential Consorts complain behind my back of my lackluster performance and think I don't know. But I don't care about any of that." He lifts a hand, then drops it. "I do care that I might die tomorrow to fix the Mirror, and never tell you goodbye. That I'll perish with you hating me."

My heart stumbles a step, and time seems to still. The air leaves my lungs and won't come back.

"Tirne," he says again, this time with the hint of a question. A plea. From the God of Death. "I miss you."

"No." This has to be some misunderstanding.

But he sent that bread to me, in defiance of his own decree. He'd caressed my cheek with a gloved hand, had sat by my bedside while I lay feverish and sick.

My voice is almost a whisper. "Do you still believe I did it? Killed her?"

". . . No. I don't know if I truly ever did. Doubted, perhaps, but after the first wave of anger faded?" He shakes his head. "No. But it was too late. You were gone. I didn't know that something of me would go with you, and I couldn't undo it."

"Because you'd lose face."

"Because everything would fall apart. But I . . ." His eyes burn now, a bonfire of inner turmoil. Then he says four words that make the earth stop spinning. "I need you, Tirne."

"You exiled me."

"I hated it," he whispers. "Forcing you away. And I hate this . . . *thing* that devours me. That has, for months. I kept hoping it would go away, but who does a god pray to for peace? Is this what it feels like for mortals? Like a knife between the ribs, a fire burning my lungs?"

I tighten my arms around myself. "Yes."

"You know me, Tirne, more than any other mortal. And I know you. Your passion, your devotion, even your stubborn pride and ambition.

All of it. Human and imperfect, but still perfect all the same." He steps nearer, a plea in his fiery eyes as he reaches toward me, ungloved. I flinch away, my own hand darting up to block his.

He freezes. His stare latches on to the Kildian cuff at my wrist, a wounded sigh slipping from him. "Oh. I . . . I see."

"No. You don't." I shake my head. "You withdrew your blessing from me, cut me off from the faith. I did what I needed to survive."

"I'm sorry."

"Are you?"

"Yes." His expression is wounded. "Did you really join the Kildians?"

My heartbeat roars in my ears, my voice cracking on the words. "No. Not truly." Not in my heart, not when I kept the leaf from his funeral bread tucked in the pages of my journal, sometimes smelling it for comfort when I needed to remember my old life.

"Tirne . . ." Again, his hand lifts, and again I step away, shaking my head as he whispers, "Please."

"No. I'm not a Consort. I'm not even allowed in the Temple anymore. This is *profane*." A trembling ache clutches me, like a fever.

"I am a god. Do I not get to choose what is sacred and what is sinful?" He takes another step closer, his fingertips reaching toward the scrap of leather around my wrist. Uncertainty flickers in his expression.

This time, when I don't move away, his hand cradles mine. Skin on skin. Warm, even in the night's chill. Forbidden. I shudder. "We *can't*."

Autumn lifts my wrist, unbuckling the cuff and sliding it free. It falls to the floor with a dull thump. "Do you truly want me to stop? To go?" He bends closer, his lips nearing mine.

I hesitate. "I'd be a heretic."

Almost a whisper, his reply. "Then be my heretic."

All my heartache and fear wash over me in a great wave. Then an aching, lonely desire drowns it all. My lips meet his, soft and yielding and tasting of apples.

He murmurs my name, and I lead him up the stairs, where we stumble to my bed. The door to my loneliness has burst open, and I pull him into it. My hands shake as I press them to his chest. The backs of my knees meet the bed and I fall onto it in an awkward heap. Still his eyes roam over me with hunger.

I scoot backward on the mattress. Somehow he makes it look graceful as he joins me there, holding himself over me. His plain cloak drapes our bodies, and I wonder what it would have been like with his usual one, surrounded by autumn leaves. He kisses me again, tenderly this time. "Such blasphemous things I want to do with you." A hand slides up my thigh, pushing my nightdress upward.

Guilt and lust swallow me whole, but I can't stop. "Show me."

He sits up and unclasps his cloak, letting it fall to the floor. The robe follows. He kneels between my thighs, his hands sliding my sleeping gown up to my waist. And heretic that I am, I lift my hips to let him.

His hands are gentle as they part my legs. I watch his eyes darken as a thumb strokes me, finds me ready, and slips slowly inside. Heresy. I've never been given the blessing of a Consort, the priests' permission to do this. I am no longer even a Herald. This is beyond forbidden.

"What happens," he asks me softly, "when a god is a sinner, too?"

My back arches. I don't answer his question, and he doesn't expect me to. Instead, he urges me to sit up and kisses me sweetly. His hands move to my hips, guiding me. I lift myself up on my knees, my legs straddling his.

I teeter on the precipice. The utmost profanity. After this, there is no going back.

Can I?

Yes.

I slide down onto him with a long, shuddering sigh. His arms wrap around my waist, hands splayed against my back and steadying me as my hips roll against his.

"Tirne," he breathes. "My Herald." I let him whisper the lie, a bitter-sweet ache.

Without thinking of tomorrow, of his Consorts or of my disgrace and misery, we drown ourselves in each other until we both lie trembling and sated.

"My beautiful sinner," Autumn says, lying beside me.

I drape myself beside him, arm thrown over his chest. I should feel guilt, but exultation fills me instead.

"Tirne," he says softly as his hand strokes my hair. Now that his passion is spent, agony once again threads through his words. "I think . . . I . . ."

"Shhh," I interrupt. "Don't say it."

But he doesn't need to utter the words. We both know.

The Lord of Autumn and God of Death has fallen in love with his Herald.

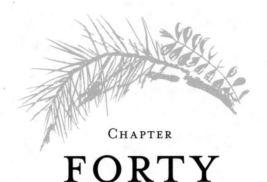

CHAPTER

FORTY

utumn makes his exit long before dawn, returning to the Temple. I watch him leave, the dead parting before him in deference to their god, no matter how mortal he has become. I wonder if the new guards gossip about his nocturnal goings-on during this important eve, and if so, what stories they tell.

No magic flows through me in the aftermath of our lovemaking, and that terrifies me. A year here, and he grows weaker even than his own children. It is as he once said: the Scions' divinity and mortality lie forever in balance, while the gods' fluctuates. They contain limitless potential but are also bound.

Surely Autumn's Consorts have noticed. Do they whisper among themselves? Does Feryn confide her worries to Vanyse? Thoughts of my lost friends leave me even more despondent, but I haul myself out of bed and down to the tiny kitchen. I barely taste the last few bites of soup I eat from the cold pot.

A god came to my bed last night.

I still wonder if it was a dream, a hallucination. But no, Autumn's scent still lingers. Hay and apples and roasted pumpkin. I breathe it in.

He risked everything by coming here, breaking his own edict to violate my exile.

In a few hours, none of it will matter.

I might die tomorrow to fix the Mirror. He knows he may be too mortal, that it may take every ounce of blood in his body to replenish that enchantment.

And mine.

I tug my cloak tight about my shoulders as I make my way to the Temple, treading a path I never thought I would again. This time, the guard lets me past with a solemn nod. She closes the gates behind me with a squeak of hinges. It is the only time I've ever seen them shut.

In the courtyard stands a congregation, the faithful assembled. The Mirror gleams in the slanting gray sunshine, melded back into one whole and somehow magically replaced in the elaborate frame. But the glass remains lifeless, devoid of enchantment. A breeze makes me shiver.

"Tirne," Autumn's voice is aloof, distant. The voice of a god, not a lover. "Stand beside me." Only I can sense his creeping dread.

I nod, swallowing and keeping my steps steady. All eyes are on me. It's mercifully a good day for the pain, only a low, dull headache, eased by Sidriel's medicine. My heart hammers, my mind jumpy as I take my place an arm's length from Autumn. Within minutes, he'll bleed for the Mirror, and so will I.

Nearby stands the Tharem, cheeks flushed pink, bald head gleaming. Autumn is motionless at my side. The magic aura that once seeped from him is gone, even the orange glow in his eyes dulled.

"Tirne," Autumn says again, more quietly. "Months ago, I gave you a task. Have you chosen?"

I take a deep breath and nod. "Vanyse." They're the steadiest person I know. If anyone could handle the responsibility of godhood, they're the one I'd trust most.

Autumn calls them over, and Vanyse stands on the other side of

Autumn in puzzlement. The god twines his gloved fingers in theirs. Vanyse's eyes search mine for answers, and I give them a reassuring nod.

The public is not invited to this ceremony, the closed gates a clear sign of that. But the faithful crowd the courtyard, high priests and acolytes alike. Bix and Jaed stand in the front row, only a few steps away. Jaed gives me a faltering smile. There's so much I want to say to him, but never will now. I cast him an apologetic look.

The sorcerers are here, too, witnessing the culmination of their hard work. Near Bix, Sidriel stands rigid, staring at me with a gaze I cannot decipher.

I am startled when Calder steps forward, not Sidriel, with Wren at his side.

"It will take the blood of many priests to fuel this spell. All those gathered here," Calder says nervously, the words a faint croak. He clears his throat and speaks up. He holds up a small, slim blade, the length of a hand. My Herald's knife wrapped in a gilt pattern of acorns and oak leaves.

"One by one, you will each pierce your hand and leave your blood on the Mirror. Wren and I will maintain the enchantment binding the blood as it seeps in. Tirne and Autumn will go last."

Murmurs ripple through the crowd.

Does this mean the process will not bleed me dry, or Autumn? I'd thought Calder a suspect, but what if he, too, had merely been trying to solve the puzzle all along?

While such thoughts batter me, the faithful line up to bleed for the Mirror. The first three bloodlettings go smoothly, a trio of Spring priests. Next is Jaed. He leaves his bloody handprint on the surface and moves away just as Bix steps forward. The large man takes the blade from Wren, poises the tip against his palm, and hesitates.

I bite my lip. I hadn't taken Bix for the squeamish type.

But faster than a breath, Bix whirls toward me—no, toward *Autumn*—and lunges with the knife aimed at Autumn's chest.

There's no time to think.

"No!" I shove Autumn back with one hand and flail to grab Bix's wrist. Wrong hand. His other still holds the knife as he whirls on me.

At first it feels like any blow, a fist to the stomach, knocking the air from me. I fall to the ground just as Jaed tackles Bix, shouting confused questions and protests.

Curling on my side, I press my hand to my belly. Pain. Sharp and fierce and shoving all other thought from my mind. I look down to see a dark stain spreading across my gray tunic. Crimson blood drips and pools on the courtyard's tile.

I feel as if I'm underwater. Movements come slow, sluggish. Sound is muffled, people screaming a mile away, my ears stuffed with cotton.

And over it all, the pain. Great, gasping waves of it.

Through the haze, I hear my name. Not shouted, but murmured with an urgency and a sorrow that seems alien in that husky voice. Autumn. Hands roll me onto my back, and I cry out at the new stab of agony.

Faces crowd over me. Nearby, Wren is barking orders, telling people to stand back.

And leaning close, his hand tangled blasphemously in my blood-slicked one, my god kneels beside me. He says my name, and it is the sound of the universe mourning, of the God of Death protesting his own dominion.

I open my mouth, but I can't form words. A wet, gasping cough racks me instead. A scuffle nearby, Wren's voice raised in anger. The words don't make sense, the world going gray around the edges. A reply, a man's voice. Familiar, but not with that tone.

Then out of the corner of my eye, a face. Pale as snow. Jaed?

My eyelids are heavy, dragged down by enormous weights. With my eyes closed, the voices become clearer.

"Stay away from her." Autumn, in a choked growl I've never heard, violent and too human. Hands press to my stomach. The searing, stabbing pain jolts my eyes back open, and I meet the colorless, agonized gaze of the man whose hands bathe in my blood.

Not Jaed.

"Stay with us," Sidriel hisses, as if furious that I'd even consider losing consciousness.

Sudden, burning heat blossoms in my belly, and I scream. My hand squeezes Autumn's tight enough to feel the bones beneath his skin.

"You're killing her!" Autumn.

"I don't care if you're a god, be silent and let me save her."

My body screams in silent anguish, tears spilling from eyes that have drifted closed once more. Too much. It's too much.

I let go and slip into the warmth of the dark that beckons.

Y ou don't have to stay," I whisper as I huddle in my blankets, curling around the stitches that adorn my belly. In those crucial moments after I'd been stabbed, Sidriel had bled over me and kept me alive, but even his magic only helped so much. The rest has taken time. Wren herself had sewn my skin together. Each day, I drink potions and other concoctions that speed the healing far beyond what would normally be needed, but it will never be fast enough for my impatience.

"You do not command a god," Autumn reminds me, placing a hand on my forehead once more to check for fever. It's still strange to feel his skin against mine. I don't know what he told the Tharem and the others, or if they even know he touches me here in the privacy of my room.

"I'm fine," I grumble. This is all too reminiscent of the days I had the Red Cough, when he tended me.

"You nearly died. You're allowed to be something other than 'fine.'"

We still haven't spoken about what happened between us, that night. "Autumn . . . ," I begin. It's too informal, saying his name out loud without the honorific, but what boundaries lie between us anymore?

He cuts me off. "No. We'll talk later, after you're fully healed."

And that is that. I'm allowed visitors, though Autumn limits them. Jaed had come to my bedside afterward, distraught, grieving. He'd reached tentatively for my hand, then withdrew. "I . . . I'm sorry."

The words had lanced some festering wound inside me, spilling out the poison that had grown between us. I took his hand. "I'm sorry, too. You were right, about everything."

"Oh"—he grinned wryly—"of course I was. But I shouldn't have made you choose. Guess I'm not perfect, either. But don't tell anyone that."

I'd smiled. "Your secret is safe with me."

We'd sat like that for a while. He started to speak twice, then stopped. When he finally got the words out, they were small and broken. "I'm also sorry . . . about Bix." I'd never heard him sound so broken. "He lied to all of us. And we don't even know why." It makes no sense. If Bix wanted to kill Autumn, he could have done so by creeping into Autumn's rooms late at night. Why wait until the Mirror ceremony?

And how did Bix know a secret only the gods did? Well, the gods and me.

"He fooled us all. It's not your fault." I held Jaed's hand and let him weep. We'd stayed like that in silence for a while, and he lay down beside me on the bed while I slept. When I awoke, he was gone.

And now Autumn rests once more at my bedside, fussing over me like an anxious mother hen. He frowns. "Bix still refuses to talk to anyone. He will be sentenced, with or without his explanation."

"Let me talk to him. If he was involved in the curse, he may speak to me at least."

"Two more days. Wren says you'll be healed enough to move about then."

"I can move now." I start to sit up, but he presses me back down with a gentle hand on a shoulder.

"Not yet."

"Fine." I flop back down. "Two more days."

Deep breaths. One, two, a third.

I stand outside Sidriel's door. Though he remains at the Temple until they restore the Mirror's magic, he hasn't come to visit in all the days I've spent forced to stay abed. Wren, Jaed, Vanyse, and Feryn, they stop by my new room frequently, but never Sidriel.

Before I see Bix, there is one thing I must do. I ring Sidriel's bell.

His voice is cold, emotionless. Does he know it's me? "Come in."

The beaded curtain slithers over my arms as I enter. He sits at his worktable, potion ingredients scattered across the surface. Our eyes meet.

"I wondered how long it would be before you came to me."

"I was bedridden."

"I know." His gaze drops back to his work. He pours the contents of one vial into a larger flask.

My cheeks burn. "Why did you do it?" They aren't the words I'd practiced. I'd rehearsed a polite speech of gratitude. Simple, quick, efficient.

He doesn't pretend to misunderstand me. "That is a very good question. But you're no fool, Herald."

"Not a Herald anymore."

"You will be again. It's all been tied in a tidy bow, hasn't it?" I don't understand the bitterness in his words.

I shake my head. "No. It's not. Not all of it." One tentative step closer, two. "Why did you save me?"

He continues to stir his potion.

"Look at me."

Though Sidriel scowls, he does. A dozen things flicker in those cold, pale eyes. Anger, loathing, desire. Fear. And something both softer and far fiercer. A matching spark kindles in my own chest. What I feel for Autumn is a gentle thing, but this . . . this thing between Sidriel and me, it has teeth.

Swallowing back the lump that forms in my throat, I utter the other question I came to ask. "Just after Ilna died, I lost an evening from my memory. And . . . there are other fuzzy spots, all through the last year. Hazy things that feel like a dream I can't quite remember. The night that's missing, someone left behind a scent of spice and sandalwood, a smell I'd know anywhere. Today I looked up the Temple's duty roster." I chew on my lip. "Bix was making incense that morning."

Sidriel's brow furrows. "Missing memory? Come here."

I do, kneeling by his chair. He lifts both hands, cradling my head between them. His eyes close. I breathe in the scent of him. Herbs and bergamot and something smoky.

He frowns. "There's . . . wait. One moment." Before I can protest, he reaches for a small blade on the table and pierces his index finger, pressing the bleeding fingertip between my eyes.

There's a sudden pressure in my head, a faint pop. And my memories return. The Tharem's smuggling. My attempt at blackmail. Then Bix and the Tharem, threatening me. Bix, controlling the thregas and the rest of the shadowy creatures that had protected Ilna's shop.

Shadows take me.

I know who he is. What he is.

With a curse, I stand, furious. But I hesitate. "Sidriel . . ."

"Go," he whispers. A dismissal as he returns to his work.

And I do.

"Bix." My greeting is bitter. He sits in an empty room with only a chamber pot for company. No windows light the space, only a pale, flickering sconce near the door. If Autumn knew I was here without a guard of any sort, he'd be indignant. But the two priests at the door don't know that. They'd let me in, locking the door behind me.

Though Bix's hands are bound before him, he's far from powerless. I know that now, but I'm not afraid. Not anymore.

He grins up at me. "Herald."

"We both know I'm not a Herald anymore. But I do know what you are. What you did to me."

Realization flickers over his face. "Ah."

"And I know who you are."

"Who is that?"

I stare straight into his eyes. "Kild. Father of Shadows. Banished, stripped of godhood. Except you're not entirely, are you? Not with your shadowy children at your beck and call. You didn't become fully mortal after all." My fists clench. "And I know why you nearly doomed the entire world. You wanted to become a god again."

"I almost did."

"Almost."

His eyes flicker dark.

"How? How did you break the Mirror?"

"I found the Tharem's little secret, same as you did. And I promised him an endless supply of water from Sylvus, if he would help me become a god. He coerced a Scion into developing the curse. An alchemist. An addict will do many things if you threaten their supply."

My mouth goes dry. "Calder."

He nods.

"And you cursed me."

"The night before autumn began. The peach."

Fire and shadow. The offering Bix had left me. Jaed had even told me Bix prepared my food that night. A sour taste fills my mouth. "What about Jaed? You used him just to get closer to the Temple, the Mirror, and me. Did you even care about him a little? Is there anything human in you?"

There. So quick I almost miss it, a twist of his mouth, something wounded in his eyes. It fades as quickly as it appeared. "I'm not human. I never have been. He's a casualty of war. Nothing more."

Bix is an exceptional liar, I'll give him that. I would believe him if I hadn't seen the cracks in his armor before, when he begged me to reconcile with Jaed. On Serrema's Eve, he couldn't have known I was paying attention to the look in his eyes when he smiled at Jaed.

It could all have been an act, but I don't think so. After mere months here, Autumn grew human enough to feel love. Bix has been here for centuries, enough for hate and jealousy to swallow him whole. What if he could feel love as well, if his plan had grown an unexpected wrinkle? I frown. "I don't believe you."

He licks his lips. "You don't have to. It doesn't matter in the end."

"One more question. Why wait for the ceremony? Why not kill him in private?"

"I needed everyone to see. To know just how pitiful the gods could be. I didn't account for you."

I don't know what to say to that.

Bix—Kild—asks, "What happens now?"

"Now"—I peer down at him and feel empty—"now we fix the Mirror for good. And I know how to do it."

The next day, I approach Autumn and outline what must be done, including Sidriel's role in it. I haven't asked him, but he promised me. *I'll fix the Mirror. Whatever it takes.* The exact same promise I made to my god.

"Bold," Autumn says when I tell him, lips pursed.

"But it can work," I insist. "He tried to murder a god. Bix is as good as sentenced to death anyway."

Autumn sighs. "Summon Sidriel."

The second attempt at repairing the Mirror is a small affair. Autumn, Sidriel, and Bix attend the ceremony, along with the alchemists Calder and Wren. I'm allowed to witness, at Autumn's insistence. Once confronted, Calder had broken entirely and sworn to help repair the damage he'd done. For once, Wren and Sidriel begrudgingly worked together alongside him for this spell.

Bix, for his part, attends his execution with dignity. "If I cannot be a god," he says to me, voice low, eyes locked on mine, "let me be nothing."

I watch Sidriel slice Bix's palms with the very blade he used to shed my blood. My stomach twinges at the sight of it, the mostly healed scar on my belly itching. Sidriel presses Bix's bleeding hands to the glass. Wren and Calder stand at either side, their own hands against the Mirror as all three recite an incantation together.

This time, it is Bix's blood that fuels the spell. Lys's brother. Divine blood. His magic may have been dampened when he was exiled, but the Mirror drinks in what's left.

Sidriel and Autumn had both theorized it would take the blood of gods to fix it.

And it does.

Bix's skin goes pale, the Mirror's surface soaking in the blood eagerly. None of it drips, all absorbed by the crimson glass. He sways, then falls to his knees. Still Sidriel holds Bix's hands against it, his voice rising and falling with the others in a low chant.

We all feel it, the moment the magic returns. The air crackles.

And Bix slumps to the ground, his magic and his very essence devoured by the Mirror. Sidriel breathes heavily. He looks at Autumn, avoiding my gaze. "It is done."

I look at the restored Mirror, my heart aching to reach out, to caress the cool glass once more. But I cannot. My hands curl into fists, and I stare deep into its surface for a long time before I turn to go.

A re you ready for this?" Wren's voice is nervous as she hands me the cup, a pale blue liquid swirling in it. We're in her room, with Calder and Autumn both standing nearby. Calder's eyes dart from me to the floor to the cup and back again as he chews on his lip.

After the Mirror was repaired, Calder begged for my forgiveness. Even though bitter anger still stewed inside me, I'd given it. I don't know how I missed the signs, his fidgeting, the gaze that never remained still, his anxious hands endlessly wringing themselves.

He'd offered to show us everything, walking Wren and Sidriel through every step of the curse's construction before the Mirror's repair. Alongside him, Wren had also managed to reverse engineer a cure for me. One I now hold in my hands.

I take a deep breath. "Yes."

It could be poison, one final betrayal by Calder, but Wren claims she understands the spell now, that she's confident in her remedy.

The potion tastes like bitter tea with tingling mint, and I swallow it all down quickly. I wait to feel something, anything. But there's no jolt, no sudden cold or heat, just . . . nothing. I set the cup on the table. "Did it work?"

My god steps forward, placing my Herald's blade in my palm. Wren hands me a vial.

And one last time, I bleed into a glass bottle for more tests.

Three days later, I seek Sidriel out one last time, the sorcerer whose claws have buried themselves deep in my soul. He could have left by now, returned to the city, but he's asked to stay until Winter arrives.

Why, I do not know.

I find him in the grove, leaning against one of Autumn's oaks, in the place he first offered the illicit bargain that drew us together. He stares up into the leaves, hands in the pockets of his dark robe. I don't bother with a greeting. "I need a favor."

He barks a jagged laugh. "I already saved your life."

"I know. I . . . I'll pay. Whatever you want. But I need you to take Autumn's blood from me, to sever our connection. For real this time."

His head snaps to the side to look at me. "Wren has removed your curse. You'll need his magic when you become a Herald again."

"I won't be." The words claw their way out of my throat, my voice cracking. My eyes burn, and I blink. No, I won't cry. Not anymore. I've already wept myself dry over this. "Herald, that is."

I watch his throat bob as he swallows. "What?"

"I . . . It's too risky." Gods, it hurts. But I choke out the rest. "Wren's tests can't detect the curse in my blood anymore, but they can't be absolutely sure it's completely gone." All my scheming, all the pain and arguments and lies, and still I lost. "So I don't want Autumn's blood anymore."

"Why?"

I don't want to feel him falling out of love with me. But I balk at telling Sidriel that. More, I don't like what my obsession for the title did to me. Sidriel may have been right about my ambition. I hurt so many. I'd told myself it was all about the Mirror, for the greater good, because of my promise to Autumn, but I can admit now it was equally my own selfishness. Laereda had told me I was haughty, and I had been, once. My recent months in the city changed that.

If I can help it, I don't want to become that woman again. I no longer need the title, and Sidriel can sever that final tie. I take a long, deep breath. "Will you do it?"

He stares at me for several long moments. "It's messy work."

"I remember." The blood welling up against my skin, the sting of a thousand needles.

"That was a show. The reality, doing it fully, is worse. Meet me in the baths when they're empty. Midnight."

I nod. "Thank you."

He doesn't reply.

That night, I wait in the baths, breathing in the steam. They're vacant, only the soft sound of running water filling the echoing space. I've never asked how the pools create their own artificial current, new water flowing in from one end and draining out the other. Some magic of the priests, I suppose.

"Tirne."

I startle at the sound of my name, to find Sidriel moving up beside me. I didn't hear his steps, his feet bare and winter-white against the brightly-colored tile. Seen through the steam, his pale skin glows. He seems a wraith, something not of this world. My mouth goes dry, and I clear my throat. "I'm ready. What do you want as payment?"

"Nothing."

My eyes narrow. "Then why help?"

He opens his mouth, begins to speak, and stops. He shakes his head. "Do you want my assistance, or not?" An uneasy glimmer haunts his normally confident eyes. He licks his black-stained lips.

I nod. "Yes."

Sidriel gives me a sweeping glance, taking in the burnt-orange robes they've granted me once more. "You'll want to disrobe, unless you plan to stain your clothing."

"It was only on my arms and forehead, last time." Droplets of blood beaded up like sweat.

"That was a charade. If I'm truly to purge your blood, there will be more of it."

I swallow and head for one of the private baths.

Sidriel follows, closing the curtain behind us. He lifts a snowy brow. "Suddenly modest?"

"Do you want someone walking in and seeing me covered in blood, with you standing beside me?"

A smile graces his lips. He nods, then begins to unfasten his belt. Heat fills my belly. I'm not ready to see him nude again, not yet. Maybe not ever. "Is that necessary?"

"I don't intend to ruin my robe for your sake."

I chew on my lower lip and slip off my own robe. First the belt, then the tie that holds the robe closed. It slides easily off my shoulders, the undergarments following. Placing them in a cubby, I turn to meet Sidriel's stare.

His gaze lingers on my stomach, the small, pink scar I will always bear, even though the stitches are gone, the wound fully healed by now. Sidriel finishes disrobing, setting his clothes near mine. My eyes trace the line of his shoulders, the planes of his chest, the thin, vertical line of snowy white hair trailing down below his navel.

He clears his throat. "In the water."

My cheeks flush at being caught ogling. I obey his order, stepping down into the steaming pool that smells like oranges tonight. The water reaches nearly to my waist, the artificial current caressing my skin.

Sidriel, too, descends into the water, stepping close.

I want to touch him. I shouldn't. He's a killer, a manipulator, a liar.

But I'm a liar and manipulator, too.

My hands move of their own will, and before I know it, they lie flat against his chest, gentle. His skin is already damp, whether from steam or sweat, I don't know.

"Tirne." There's something strangled in the sound of my name. He grips my wrists and urges my hands down to my sides. "I agreed to remove Autumn's blood. I neither offer nor request anything more."

"Why?" The question I keep asking him but have yet to receive an answer to.

He frowns. "I don't need to explain myself to you. Take my assistance or leave."

My eyes squeeze shut, preparing for the pain. "Then do it."

His touch is gentle, palm and fingertips against my breastbone. Warm. Then agony racks me. Burning, venomous, a million bee stings. I bite my tongue and clench my fists, determined not to cry out. I don't know how long I make it before my knees give way. Sidriel catches me in the water, urging me to sit in the submerged bench.

It could be seconds or minutes or hours. Time becomes meaningless, my world enveloped only in the waves of pain.

Then it's gone. I open my eyes to find the pool stained pink, dark ribbons of blood trailing away in the flow. I glance down, and the blood coats my chest, my shoulders. Wiping a hand across my cheek smears it there, too. I grimace and duck under the water, scrubbing my face. When I emerge, blinking away orange-scented droplets, I find Sidriel standing in the center of the pool, watching me. The water already clears, the blood drifting away down the drain on the far end.

His chest rises and falls, one long breath. Weariness clings to his features.

I ask him one last time. "Why help me if you've nothing to gain?" I need to hear him say it. "Before, I always had something you wanted. Not anymore. Now all I have left is me. So why?"

Save his soft breathing, Sidriel is motionless. "Maybe," he says very quietly, "you just answered your own question."

I hold his gaze. Longing and fear, and a deep, mocking self-loathing. *All I have left is me.*

He tries to slip past, but I reach out to grasp his wrist. "Do you . . . Do you want more? Of me?"

"No." But his expression is pained.

I stare at him a second longer. "That's the first time you've lied to me, isn't it?"

He flinches.

I loosen my grip on his wrist, tracing a line up his arm with dripping fingertips. He trembles, his breaths quickening. I speak again before he can. "I think this lie . . . you almost believe it yourself." I lean closer. My lips brush his shoulder and I murmur, "Maybe, just this once, we could stop lying. To each other, to ourselves."

He makes a small sound, a plea, and his hands come to rest on my hips.

I keep talking. "I don't know what this is," I admit. "But I don't think I want it to be over."

"It has to be."

"Why?"

"Because you're a liar, but you're not a killer."

I suck in a breath and jerk back.

"That." His smile is sharp, full of self-loathing. "The look on your face. That's why. What I did to Laereda . . . you could never do." He strokes my hair. "And you deserve your match. Someone with a good heart. Ambitious, maybe, but good."

I lean into his embrace. He shudders, and I press my advantage. "You don't get to make my choice for me." My hands slide up his arms, drift over his shoulders, and tangle in his hair.

Beneath my fingertips, he trembles.

Sidriel closes his eyes. Takes a deep breath. And lets his walls crumble. In a single movement, he pulls me close, his mouth meeting mine, teeth scraping my lower lip. The sound that escapes me is barely human. Then my feet are swept out from under me, his arms lifting me up to sit on the edge of the bath. My legs wrap around him as he plants a row of kisses down my throat, my chest.

Yes.

"Tirne." I open my eyes. With his armor now shattered, Sidriel is raw, exposed. There's a deep vulnerability in his eyes I've never seen before. That pale, anguished gaze drowns me, and I ache from the desperation in the grasp of his fingertips. Like a prisoner devouring his last meal.

It chokes the words in my throat, and all I can do is pull him closer.

"One last time," he says, his face buried in the crook of my neck as he finds his position and slides into me. Gently, cautious of my new scars. I groan, urging him deeper with the press of my legs around his waist.

The final time.

I want to deny it, but the determination in his words is as strong as the despair.

"After this," he breathes as his hips rock against mine, his voice ragged, "please . . . I can't . . . if you're near me . . . After tonight, we part ways. Promise me."

For a long, shuddering heartbeat, I savor this moment. The feel of our bodies locked together. The taste of his skin, damp with steam and tasting of bitter orange rind. I memorize every detail. I suck in a painful breath and realize my eyes burn. I clutch him tighter so he can't see my tears.

"I promise."

⁂

One more farewell remains. When I return to my room, my skin still damp and my soul scraped bare, Autumn waits for me there. A single tallow candle burns on the nightstand.

He stands in the center of my room, my humble new surroundings. The lavish chambers of a Herald are no longer mine. A god looks uncomfortably out of place here, too glorious for unfinished wood and rough sheets. Leaves skitter across the floor in his eternal breeze, his cloak like a shield, a barrier between us.

"It's gone," he says by way of greeting. He doesn't have to specify what. "I felt you go."

I nod. "Sidriel didn't take your blood last time. Not all of it. Now he has."

"Why?"

With a long, slow breath, I perch on the edge of my bed and stare at the back of my hands, fisted in my robe. "It's better this way. A clean break."

He clears his throat. Too human, that gesture. "And I have no say?"

I shake my head. "I couldn't spend months feeling you drifting away. You can't ask me to endure that."

Autumn tilts his head to take me in, my damp hair, my bare feet. "You were with him."

I don't pretend to misunderstand his implication. "Yes."

Anguish in my god's eyes, then a pained sort of peace. ". . . Good." His hands twitch at his sides. "He'd best treat you well." His shoulders slump as he lets me go.

It's too much. A god stands before me, telling me goodbye. The second painful farewell I've endured this evening. The sob that rips through me is sudden, violent, the tears following in rapid succession.

Within a moment, his arms are around me, his cloak encircling us both with the scent of dying foliage and roasted apples. I'm too raw, too unsteady, my parting with Sidriel cracking something open that Autumn now shatters completely.

In the span of hours, I've lost them both.

He holds me gently, knowing this is our parting, that we cannot stay like this.

I want to. I want it all. Autumn's gentleness and prickly pride, Sidriel's fierce challenge and devotion. They each fill empty spaces inside of me. But Autumn's love is an elusive thing, a tide that will ebb and flow as his mortality drains. And Sidriel has made his decision. I cannot change it.

My god places gentle kisses on top of my head, and I don't protest.

"Please," I say softly, and I hear the cruel echo of Sidriel's words in my own. "Please go. I . . . I can't . . ."

"I understand." His embrace tightens, but only for a moment. "Good-bye, Tirne."

When he leaves, I blow out the candle, curl up in my blankets, and stare into the dark, alone.

CHAPTER

FORTY-THREE

ays later, the congregation meets in the courtyard at midday.

"Red suits you," I tell Vanyse. And it does. The crimson robe of Autumn's Herald makes their skin practically gleam like polished bronze. The ceremonial crown of autumn leaves nestles atop their dark hair.

Vanyse brushes the collar of my robe with slim fingers. "You as well." My new robe is an acolyte's shade of pumpkin, but a scarlet trim adorns the edges. A sign of my service as Autumn's retired Herald. My name already lies on the tablet in the corner, my place in history secure.

A rare wrinkle forms in Vanyse's brow, their eyes going distant, chest rising and falling in a long, slow breath.

"You'll do fine," I assure them. "Just like we practiced."

They nod and step back toward the Mirror. I stand with the rest of the crowd, though I at least merit a spot in the front row. Feryn launches herself forward, wrapping Vanyse in a tight hug.

"Oof," Vanyse mutters, pushing their friend gently away, but not without a grin. "Careful, or you'll squeeze your baby right out."

Feryn laughs, resting a hand on her growing belly. "Not quite yet."

It eases the ache of it all, to watch my friends share such merriment.

Still, my eyes keep drifting to the ruby glass of the Mirror, restored to its former glory. It once again hums with magic. Only one thing remains, to lead Autumn through it. But not me. I will never touch its surface again.

Jaed stands to my right, and his questing fingers find mine with a reassuring squeeze. Every breath hurts. But I take them anyway, one after the other. Stabbing, cold. My gaze wanders the crowd, searching. I find what I'm looking for. Sidriel watches me, too. The moment my stare locks on his face, he looks away.

Peace. I gave him my promise, and I will not break it. Today is not forever, and perhaps someday our paths may flow together once more. And maybe not. For now, my heart bleeds nonetheless. I straighten my shoulders and turn back to the Mirror. I watch Vanyse pierce a palm with the ceremonial blade and lift their hand to the Mirror, my god beside them. Autumn casts one final look over the crowd, and our eyes meet.

His blood no longer burns in me, our connection severed. But right now, I don't need a magical bond to catch the aching sorrow in those ember eyes. Regret paints them dark, and grief.

And a farewell.

The Mirror yields to Vanyse's touch, and Autumn turns away to pass through it, forever lost to me. He'll return in nine months, once again cold and unknowable. Not strangers, no, but no longer beloved.

How long until he forgets this jagged yearning, this hole that's been carved into our souls? Days, weeks, months? I don't think I'll ever be free. The feel of his hands tangled in mine, the apple taste of his kisses, those I'll carry with me until my body fails and my soul is carried through the Mirror one last time.

Then he and Vanyse are gone, the glass surface still, reflecting our eager, nervous faces back at us.

And we wait.

In moments, Winter emerges, followed by her Herald. An icy breeze skitters through the courtyard.

Winter has arrived.

EPILOGUE

A chorus of summer insects fills the air, the sun beating hot on my skin. I stand at the front of the crowd, facing the Mirror. Summer—and only I know she is truly Serrema—faces away from us, beside her Herald.

"Are you all right?" Jaed's whisper is low as he leans in toward my ear.

I'm not, but I nod anyway. My heart races, my chest tight.

Autumn arrives in minutes, and I'm not ready.

It's been a long nine months. Winter was hard, after the prolonged autumn. The plague dwindled, but not before claiming more lives in its greedy clutches. But spring came smoothly, bringing with it the early fruits of its harvest, then summer. A leaner summer than most, to be certain, but still a welcome boon after the long months of cold and tight resources. We heal. Slowly, but we heal.

I've only seen Sidriel twice since we parted. Once, a fleeting glimpse in the market, his sharp profile still so familiar. He didn't see me, and I turned down a side street. The second time, our gazes met, and I hated the way my gut twisted to see the naked hurt in his eyes. But I've kept my promise and left him in peace. The wound scabs over. There will always be a scar left by his passing, but only that.

Life at the Temple has regained a routine. With my Herald's position no longer in danger, my affliction has come to light, and I'm allowed the days I need to lie abed when needed. Every month, a bottle of medicine arrives at the Temple, delivered by Sidriel's young apprentice. I use it sparingly now, choosing rest instead when I can. I remember what it was like when I was suddenly bereft of it, and no longer wish to be its prisoner.

Jaed has been a comfort, doing his own healing. Though he may not have felt romantic attraction to Bix, he still cared deeply. We help each other, when the nights are cold and dark, when we need to be held while we weep. I told him of my suspicions that Bix did truly care, but Jaed said that only makes his betrayal worse. He's probably right. Jaed has yet to take another lover, and I don't know if he will. But we have our friendship, and for now that is enough.

Feryn is a bright light as well, though motherhood keeps her too busy to play our games of Spinner quite as often. Today, she stands beside me, her babe napping in a covered basket at her feet, well shaded from the summer sun. The child has the look of Autumn about her, with a dark tuft of hair and eyes that glow like embers. Someday, she'll grow into her magic, joining the priesthood or leaving the Temple as a sorcerer.

Speaking of sorcerers . . . I glance around the crowd and see Wren's familiar dark braids and flashing eyes looking back at me. She gives a soft smile and a nod. I visit her shop in town often, just to enjoy a cup of tea and catch up. Our rift has been mended, and we've shared too much together to part ways entirely, though we carefully avoid the topic of Sidriel.

My traitorous eyes search for him in the throng, too, but though two of Winter's children are present among those outside the priesthood, none are the face I know. A strange mingling of relief and regret washes over me.

Then it is time. Summer's Herald lifts her hand to the Mirror, and it ripples at her touch, the way it once did at mine. Then they pass into the gleaming red glass, and Vanyse emerges with Autumn in their wake.

He looks magnificent enough to make my breath catch. Dead leaves eddy around him, shed by his cloak and scattered in his breeze. His crown is a gilded match for Vanyse's, who stands lovely and elegant in their crimson robe of station.

Autumn scans the crowd, and his eyes latch on to mine. Does he feel anything for me now? His expression is stone, immovable, his eyes glowing. No smile, no frown, only an inscrutable divinity. A god now, no longer a mortal man. It feels like being stabbed all over again, a sharp and sudden pain.

Gone. All gone. Whatever he felt for me has been sapped away by the godly magic of Sylvus.

I break the stare, looking down at his feet as Autumn begins the traditional speech. It buzzes in one ear and out the other as I try to remember how to breathe. Beside me, Feryn's hand comes to rest on my shoulder with a squeeze, and Jaed's fingers twine with mine.

One deep breath, another, and the agony fades. It hurts, yes, but I have my friends, and I will heal. Strangely, I do not ache to rekindle what we had. It would never be the same. The pain comes from the knowledge that he has forgotten. That Autumn is incapable of feeling the warmth of happy memories, the quiet confessions we shared. That our night together holds no emotion for him now, merely a thing that once happened.

He finishes his speech and sweeps into the Temple, Vanyse leaving his side to find us. They grin at Feryn and share an embrace before cooing over Feryn's daughter, waggling fingers until the babe grasps one, babbling softly.

"Come," they say, gesturing us inside. "I need to untangle this thorny mess from my hair, and I nominate you two to do it."

I laugh. "I know a few tricks."

It's surreal to spend an hour in Vanyse's room, the one that once was mine. I've since been moved to chambers of similar luxury in my retired state, but the official Herald's rooms are theirs now. In an echo of my old nights with them both, Feryn and I catch Vanyse up on all the Temple news and gossip as we carefully extract the leafy crown from their sleek, dark hair.

I don't ask them about Autumn. It wouldn't help me to know, either way.

It little matters. Later that evening, after devotions, when most should be abed, he comes to me.

I would be lying if I said a part of me hadn't wanted to hear the tiny jingle of the bell in my curtain, but it had been a slim hope. I answer, and gesture him in.

He's not the man I knew last year, that much is clear. A coolness seeps from him. The warmth I'd come to see in those eyes is gone. But they do hold something else: sorrow. Not the deep, agonizing stare he once gave me as he spilled his fears to me. No, never that, not anymore. But sadness nonetheless.

"Tirne," he says, and the timbre of his voice kindles a hollow ache in my chest. I remember what it felt like to hear him say my name while our bodies joined, the rough, awestruck tone it had once held.

"Your Holiness." I bow, as I must now. But I can't stop my tongue from blurting, "Why are you here?"

"To apologize."

I shake my head. "You don't have to. I know where this stands. Where we stand. It's done."

"Is it?" There's a softness to the question, if not a warmth. He lifts a hand to stroke my cheek, and against my better judgment, I lean into it.

I don't want to ask the question. No matter the answer, it will hurt. But I do. "Do you . . . do you feel anything anymore? For me?"

His silence is response enough, and I pull away.

I wrap my hands around my waist, as if to hold myself together. "Of course not. You're a god again."

"Even gods can regret."

"And do you regret it? What happened?"

"No. But I regret causing you pain. It was foolish."

A bitter laugh slips from me. "Humans are often foolish."

"Yes."

"And that's it? Just an apology?"

"I'm sorry, Tirne."

"I'm not." And I realize it's true. This ache will pass, and I will never regret those months, or that night he came to me and we committed the deepest heresy. Instead, I ask, "You're going to choose Feryn, aren't you? As Consort?"

". . . Yes."

I smile, and I'm surprised to realize I truly am happy at the news. "Good."

And there's little else to say. "Thank you," he says as he turns to leave. "For everything."

The curtain clatters behind him, and I murmur, "You're welcome."

Perhaps it's a spark of madness that possesses me the next day. Autumn announces Feryn as his Consort that morning, and Vanyse and I congratulate her by uncorking a wine jug before noon. But I can't seem to find it in me to celebrate. I share a glass and leave them both to their revelry.

I am consumed by the need to close the other open book in my life, the other ragged thread left untied. I make my way to the corner of Yarrow and Hedge Streets, to the tidy apothecary I've studiously avoided for months. The sun is high, afternoon light casting deep shadows. I half expect to see them move, but they remain still.

A friendly bell chimes as I walk into the apothecary. Sidriel emerges from a back door, then halts in his tracks.

Several heartbeats pass in stunned, awkward silence.

"I miss you." The words fall from my lips before I can stop them. I should have prepared a speech. Now that I'm here, my thoughts and feelings are all a jumble. I want to hit him, I want to kiss him. I want to drag him up that thin set of stairs to that loft and the bed in it.

He flinches at my admission, but a studied, stone-faced expression settles over him. "You made a promise."

"And I'm breaking it."

The coldness in his eyes cracks. "Leave." A pause, then a soft, "Please."

"I can't."

He steps closer, as if he can't help himself. And perhaps he can't, for I find my own feet dragging me toward him like a rock tumbling down a hill. Inexorable.

We stop just within one another's reach. My voice shakes. "Months ago, you told me what I needed. But you were wrong."

"Tirne . . ." My name is a plea, though I don't know what for.

"You gave me that nonsense about what's right for me, but I'm not a good girl anymore."

His smile is infinitely sad. "Liar." This time, it's not a term of endearment, but a farewell. He steps forward and caresses my cheek once, softly, before he turns to retreat. "Goodbye, Tirne." And this time, a heavy finality lies in the words.

I should be angry, perhaps, but instead I feel only mournful relief. He made his choice, and I can be at peace. I have a new life now, a good one. One that I can be happy living, even without him.

And like that, a book closes. My new story begins as I leave his shop, walking out into the slanting sunlight of early evening.

A heart can hold more than one love. A piece of Sidriel will always belong with Oluryn, and facets of me are buried in Autumn, in Jaed, in Feryn and Vanyse. Sidriel and I will carry parts of one another through the rest of our lives. There's a peace in acknowledging that, in grieving, and in moving on.

Hearts will heal. The season will give way to spring, to summer, to winter, on and on and on.

But we will never forget that longest autumn.

ACKNOWLEDGMENTS

While it's a romantic notion to think of an author as a lone genius, penning books in solitude, that has never been my experience. *The Longest Autumn* has been raised by a village of family and friends from day one.

It's since been reshaped with the help of my wonderfully compassionate agent, Amanda Rutter, who saw the potential in it and guided me in ironing out its many wrinkles. Then it was further refined by my brilliant editor, Maxine Charles, who found the heart of the story and helped me chip away the excess to reveal the diamond within.

Most importantly, I could never have done this without my husband, Nathan. Thank you for calmly weathering storms of frenzied deadlines and neglected chores, for never complaining about all the fast-food meals quickly scarfed so I could write all evening, for talking me through my own dark nights of the soul, and for always believing I could do this whole author thing, even when I didn't.

I owe so much to D. C. McNaughton. Your prompting sparked the idea that would become this book. You have watched it grow, helped me refine it, talked me through some truly epic panic spirals over plot holes, and brought beautiful life to my characters with your art. I wouldn't be the writer I am without your friendship.

So many thanks to all the others who stood by me through drafting and innumerable revisions. Thank you, Renee, for letting me fling early concepts of *The Longest Autumn* at you, and for assuring me there was something worth pursuing in it. And to Elina, for knocking a little sense into me whenever I needed it (and for being a founding member of the Sidriel Fan Club).

Thanks go to Abi, for your endless optimism and encouragement. To Alicia, for wowing me with word counts that inspire me to keep typing even on the hard days. To Audely, for being a calming influence and an inspiration with your own dedication to your work. To Emily, for poking holes in my mystery plot and helping me patch them up. To Lesia, for being a voice of reason and the source of the group chat's best quotes. To Naomi, for all those writing sprints and patiently letting me prattle at you between them. To Sifa, for your endlessly useful fountain of publishing industry knowledge.

A special shout-out to Rebecca McMahon, horticulture agent, for humoring me and answering my questions about fall crops and growing seasons.

I'm also eternally grateful to everyone behind the scenes, those who championed and fostered this book through the publication process: Bob Miller, Megan Lynch, Erin Kibby, Cat Kenney, Bria Strothers, Devan Norman, Frances Sayers, Emily Walters, Kelly Gatesman, Keith Hayes, and Jonathan Bush. And many thanks to literary agent Jennifer Azantian for ushering it across the finish line.

I've saved the lifelong supporters for last. Thank you to my parents for always encouraging my penchant for wild storytelling. My love of books started with you, with the stories you read to me from the moment I could begin to understand them. (Yes, even that awful scarecrow one you loved to frighten me with.) I'm sorry for all the terrible plays I wrote and made you watch, but I'm so grateful that you did.

A special thank-you to my brother, Adam, and cousins Laurie and Andy, my earliest partners in crime when crafting new worlds and characters. I will always treasure the days we spent playing games of make-believe, of elves and vampires and dragons, building our grandparents' farm into a fantasyland of pecan groves turned into spooky forests, of tiny ponds as grand silver lakes.

This book would never have happened without each and every one of you. Thank you.

ABOUT THE AUTHOR

Amy Avery is a graphic designer and a lifelong lover of fantasy living in Wichita, Kansas. In her spare time, she cohosts the writing-craft podcast *And It's Writing*. She can also be found watching cooking shows with her husband, crafting cocktails, or catering to the whims of a rather demanding tuxedo cat.